A LOVELY DAY TOMORROW

LYNN KURLAND

First Edition: 2021
Print ISBN: 978-1-7341207-4-5
eBook ISBN: 978-1-7341207-5-2
Cover Layout and Formatting: Streetlight Graphics

Praise for *New York Times* Bestselling Author Lynn Kurland

"One of romance's finest writers." — *The Oakland Press*

"Kurland weaves another fabulous read with just the right amount of laughter, romance, and fantasy." — Affair de Coeur

"A story on an epic scale. Kurland has written another time-travel marvel … Perfect for those looking or a happily ever after."
— *RT Book Reviews*

"Woven with magic, handsome, lovely heroines, oodles of fun, and plenty of romance … Just plain wonderful."
— Romance Reviews Today

"Spellbinding and lovely, this is one story readers won't want to miss." — Romance Reader at Heart

"Kurland infuses her polished writing with a delicious dry wit … Sweetly romantic and thoroughly satisfying."
— *Booklist*

"A pure delight." — Huntress Book Reviews

"A disarming blend of romance, suspense, and heartwarming humor, this book is romantic comedy at its best."
— *Publishers Weekly*

Titles by Lynn Kurland

STARDUST OF YESTERDAY
A DANCE THROUGH TIME
THIS IS ALL I ASK
THE VERY THOUGHT OF YOU
ANOTHER CHANCE TO DREAM
THE MORE I SEE YOU
IF I HAD YOU
MY HEART STOOD STILL
FROM THIS MOMENT ON
A GARDEN IN THE RAIN
DREAMS OF STARDUST
MUCH ADO IN THE MOONLIGHT
WHEN I FALL IN LOVE
WITH EVERY BREATH
TILL THERE WAS YOU
ONE ENCHANTED EVENING
ONE MAGIC MOMENT
ALL FOR YOU
ROSES IN MOONLIGHT
DREAMS OF LILACS
STARS IN YOUR EYES
EVER MY LOVE
A LOVELY DAY TOMORROW

The Novels of the Nine Kingdoms

STAR OF THE MORNING
THE MAGE'S DAUGHTER
PRINCESS OF THE SWORD
A TAPESTRY OF SPELLS
SPELLWEAVER
GIFT OF MAGIC
DREAMSPINNER
RIVER OF DREAMS
DREAMER'S DAUGHTER
THE WHITE SPELL
THE DREAMER'S SONG
THE PRINCE OF SOULS

Anthologies

See www.LynnKurland.com

Dear Friends,

Just a little note to let you know that we're going to be doing some, ahem, potential *time traveling* with the next few entries into the de Piaget and MacLeod chronicles.

(Because really, if I sent out a newsletter that said I'd found a portal near a certain castle we all adore, promised that Robin de Piaget had a buffet set out on the lord's table with a few empty seats waiting for us, and we had a semi-guaranteed return trip back to the future, who among us *wouldn't* be booking our plane/train/bus tickets right away?)

There are characters who want their stories to be told and apparently I'm going to have to do a little time slipping to accommodate them.

I wasn't going to argue, because, you know, they insisted …

Happy reading!

Lynn

Prologue

A tall, bekilted man walked briskly along the faint path that led to a bluff overlooking the coastline. It gave him a sense of purpose, that striding, with his sword strapped to his back and his unease firmly in check. He was lacking neither in courage nor an ability to face impossible odds and come away the victor, but the task that lay before him would require a greater-than-usual amount of both.

The pathway terminated quite suddenly, which he had expected given that he'd been to its end many times in the past. He stopped and looked over the edge at the sea churning below. 'Twas fierce and savage that stretch of ocean there, untamed by either man or nature. The morning sun reflected onto the ocean with a bright golden hue and cast its light upon the grassy terrain around him just as sharply. He closed his eyes, relishing the smell of the sea and the brisk sting of the wind against his face—

"As if you could feel it now," snorted the man suddenly standing next to him.

Ambrose MacLeod, laird of the clan MacLeod during a previous tumultuous and glorious century, took a possibly non-existent breath and left his mighty Claymore strapped to his back instead of drawing it to use in skewering his companion.

The man was, after all, his brother-in-law.

He opened his eyes and looked at Fulbert de Piaget, second son of the earl of Artane in a similarly bygone century, and was only faintly surprised to find his sweet sister's husband wearing a slightly uneasy expression.

"Afeared I'll push you over the edge?" Ambrose asked.

"'Tisn't as if you haven't tried before," Fulbert said with a shrug. "But nay, that doesn't trouble me. 'Tis the other." He nodded knowingly. "Dodgy business, that."

Ambrose pursed his lips. "More for you than me, I daresay."

"I wasn't speaking of meself, though the thought of having missed me turn with matrimony does give me pause."

Ambrose glared at his companion on principle alone, then turned back to his contemplation of the sea. He noted that Fulbert had shielded his eyes against the sunlight as he squinted toward the north. Ambrose refrained from pointing out that his companion hardly had the frailties of mortal eyes needing shielding from anything. He had learned, as the centuries had worn on, to refrain from many otherwise pithy and pointed remarks.

"A pity Raventhorpe hasn't weathered the years well," Fulbert noted. "'Twas a formidable place in its day."

"You would know, having once hidden from my wrath inside its gates."

"I couldn't let me bride nip inside and leave me with me innards adorning the outsides, now could I? And don't think I'm not well aware that ye foisted yer sisterling off on me to rid yerself of her endless yammering on."

Ambrose couldn't deny the truth of that, though it had taken a good three centuries—or thereabouts—not to want to shove the aforementioned Claymore into his compatriot's chest every time he saw him.

Family reunions had been unpleasant during that time, to be sure.

"Well, of course," Ambrose said, clasping his hands behind his back and ignoring his sword. "It couldn't possibly be because she was daft enough to fall in love with an Englishman—and a second son, at that."

"Second of five," Fulbert agreed. "Free to kick up me dainty heels and indulge in riotous living whilst leaving the weightier matters to more sober and serious souls."

Ambrose smiled to himself. Fulbert's elder brother had been fortunate to have such a one as that standing behind him, hiding the key to the wine cellar and attending to most of the parleying with allies and enemies alike, else Artane would likely not be standing.

Fulbert had also turned out to be a decent husband to the admittedly irascible Fiona MacLeod, which was perhaps the more important thing.

"Now, about this other perplexity," Fulbert said slowly. He looked at Ambrose. "I'll tell ye plain, Ambrose. I worry about this whole plan."

"Which part?"

"Where shall I begin?"

"In the middle?"

Fulbert frowned fiercely. "This is serious business. More than just one happy match depends on it."

"Which is why we've done what we can and left the rest to Fate."

"Fate," Fulbert echoed in disbelief. "Aye, perhaps when one cannot control the past, but this is the future we speak of. I cannot believe you allowed Hugh McKinnon to travel to the Colonies again."

"You know why."

"And in that company!" Fulbert shook his head. "There will be bloodshed, I guarantee it."

"John Drummond has a particular interest in the gel, as you well know. Besides, how much trouble can two shades possibly combine in that northern territory? It rains endlessly there."

"Not as much as you might think, and 'tisn't the rain that concerns me." Fulbert shuddered. "Mythical creatures roaming the forest."

"No doubt that was John Drummond dressed in winter woolens and out for a brisk stroll."

Fulbert grimaced. "I suppose the best we can hope for is that he and Hugh don't come to blows before they accomplish the goodly work laid before them."

"The twigs were laid months ago," Ambrose said confidently. "All they must do is make certain the final pieces fall into place. How hard can that be? A discreet cough at the right time or an almost imperceptible tap on the shoulder when a direction needs to be altered. Easily done, even for those two."

"Hugh McKinnon possesses all the subtlety of a rampaging boar."

Ambrose had to concede Fulbert had a point there. "No doubt the Drummond will balance him out."

Fulbert looked at him in astonishment. "Aye, if he can keep himself from rolling in vermin and screeching like a banshee long enough to do so."

"That happened decades ago. I'm sure he's given all that up now."

"Tell yourself that if it eases you. I can scarce begin to think on all the things that could—and still could in the past!—go completely awry." He took a deep breath, then shook his head. "Know ye, Ambrose, how close I came to stabbing Hugh in the gut instead of agreeing to quaff a companionable mug of ale with him?"

"And if my sister hadn't disguised herself as a McKinnon—"

"And then taken work in an alehouse in Edinburgh—"

"And spilled a pint of their finest down your doublet—"

"After I'd taken me life in me hands to travel there in the first place—"

Silence fell, as it always did at the end of reminiscences on those fortuitous events. Fulbert looked off into the distance.

"I love ale," he said wistfully.

"You love my sister more."

Fulbert smiled, but didn't look at him. "I might."

Ambrose took off his sword and sat down on the edge of the cliff with his brother-in-law. Memories were best enjoyed with something tasty in one's mug, so he plucked a bit of that still-existent pub's finest out of thin air and enjoyed a sip. Fulbert did the same, then discreetly dashed a tear from his cheek.

Ambrose refrained from comment. Some moments of great emotion were best left unmarked.

He waited until Fulbert had tossed his empty mug over the edge of the cliff before he spoke.

"We'd best go scout out Artane and the surrounding environs," he said. "To make certain all is in readiness."

Fulbert slid him a look. "You might want to pop over to the Boar's Head first to make certain of the same for yourself."

"Ah," Ambrose said uneasily. "Too far out of the way, to be sure."

"Mrs. Pruitt leaves the light on every night, or so I hear."

Ambrose shivered. He'd had enough adventures over the course of his very long mortal life, never mind his undeath, to think he might have had enough—especially if the adventures were of a more romantic sort. He leapt to his feet and sent his own mug into the ether. Would that he could have sent his companion there as well, but alas, there were limits to what even he could do.

Fulbert stood up and smiled pleasantly. "I suppose that means I'm for home. Come along, if you've a be-curlered innkeeper to avoid."

Ambrose nodded and followed his companion as he started toward the south. Any conundrums his own life might contain at the moment could safely—and not at all in a cowardly manner—be set aside in favor of the task that lay before them. Action would need to be taken, though he was the first to admit that there was only so much he could do to see to the happiness of his chosen vict—er, beneficiaries before he had to simply allow nature to take its course.

Unfortunately, given the stubborn nature of the two he was determined to make a match for at present, he suspected that course might be a rather bumpy one.

Fortunately for them both, he wasn't above leaving the odd clue lying about, or giving Fate—or anything else that needed it—a wee push.

He hoped it would be enough.

He took a deep breath, strapped his sword to his back because one never knew when a bit of steel might be what turned the tide, then hastened to catch up with his sister's husband.

One

The Cascades, Washington State
2008

SHE WAS FINISHED WITH ANTIQUES.

Olivia Drummond repeated that under her breath like a mantra as she deposited a final bejeweled kitty figurine into a moving box with half a dozen of its equally well-wrapped litter mates and taped the top shut before anything could escape. How she'd gotten roped into packing up all her aunt's junk was a complete mystery—

She paused and blew a stray hair out of her eyes. Actually, there was no mystery to it at all. She had owed her aunt an enormous favor and that same aunt had wanted to kick up her vintage Hush Puppies and jet off to rendezvous with her soul mate in Belize. Given that said favor-repayment had consisted of packing up the family cabin, she'd resigned herself to her fate and trudged home to pay the piper.

But now after a week spent cleaning out every nook, cranny, and familial hiding place, she could safely say that her duty was done.

Or, almost done.

She pushed herself to her feet, then looked uneasily at the final treasure sitting prominently on the mantel, a meticulously crafted cross stitch that her aunt had no doubt created under the watchful eye of her own mother. It was a no-nonsense axiom that had guided three generations of Drummonds to barns, haylofts, and sheds where they never should have gone.

To the seasoned treasure hunter, the lure of
the unopened box is irresistible.

Considering the number of treasures she had packed up over the past week, Olivia thought she might have an opinion on just how thoroughly her family had been unable to resist that lure.

Maybe it was time to draw a line in the sand.

All she had to use was brown shag carpet, but that would have to do. She dragged the toe of her floral-patterned ked through it, made certain she was on the non-treasure-hunter side of the line, then faced off with that stitchery that should have been stuffed in a wooden crate and hidden away in some unidentifiable governmental warehouse.

"No more treasure hunting, mysteries, or collectible anything made prior to the year 2000," she announced. "I, Olivia Grace Drummond, am *making a change.*"

She waited for possible repercussions, but the world didn't end, deceased ancestors didn't howl, and that cross stitch adorned with a couple of saucy, emerald-eyed felines didn't leap of the wall and wrap itself around her face to smother any more possible declarations of independence from her former life.

So far, so good.

After all, wasn't making big changes why she'd put all her eggs in the basket of a potential job in London? She was striding off purposefully into a future where the only old things she intended to encounter were managed by some British governmental body dedicated to the tidy preservation of historical structures of note too heavy to move.

Well, she might have to make an exception for swords, but those would probably be behind some sort of barrier where the average person couldn't get at them.

But that was it. The only steel she was going to be encountering on a daily basis would be in her yet-to-be-found shiny, modern London apartment. Her yet-to-be-secured job would entail dealing with very expensive, potentially very old art, true, but as long as someone else would be doing the unearthing of it from dusty locales, she thought that might not interfere with her vow.

Her heart leaped a little at the sound of the front door opening because that meant that the last of her aunt's junk had been packed into the truck to soon grace the nooks and crannies of the local thrift shop. She picked up the final box, promised herself a decent massage at some point in the future, and limped over toward the hallway.

The head of the moving crew, a man who looked as if he'd seen it all, was standing there looking as if he might have finally seen too much. She sympathized, but handed him the last box anyway.

"Finished, Greg?" she asked, trying to put just the right amount of enthusiasm and expectation into her tone.

"Would be," he said slowly, "but we have a situation out front."

Oh, no, not that. She had a plane to catch and no time for situations. Fortunately for her schedule, she came from a family of antique-store owners and knew there was nothing that couldn't be fixed with packing tape, permanent markers, or a good shove. She followed Greg outside, ready to roll up her sleeves and do what needed to be done.

The truck was definitely overflowing with stuff, though an open spot remained for the brown Naugahyde recliner still sitting on the driveway. She watched Greg's crew struggle to hoist the chair up and into place, but the chair was having none of that. It flung itself into a reclining position and came close to flapping its beefy arms at the men trying to keep hold of it. They were left with no choice but to set it back on the ground.

The recliner gathered itself back upright in a bit of a huff, then settled into place without help while the movers settled themselves around the corner of the truck without delay.

She could have sworn she saw a flash of tartan disappear behind the chair as well, but that was probably her imagination. She looked at Greg and saw her own well-honed willingness to ignore anything odd mirrored in his expression.

"Like I said," he said with a vague wave in the direction of the recliner. "A situation."

She sniffed suddenly. "Is your truck on fire?"

Greg shook his head. "It's pipe smoke, but I can't find where it's coming from."

Considering the number of her aunt's vintage treasures cluttering up the insides of his truck, Olivia thought she might have an opinion on that, but maybe that didn't need to be said.

"As long as it's not coming from the chair itself," she said confidently, "I think we're safe."

Greg didn't look as though he felt safe, but then again, he and his crew had already spent some quality time with that renegade recliner.

"Any suggestions?" he asked.

She recalculated quickly. The cabin's new owners had asked that it be empty, but people needed a place to sit and rest while they contemplated their remodeling plans, didn't they? Besides, they might look at that piece of fake-leather goodness and fall immediately in love. She pushed the front door back open.

"It'll look great back by the fireplace," she said.

"Couldn't agree more."

She left them to it and went to grab her bag from her rental car. She waited for Greg on the porch, trying to avoid being trampled by his guys bolting out the front door, then handed him a check.

He took it, then paused. "I don't usually say this, but maybe there's something hidden in that chair that you're supposed to find."

She laughed politely when what she really wanted to do was do her own bit of bolting off into the woods before any involuntary reactions to Possible Items of Great Value kicked in and left her taking the time for a final rummage through recliner pockets.

Greg bounded off the front porch with the enthusiasm of a man leaving trouble behind, packed himself and his crew into the cab of his moving van, and wasted no time hitting the road.

Olivia pulled the house key out of her pocket, fully intending to lock the front door and do the same, then paused with her hand on the doorknob. Was that a squeak? The last thing she needed was to blow the sale for her aunt because she'd left a window unlatched or a door still open. Maybe it wouldn't hurt to have a last look around.

She walked back inside, checked all the doors and windows one more time, then found herself coming to a stop as she met the ghost of her younger self there in the den. It had been a good place to land after her unsettled childhood, though why her grandfather had agreed to take a wild-eyed, wild-haired ten-year-old girl under his wing was anyone's guess. Unconditional love, maybe.

A prince of a man, definitely.

She smiled faintly at the sight of her grandfather's recliner sitting in its accustomed spot by the fireplace and her aunt's stitchery on top of the mantel. The new owners would probably love—

The chair suddenly kicked up its foot rest.

She almost went reclining as well, but got hold of herself just in time. The chair was at least fifty years old and the mechanics were probably going. That was obviously the answer for the squeaking she'd heard a few minutes ago and what looked like some serious paranormal activity at the moment.

She started to turn away, then Greg's words came floating back to her. What if there were something hiding inside that chair? She looked frantically for her line in the carpet only to find it had been obliterated by work boots. Her will-power was vanishing just as quickly because apparently the lure of a possible find was just too strong to resist while standing on familial ground.

"All right," she said slowly, setting her bag down out of the way. "A quick look for old time's sake."

The chair refrained from comment.

She faced trouble head-on because she was a Drummond and

Drummonds didn't shy away from the difficult. *Gang warily* was the motto her grandfather had always attached to the end of standard discourse on their glorious heritage, and she suspected *warily* was exactly how she was going to be ganging at the moment. The last thing she needed was for that chair to close up while her hand was inside it.

She checked the outside pockets to find them just as empty as she'd left them earlier that day, then got down on her hands and knees where she could more thoroughly explore the undercarriage. She was fairly sure she wouldn't find anything past a few petrified butterscotch candies or a stray cat figurine, but she'd been wrong before. She reached into the cavernous area under the seat and came away with nothing more otherworldly than a book.

Well, she found more hard candies than she'd expected, but she tossed them back inside and decided they could be a bonus for someone else.

She pushed the chair back into its locked and upright position, then sat back on her heels and examined her find. She had a weakness for old books and what she held in her hands was a stunner. The blue linen cover was as mint as the heavy paper inside. She opened it and checked the printing details: 1910; Wright & Sons, London. She closed it and looked at the title.

Northumbrian Ghosts and Legends

She almost put the book back in the chair. She had no idea where Northumbria was and she wasn't interested in any paranormal doings to be found there. It was the sort of thing her Aunt Phyllis would have considered fascinating reading, though, so the book had probably slipped down the side of the seat as her aunt had rushed off to investigate another unopened box. She would just have to pop it in the mail once she'd landed in England.

She stood up, then realized there was one last piece of business to take care of. She sighed gustily.

"I do *not* need anything else—"

The stitchery fell off the mantel.

She stood there and surveyed the battlefield. Her common sense was there to the left—huddled there, admittedly—while off to the right stood bekilted foot soldiers representing at least three generations of American Drummonds off to gang in directions they shouldn't.

And there in the middle of the field lay the words that had inspired all that business.

She sighed gustily, picked up the stitchery, then freed it from its pink plastic hoop and put it in her pocket. She could send it along with the book.

She put the hoop back together, stuck it in a side pocket of the recliner for someone else to enjoy, then grabbed her bag and ran for the front door before the chair could come galloping after her and demand more attention. She locked the door, turned, then realized abruptly that she was still holding onto the house key.

Short of hiding it under the doormat, all she could do was take it with her. She shoved it into her pocket to keep the stitchery company, then turned and stepped off the porch.

Her future was waiting for her, and she couldn't wait to get to it.

Five hours later, she found herself sitting in a different fake leather chair, counting the minutes until her flight would begin boarding while simultaneously trying to ignore all the hemming and hawing her aunt was doing on the other end of the phone. Fortunately there was plenty of distraction in the persons of two elderly gentlemen sitting across the aisle from her in full Highland dress. She wondered why someone hadn't spoken to them about their enormous swords tucked between the seats, but maybe they'd gotten some sort of special permission for their re-enactment gear.

"I had a bit of a snag, sweetie."

Olivia dragged herself back to the conversation she was having with her aunt over a very bad connection. The fact that she could hear that same aunt purposely crumpling a piece of paper near the phone was perhaps something she didn't need to acknowledge. There was trouble ahead, she could hear it coming.

"What kind of snag?" Olivia asked uneasily.

"You remember Irma, don't you?"

Who wouldn't remember Irma? She owned half the local town and had the goods on the other half. Everyone had warned Phyllis not to take her on as a business partner, but her aunt hadn't listened.

"I'm mortally embarrassed to admit this," Phyllis said, sounding very embarrassed indeed, "but I've been bamboozled."

Olivia nodded sagely. Par for the course.

"Envision your poor aunt being blindfolded with a fake Hermès scarf and carried off to an undisclosed location where she was bullied into a state of financial peril. There was a bare bulb there, sweetie, and brawny helpers in sunglasses. It was terrifying."

Olivia suspected there had been less brawn than scrawn and the undisclosed location had likely been the local diner, but no sense in bringing too much reality into things. Irma was, as any of her tenants would have testified, very fond of movies where kneecaps were targeted. Whether or not her sunglasses-wearing nephews could have broken anything including a sweat was debatable.

"Financial peril," Olivia repeated. "How terrible."

"It was, cupcake. You see, it all began a couple of years ago when Irma started using the business credit line to feed her unwholesome addiction to Bakelite bangles and her initial foray into vintage bell bottoms. I told her that the cusp between the 60s and 70s was a very tacky place, but she didn't listen."

Olivia put her hand over her eyes to block out any more reality than what she was having to listen to over the phone, though she definitely agreed with her aunt's fashion opinions.

"I should have been paying more attention, but I was distracted by looking for love in the classifieds." She sighed rapturously. "I had just met Randy thanks to an ad in the back of Yesterday's Treasures, which as you know is my favorite trade journal."

Olivia had very vivid memories of boxing up a decade's worth of the same, memories she was more than ready to put behind her.

"By the time I noticed what was going on," Phyllis continued, "the business was in a deep vermillion color. Irma was happy to take the inventory and try to sell it to her connections, but that didn't seem to go very well. Thank heavens the cabin sale got me pretty close to paying off the business debts."

Olivia only managed not to moan because she was a Drummond and Drummonds didn't moan. They squared their shoulders and marched into battle with heads held high. Warily high, maybe, but high nonetheless.

"Pretty close?" she managed.

"Within spitting distance," Phyllis admitted. "If you can spit a long way, which isn't ladylike so I don't do it. You know I was just so thrilled to have someone who wanted a quick close that I didn't ask any questions. Did I tell you that Irma was my real estate agent?"

Olivia understood why her grandfather had left her a yet-to-be-disbursed inheritance in the care of a former law student, not her poodle-skirt wearing aunt who was at that very moment calling from the beach where she was no doubt gazing lovingly at Randy from Fresno who had big plans to open a daiquiri bar.

Not that there was anything wrong with Fresno, daiquiri bars, or beaches. As for anything else … she took a deep breath. Actually, she took several. It seemed wise.

"So, sweetie, I'm afraid I'm going to have to sell a few drinks before I can pay you back for the movers—"

"No," Olivia said, dredging up a smile, "no, don't worry about it. I have plenty of money in my account." She did, though it would be substantially less plenty once the movers cashed her check. She would just have to be frugal until she landed her dream job. "I still have the key to the front door, though. Where should I do with it?"

"Toss it in a planter and call it good. One of Irma's kids is a locksmith."

Of course he was. Olivia shuddered to think what that meant for the locals, but perhaps she was too cynical.

"Now, you have Randy's address and phone number, don't you? Call me when you get a new phone in England. And you brought lots of skirts and those cute sweater sets I left you, right? You might meet a handsome lord over there and you'll want to look your best. Make sure you put on makeup every day and sleep in curlers."

Olivia made noises of agreement because there was no point in stating for the record that she was *not* heading across the Pond to look for a guy, no matter how handsome or lordly he might be. She was tempted to add *swear off men for a least a year* to her list, but after what she'd been through so far that day, she suspected it might be best to just keep her big mouth shut.

She did cross her fingers in her jacket pocket and make a no-dating vow silently, but that was just between her and her self-control.

She listened with one ear to her aunt extolling the virtues of sturdy woolen socks and looked around herself for some kind of distraction. She found it in the persons of those two elderly Scots who looked as if they'd just stepped off the pages of some lovingly illustrated history book. Given how many of those she'd seen thanks to her grandfather's enormous pride in his Drummond heritage, she thought she might know what she was talking about. One of them was reading a newspaper and puffing industriously on a pipe while the other had his nose buried in a book entitled, *Genealogy: It's Not Just for Boomers, OK?*

Pipe smoke. Was she going to be haunted by that for the whole trip? She almost pointed out to the grandpa on the left that smoking was illegal inside the airport, but then what her aunt was saying registered.

"Wait," she said. "A what?"

"A dream about a castle," Phyllis repeated. "That's why I'd gone into Andrew Fergusson's bookshop. I was on the hunt for a particular book on them—dreams, not castles—and I almost ended up brawling with some Scottish man in a kilt. I told him he shouldn't smoke a pipe in public and he swore at me. In Gaelic, of course, which I understood. As Daddy always said, *Drummonds speak the Mother Tongue.*"

Olivia wished she'd had a nickel for every time she'd heard *that* over the course of her life, in Gaelic. Then again, she wasn't sure there was enough money in circulation to mitigate the effects of looking at a bekilted grandfather sitting across from her, smoking a pipe that she honestly couldn't smell, while listening to her aunt describing having seen someone very like him in an entirely different place.

She was, she had to admit, having a very strange day.

"Randy stepped forward and displayed a serious bit of chivalry by hustling us away to avoid any unpleasantness or I do believe I would have punched the man," Phyllis said. "I didn't have a chance to properly search for the book I needed to replace the one I'd surrendered to my new friend in London."

Olivia pounced on that opening without hesitation. "About that friend in London, Aunt Philly, and her company that I'm interviewing with—"

"I told you before, Livvy honey. We both ordered a real peach of a book about interpreting dreams. Since there was only copy to be had and she seemed to need it more than I did, I told the dealer to just send it to her. We got to chatting as you do with new friends, and when I told her about your background in art history, she was interested."

"But didn't she used to have a jewelry business?"

"Still does, but she's branching out."

"By going into art?"

"Funny, isn't it? She'd had a dream about a McKinnon clansman who visited her like a Dickensian specter and apparently encouraged her to pursue a new direction in *that* direction. That's why she wanted the book, you see, to unravel all that. Who knew that it would lead to her wanting to interview you? And you know, sweetie, the connection's getting really bad."

Olivia could hear the paper-rustling intensifying. "Aunt Philly, you promised you'd tell me everything before I got on the plane and I'm about to get on the plane."

"Must dash, sugar."

"But, the book you left me in the chair—"

"Glad you found it, we'll catch up soon!"

Olivia listened her aunt hang up, then closed her phone and put it in her pocket with the stitchery. That was a completely unsatisfactory end to the conversation, but for all she knew Aunt Phyllis had also been visited by some McKinnon-plaid-wearing ghost and advised to stay mum.

She pulled her bag onto her lap, then looked around to find something to take her mind off what would soon be her decimated bank account. Fortunately for her, there was an enormous distraction in the person of that flame-haired grandpa who was making a production of reading his book.

The man was wearing a McKinnon tartan.

She realized with a start that his pipe-chewing companion was wearing what she should have noticed immediately was the Drummond plaid.

She felt her nose twitch, but she rubbed it quickly and used all her will-power to ignore those catastrophically unusual coincidences.

She did jump a little when she realized the McKinnon genealogist was looking at her expectantly, but she wasn't quite sure how to begin a conversation with an utter stranger dressed in that kind of gear. Should she start things off in the Mother Tongue, hoping that would lead naturally to a discussion of clans and their mottos, or should she instead announce that she was completely opposed to the sort of extended family get-togethers she was sure had inspired most of the content of his book?

The pipe-puffer rolled his eyes, used his pipe to gesture toward her with a fair bit of impatience, then made exaggerated book opening-and-closing motions.

She frowned. She didn't have any book—

Oh, but she did, didn't she? And why not, when most people brought things to read on a flight, especially a transatlantic one? For all she knew, those two grandfatherly types were just being polite by reminding her of a handy way to keep herself amused on the plane. She smiled politely, then retrieved her vintage treasure from her bag.

She looked at that marvel of century-old publishing and couldn't suppress a brief twinge of curiosity. Old books sometimes contained extra items of interest. Maybe she would find a four-leaf clover, or a secret love letter, or perhaps directions to a secret chest of doubloons buried in a Scottish garden—

She stomped on the mental brake pedal before her former self ran away with her. What she had in her hands was an old but no doubt very ordinary book on fanciful Victorian imaginings. She was perfectly capable of examining it with a jaundiced eye and absolutely no rampant speculation.

She gently opened the cover and fanned the pages. No spiders or pressed flowers dropped into her lap, though she did find a fancy little travel folder tucked inside the back cover. She took it out and examined the goods.

There was a one-way train ticket made out in her name for the next day as well as a reservation—paid in full—for a trio of days in what she assumed was a spot somewhere near where the train would drop her off. She had no idea where Artane was, but the brochure she found behind the reservation confirmation had pictures of an enormous castle right on the coast.

She also found a note scrawled on the back of a faded receipt.

Olivia, honey, I wanted to give you a little good luck journey before the big interview and my travel agent friend Maxine suggested this spot. Maybe you'll find a mystery there to keep you busy …

Olivia closed her eyes briefly. She was half tempted to call her aunt back and first curse her for suggesting anything to do with what she'd just given up, then thank her profusely for something she wouldn't have done for herself. Maybe a thank-you note posted with a royal stamp would make a better impression. She folded up the reservation and tucked it along with the brochure and the train ticket back inside her book.

It was probably crazy to do anything besides huddle in a budget hotel near London and gnaw on her fingers while she waited to dazzle in her interview, but the chance to stay at the feet of a castle that looked like that …

Something washed over her, something that seemed like equal parts hope that she might find something she couldn't walk away from and terror that she might find something she absolutely couldn't walk away from.

Gang warily, sweetheart, but make sure you go just the same.

She could hear those words as clearly as if her grandfather had been sitting next to her, saying them right then.

She took a deep breath and decided she would go and make the most of it. Three days in a charming bed and breakfast, a train ticket that was already paid for, and something very old to casually look at more than once? It was the perfect way to start what she hoped would be a very long stay on yon blessed isle.

She realized what she was hearing wasn't her heart pounding in her ears, it was the announcement that her flight was boarding. She couldn't go wrong with a quick thank-you to those Highlanders as well. She might not have opened that book if it hadn't been for them.

She looked over their way to find they were already gone. No doubt they had better seats than she did, especially with all their unusual gear. For all she knew, they were famous.

She put her book in her bag, sent Aunt Philly a mental hug, and got up to walk confidently into her normal, unmysterious future.

TWO

Artane, England
Spring 1258

JACKSON ALEXANDER KILCHURN V, HEIR to Raventhorpe and all its marvelous gloominess, leaned over and clutched the sharp pain in his side. If he never managed to outrun his demons, it certainly wouldn't be for a lack of trying.

The present moment was proof enough of that. He'd begun to run along the shore as the afternoon sun had been dipping below the walls of the castle behind him and now the moon was rising over the sea into a sky beginning to wear the lovely colors of dusk. Perhaps he'd been out for longer than he'd realized.

He heaved himself upright and ignored the twinge in his back that never should have been felt by someone his age. In his defense, he'd spent the morning sparring with his uncle without leaving the man yawning even once, no mean feat considering who his uncle was. He had then passed a trio of hours in an equally pleasant fashion with Artane's garrison until he'd run through them all. That had left him with nothing but time and decent weather for a leisurely stroll along the strand.

If he had instead sprinted along the water's edge in an effort to escape a sprightly selection of Hell's fiercest, perhaps that was something he could keep to himself.

He turned away from the water and looked at the monstrous

pile of stones that had been fashioned into a castle atop the bluff there. He was particularly fond of it, partly because it was the backdrop for countless memories of long days spent with his cousins and partly because it had given him an equal number of hours full of running along the sand in its shadow. Artane was lovely, well-behaved, and tidy.

Not like his father's hall to the north. There was no endless stretch of sandy shore where a man might attempt to outrun subversive thoughts. Below Raventhorpe lay nothing but jagged, perilous rocks against which the sea crashed endlessly no matter the weather. Handy for use in tossing an enemy to his death, but perhaps not quite as useful for running until all and sundry demons were left behind. It was a glorious place, though, that sturdy keep that belonged to his sire who had sacrificed so much to obtain it.

That keep that would belong to him in time.

He rubbed his hands over his face and blew out his breath. Any man with any wit at all would have been overjoyed to have that future, *his* future, stretching out before him. His younger brother Thaddeus would have leapt at the chance to carry the title on his shoulders—

That younger brother who was trotting up the strand toward him.

Jackson stepped forward in alarm, then forced himself to stop and wait. Thad didn't look as if he were in haste to deliver ill tidings, but his brother was like that. Steady. Sensible.

Worthy of whatever their father might see fit to gift him.

He viciously suppressed the urge to turn and flee into the deepening twilight until he found the good sense he was convinced lurked there. He had many siblings, true, but he and Thad were closer in age of any save the span that lay between him and his elder sister. It made them ideal choices to guard each other's backs, which they had done for each other from the moment they'd both understood what that meant.

Thad came to an easy, graceful halt and inclined his head in his usual show of deference. It amused him to do so, Jackson knew. He knew Thad knew how much it irritated him, which no doubt made it all the more amusing.

Brothers and cousins. He had far too many of them.

"What is it?" he asked shortly, almost not daring to voice the question. "Mother? Nay, Father—"

Thad waved away his words. "Nothing so dire, though they arrived at the keep a pair of hours ago."

Jackson scowled at him. "Then why are you here? Were you afraid I would run into the sea?"

Thad lifted his eyebrows briefly. "The thought has occurred to me more than once, aye, but today I simply came to fetch you before you stubbed one of your tender toes in the gloom."

"Given that it might slow my pursuing you to beat good sense into your thick head, I can see why you would want me to avoid it."

"You could only dream of catching me did I truly wish to escape you."

Jackson regretted having left his sword behind in his chamber—a place he was fortunate enough to share with whatever cousins found themselves loitering at Artane at any given time—though he supposed he didn't need steel to do damage to his brother. Sadly, Thad knew those same sorts of unapproved tactics, so perhaps the exercise would have finished as it usually did with both of them rumpled and winded.

Brothers and cousins. What wasn't to love about them?

He turned away and looked at the moon hanging just above those endless waves. He loved his parents and his siblings and his numerous relations, loved them with a fierceness that he never showed if he could help it. Unmanly, that sort of emotion. Hard to think about too often lest it render him unfit for company.

Because the truth was, he wanted something different, something he hardly dared even admit to himself much less wish for on any heavenly body.

A woman to love would have been glorious as well, but he was realistic about the odds of that happening.

"Petitioning the moon for a bride, my lord?"

Jackson turned back to his brother. "Run," he suggested.

Thad only laughed and bolted back the way he'd come.

Jackson caught him, though it took him almost all the way back to the keep to manage it. He slung his arm around his brother's shoulders and delivered a friendly slap to the back of his head as a reward for his cheek, then accepted the elbow in his ribs as nothing more than his due.

"Look you there," Thad said cheerfully. "Someone else come to make certain you hadn't gotten lost in the surf."

Jackson rolled his eyes at the sight of yet another cousin, though he wasn't unhappy to leave his brother in Parsival de Seger's capable hands. He was certain they would amuse themselves by speculating at length about his own impending descent into madness, so he left them to it and continued on through the gates.

He paused by the stables and found them darker than he cared for, but horses and fire didn't exist well together. He forced himself to ignore the pang that the sight of that shadowy opening caused him. He wasn't one for indulging in ridiculous displays of emotion when a well-chosen curse or two would do, but he had to admit that every time he passed those bloody stables, his heart felt as if a fist had reached inside his chest and given it a hard wrench.

His cousin, Maryanne, had haunted those stables for as long as he could remember, but she was gone now. She had fallen ill and passed away a fortnight ago.

Or so the tale went.

He turned away from that thought immediately, then kept himself warm with a few things he wouldn't utter in chapel as he continued on his way into the hall. He had obviously missed not only supper, but the arrival of his parents as well. He nodded to his sire's men who were warming themselves at the fire there in the great hall, then made his way toward the kitchens to see if there might be something left on the fire.

What he found first was a pair of lads of ten-and-six with their blond heads close together and their ears pressed to the wood of a certain door. He stopped behind them, put an arm around each of their shoulders where clacking their heads together might be more easily accomplished, then leaned in closely.

"What are you doing?" he whispered.

They froze, then looked at him cautiously.

"Nothing," Samuel de Piaget breathed.

"Nothing at all," Theophilus de Piaget agreed.

"Save holding the door up with your heads, as I see," Jackson murmured. "How generous of you both."

"You're wise and observant," Sam noted.

"The mark of a superior warrior," Theo agreed.

"Hear anything interesting?"

Sam and Theo exchanged a wide-eyed look, then shook their heads slowly and in a way that was somehow not at all reassuring. Jackson sent them both a look of warning he was certain they would ignore, then released them and walked away before he found himself tempted beyond reason to slap sense back into them. They were a menace, those two, but possessing an almost magical ability to uncover information that likely should have remained hidden.

He, of course, had no use for anything of a fanciful nature, a belief he hardly had to remind himself of more than once a day. Samuel and Theophilus de Piaget were peerless eavesdroppers, no more.

He made his way to the kitchens where he exchanged the usual nod with Cook, then fetched himself his own bowl of what promised to be a delicious stew. He sat at the worktable, then found himself joined by Cook himself. Cook broke a hunk of bread in half to share and Jackson poured them both wine.

"Full moon tonight," Cook noted.

Jackson would have choked, but Artane's chef's timing was as excellent as his victuals, leaving him only having to avoid dropping his spoon into his bowl.

"Is it?" he asked mildly.

"If it isn't, it should be," Cook said with a smile. "Hard to tell now with the fog rolling in."

Jackson grunted at him, then applied himself to his meal, fetching himself more stew when required and accepting more wine from his companion when needful. He finally rested his elbows on the table and looked at his aunt's best acquisition.

"Perfect, as usual."

"Considering the breadth of your travels, my lord, I'm honored by the praise."

"Considering your years spent in Paris before the lady Anne convinced you to come to our barren wasteland here, I'm delighted to have your offerings to enjoy. I'm only surprised my father and my uncle haven't come to blows over your skills."

Cook smiled. "My cousin is quite happily tending the fire at Raventhorpe, and he is the far superior chef."

Jackson nodded, because a decent argument could be made for that. The rumor that men lined up to vie for the privilege of cooking for Amanda of Raventhorpe, his terribly beautiful mother, was absolutely true. The number of masterpieces he'd eaten over the course of his life would likely come back to haunt him in the future.

He remained there in companionable silence with his aunt's cook, grateful for the chance to simply sit and think of nothing. That was a rarity, that peace, for it seemed that his life was continually full of this cousin or that sibling or some other concern that hounded him simply by virtue of his place in his father's house. He couldn't even escape by rushing off and leaving the title to his older sister. She was happily if not very dangerously wed and leaving every man in her vicinity fainting from her beauty alone.

He took a deep breath, then nodded at Cook. "Thank you, good sir, for yet another spectacular offering."

"A place at the table is always yours, my lord Jackson."

Jackson rose and ran bodily into one of Artane's bolder serving wenches who had obviously come to clear away his cup and bowl. She lifted an eyebrow, which he supposed in another place and time might have been the start of something that would have finished elsewhere. He managed not to scowl at her because he was a knight of the realm with decent manners, but that took more effort than he wanted it to. The fist that had been clutching his heart in a relentless grasp for the past fortnight was simply too much even for his decent manners to overcome. He took a deep breath, nodded politely to her, then escaped before he felt compelled to make any excuses about his behavior.

He made his way to his bed, alone, and hoped if the world ended before daybreak, he would sleep through it.

He woke to the blinding light of a score of scorching suns pouring directly into his eyes.

"The world had best be ending in truth," he said throwing his arm over his abused eyes, "or you'll be meeting yours, whoever you are."

"Jack, come now."

'Twas his brother, of course, no doubt with tidings he wouldn't want to hear. "Mother?" he mumbled. "Father?"

"Zachary Smith."

He sat up so quickly, he almost singed his face on the torch Thad was holding. "*What*? Alone?"

Thad looked as if he'd just seen a ghost. "Aye, and he left Mary—well, you know where he left her. You can come ask details yourself if you're curious, but make haste. Uncle's reportedly making for the barn to send horses with him to, ah—"

Jackson pushed him aside and fumbled for clothes.

"Are you going to bring the sword you had made for him?" Thad asked.

"Aye and leave it lying where he might fall upon it and thereafter breathe his last," he muttered.

"Mary loves him, you know."

Jackson rolled his eyes. "I know that, dolt."

"I think you're envious of her having found someone to wed whilst you are—"

"Exactly three heartbeats away from ending your life, as I threatened to do a moment ago," Jackson growled. He jerked on boots, shoved knives down the sides of them, then belted his sword around his hips. Perhaps he might find a use for it very soon indeed.

He looked about him for a different sword only to find Parsival standing at the doorway, holding that blade casually. Jackson threw a cloak around his shoulders as he walked across the chamber and took it without snarling, which he thought showed remarkable restraint on his part.

Parsival smiled gravely. "She is well, if Zachary is to be believed."

"Is she happy?" he demanded. "Nay, don't answer that. How can she possibly be happy with that unpleasant whoreson—"

"She is alive," Parsival said. "Perhaps she can ask for no more than that."

Jackson had thoughts he supposed he might not want to share, so he pushed past his cousin and his brother. It took hardly any time at all to reach the stables, collecting more cousins along the way. He took up a post just outside the torchlight and waited, keeping himself company with a few surly thoughts.

He hadn't thought to see his cousin's, ah, *friend* again in the current lifetime, though he certainly wouldn't have been unhappy to repay the man for one particular slight that he was certain would never have happened if he hadn't been stupid enough to cling to those damned ideals of nobility and common curtesy—

He paused and with great reluctance supposed he might as well be honest and admit—silently—that he'd attacked a man whilst he himself had possessed a sword and the other man hadn't, so perhaps his recompense had been nothing more than he'd deserved. He contented himself with the thought that his cousin's happiness had been at stake.

Her happiness with the man walking into the stables who he wouldn't admit under pain of death was eminently capable of keeping her safe.

He fought to remain calm when what he desperately wanted to do was find somewhere to sit before he fell down from surprise. That man there ... well, there were several things he could call him that wouldn't do anything to improve matters. He settled for a frosty expression when Zachary turned to greet him.

"For someone who reportedly died unexpectedly almost a fortnight ago," he said, "you're looking very well."

He supposed Zachary replied, but he couldn't make sense of it. He was honestly too shocked to do anything but stare at the man and try not to babble. He listened to his brother and cousins trip over themselves to make polite and vacuous speech with the man. He was fairly certain the twins had offered to go along with Zachary on whatever adventures he seemed to be planning, which likely should have horrified them all.

He listened to Zachary promise to care for Mary well, heard himself snarl something impolite, then pulled out the sword he and his uncle had seen fashioned for the man who would, unless there was any justice left in the world, wind up as Maryanne de Piaget's husband. He took a deep breath, then handed the blade over, hilt-first. That was the absolute extent of the concessions he was willing to make.

"What's this?" Zachary asked.

"Uncle and I had it made for you," Jackson managed. He listened to himself describe the blade's history, because it gave him time to regain control of his desire to take the blade back and stab the man in front of him with it.

Truly, he needed another very long run on the shore sooner rather than later.

"Are you satisfied with it?" Zachary asked.

Jackson attempted a shrug. "I was merely hoping you would trip and impale yourself on it, so I didn't much care how it was fashioned."

"Oh, Jack," Thad said with a long-suffering sigh, "just stop, would you?"

"I don't like this," Jackson managed.

"I imagine you don't," Zachary said quietly, "but there is no going back now. I will take care of her."

"Not that I'll have any means to verify that," Jackson said through gritted teeth.

"Oh, I don't know about that," Thad offered cheerfully.

"Shut up, Thad," Jackson said, whirling on his brother. It was all he could do not to draw his own sword and use it on his sibling until perhaps the entire lot of them turned on him and sent him into oblivion.

Because he would have taken his life in his hands and marched straight into the Future if he'd dared.

He stepped back from that place of madness and ran directly into the latch of a stall door. He took a moment to catch his breath and let the sharp pain of metal meeting a tender place on his back subside, then limped after the company who had gathered around Zachary to aid him in leading Mary's beloved horses from the stables. It would have served him right to have been kicked in the gut by one of them. The horses, not the lads, though that would have rewarded him properly as well.

He nodded to his father and his uncle who were waiting in the courtyard, then pretended to stand there, unconcerned and uninterested, as the elder statesmen left with Zachary to points unknown and uninvestigated.

Of course, he trailed after the twins, their older brother Connor, and Parsival and Thad, but they were too concerned with what was before them to notice what was behind them. He followed the company as they made their way carefully out the front gates, skirting the village, then coming to a careful and silent stop on the south side of the keep, far enough away from the bluff to be out of its shadow. He imagined he wouldn't see anything more interesting than perhaps one of the lads stepping in horse droppings.

He'd heard tales of otherworldly things, of course, because hadn't they all? Whether or not he'd had a look inside his uncle Nicholas' trunk was something he refused to discuss. Even looking inside was enough to cause nightmares for months to those who dared, or so the rumor went. He had, of course, never seen anything untoward from his sire unless the man's ability to sketch anything and bring it to life on paper could be considered magic.

But anything else, including the possibility that his sire was from a time not their own, was nothing but ridiculous speculation no doubt begun by his uncle Montgomery who was convinced that anything untoward had been spat up directly from Faerie. His father's command of other languages was due to his many travels. The very strange peasant's tongue that he occasionally spoke with his wife when they thought they were alone was perhaps something he'd picked up in an unusual part of London. That a handful of other family members of that generation managed to speak it as well was nothing more than an attempt to converse in a manner their children couldn't understand.

If he had stood to the side and snorted as his brother and cousins had endlessly practiced that same tongue with each other, well, that was also something he didn't like to think about. There were lines a man of sense and reason simply didn't cross.

He supposed he had just crossed one of those lines at the moment, but what else could he do besides remain with the company and feign confidence that they hadn't lost their collective wits somewhere along the path from the keep to the middle of a bloody field where nothing but grass grew? Yet there they all stood on that spot he wouldn't have visited without a pressing need. Too far from the strand, not close enough to the village for a quick mug of ale.

The day was beginning to dawn, which left him with a far

better view of a particular patch of earth than he'd ever taken time to look at before—

He looked heavenward and shook his head. He was, at some point in his life, going to have to stop lying to himself.

"Look, Sam," Theo whispered in awe.

"I'm looking, Theo," Sam managed. "Bloody hell, 'tis a gate!"

Jackson caught his wee cousins as they backed into him. If he leaned on them more firmly than perhaps he should have in an effort to hold himself up, he didn't imagine they would notice. They were too busy squeaking like mice, and he was too busy watching a door simply appear there in the fabric of the world, shimmering in the morning mist as if it were actually made of something besides some bard's most deranged imaginings.

Zachary stepped forward onto that spot and the door swung open.

Jackson gaped not only because he was watching magic be made before his very eyes, but because he could see his cousin standing on the other side of that magic.

Maryanne de Piaget, safe and whole.

He wanted desperately to blurt out to anyone who would listen that he couldn't believe what he was seeing, but apart from one notable exception in his youth, he did not lie.

And the unfortunate truth was, he had thought of the possibility endlessly.

He'd known damned well that peasant's tongue his father and aunts spoke was something they'd learned in the Future. He'd told himself over the years that he was content with the marvels he'd seen on the continent, things that had left him speechless with wonder and grateful beyond measure that his sire had been so determined to see as much of the world as he could manage and his mother terrifying enough to be equal to going with him. He'd seen colored glass, gardens, exquisite fabrics. He'd heard music in places where it seemed as if the very walls had joined in the liturgical song.

But even with all that, even with what he had always suspected might lie beyond the world that he could see with his mortal eyes, he had honestly never been able to fully believe that magic might exist.

Not truly.

Not until that moment.

He paused to question whether or not he might have spent too much time wishing death after a hearty case of boils on the man leading those horses into that accursed spot, then it occurred to him that things weren't going to Zachary's plan. A horrendous noise rent the world in two, then the horses bolted. Zachary himself began to fade, as if not even Hell and all its demons wanted anything to do with him.

Maryanne started forward to save him. Zachary called for her to stop, but 'twas obvious that something more needed to be done.

Jackson swore viciously, then pushed his cousins out of the way and rushed forward. If he did nothing else that day, he would bloody well make possible a marriage for two souls who obviously loved each other very much. He would have wished the same for himself, but that was likely too much to ask of Fate.

He tripped over something but managed just the same to shove Zachary Smith through the damned gate and into his love's arms.

He just hadn't expected to find himself pushed as well.

He stumbled forward into that rent in the world, fell endlessly, then felt his head come to rest rather ungently against a rock.

Or at least he hoped it was a rock. With the way his luck was running at present, he wouldn't have been surprised to discover that he'd clunked his head against the slag-lined pit of Hell. He would no doubt wake to find himself surrounded by that same clutch of demons he'd spent so many years attempting to outrun.

He fought the darkness until he could fight it no more, then he surrendered.

THREE

OLIVIA STOOD IN THE DOORWAY of her cottage and gaped at the honest-to-goodness castle on the bluff in front of her with all the enthusiasm of a Scottish-ancestored Yank staring at her first piece of British history.

She patted the little entry-hall table for her camera and only succeeded in knocking off a pile of brochures that she was sure would tell her everything she wanted to know about the fortress up on the hill. She gathered them back up, made certain her camera and the book her aunt had given her were safely out of the way, and decided that maybe for the moment it was enough to simply look.

She could hardly believe she hadn't paid any attention to her surroundings the night before, but in her defense she'd spent a plane ride not sleeping followed by a train ride that had felt like a waking dream. If it hadn't been for an extremely handsome blond guy sitting down next to her and waking her up when she'd reached the right train stop, she probably would have slept all the way to the northern tip of Scotland.

That gorgeous guy had also pulled her suitcase down for her, then very helpfully pointed her in the direction of the bus that had subsequently left her just a block away from her little spot in the village of Artane. She had staggered to her B&B in a fog of weariness that fortunately hadn't gotten her a second look from the local constabulary, but maybe they were used to jet-lagged tourists. She was fairly sure her hostess had sent her off to bed with cookies and a bottle of water, but that might have been an actual hallucination.

The one thing she could say for certain was that the castle in front of her was the biggest thing she'd ever seen in her life.

She wondered if they had an armory inside with a few samples of original weapons, then put her hand over her heart to calm the flutter that generally accompanied any thoughts of well-crafted steel. She had once mentioned her interest in swords to her grandfather—in passing, just in case he thought she was crazy—only to have him a week later hand her a vintage treatise on English weapons through the ages. If that book happened to be currently lurking deep in her suitcase under the lone aqua-colored sweater set she'd kept, that was probably something she could keep to herself.

There was no time like the present to go see the real thing, though, so she briefly examined her plans for the day. She'd already showered and changed into something appropriate for a cloudy fall day, woolen socks accounted for. She'd exchanged enough money at the airport to survive for a bit, and she'd slept like the dead the night before so she was fairly sure she could power through till bedtime. All that was left to do was find her key and be on her way.

She reached for her jacket, then caught sight of the mysterious book she'd been given sitting there on the little table. If anyone would have a finger on the pulse of vintage Northumbrian tourist attractions, it would be a Victorian travel blogger. It might be wise to venture out prepared.

She opened it to find a black-and-white photographic plate of the author, the illustrious Eugenie Kilchurn. Olivia smiled briefly at the woman's clothing, then read her biography. Miss Kilchurn had not only been born and raised in the area, she'd made a career out of writing about her favorite English county of Northumberland, including its many structures of note.

That and its paranormal idiosyncrasies, of course.

Olivia decided she would give the woman a pass on that. In a former life she had left behind a distant thirty-six hours ago, she too had been obsessed with the mystery of the next unopened box. Maybe Miss Kilchurn had felt the same way about things that went bump in the night.

She studied the photograph for a moment or two longer, then blinked in surprise. That wasn't a walking stick the woman was holding.

It was a slim, Victorian rapier.

Olivia laughed briefly only because the goose bumps she'd just gotten gave her no choice. She put Miss Eugenie firmly in the Kindred Spirit column, then read over the table of contents to see what had caught her new friend's attention.

There was a list of castles, manor houses, and what she assumed were landmarks with some sort of unusual legend attached to them. She found the chapter on Artane and prepared herself for some juicy details.

> *Ah, Artane, where to begin to describe the glories of your ancient passageways and shrouded nooks? Nary a night has passed inside your hallowed hall that I haven't been delighted by visions of times—and beings!—past.*

Olivia had to wonder how much time Miss Kilchurn had spent in the castle up the hill and how she'd gotten herself inside to do said ferreting. Friend of the owners, probably. She glanced at the brochures she'd rescued and wondered if there might be a tour available for those who'd recently given up their antiquing ways but weren't opposed to ogling some really old things.

She set that idea aside for the moment and continued to read. She turned another page and found a color illustration of the castle in front of her. It was very well done, as if the artist had been thoroughly familiar with the place and very fond of it. She realized with a start that it had been done by Miss Eugenie herself. A very talented artist, an engaging writer, and a terrible snoop, too? She would have pointed out where the last one led, but she suspected that not even a little jaunt in a time machine would have convinced that Victorian ghost hunter to give up her sleuthing ways.

She turned to the next chapter to see what else the woman might find interesting.

Today, Dear Reader, we shall turn our sights to a different fortress on the sea, one that is no less beloved to this authoress's heart . . .

Olivia looked above the chapter title and noted the name of the castle she was on the verge of describing.

Raventhorpe.

She shivered as something washed over her briefly, a breath of air full of the smell of the sea and the fierceness of its endless roar. That might have been a little unsettling if it hadn't been for the fact that she was probably a quarter mile from the ocean and the air was full of its breezes.

She flipped through the next few pages, noting the ruins of a castle that was indeed sitting right on the edge of the ocean and the illustration description indicated that it was indeed Raventhorpe in its present condition. Well, that of a century ago, of course. She wondered what it might have been like in its heyday, sitting right there on a cliff with the sea crashing beneath it.

Glorious, that's what it must have been. She had spent the whole of her life that she could remember by a mountain lake, too far inland to have much chance to get to the coast, but near enough to water to fix in her heart a deep longing for the same.

If she had the chance, she thought she might like to live near the sea—which might be a bit dangerous if she couldn't pay more attention to things like tides and weather and teenagers who might or might not have been standing in front of her, watching her get a little worked up over an ancient castle.

She thought the girl might be the owner's daughter, which was reassuring, but she wasn't entirely sure she hadn't just been arguing out loud with phantom relatives, which was not. The girl only sighed and held out an envelope.

"My mum says it came last week."

"Please tell your mother thanks," Olivia said, trying not to shudder as she took it. It wasn't a box, true, but it was giving off a definite open-me-at-your-peril sort of vibe.

She set it down on the entryway table, then resumed her nonchalant pose against the doorframe.

"Don't you want to know what's in it?" the girl asked, looking almost surprised.

Olivia laughed lightly. "Oh, I'm not at all curious about that kind of thing."

The girl rolled her eyes and retreated back the way she'd obviously come. Olivia continued her vigil in the doorway, completely comfortable with not investigating what she'd just been handed. It was obviously too small to hold another vintage book, though big enough to hold maybe a treasure map or a key to something—

She put her foot down. She was *not* going to succumb. She was just going to shift to the entryway-table-side of the doorway so she could have a bit more shelter from the light breeze. She took the opportunity to stretch a bit, just to work out the residual stiffness lingering in her back from all that packing. If she happened to lean over and take a gander at the addressee on the new arrival while she was at it, who could blame her? Nothing but a commendable sense of responsibility compelled her to make sure her hostess hadn't delivered something to her that had been meant for someone else.

Well, it was definitely addressed to her, but that didn't mean she had to open it. Then again, maybe there was some sort of British postal regulation that required that she do so, which would leave her still on the right side of her vow. Besides, it was an envelope, not a box. How dangerous could that possibly be?

She casually picked it up and opened it to find a ticket to a performance of Henry V that very night, set on a stage in the field below the castle, and co-starring none other than her uncle, Richard

Olivier Drummond. There was also a receipt indicating that it had been purchased by one Phyllis Drummond as a gift for her beloved niece who would surely appreciate the chance for a little reunion with her cousins.

Ah, the tug of familial guilt that reached across time and distance. Olivia had to give her aunt credit for not only sending the ticket to a place where it wouldn't go uninvestigated, but anticipating any resistance to a potential get-together.

But those East Coast Drummonds? Just the thought of them made her uneasy. Richard was actually her grandfather's brother's son, which made him less an uncle and more a first cousin once removed, but since that had been a mouthful and he had never seemed to mind what she called him, she'd chosen Uncle Richard.

His wife Louise was another story and terrifying enough that most of the family addressed her as Mrs. McKinnon-Drummond. Olivia half wondered if her cousins didn't call her the same thing.

She put the ticket back inside the envelope and considered tossing it so it would land behind the table where she couldn't reach it, but she was distracted by pipe smoke wafting toward her with all the delicacy of someone blowing it deliberately into her face. She would have dropped the goods if she hadn't had so many years of practice holding onto treasures while being confronted by spiders, snakes, and the occasional renegade rooster.

She did manage to jump outside to look for the offender, but her little courtyard was empty.

She could have sworn she saw a flash of plaid disappearing around the corner, though, so maybe someone had been out for a run in tartan-patterned shorts, puffing away, and the breeze from their passing had come her way.

Maybe that same gust of wind had also accompanied her back inside and blown a brochure onto the floor. She picked it up and set it back in its place, but not before she'd read its message.

The Artane Genealogical Society:
Your Family Needs You!

Not when it came to her family, they didn't. Those East Coast Drummonds were penny loafers and Dockers types; she and her family wore Birkenstocks and duck-canvas jackets they'd been passing down through the ranks since the 80s. If nothing else, a reunion would have been a fashion nightmare.

Unfortunately, she just couldn't get away from the fact that the show was right up the street. At the moment, she wasn't sure she could muster up even a sore throat, low-grade fever, or upset stomach to get out of attending. What she should have done was leave the envelope on the table, unopened and unexamined, but apparently giving up the family business was going to be a bit harder than she'd expected.

And why not? Her most cherished memories were inextricably linked to long road trips taken with her grandfather to investigate estate sales and out-of-the-way barns.

She'd hated it at first, of course, because she'd been ten and her granddad's truck had lacked creature comforts like Cheetos and air conditioning. But then a couple of years later had come The Box.

They'd been on yet another of their weekend jaunts, leaving her as miserable as any kid would have been with only a baseball game on the radio and no decent junk food in sight. Her grandfather had followed his nose to a barn and she'd followed along only because he'd promised her ice cream if she joined him on his hunt.

She'd been the first to spot it, that weathered wooden box that someone had obviously used for their most precious possessions. She'd unearthed it from a pile of hay, then made a noise of triumph any pirate would have been proud of after she'd opened it and found it full of antique silver dollars. She would never for as long as she lived forget the look on her grandfather's face. At the time, she'd thought he'd just been proud of her for finding a great stash.

Now, she understood that along with that pride had been a

great deal of love and maybe an equal amount of relief that her surly twelve-year-old self had taken pleasure in something.

Well, he might have been a little envious of her find, but the ensuing friendly competition had become an integral part of their subsequent outings. She'd learned to love those long, dusty trips where they'd sometimes had a destination in mind and other times no idea where they were headed. She'd become an expert navigator and he'd given her endless opportunities to know how it felt to be trusted with something as important as a map. Powerful stuff, that.

It had occurred to her a year or so after his passing that he hadn't needed to spend his weekends that way, or retire from his university position to teach at the local college to have more free time to spend with her, or eventually open an antique shop where people came to haggle with him over the price of things he basically gave away unless they were hers. He'd done it because when they got out on the open road, she had loved to talk and he had loved to listen.

Again, a prince of a man.

That had most likely been the problem with any of the guys she'd dated. They had just never measured up to a man who would have sent them scampering with just a look—if she'd ever had the desire to bring anyone home to meet him, which she hadn't.

She wondered what it might have been like to have found a man her grandfather would have approved of.

Which was absolutely not going to happen any time soon because she had a job to land, a new life to start, and absolutely no time to get involved with any sort of dating distractions. She pushed away from the doorway with an energy that came strictly from her imagination, then grabbed her jacket and hurried out the front door.

She made it without incident to the sidewalk, then looked up at the castle. They probably had some sort of tea shop, but she wanted to be wide awake before she ventured inside those amazing walls. There had to be some sort of fast food place nearby—

"Olivia?"

She jumped a little at the sound of her name, wondering if one of Eugenie Kilchurn's ghostly friends had decided to pay her a visit, then turned to find a trio of people standing ten feet from her. There was an older gentleman there, a fairly pregnant woman about her age, and an extremely handsome man holding the hand of that woman.

It took her a moment or two to come to terms with the fact that she wasn't looking at strangers, she was looking at those nattily dressed East Coast Drummonds.

"Sam," she said in surprise. "And Uncle Richard." She had no idea who that gorgeous guy with them was, but she'd heard a rumor that Samantha had gotten married the year before, so maybe that was her new husband.

"Olivia," Samantha said with a laugh, coming and throwing her arms around her. "What are you doing here in England? And here by Artane, of all places!"

"Aunt Phyllis sent me," Olivia said. "Well, I'm actually here for a job interview in London, but she bought me tickets to all this." She watched any hope of skipping the show vanish with yet another of those brisk ocean breezes, then looked at her uncle. "To your play tonight, actually."

Richard Olivier Drummond swept his metaphorical cape back over his shoulders and strode artistically forward to envelope her in a hug.

"Livvy," he said kindly, "I am thrilled you're here. I understand via the family newsletter that your aunt has jetted off into the sunset with a beau, leaving you to fend for yourself. Never fear, my dear, we shall pull you into the welcoming bosom of the family and take care of you from this point forward. No Dickensian slumming in London for you!"

Olivia would have protested, but apparently her input wasn't going to be necessary. Uncle Richard was on a roll and she knew from both experience and rumor that there was no stopping that train once it had left the station.

"You know Sam, of course," Richard continued, gesturing to his daughter. "This strapping lad here is her husband, Derrick Cameron, a young man worthy in every respect to share a stage with your humble relative. He will be taking on the role of Henry tonight, of course, while I will try not to upstage him as the king of France."

She looked at Samantha and her husband in horror, wondering if they were completely offended by her sort-of-uncle's words, but they were only smiling fondly. She looked up at Richard to find his eyes were twinkling. She couldn't quite lay her finger on what was different, but there was definitely something.

"Um," she began.

"I've mellowed?" Richard shrugged. "Surprisingly, perhaps, but such is the influence of these blessed shores. It also helps that Louise has cast me aside for a thin, bespectacled fellow who smells strongly of mothballs and halitosis, but what can one do in such straits?"

"I have no idea," Olivia said faintly.

"One strides off into the future with dogged optimism, that's what one does." He took her hand and patted it. "Still suffering a bit of jetlag, are you? You might want a brief nap this afternoon so you don't miss any of the excitement tonight. Then we'll make plans to heal the breach! I daresay that will be more easily done now we're all so happily ensconced on Shakespeare's home soil."

Olivia was tempted to look around to see if there might be any stray genealogy-endorsing Scots lurking behind lamp posts or red phone boxes, prepared to nod knowingly, but she couldn't find any. What she could see from her new vantage point near the street was the set for what would no doubt turn out to be a fantastic production.

Richard looked at Samantha's husband. "Derrick, my boy, let us stride boldly ahead and secure a table for our ladies fair. Sam, you and Olivia come at your leisure. Never fear, my dears, we shall fight our way to a choice chippy!"

Olivia watched Samantha's husband walk off with his father-in-law after sending his wife a wry look Olivia suspected they had exchanged more than once in the past, then she turned to her cousin.

"Interesting."

Samantha smiled. "You have no idea." She linked arms with her and nodded her head in the direction their champions had gone. "Dad adores Derrick and Derrick seems to like him as well, so don't be fooled by their artistic rivalry. And I'm sorry I didn't send you a wedding invitation. We kept things pretty much under wraps to avoid any craziness with my mother."

"I understand completely," Olivia said with a smile. "You look very happy. Is he English, then, and an actor?"

"Scottish to the bone," Samantha said happily, "and he has an antique business based in London. He and Gavin have a rivalry that may reach my father's level of legendary someday."

Olivia knew she shouldn't have been surprised. Antiques at every turn? Obviously, Karma was testing her.

"I'm actually authenticating rare textiles for his company," Samantha said, "if you can believe it. I'll give you details later if you're interested, but I'd rather hear about you now. You're here for a job?"

Olivia took a deep breath and nodded. "Next week in London. Aunt Philly gave me this little trip as a good luck present."

"She couldn't have picked a more magnificent castle for you to see," Samantha said. "You should also come stay with us in the city until you get settled."

"Oh," Olivia said, suppressing the urge to bolt, "I couldn't impose."

"You wouldn't be," Samantha said cheerfully. "We're sort of between houses right now, what with the baby and all, but we have plenty of room in both spots. We'd love to have you."

Olivia felt a small stirring of something in the vicinity of her heart that she was fairly sure wasn't panic at the thought of making nice with other Drummonds.

It felt, surprisingly enough, like happiness over being included.

"That would be very nice," she managed. "Thank you."

"We can make up for at least one truly awful reunion in Nebraska that I remember."

"Mid-point, almost to the foot," Olivia agreed.

"Let's blame my mother because I'm sure she was responsible for that. And as for the other, I'll get you a key."

Olivia wasn't quite sure what to say, but Samantha didn't seem to expect any response. She merely smiled and nodded ahead of her.

"There are our knights in shining armor," she said with a smile. "Fish and chips okay with you?"

"Wonderful," Olivia said.

"I think I might have to have a lie-down after," Samantha admitted, "but I've had plenty of time to wander around the village this past week. I'll give you a list of cute shops to visit unless you're headed to the castle."

"I thought I might wait for that until I was awake," Olivia said. "I don't want to miss anything."

"It's definitely worth the wait, but I find myself saying that about a lot of things these days."

Olivia walked on with her cousin to join the scouting party, finding herself a little surprised at how nice it was to have a little family around. Unexpected, but nice.

Maybe her new life was going to be a little more miraculous than she'd dared hope.

Four

JACKSON WOKE, THEN REMAINED PERFECTLY still as was his habit. His head felt as if it had been cleaved in twain, which led him to believe he'd dashed it against something unyielding such as the hilt of a sword or perhaps one of his cousins' damned knees.

Then again, for all he knew he was simply suffering the aftereffects of a particularly foul dream. He could feel the remains of it tromping through his head with all the delicacy of a weary garrison, a dream of demons that tugged at him and his cousin Maryanne who had stretched out her hands toward that bloody Smith whoreson. Now that his wits had returned, he was certain that he'd merely imagined seeing his cousin, whole and sound, standing there waiting for her bastard lover to cross the centuries to her.

He lay there for several minutes as the fog receded from his mind, then realized that it wasn't a clutch of demons pulling him toward Hell, it was a youth trying to pull off his boots. He sat up with a snarl and the lad scampered away. He lay back down and threw his arm over his eyes to keep from having to watch the world stagger about drunkenly.

At least the roar of the sea was reassuringly familiar. That was balanced nicely by wondering why the hell he found himself outside, but that was likely a poor jest on the part of some cousin he would do bodily harm to as soon as he could stand up. He forced himself to count to a decent number—in Latin, to bring his rampaging imagination fully under control—then opened his eyes.

The sky was just as he was accustomed to seeing it, which left him feeling very foolish that he had even entertained the thought that it might be something different. 'Twas obviously well past noon, though. Just how long had he been senseless?

He attempted to turn his head to scrutinize his surroundings, but stopped at the twinge of pain. He carefully reached up and encountered a very tender place on the back of his skull, but scraped his knuckles against a rock as he did so. Answer enough there.

He closed his eyes until the pounding abated enough that he thought he might attempt to sit up and not lose whichever meal it was he'd eaten last. Supper the night before, if memory served, which left him with hope he might enjoy something akin to it if he could get himself back to the keep before the afternoon completely waned. He heaved himself upright, waited until the world stopped spinning, then looked around him.

Artane was behind him, perched atop its usual spot, its flag snapping with its accustomed crispness in the breeze. It was exactly as he'd left it . . . earlier . . .

He felt his jaw slide south. He was very familiar with his uncle's keep and thought he could safely say that those outer walls hadn't been there earlier that morning. And what were those large openings near the top of those walls? Or those long black protrusions coming from those unusual openings?

He looked down at the grass under his hands. That, at least, seemed to be of the usual sort. The cries of gulls overhead were also reassuring, though somewhat less reassuring was the sound of shouting coming from over the gentle rise that obscured all but the tops of the village houses—

He felt his mouth fall open again. That was more village than he remembered and those houses were definitely not of the fashion he was accustomed to seeing.

By all the bloody saints, had he actually flung himself forward to a different time?

A time full of the bellow of war cries, apparently, along with the distinct ring of swords. It would be best to see which way the wind was blowing before he walked up to men possibly from a different time and asked to hoist a tankard of ale with them. *Be invisible until you choose to be visible* had been his father's sage advice when it came to almost anything of note. He'd watched his sire do exactly that countless times, blending in until he had studied the situation to his satisfaction before committing to a course of action.

Not like his uncle. Robin of Artane threw himself heedlessly into impossible tangles simply for the sport of seeing how much trouble it might be to unravel them from around his arrogant self. Jackson the Fourth tended to leave the shouting and blustering to his brother-in-law whilst he waited a bit until he could cut through any situation like a polished, lethally sharp blade.

Jackson would have followed his uncle into any battle.

He would have followed his father to Hell and back.

Hell was, he suspected, a destination he would be visiting all on his own if he didn't determine where he was and what those sounds of battle might be. He glanced around himself to see if there might be anyone lurking behind him, dagger in hand, only to find a man lying very still a dozen paces away.

He kept himself out of sight as he crouched low to the ground and scrambled unsteadily over to the unconscious soul who turned out to be a priest. He leaned over, sniffed, then drew back and clucked his tongue. Any guilt he might have suffered over what he intended to do was immediately swept aside.

He relieved the man of his liturgical cap, popped it atop his own head, and indulged in a quick prayer that those efforts would be enough. He did the priest the great favor of resettling his cloak so he didn't die of the ague, but that would have to suffice until the man could regain his senses and reconsider his life of drunkenness.

He stood and checked his disguise. His sword was visible below his cloak, but there was nothing to be done about that. He would see where he was, avoid encountering those who might want him dead simply for sport, then get himself to Raventhorpe—

Where he might not have found any of his family.

That thought almost left him sitting down in surprise, so he turned away from it immediately and concentrated on what lay before him. A pity he didn't have that damned Zachary Smith to threaten to put to the sword unless the man provided a few answers to pertinent questions.

He paused with his hands fixing a bow under his chin and considered the improbable. Had his uncle Robin known where, er, *when* Zachary was from and where he intended to take Maryanne? Did Robin further hope that the unpleasant whoreson might heal her and she would continue to live a life in a different time?

He finished his bow thoughtfully and decided that his uncle had to have known. Robin had also likely known that even a life without her family had surely been preferable to death for her.

What a terrible choice that had to have been.

He considered his own possible choices and decided the first thing to be done was see if he couldn't get that damned gate to work again. He made his way back to that particular scrap of earth that had sent him to a time he had no choice but to believe was not his own, looked about him to make sure he wasn't being observed, then walked onto the spot where he thought the gate might find itself.

There was nothing there but late winter grass.

He was tempted to jump up and down, but found that to be too absurd even for his current straits. He settled for a bit of vigorous stomping, but that produced absolutely no reaction at all from the earth beneath his boots whilst simultaneously giving him renewed pains in the head. He blew out his breath in frustration. He had never intended to find himself out of his time—

Nay, he couldn't be anything but honest. He had absolutely planned to use the magical spot he was currently standing on, only he'd intended to leap into it prepared with a rucksack full of important things like food and maps and gold. What he hadn't intended was to simply stumble into a portal between centuries with only his sword and his wits to use as bargaining tools.

"Where's the bloody priest—ah, there ye are, damn ye!"

Jackson realized he'd been spotted. 'Twas tempting to turn and flee, but the trouble was, he had nowhere to flee *to*. Damnation, but his very life was unraveling more quickly than he could attend to it. He honestly had no idea why his uncle enjoyed that sort of thing so much.

Unfortunately, he had no more time for assessing the battlefield. He strode forward as if he had business with the two groups of men who were motioning impatiently for him to approach.

The lads on the left were obviously Scots. He found it reassuring to see bare knees below their plaids and dirks poking up from their boots whilst enjoying the familiar sound of Gaelic being shouted across the field.

The men to his right were wearing Artane's lion rampant on their tabards, which would have been equally reassuring if he'd been able to understand them. Whatever tongue those de Piaget lads were speaking in the present year was almost unintelligible. That didn't begin to cover their style of dress, which, as it happened, didn't cover nearly enough.

He preferred a tunic that came properly down to his knees and left enough room at his neck for him to breathe easily. He was surely no innocent, but the thought of drawing attention to things that should have been hidden discreetly behind a substantial drape of cloth was absolutely appalling.

He considered briefly, then decided he might venture to affix a date to where—*when*—he was. A bit beyond the year 1600, surely. He knew that because despite being willing to deny it to his grave, he had made a brief but terrifying study of one of the books housed in his uncle Nicholas's sacred trunk, a study made with his uncle's fourth son, Connor. If they had done so in absolute silence, who could have blamed them?

They had just as soundlessly locked the bloody thing back up, then never spoken again of what they'd seen. He had retreated to his position of insisting that anything to do with traveling between centuries was utter bollocks and Connor had returned to sighing deeply over whatever it was he sighed over.

That he was himself now loitering in a time of ruffs and codpieces was a bit more irony than he was comfortable with.

He realized the men were still looking at him expectantly. He held up his empty hands as a gesture of good will as two of the obvious leaders approached and scrutinized him. He attempted a *good morrow* in French and a *good day to ye* in Gaelic, just to, as his father would have said, cover all his bases.

Jackson Alexander Kilchurn IV had many things to answer for, that was for certain.

The Scottish clansman frowned darkly. "Why do you bear dirks and a blade?"

Jackson decided he would definitely fare better with those de Piaget lads than the Scots, so he shifted slightly so he might appear as part of their company. "These are perilous times," he said carefully in Gaelic. "Even for one such as I."

"You look like Kilchurn spawn," said the de Piaget relative.

The saints preserve him, he might be pretending to be his own grandson, however many generations removed that might be. The thought gave his belly, solid as it usually was no matter what the trencher supported, an unsettling turn.

"Ah," he said, scrambling for anything useful, "I don't care to speak of it openly." He leaned in and lowered his voice. "Natural son and all, if you know what I mean."

That generally worked for quite a few men claiming Robin of Artane as their sire, so why not for him?

The man on his right extended his hand. "Fulbert de Piaget," he said. "And ye wouldn't be the only one, man, so no need for shame." He nodded toward the Scot. "That's Laird Ambrose MacLeod, but don't bother trying to dig for any of his accomplishments as ye won't find any. Me name speaks for mine."

"And my sword speaks for mine," Laird Ambrose said smoothly. "You may test that, Lord Fulbert, if you've the courage to."

Jackson struggled to identify the slurs that were then exchanged by the two men. The strangely accented peasant's tongue would no doubt be intelligible enough if he had the time to accustom himself to the sound of it, but he had no intention of remaining in a year where the men were practically parading about in their altogethers. Gaelic would be easier and that because he spoke it very well himself. His cousin Kendrick had been convinced they should learn it properly so they could skip across the border and engage in dangerous activities, and he hadn't disagreed.

Laird Ambrose finally folded his arms over his chest and glared. "You stole my sister."

"I stole nothing that didn't care to be free of ye," Fulbert said with a shrug.

"To then be chained to you? Are you daft, man?"

Fulbert stuck out his chin. "She could do worse."

"She'll do much better after I cut you to ribbons!"

Jackson listened to the discussion descend into threats of dismemberment and death and thought he might understand why the priest had snuck off to drink himself into a stupor. It also occurred to him that perhaps he and Kendrick should have practiced a few more things that hadn't been quite so polite.

He had scarce entertained that thought properly before a flame-haired woman walked over and placed herself between Laird Ambrose and Lord Fulbert.

"No one's asked me if I want to be wed," she said tartly. "Do you think I want to be a bride to a bloody Englishman? 'Tis worse than going back home with an overbearing brother!"

"'Twas love at first sight," Fulbert growled, "which ye know very well, ye vexatious wench."

Ambrose pulled the woman over to stand next to him. "My beloved sister Fiona's eyes aren't that good."

"They're better than what she'll leave of me ears with all her screeching!"

"Your ears will remain unassaulted, for I say you'll not have her."

"And I say I shall!"

Fiona MacLeod stepped again between her brother and her intended and held them apart.

"And if death comes to the both of you, where would I be?" she asked. "Weeping endlessly along the shore, keening for my dearest love and my favorite brother?"

Jackson suspected not, but what did he know? He watched the men chew on that for a moment before Laird Ambrose looked at him sharply.

"Wed them."

"Of course," he said, because he suspected he didn't dare do anything else. He would likely need to apologize to someone in his family for it at some point, but given the day he'd had so far, perhaps not.

A scribe was provided and the negotiations were begun, accompanied by snarls and curses—and those were just what was coming from the bride and groom. He did his damndest to arrange a proper settlement between a Scottish lass who was too shrewish by half and a bloody relation who was more surly and arrogant than he should have been, but the whole thing was a bit of a slog. The sun continued to sink toward the west and the trio in front of him continued to argue.

He began to wonder if Lord Fulbert and Lady Fiona would gain their wedding bed without murdering each other first, but then he caught a look they exchanged when they obviously thought no one was watching them. It fair singed him on the spot, and he was standing ten paces away from them.

The vagaries of romance were, he had to admit, occasionally lost on him.

He married them—eventually—in eminently functional Latin, committing not only to a bit more time in chapel as penance, but a hefty contribution to his father's priest's coffers for having taught him so well. The bride was kissed, the groom congratulated, then the bride simply walked away and hopped up onto her newly made husband's horse.

"Where go you, wife!" Fulbert bellowed.

"Raventhorpe," came the screech, "to escape ye, ye blighted Englishman. Besides, they've a wondrous chef and I'm famished."

Jackson wondered if that senseless priest might have anything strong hidden in some purse or other. He thought he might want to borrow that as well and very soon.

"Lock yourself inside the gates!" Ambrose shouted at his sister. "I'll come rescue you after I've slain your husband."

"Not if I get to those bloody gates first," Fulbert snarled. "Damned woman. I'm liable to lock *her* out. At the present moment, I'm not sure which would suit ye better."

"Don't ask."

"Shall we have a bit of sport whilst we consider the tangle?"

"Nay, I must away to Edinburgh," Ambrose said heavily. "I've a McKinnon to slay."

"Because he helped yer wee sisterling find work in an alehouse?"

"Aye, to escape the plans I had to wed her to a Scottish lad, not to indulge in the same with you!"

"'Tis hardly *my* fault she spilled ale down me front."

"Hugh pushed her," Ambrose said pointedly, "and look where it's led."

Lord Fulbert twitched back his cloak and drew his sword. Jackson supposed there was no reason not to take a moment to appreciate the unusual noise it made as it cut through the evening air, though he was also quite impressed with the sword Laird Ambrose pulled from the scabbard on his back. He committed both designs to memory for use in a future discussion with his father's blacksmith, then watched as the men indulged in a brief skirmish.

He couldn't help but note, though, that there was less fighting and more watching on both their parts as the bride trotted slowly off north. He knew the path to his home so well he likely could have run along it in the dark and not come close to tripping even once, but obviously Lady Fiona would not.

Curious, though, that those two men only watched her scamper off without giving chase.

He absently accepted a handful of coins from one of Artane's men because he assumed he shouldn't refuse. Perhaps that had been one too many things for Fate to stomach, for 'twas at that moment that priest came staggering out of the fading daylight into the battle.

"You stole me cap!" he bellowed.

Jackson had to admit that was true, though he imagined doing so silently would be enough. He hardly had time to draw his own sword before he found himself fending off Laird Ambrose and Lord Fulbert both. He managed to leap aside to avoid being skewered by a mighty Scottish sword, but he heard the blade go through his tunic just the same.

"Away lads," shouted a voice suddenly from his right. "To the north! There be ruffians after the bride!"

Both companies turned as one and rushed off to rescue a woman Jackson suspected could have defended herself with curses alone. He resheathed his sword, then pulled the cap off his head and tossed it to the priest.

"You might want to marry them again," he suggested.

The priest glared at him and staggered off toward the keep. The man who had identified the menace to the north laughed as he walked over with his hands in plain sight.

"You'd best be away, friend," he said from within the depths of his hood. "To the south, I daresay."

"We're going that way ourselves," said a second man, coming to stand next to the first. "You won't be popular here, I imagine."

Jackson couldn't disagree with that, nor with the realization that whoever those two men might have been, they weren't coming at him with blades bared. One against two was also better than one against two score, so he headed south with them, prepared to fight if necessary.

They said no more, but instead strode alongside him until they came to a spot in the field that he recognized. It helped that the gate he'd fallen through that morning was again visible in the twilight. He wondered how he might nip inside it without having to discuss the same with his escorts, then made the mistake of looking at them just as they were pushing their hoods back from their faces.

They resembled Connor of Wyckham so greatly that he gasped. Then it occurred to him that he wasn't looking at Connor divided in twain, he was looking at Samuel and Theophilus de Piaget, only they were men, not lads.

"What the *hell*—" he began, then he shook off their hands as they reached for him, no doubt to pull him into their madness. "Leave me alone, you fiends, and explain yourselves!"

"Now, cousin," one of them began soothingly, "calm yourself."

"Aye," added the other, "there's no need to work yourself into such a womanly state."

"You cheeky little bastards," he spluttered. "What are you doing here—nay, I don't want to know. How did you—nay, I don't want to know that, either." He pointed his finger at them accusingly. "You've done this before."

"Aye, a time or two," Sam said. "We'll help you now, if you like."

Theo nodded in agreement. "But before we can, you must decide where you want to go."

Home was almost out of his mouth before he called the words back, unspoken. There were things he should do, of course.

There were also things he *could* do, even just for a handful of days.

A terrible longing rose up in him, a longing to see what he'd dreamt of for as long as he could remember. He understood at that moment what drove men to leave their homes and risk danger and death to explore unfamiliar lands. The idea that he might actually see for himself what others had seen and perhaps find other things they might have missed …

The very air around him was suddenly still with a particular sort of quiet that he rarely stopped long enough to heed. He wondered if every man when faced with something completely unknown that he wanted so badly he could taste it had such a heart-stopping rush of emotion wash over him.

"I'm not sure," he said carefully.

The twins exchanged a brief glance. Jackson had spent most of their lives coming to instant conclusions about what those looks might mean, but he'd obviously missed out on a few years. The saints only knew what they were thinking at present.

"I daresay you are sure, Jack," Sam said seriously. "Don't you agree, Theo?"

"I think he's been thinking about it for ages."

"Then what do I do?" Jackson blurted out, feeling as green as … well, those lads there had never been green. He'd found them terrifying even before they'd managed to find their feet and toddle off to make mischief.

"Focus your thoughts on where you want to go," Sam instructed.

"Best make it more specific than *I'm off to do good*," Theo added solemnly. "Look what that got you the last time."

"That's not what I was thinking," Jackson growled. He imagined he didn't need to destroy the innocence of his two young cousins with the vile things he had been thinking about Zachary Smith. Then again, his cousins didn't look all that innocent at the moment so perhaps they would survive. "I believe my thoughts were centered more around an intense desire to wrap my fingers around Zachary Smith's throat and squeeze the life from him."

Sam smiled. "Are you sure?"

Jackson opened his mouth with the intention of assuring him that he knew his own damned mind, but then he felt that uncomfortable stillness descend again. He hadn't been thinking about slaying Zachary Smith, as enjoyable as that would have been; he'd been thinking about making certain a marriage happened.

By the saints, had he wished himself into a priest's cap?

"He looks indecisive," Theo remarked.

"Let's give him a push."

"We pushed him before."

"Ah, but we didn't know what we were doing then."

"I'm not sure we know what we're doing *now*."

Sam laughed uneasily. "We're better at it than we used to be, at least. Let's send him into the waiting arms of a beautiful woman."

"Poor gel, whoever she might be."

Jackson cursed them mostly because he couldn't deny having wished more than once that there might be just one woman in the great, wide world who might look at him and find him … tolerable. He knew he was too serious and spent far too much time in the lists, but surely there had to be a wench somewhere who might not faint at the sight of a well-fashioned blade or scorn his devotion to the same.

The twins stepped forward and he stepped backward instinctively, right into that swirling void between worlds. The dizzying nature of that particular piece of soil was terrible.

"Shall we stay here for a bit, Theo?"

"Nay, Renaissance food gives me tummy upset. Let's clean up the details here, then go back to the flat."

"Curry take-away?"

"Brilliant."

Jackson had a score of questions to ask them, but he could feel the gate pulling him fully into its foul embrace. He sent his wee cousins a look of promise and had a pair of languid waves as his reward.

He would kill them first, then Zachary Smith, then … well,

he wasn't certain what he would do then, but he was fairly sure it would involve doing extensive damage to anyone else associated with the present madness.

The gate spat him back out as forcefully as it had pulled him into itself and he found himself suddenly on his hands and knees without knowing quite how he'd gotten there. He heaved himself to his feet and looked around him.

The twins were gone. There was grass under his feet and a deepening sky above his head. Artane was hovering over the village as it always did, which was ... ah ... not at all reassuring given that the walls were lit by what he could only assume were torches of a Future nature.

He was beginning to very seriously regret having gotten out of bed that morning.

He looked behind him to find that the gate had retreated back into the ether, which left him trapped where he was at least for the moment. He took a deep breath, trying to decide if he should have been elated or terrified. Perhaps that was something to think on after he'd discovered where—er, *when*, rather—he was.

There was a gathering of some sort in the distance, almost exactly where he'd impersonated a man of the cloth not half an hour earlier. If nothing else, perhaps he could at least see how the local villagers were dressed. He put the coins he realized he was still clutching into the purse at his belt, then put his shoulders back and walked on.

He soon reached a group of men milling about, babbling rather poorly in that Elizabethan tongue he'd just escaped having to listen to any longer. He looked at their dress, then he felt his mouth fall open.

By the saints, more men in tights!

"You're late."

He looked down to find a wee granny taking hold of him with a grip that warned there would be consequences for arguing. She pushed him toward a collection of men fussing with swords fashioned in the style of Lord Fulbert's.

"Go over there for help with your costume. I am occupied with Mr. Drummond."

Jackson was grateful for all those hours he had indeed spent hovering on the edge of endless conversations between Kendrick and a select group of cousins as they'd practiced their Future-speak, as Connor had called it. He had never participated, of course, because he was a man of sense and intelligence. He was also no fool, which meant he'd practiced endlessly on his own. It would take him a bit to adjust his ear to the local vernacular, but it wasn't anything he hadn't done in numerous other countries with his family.

He took a moment for another round of counting in Latin, but that didn't sharpen his wits. Perhaps he had no wits left to sharpen. All he knew was that he hadn't remained in a time of lacy neck gear and appalling things worn over a man's ... He took a deep, restorative breath. He now seemed to be in a time of short tunics and strange trews that did not reach to the knee but instead stuck out as if they'd been designed to be as wide around the thigh as they would have been around the waist. Each leg, even!

He watched the souls milling about for a bit longer, then a shocking thought occurred to him.

Had he fallen in with a band of players?

He decided abruptly that he wouldn't ask lest the present madness increase. If he ever had his hands and Zachary Smith's throat within the same span, there would be hell to pay.

But until that happy time arrived, the best he could do was wait until he could return to the gate and insist that it carry him back home.

He took a deep breath and prepared to hide in plain sight.

FIVE

OLIVIA RAN DOWN THE STREET, braiding her hair as she went and hoping jeans and a very wrinkled shirt under her grandfather's jacket would get her into the show. With Richard Drummond involved, she wouldn't have been surprised to find the dress code including opera pearls and strappy shoes.

Fortunately for her, the venue was outside and the people she saw taking their seats were dressed for the weather. She almost plowed right over a guy in a trench coat and fedora who stepped into her path, but she hadn't grown up avoiding bugs dropping from barn rafters for nothing. She sidestepped him, flashed her ticket at the appropriate taker, then stopped to catch her breath and have another look at the castle behind the stage. Uncle Richard certainly could pick his backdrops. She'd never heard of his doing outdoor theater, but maybe this was part of the new, more accessible him.

She was half tempted to pop backstage and tell everyone to break some bone or other, but her uncle's pre-show rituals were the stuff of legend. Regardless of whatever leaf-turning he might have recently done, interrupting that might get her booted from the family before she'd had the chance to settle in. She started to turn away, then realized Samantha was peeking around the backstage curtain, waving at her. She couldn't decide if it was a welcoming wave or one that indicated a need for a rescue, but maybe a quick hello wouldn't damage her uncle's descent into character.

She stopped in front of her cousin and looked her over. "Maybe you should sit for a minute."

"I wish I could," Samantha said, pushing her hair back from her face. "The stage manager called in sick two hours ago and my father doesn't trust anyone besides me to take over. Things are on the verge of becoming a situation, if you know what I mean."

Boy, did she ever. She suppressed a shudder and shoved her ticket into her pocket. "Put me to work."

"Really?" Samantha said in surprise. "I hate to ask, but I definitely could use help backstage."

"I'd love to." She wasn't a theater person by any means, but she was used to antique shows. The chaos behind the curtain couldn't be much different.

Samantha pulled her backstage, then pointed. "See that woman fawning all over my father? That's the costume mistress, Mrs. Sutcliffe. She'll have what you need."

"Ah," Olivia said, "but I—"

"Can't understand why we're doing Henry V with Renaissance costumes?" Samantha finished. "Neither can I, but I'm guessing Dad's trying to be edgy. We had to borrow a few guys from the local company for tonight's show so who knows what they'll be wearing. Just try to get everyone to match as best you can and make whatever repairs they need. I'll check in later, thank you!"

Olivia watched her cousin hurry off to marshal her forces, one hand pressed against the small of her back.

"—can't sew," she finished, but no one was listening.

Well, bad help was probably better than no help at all. She walked over to the white-haired costume mistress who was staring worshipfully at Richard Drummond as if he'd been the second coming of Sir Laurence himself. She almost hated to interrupt that level of ogling, but sacrifices had to be made.

"Um, Mrs. Sutcliffe," she began carefully, "I'm here to help?"

Mrs. Sutcliffe held out a basket without taking her eyes off the prize. "Wonderful," she said absently. "I will be tending to Mr. Drummond's sartorial concerns personally. You will be seeing to everyone else."

Olivia nodded, took the collection of tools of the trade, then went to stake out a bit of backstage real estate. She set her gear down on the ground, donned a little strawberry pincushion bristling with straight pins, and braced for the onslaught. She didn't hold out much hope for her efforts, but being so near the Motherland left her feeling an increased pressure to do the family proud.

"I need this sorted right now," a tights-wearing, sword-bearing guardsman said impatiently, shoving a sleeve in front of her face.

Olivia bit her tongue partly because she was in the habit of making nice with all sorts of customers and partly because the current gig wasn't hers and she didn't want to spoil it for her cousins. She dug around in her basket for the appropriate color of thread, then examined the tiny bit of braid that had come undone from the soldier's cuff. She tried to pin it, but he jerked it away.

"Oh, you are useless," the guy growled. He shoved his sleeve into her face. "Just sew the bleeding thing and hurry before I have to use sello tape instead!"

She tried, honestly, but she was having trouble keeping up with a constantly moving sleeve that was being flapped in her face by a guy who was hopping with impatience and frustration. If she accidentally jammed a needle into his wrist while she was trying to fix his braid, who could blame her?

He could, apparently, and did. She realized he was about to shove her, then watched in astonishment as a different hand caught her surly sleeve-wearer by the wrist in a grip that even she could see was much too tight for comfort. Her current victim spun around to look at whomever was holding onto him.

He fell silent. Olivia looked as well, then almost dropped her needle.

There was a man standing there. That shouldn't have been

unusual given that she was surrounded by a small army of them, but that one there looked as though he'd just stepped off the pages of Medieval Nobleman's Quarterly. She found herself standing shoulder-to-shoulder with her sewing project and heard someone whimper. She wasn't entirely certain she hadn't heard two someones whimper.

The first thing she noted was that her rescuer was taller than she was by several inches and she was tall enough that she'd occasionally had trouble during her teenage years finding jeans long enough to suit her. He had dark, windswept hair, pale eyes, and a face that angels must have wept over—angels and most of the artists whose works she'd studied and loved, actually. She was half surprised her uncle hadn't spotted him already and insisted that he wear a hood that hid his face.

She wasn't sure how they would have hidden the fact that he was standing there surveying his domain with a strange sort of noble presence that left her wondering if he might be the son of someone nobleman. Local earl, probably.

He fixed his captive with a warning glance. "Do not," he advised.

Olivia resisted the temptation to swoon. Gorgeous, chivalrous, and possessing an accent that would require a great deal of time spent listening to in order to place.

"I wasn't going to do anything," her current project said, carefully peeling the other man's fingers away from his wrist. He held out his sleeve toward her. "See?"

Olivia forced herself to turn back to what she was supposed to be doing, but she had a hard time concentrating. She managed not to stick the guy again, but she couldn't say that his sleeve wouldn't come unraveled again very soon. She cut the thread, then caught the tail-end of the look he'd sent her rescuer. She backed up in spite of herself, then caught her foot somehow in the strap of her bag and almost went sprawling.

Or she would have, if her rescuer hadn't casually caught her by the arm and steadied her while simultaneously sending her initial sewing project a bland look that spoke very clearly about just how little the implied threat concerned him. She was surprised he didn't yawn as well, but maybe he had good manners.

The guy with the still-unraveling braid slunk off, muttering to himself. That left her with absolutely no choice but to face perfection. She took a deep breath, made sure her feet were no longer tangled in the strap of her bag, then bravely took one for the team by giving her knight in shining armor the closest scrutiny possible.

Unfortunately for the production, not even her current victim's face could make up for the fact that his clothing was better suited to a medieval faire than Uncle Richard's Renaissance mishmash. Even his sword was such a great medieval reproduction that she could hardly believe it wasn't the real thing.

She fanned herself briefly with the edge of her jacket, not because she was flushed from her recent brush with gaping at a complete stranger, but because she was, as she had noted before, the kind of woman to get giddy over a good-looking blade.

"*Demoiselle*, are you unwell?"

It took her a minute to realize he was speaking in French. Actually, less French and more a charming sort of English that sounded as it if had been run through a rustic French filter with a little of the latter tossed in for seasoning.

"I'm fine," she managed, "but you don't match."

He looked at her blankly.

"Your clothes," she said. She pointed at the other cast members, then took a stab with her own French that was only as good as a couple of years in college and a summer spent antiquing with Aunt Philly in Provençe could make it. "You don't look like them. You should remove your, ah, cloak, *oui*?"

The man looked around himself casually, then froze, as if he realized just how right she'd been. He slowly unfastened the clasp of his cloak and took it off, then studied her for a moment or two before he held it out. "You shall watch it, yes?"

That wasn't all she was going to watch, but that was only because she felt duty-bound to make sure her repairs held up. She took his cloak and put it under her basket just the same, spared a brief moment of regret that he didn't ask her to watch his sword as well, then looked at the rest of him as dispassionately as possible.

He was wearing a tabard that was substantially longer than anyone else's, but she didn't imagine she was going to get him to hike it up so he would just have to hang around in the back. She checked his sleeves for the sake of something to do, then realized he had an enormous rent down the side of his tunic. Either he'd caught himself in the door of his car or he'd been hopping fences to evade the local authorities. He also might have just participated in a friendly little sword fight, but that seemed a little unlikely so she let that one go.

She threaded another needle, then popped a few pins in her mouth and motioned for him to lift his arm so she could get at his shirt.

A hand gently removed all the pins from their dangerous roost and put them in a facing palm. He held that hand out, then held his other arm behind himself to reveal the tear in his tunic.

"There go you," he said gravely.

Yes, there she went indeed, right to ye olde metaphorical fainting couch. She wondered if anyone would notice if she took a very long time fixing her medieval knight's shirt—not because she was interested, of course, but because he looked as though he'd gotten his clothes from a vintage store and she was, her earlier vows aside, a dedicated appreciator of old things. She'd already made an exception for very old items of note managed by English historians, hadn't she? With the right amount of enthusiasm, the man in front of her could definitely be given a good shove into that category.

She pinned his shirt together, apologizing for each time she poked him. She looked at him after a particularly egregious pinning of his shirt to his flesh only to find him watching her and shaking his head occasionally, as if he weren't sure quite what to make of her.

She finished her very poor seam, then looked at the rest of him.

That was, she had to admit, another in a series of horrible mistakes she seemed to be making while standing two feet away from someone who should have been plastered on the side of every bus in the world. She looked at his tabard and had to pause for a moment to admire. That was definitely an eagle and it was absolutely looking at her with its vivid aqua eye.

It was, oddly enough, the same color as that man's eyes, that amazing shade of turquoise, like some coastal bay in an exclusive part of the Caribbean she'd seen pictures of but never thought to visit.

She wondered why he'd chosen that because wondering that sort of thing was better than noticing how the material stretched over shoulders that were just the right height and width to rest a weary head on after a long day of reminding oneself that one was in England to get a job and start a new life, not melt into a pile of mush at the feet of a man who probably used more hair gel than she'd ever owned.

She looked up at his hair that was definitely a bit too long for a professional-type office and considered. She wasn't sure how anyone got that sort of windblown perfection without a stylist, and then she watched him rake his fingers through his hair. Mystery solved.

"You're fine," she said before taking a step back and waving him on to his fate. "Off you go."

He nodded, started to step away, then stopped. He turned back and looked at her. "Encounter me later."

She nodded weakly, then put a stamp of approval on the rest of the guys who filed by her without remembering whether or not she'd actually looked at any of them. Hopefully none of them would come unraveled during the show.

She stowed her sewing gear next to a post, grabbed her bag and her new friend's cloak, then looked for somewhere to loiter that might give her a good view of the action. One never knew when one's sewing skills might be called upon.

"Keeping a close eye on things?"

She jumped a little, then looked at her cousin standing next to her, watching her knowingly.

"I'm responsible like that," Olivia said promptly. "And in the interest of full disclosure, I can't sew. Well, I tried with that guy over there, but I got distracted."

"I can see why." Samantha studied him for a bit. "That's not exactly a Renaissance costume, is it?"

"That's also not a 17th-century sword."

Samantha looked at her in surprise. "I thought you majored in art history."

"I did."

"Why do I get the feeling there's more to this story?"

Olivia cast caution to the wind and watched it flutter away. She looked at her cousin. "Because I have a secret."

Samantha smiled. "So do I. Let's trade."

"I love swords."

"I hate Victorian everything."

Olivia looked at her cousin and almost hugged her. "Today has been a good day."

Samantha laughed and linked arms with her. "It has. Let's go grab a seat and watch the show. Mrs. Sutcliffe can handle things back here for a bit while we see if your new friend can compete with my husband."

"I'm not in England to date a man that pretty."

"You don't have to date him," Samantha said, tugging on her. "You can just window shop. I'll memorize a couple of my father's highlights to use for compliments later, then I'll spend the rest of my time drooling over Derrick while you drool over someone we won't talk about ever again. It'll be great."

Olivia wasn't sure that would be anything but crazy, but at least she would be safely anonymous in the audience.

Three hours later, she had to admit that while she'd certainly kept her eyes peeled for that guy who seemed far more comfortable with his sword than anyone else in the cast of extras, she'd had a hard time not being wowed by Derrick Cameron right along with her cousin. Her Uncle Richard was his usual stage-stealing self, but Derrick had given him such a run for his money that she'd never forgotten who was the star of the show. She looked at her cousin.

"I'm almost speechless."

Samantha smiled. "I keep telling him that he should do it full time, but it's complicated. My father is, as you know, another story entirely."

"Uncle Richard was amazing, as usual." She looked around, but didn't see her costume triumph. "I think I'd better go find you know who and give him back his coat."

"I wonder if he has a girlfriend?"

"I wonder if I should go back to my cottage and hide?"

Samantha laughed briefly and used her to get to her feet. "I'm happy you're here. I think we'll be good friends."

"I think so, too," Olivia said, wishing she had that red-haired Scottish grandpa nearby to thank for the little nudge in the right familial direction. "I'm not sure why we didn't do more together at reunions."

"Louise Theodosia McKinnon," Samantha said dryly. "We should have left her terrorizing her staff at home instead of forcing her to come to reunions so she could terrorize us." She put her hand over her belly, took a deep breath, then smiled. "I'm so glad you came before the show closed."

"I am, too," Olivia agreed, ignoring the slightly queasy feeling she had over how easily she could have overlooked that book in her grandfather's chair, never mind the train ticket inside that book which would have had her missing the ticket to the show. Not, of course, for any other reason than she would have missed her cousin and associated family.

"We're having a cast party down the street in the grange hall in an hour," Samantha said. "If you can stay awake until Dad has accepted all his accolades, you're more than welcome to come with us."

Olivia nodded and watched her cousin walk off to find her husband and father, then waited a bit longer while the crowd began to clear out. She didn't see the owner of the coat she was holding, so she kept herself busy by having a little peek at the clasp.

It was in excellent condition, hand-forged, and definitely medieval in design. She knew that because her love of historical sharp things had actually begun with a rather obsessive study of jewelry though the ages. She supposed it was possible that her own unwholesome fascination with Bakelite bangles had started her, like Irma, down a path of no return.

She studied the clasp a bit more and decided that the most likely explanation was that it had been made by a blacksmith with a love for vintage tools and what they would produce. Maybe the cloak's owner had hidden talents and doing shows was a side gig to help pay for forge rental somewhere in the area.

She looked up suddenly to find that she was the only one still sitting in the audience, though she could hear voices in the distance. She pushed herself to her feet, then made her way backstage. She could see a collection of cast members standing in a group in the distance, no doubt surrounding Uncle Richard who would absolutely be in his element. That was expected.

What she didn't expect to see was someone skulking around in the shadows, rifling through any gear that had been left behind.

She realized with an unpleasant start that she was looking at that stunning man she'd stuck several pins into and he was going through everything that had been left backstage.

Actors were one thing; thieves were another.

She leaped up onto the platform and pointed her finger at him. "Stop, you foul fiend," she said sternly.

He looked up and tilted his head as if he didn't have a clue what she'd just said to him. Obviously she was suffering from the after-effects of too much Shakespeare, but what she wasn't suffering from was indecision. She hoisted her bag more securely onto her shoulder and rushed forward to catch her sewing project before he could escape.

She decided abruptly that her ancestors had been onto something when they'd given such pithy advice about how to put one foot in front of the other. That sort of realization should have come before she'd tangled her own feet up in someone's gear, but lesson learned. No more unwary rushing.

Unfortunately, that didn't solve the problem of going sprawling off the edge of the stage in front of the most handsome man she'd ever seen. She frantically reminded herself that she couldn't care less what he thought because she had sworn off men and the guy she was flying past was definitely one of those.

But for the second time that night, she didn't fall.

She felt herself be caught and swooped up into strong, manly arms. She squawked and threw her arms around her rescuer's neck to keep from falling, narrowly missing elbowing him in the nose. She started to protest that she was probably too heavy to be held and that it was perfectly fine to put her down, then she realized that her knight in shining armor wasn't huffing or puffing.

And his eyes were still the color of a Caribbean bay on a sunny morning.

"*Demoiselle*?"

She tried to focus, truly she did. "Ah, it's Olivia." She realized he probably hadn't been asking that, but it seemed like the sort of thing a rescued damsel in distress should offer right away. "Olivia Grace Drummond."

He carefully set her back down onto her feet, then held her by the arms until she nodded and stepped back. She looked behind her for stray gear before she did, which she thought was very wise, then looked at the man who had saved more than just her pride, which she suspected was less wise.

He took a step back and made her a small bow. "Jackson, ah, Kilchurn," he said. "A good e'en to you."

He repeated his greeting in Gaelic, but she wasn't sure she wanted to start a conversation in that language so late at night. That he could say anything in it seemed unusual, but maybe he thought she was Scottish. Who knew what the conversational rules were in the apparently haunted county of Northumberland?

The fact that his name was Kilchurn and she had a book back in her cottage written by a woman with the same name was a bit of a coincidence—

She stopped herself before she took even a single step down that path. If Miss Eugenie Kilchurn had lived close enough to Artane to write about it, and Jackson Kilchurn lived close enough to Artane to come act in a play at its feet, then the whole countryside was probably full of Kilchurns of all kinds.

She realized Jackson Kilchurn was simply watching her as if he weren't quite sure what she might do next. Given their shared history, he probably had good reason for it.

She gestured briefly in the general direction of backstage. "You can't just steal other people's stuff."

He looked genuinely shocked. "I do not steal."

"What were you doing, then?"

"I lost my … key," he said. "I must for it look."

"Oh," she said, imagining several reasons why that might be a problem. Maybe he had a cottage somewhere in the area with tasty snacks waiting. Maybe he had a screaming BMW with a great heater and absolutely no Cheeto residue stashed in some deserted corner of the village.

It was probably sensible to wonder if the key might belong to a girlfriend who would kill him for losing it, but she didn't like that one so she ignored it.

"What's the key ring look like?" she asked.

He was still doing that translation thing, but it apparently wasn't working for him at the moment because what was coming out of his mouth was still that same sort of French that was absolutely beyond her experience. Vintage linen or hat pins? No problem. Everything else? She'd have to start on it earlier in the day.

She settled for using her fingers. "One key? Two? House key? Car key?"

"One key," he said slowly. "No car key, to my sorrow."

He was back to that English that made him sound like an escapee from a British mystery series who'd had a brush with East Coast prep school. Given how recently she'd talked to her Uncle Richard, she thought she might be qualified to judge. It was a little too charming for her peace of mind, so she decided that maybe they needed to try something else.

She dug around in her bag and pulled out pencil and paper. She was reluctant to use that little notepad she'd poached from her cottage because Artane was sitting so majestically at the top of every page, but sacrifices had to be made. She handed the goods over.

"Can you draw it?"

He took both pencil and paper as if he'd never seen anything like them. She watched him consider, then sketch something with his left hand. He looked at her quickly, then switched hands. She pretended not to notice, mostly because in spite of the stern warnings she was giving herself, her perfectly calibrated mystery meter was going off with the dulcet tones of a ferry horn. A southpaw who looked like he'd never seen a note pad before in his life and who had hauled her up into his arms with nary a huff of exertion?

She didn't want to know more, truly.

He held out the pencil and paper. "This it is."

Well, that was definitely a key, but it looked like something made to fit some sort of high-tech container that would probably blow up if the key were inserted improperly. She put her notepad and pencil back in her bag, then handed him his cloak.

"I'll help you look," she said.

He paused, then took his cloak and put it around her shoulders. "'Tis cold this night."

It was cold, he was stunning, and she was losing what was left of her mind. She didn't even really have the excuse of jetlag to hide behind any longer. She settled her bag more securely over her shoulder but under his cloak and started to help him search, doing her best to completely ignore exactly how crazy her life had suddenly become. She was rifling through the belongings of complete strangers in the company of a man who looked as if he'd just stepped out of a medieval history book, who could barely string two words together in English before adding a French twist, and she was wearing a cloak that smelled fairly good for boasting as many travel stains as it did. She wished Samantha would show up so she could get an opinion on the age of the cloth.

"What in the world is going on here!"

She found herself pulled behind her new friend and could have sworn she heard the whisper of a sword coming from its sheath. She tried to look around Jackson Kilchurn's shoulder only to have him step in front of her again.

"Who are those souls?" he asked over his shoulder.

"My cousins."

He sighed deeply. "Of course."

Olivia peeked around him to find that her Uncle Richard was gaping at them, Derrick was watching with no expression at all on his face, and Samantha looked as if she might be trying not to laugh. Jackson put his sword away, then made her family a low bow.

And then he gasped. She did too, because in the end she was a first-rate treasure hunter and there was something shiny there in the grass. Ganging warily be damned, there was bounty to be had.

She just hadn't expected to meet her match on her way off the stage.

SIX

JACKSON NARROWLY AVOIDED DASHING HIS head against Mistress Olivia Drummond's only because he'd spent a lifetime wrenching out of the way of someone else's sword. The hilt of his own caught him firmly in his side, but he shifted to dislodge it and dove for that glinting piece of pale gold.

The world suddenly exploded into a light that almost drew an unmanly noise of surprise from him. He looked up to find not the sun having made an unexpected appearance, but rather Future torches that had somehow been lit all at once. Not even squinting at them allowed him to study them for more than a heartbeat or two, so he looked away and added them to his list of things to investigate later.

The light did allow him to see that he was holding onto nothing but a simple coin. Half a coin, as it happened, given that Mistress Olivia was holding onto it as well. She looked closely, then released it.

"Just a new one," she said as easily as if she dismissed something inedible on her trencher. "Queen Elizabeth looks great though still, doesn't she?"

Jackson looked at the coin he now held. There was indeed a woman wearing a crown stamped on its face, along with the date of the coin's minting.

2008.

He felt himself sway. If he hadn't believed what had befallen him already that day, he would have believed it right then. He felt a hand suddenly on his arm.

"Are you okay?"

Okay had been one of Kendrick's favorite Future words—along with *whatever* and *awesome*—so he wasn't unfamiliar with it. Whether or not he was indeed okay was something he thought he could add to that ever-increasing list of things he would think about when he was equal to the same. He looked at the woman kneeling next to him.

"Aye," he said confidently, "I am okay."

"If you say so," she said slowly.

He heaved himself to his feet and held out his hand to help her up. Knight of the realm before more pressing personal concerns, or so his father would have advised.

He wondered what final words his father would have offered before he found himself put to the sword for not having volunteered answers to questions Jackson had never dared ask.

The pointed clearing of a male throat brought him away from thoughts of just desserts and back to the present moment. He nodded slightly at Mistress Olivia, then turned to assess the trio of souls who had gathered nearby.

He recognized the man on the left as the player who had done such a credible job of bringing King Henry V to life. He spared a brief moment to acknowledge their numerical kinship whilst doing his damndest to ignore when that same king had reigned, then made note of the older gentleman there—a player as well—and a woman who was obviously blossoming with child. He made them all a low bow.

"Good e'en to you all," he said politely.

The elder gentleman frowned. "Your name, young man?"

"Jackson … Kilchurn," he said, finding that method of introducing himself still to be strange on his tongue. "My lord."

The older man beamed, so perhaps offering that courtesy had not gone amiss.

"I am Richard Drummond," he said, looking every inch the proud patriarch. "This is my daughter, Samantha, and her husband, Derrick. You've apparently already met my young cousin, Olivia, though don't think to get any friendlier with her until I've seen your resumé. We're off to a fête, if you care to come."

Jackson cursed himself silently for needing time to unravel Lord Richard's words. He understood that he'd been invited to some sort of meal which at any other time he would have agreed to without hesitation. Unfortunately, things were what they were and he had a key to find. It also occurred to him that once he found it, he should likely return home.

He wondered how long he could put off thinking about that.

"My gratitude," he said, turning his attentions back to the matter at hand and hoping his Future words were more intelligible than they sounded to him, "but I cannot. I will accompany you until you reach your home, then I must seek out mine."

He realized he'd begun in English and ended in French, but considering the length of the day he'd had so far, perhaps he could be forgiven for it.

"Suit yourself," Lord Richard said, in oddly accented but decent French himself. "The offer stands if you change your mind. Let us be off, my dears. I suspect we're holding up the celebrations."

Jackson accepted his cloak back from Mistress Olivia, then watched her cousins gather her up and lead her away. He fell in behind them as they made their way from the location of the entertainment, partly because he needed to go south as well but mostly because he thought he might want to have one last look at that Future gel who had so ferociously accused him of thievery.

He suspected his mother would have approved of her.

The torches extinguished themselves, which startled him, but he followed after the company just the same, trying without success to ignore the feeling roiling inside him. He refused to call it *panic* because that would have been an absurd thing for a man of his maturity to allow himself. After all, he had lost nothing more important than a key.

Then again, he'd been in possession of the same since the day he'd turned ten-and-two and found the damned thing lying on the floor directly in front of his sire's solar door. He had picked it up, felt the slight weight of it in his hand, and studied the strange and wondrous color of the smooth silvery gold.

Then he had done something he hadn't done before or since.

He had lied.

He'd shoved it down the side of his boot—never mind sewing it into the seam of every pair of boots he'd owned thereafter—and denied having seen it when he'd been asked. He'd told himself that it was merely something useless his sire had dropped. He had soothed his tormented conscience by assuring himself that it had likely just fallen off his mother's ring of keys. It wasn't as if a key couldn't be remade or a lock opened without any key at all, was it? Hell, Kendrick had taught him how to best any lock in front of him by the time he'd been ten and he knew that was a skill his cousin had learned from Jackson IV himself.

His father had asked him casually on his fourteenth birthday if he wanted to know how, but he'd pretended great offense and stated arrogantly that he would never stoop to such unknightly tactics.

He suspected his sire had known already what he knew how to do, yet his father's only response had been to smile, clap him on the back, and invite him out to the lists to do what real knights did.

Again, to the very gates of Hell and beyond. His sire was responsible for absolutely everything he knew about being honorable, honest, and relentless.

And that key had come near to burning a hole into his soul from the guilt of having kept it.

He'd suspected over the years, deep in that same place in his soul where he didn't dare look all that often, that it was a key from the Future. He had no idea what miraculous thing it might open, though he'd speculated endlessly when he'd been too weary to fight the impulse any longer. And to lose in the very place he was standing the one thing that had led him to that same place?

He swore silently. He didn't like irony. It made him want to take his sword and stab something.

He glanced to his left at that hulking pile of stones up on the bluff. The fact that he was a fraction of a league from his uncle's gates whilst being several hundred years from any family inside whom he might recognize was perhaps something he could also refrain from thinking about lest the absolute improbability of it overwhelm him.

He paused with the company as they came to the edge of what he recognized as a main thoroughfare through the village in his day. He kept his mouth shut thanks solely to a lifetime of traveling to unfamiliar places. He watched Lord Richard gather up the ladies and walk ahead across the road, then he followed with as much confidence as he could muster.

Their path led along a small cobbled road to a small courtyard. The courtyard was not a surprise, but the house that lay to one side of it surely was. He had never seen anything so marvelously built. He stood next to Mistress Olivia as the men in her family went inside, no doubt to make certain the hall was secure.

"Is this your home?" he asked.

She looked at him in surprise. "No, it's just a hotel."

"Where is the innkeeper?"

"She's probably asleep."

He could scarce believe his ears. No servants, no guardsmen, just a woman by herself? It beggared belief. He watched as the lords Derrick and Richard returned to announce that all was secure inside.

"I think I'll call it an early night," Mistress Olivia said. "It was a great show, though. You guys were wonderful."

"You have my UK number," Lady Samantha said. "Just call me when you get to London and we'll get you settled."

Jackson refrained from pointing out how little good calling anyone's name in a London crowd would do only because he suspected there were perhaps Future things afoot that he didn't understand. He watched Mistress Olivia step onto the threshold of her hall, then turn to bid her family a final goodnight.

The light from inside her hall fell softly onto her lovely features. He would have stopped to have a second look at her if that had been the extent of her charms, but he had also listened to her call him a thief and battle him for a coin.

Those were things a man didn't take lightly.

He was, admittedly, an admirer of women. He adored his mother, who was not only lovely beyond belief but fierce and courageous, and his grandmother Gwennelyn, who even with her well-earned years wrapped around her like a delicate shawl, was still the sort of woman bards traveled great distances to have a proper look at so they might use her as inspiration. His aunts and cousins were, to a woman, worthy of admiration and his best comportment.

He was also a man, though, and he had definitely over the course of his score-and-eight years clapped his eyes on a great number of women not related to him in any fashion who had left him simply speechless with their beauty and wit. If he'd availed himself of a discreet number of private interviews with those breathtaking creatures, he wasn't going to admit to it in mixed company.

What he would admit, however, was that never in all those years of looking wherever he pleased had he ever felt the need to simply settle in and admire.

She was … enchanting.

"Coming, son?" Lord Richard asked.

Jackson dragged his attentions away from that glorious woman standing on the threshold of her small hall and tried to balance his annoyance over being interrupted in his looking with not wishing to offend by correcting Lord Richard about his manner of address.

Things in the Future were, he was finding, very different.

Some things were unacceptable no matter the year, however, and one of those things was leaving a woman unprotected. He turned to the two men standing there, then gestured to Mistress Olivia.

"Surely you will not leave her here without a guard."

Lord Richard frowned. "The village is very safe, Master Kilchurn. We've checked the premises for ruffians and found none. My young cousin will be fine."

Jackson looked at Mistress Olivia who was still standing in her doorway. "Have you a weapon?"

She looked at him as if he were babbling nonsense, but he was fairly sure he hadn't spoken amiss. Her family was looking at him the same way save Lord Derrick, but that one there had a wife to keep safe.

He didn't like the situation, but perhaps he had done all he could. He made her a low bow, then motioned for her to go inside. She exchanged a look with the lady Samantha, then shook her head as she walked inside. She turned and looked at him.

"I'll lock my door."

"I'll wait to hear it."

"I hope you find your key."

He nodded his thanks, then looked at her pointedly.

She smiled briefly, then shut the door. He heard some bolt or other slide home, which was perhaps the best he could hope for. He turned to find her family apparently waiting for him.

"Are you certain you don't care to come with us, Master Jackson?"

"I am grieved, my lord, but nay," he said politely. "Many thanks for your kindness."

More pleasantries were sent his way, though he honestly was too weary to make note of them. What he did understand very clearly was just how unwilling to move Lord Derrick seemed to be. Ah, something reassuring. He never would have left a stranger near any of the women in his family without a decent guard, never mind completely alone. He made the entire family a small bow, then walked away and started across the road.

It was there, within sight of his uncle's keep, that he almost lost his life because it hadn't occurred to him how quickly something might come out of the darkness to slay him. He realized he'd been pulled out of the way of some massive beast by none other than Lord Derrick himself.

"Cars move quickly," he said mildly.

Jackson took a deep breath. "My mistake," he said without hesitation. "Many thanks."

Lord Derrick only released him and stepped back.

Jackson looked to both sides of himself, then walked without lingering across the road. He supposed that had been no worse than an encounter with a bolting horse—or being atop a horse whilst it was bolting, which he had also been—so he took a deep breath and carried on.

He continued on, trying to ignore the sight of Artane looking not at all the same as it had the day before, then finally had to stop and breathe for a moment or two. He looked heavenward to see where the moon might find herself, then stopped still at the sight of a slender crescent.

He gaped at the heavens in astonishment. He was certain the moon had been full not two days earlier.

He was going to have a word with … well, he wasn't sure with whom, but there was a body who would hear of his displeasure. He muttered a curse under his breath to keep himself company, rubbed his arms against a chill that felt more like autumn than late spring, and continued on toward the keep. The terrain was more unfamiliar than he'd suspected it might be, but perhaps he couldn't expect anything else.

He retraced his steps to the ground on which that accursed time gate had opened for him earlier. It was unsteady beneath his feet, which he found alarming, though he carefully walked over it just the same.

He stopped finally and folded his arms over his chest as he considered the events of the day. He was certain he'd still had his key inside his boot when he'd donned them that morning. He hadn't brawled with anyone or stumbled in surprise, not even when he'd been in that foul time where the lads wore too much lace about their throats and not nearly enough cloth everywhere else.

There had been that cheeky lad who had been trying to relieve him of his boots when he'd woken that morn, but he was certain nothing had been dislodged from inside them. The only spot where he'd gone down fully to his knees had been as he'd been shoved into his current day by those damned twins who were no longer children. He'd been too unnerved at the time to know whether or not he'd lost anything but his wits.

Perhaps he'd lost it on the way to the frolic. He carefully made one final search of the soil surrounding the gate, then retraced his steps to the location of the play. He searched in ever-widening circles until he was certain he was walking over ground he hadn't that day.

He finally simply stopped and stared into the distance. He was fortunate he'd been raised to manhood by a man who never panicked. He honestly couldn't bring to mind a single time when his father had appeared anything but fully in control of himself even when he hadn't been in control of the events swirling around him.

Obviously, he would do the same thing.

He didn't like to leave anything undone overnight, but he could tell nothing more would be accomplished without daylight. Given that such was the case, perhaps he could at least be of some service to Mistress Olivia by acting as her guardsman during the night.

He retraced his steps and found her dwelling easily enough, but the torches inside had been extinguished. He paused by the door and listened, but heard no sound. He could only assume she was safely tucked in her bed, which left him with the task of simply securing her front stoop.

He made himself comfortable on a slab of flat stone, unclasped his cloak so he didn't choke himself in the night, and laid his sword down next to him where he could rest his hand on the hilt. He leaned back against the wall of her house and closed his eyes. He wasn't much for sitting, but it occurred to him that the present moment was the first time he'd sat down for the whole of a day that had felt more like a year—

He heard the faintest scuff of a footstep only because he'd spent so much of his life listening for the same. He didn't imagine his sword would be of any use against any weapons of the current day, but a man couldn't go wrong with a pair of knives.

He was on his feet and halfway to killing his visitor before he realized it was simply Lord Derrick. He wondered how he might have explained to the local authorities that he'd almost cut out the man's intestines and was still holding onto the very sharp knives he'd intended to use in that same business, then realized he wouldn't need to. Lord Derrick also had a pair of knives, ones that were currently keeping his gut unpierced. Obviously no explanation would have been necessary.

Lord Derrick remained exactly as he was for a protracted period of time, then very slowly and deliberately pulled his knives back and slid them into sheaths that Jackson could see were strapped to his sides under his close-fitting cloak. The man then took a pair of steps back and simply stood there with his hands at his side.

Jackson returned his knives to their accustomed spots in his boots, then folded his arms over his chest and settled for silence. He wasn't one for mindless chatter on the best of days and he was certainly not at his best at the moment. He could see no other weapons on his companion's person, though the man gave off the same sort of aura he was accustomed to from his sire, that of someone who didn't need steel to be dangerous.

Interesting, that.

His companion watched him just as patiently before he finally nodded slightly and extended his hand. "Derrick Cameron, cousin to Robert, laird of the clan Cameron."

Jackson shook his hand, appreciating not only that it was dirk-free at present but that the man standing there hadn't shied away from keeping himself alive by means of the same. He also appreciated that Lord Derrick—if that was his appropriate title—was speaking in Gaelic, which would definitely make communication easier than it might have been otherwise.

"Lord Derrick," he said, inclining his head politely.

"'Tis simply Derrick. And you are?"

"Jackson of Raventhorpe," he said, though he supposed that might have been more than he should have said. "Kilchurn, I mean," he added. "As I said before to your father-in-law."

Derrick Cameron showed no reaction to that. He merely clasped his hands behind his back and tilted his head slightly. "Guarding the door?"

"I thought it wise," Jackson said. He hesitated, then supposed there was no point in not being blunt. "I daresay you should have considered the same. Why did you leave her alone here?"

"I saw my wife safely settled, then returned to make certain Olivia's cottage was secure."

Jackson nodded. "I stand corrected, then."

Derrick didn't seem particularly flattered by the apology. "How do you know my wife's cousin?"

Jackson noted the unmistakable warning behind the question, which left him suddenly entertaining a few kind thoughts about the man standing there.

"She stuck me with her small pieces of steel whilst attending to a rent in my tunic," he said. "I thought to repay the kindness by keeping watch over her for the night."

"Did you find the key you lost?"

"Nay," Jackson said, in as off-hand a manner as he could manage. "I need daylight for a proper search."

"Understandable." Derrick considered, then nodded toward the sword lying near the doorway. "During the daytime you should leave that inside Olivia's cottage, if she'll allow it. And keep your knives hidden."

Jackson nodded as if he understood, though he couldn't imagine why a man would want to give up his sword. 'Twas no wonder Zachary Smith had known so well how to use his hands and so poorly how to protect himself with a blade if this was how they comported themselves in the Future.

"I noted the way you looked at my cousin before," Derrick continued very quietly. "If you harm her, I will hunt you down and slay you. The latter will not happen quickly."

Jackson nodded in appreciation of the warning. "I have sisters and gel cousins. She will remain perfectly safe in my care."

"Well, if you forget your honor, she does have her small pieces of steel."

Jackson drew himself up, then realized the man was poking at him, no doubt to test him.

"My honor is beyond reproach," he said crisply.

"I'll trust that it is."

Jackson imagined that such trust would only go so far, which he understood. He also had no doubt that Derrick Cameron would make good on his threats. Admittedly his head pained him and he was in a foreign land, but he hadn't heard the bloody whoreson until he'd been almost next to him.

"I brought you supper and clothes."

Jackson didn't imagine falling on the man's neck and weeping with gratitude would improve things any, so he simply nodded and watched Derrick melt into the darkness. Scots were, as he knew thanks to a lifetime of living on the border with them, canny lads, indeed.

Derrick returned with two rucksacks made of a fabric that crackled as he held it out. Jackson didn't consider himself unlearned or cowardly, but he had to admit that was the first Future thing he'd encountered that left him truly unnerved.

Or at least it did until he caught a whiff of what obviously resided inside one of the marvelous sacks.

"Fish and chips," Derrick said.

He looked up. "Chips of what?"

"Potatoes, which weren't cultivated in England until a bit before 1600—" Derrick paused and smiled briefly. "Sorry. Too much research for Shakespeare. Apologies as well that supper isn't as hot as it could be."

Jackson would have eaten anything straight out of a pile of snow and been overjoyed to fill his belly, so he wasn't about to complain.

"You'll likely want to change out of your costume as quickly as possible," Derrick added. "The clothing is mine, but it's clean. You've no need to return it."

Jackson took a deep breath. He hardly knew where to begin to express his gratitude for the kindness of a complete stranger, so he would, as his father had also endlessly advised, pay it forward. "Thank you."

"You're guarding my cousin," Derrick said easily, "so 'tis an even trade. Don't kill anyone with your sword, though. It would inconvenience me to get you out of the local dungeon."

And with that, he smiled and walked away. Jackson watched him walk into the darkness, then shook his head over the unexpected gifts. The kindness of strangers, indeed.

He considered what he'd been given, then decided the first thing to do was to look as if he belonged in the current day. He set his supper down by the door, then examined the clothing Derrick had given him.

He was relieved to note that the pieces designed for the lower half of a man covered what they should, though the undertunic was shorter than he was accustomed to. There was also something he supposed might pass for a tabard. At the very bottom of the pile was a close-fitting cloak such as he'd seen Derrick wear. He imagined his boots would continue to serve him as they always had.

He found himself a patch of deep shadow, quickly exchanged his own clothing for Future gear, then folded everything of his up and put it in the noisy rucksack. That attended to, he made himself at home again in front of Mistress Olivia's door and acquainted himself with his supper.

He wondered halfway through the meal if he hadn't bypassed the Future and gone straight to Heaven. Considering he'd always suspected that the main course in Hell was cold eel, perhaps he had yet again managed to avoid a lengthy encounter with his usual demons.

He finished his supper, then looked at the bottle of liquid that had been so thoughtfully provided. There was no cork of any kind, but the container seemed flimsy enough, so he poked a hole in it with his knife and had the best water he'd ever tasted.

He returned his strange Future bowls to their sack, cleaned his teeth with what Derrick had obviously provided for that activity, then pushed himself to his feet and had a final look around the outside of the cottage. He paused at the edge of the dwelling and looked up at the castle sitting so comfortably on the bluff there. 'Twas odd to consider how often he'd thought about the Future and what a marvelous place it might be.

And there he was, standing in the midst of it.

He shook his head over the improbability of that, then returned and made himself comfortable on the stone in front of the doorway. He supposed it might not be unthinkable to indulge in the luxury of feeling like a proper Future lad.

It wouldn't last, he knew, but the other thing both his parents had taught him was to never take a moment of wonder for granted.

And the Future was indeed a wondrous place.

SEVEN

OLIVIA STOOD WITH HER HAND on the door of her little cottage and wondered if Miss Eugenie Kilchurn had been onto something with all her tales of Northumbrian things that went bump in the night. She'd had uneasy dreams, but it could have been worse. She could have enjoyed the full paranormal experience of having some ghost or legend popping in during the middle of the night for a cup of tea and a wee chat.

She took a deep, cleansing breath and mentally put everything strange behind her. She was probably just suffering from jetlag, not enough dinner, and the lingering vision of Jackson Kilchurn, medieval re-enactment aficionado, who was definitely wasting himself in the cast of his local shows.

She couldn't deny that it had been with a twinge of regret that she'd had one last look at him the night before, but she'd at least done so feeling properly championed. It was the first time any man besides her grandfather had reminded her to lock her door before she went to bed.

But that was yesterday, today was today, and she was free of needing to puzzle over the chivalrous habits of handsome locals which left her free to go gawk at an enormous castle. She only had two days left to investigate nailed-down Northumbrian items of historical significance and time was precious.

She opened the door, then almost went sprawling over an addition to her doormat. She caught herself with her hand on the doorjamb and supposed she could apologize in a minute for dropping her bag on that something's stomach.

Jackson opened his eyes and looked at her for an endless moment before he simply reached up and handed her back her purse.

"What are you doing here?" she managed.

He rubbed his hands over his face, then heaved himself to his feet and turned to make her a slight bow. "I was guarding this door of yours," he said. "I was not called upon to dispatch any ruffians."

Well, thank heavens for that. She supposed she didn't need to point out that he'd probably been in more danger from fangirls than thugs. Whatever could be said about the guy in medieval gear didn't begin to describe the entirely new level of luscious that was Jackson Kilchurn in jeans and a black leather jacket.

She was tempted to look over her shoulder to see if Karma was gunning for her, but there was probably a good reason why that gorgeous man had decided she needed her doorway guarded. Maybe he still hadn't found his key and wanted another pair of eyes to help in the search. Maybe he'd lost his wallet and wanted her to buy them both breakfast. Maybe he was afraid that if he went out into general circulation, he would be mobbed by that stampede of women who hadn't known where to look for him the night before.

"Mistress Olivia, are you unwell?"

She pulled herself back to the present. "Faint from hunger, probably."

"Then we should seek out sustenance." He reached for something lying on the stone near his sword and held it up. "I have this golden coin to use."

She looked at the pound coin they'd found the night before, then considered. Had his parents not only hidden him away in the barn to save the local female population from brawling over him, but also kept him completely in the dark about the cost of modern-day life? She didn't want to embarrass him, but she'd also enjoyed that old I-forgot-my-wallet ploy more than once in the past. She would need to proceed with caution.

"Oh, don't worry about that," she said casually. "I have money—"

"A woman pay for my meal?" he said, looking almost as appalled as he had when she'd accused him of being a thief. "Unthinkable. I will find a labor to do, then see us both fed."

Maybe it would be best to hold off on trying to figure him out. What she did know, though, was that neither of them would last long enough for him to chop a little wood, so she dug around in her bag for the cookies she'd found on the tea tray that morning—and already sampled, as it happened—then held the tube out.

"Breakfast," she said, on the off chance his usual meal consisted of something healthy, like porridge. "Chocolate is involved."

Jackson took a digestive biscuit and studied it with a frown before he hesitantly tasted it. He chewed, then looked at her in surprise. "This is chocolate? I've heard tell of its wonders, but—"

He stopped speaking abruptly, looking as if he thought he might have said too much. He focused on his biscuit and she indulged in a moment of silent outrage on his behalf that his parents had apparently deprived him of one of life's best food groups. She took a couple of chocolate-dipped staples for herself and handed him the rest. It was the least she could do to welcome him to the twenty-first century.

She crunched with him in companionable silence until there was nothing left to eat, then she took the package away and tossed it into the trash.

"Did you find your key?" she asked.

He shook his head. "Daylight was required."

She cast caution to the wind for the second time in as many days. "Do you want help looking? I'm going up to the castle anyway."

"I do not like to ask for aid," he admitted, "but I would welcome it this morn." He leaned over and picked up his sword. "Your cousin Derrick advised that I leave this hidden, but I wouldn't presume—"

She hoisted her bag more securely over her shoulder and held out her hand. "I'll put it under my bed."

He rested that sheathed sword point-down on the stone and studied her. "'Tis sharp."

"I promise I won't stab you with it."

He lifted an eyebrow briefly. She tried to ignore the way that drew her attention to the color of his eyes, but that was harder than it should have been. She realized he was speaking, but he was peppering his sentences with enough French that she only caught *clothing* and *keep you safe*.

"I'm sorry, what?"

"Your cousin loaned me this clothing," he repeated carefully.

"He's a great guy." She was starting to feel a little silly holding out one hand, so—in for a penny, in for a pound—she held out both and looked at him with just the right amount of expectation. She knew what that right amount was because it was hard-wired into her antique-store-owner DNA.

Jackson pursed his lips and put both hands over the hilt of his sword. "My sword is *very* sharp," he said, "and you make me uneasy."

"Me?" she said, stopping just short of putting her hand innocently over her heart.

"Aye, you." He considered, then held the blade out to her, hilt-first. "If you cut yourself, your cousin will slay me."

She seriously doubted Derrick would do Jackson Kilchurn any damage, though she appreciated the sentiment. She was also torn between looking at a man she didn't have time for and ogling a sword she could make a great deal of time for, but it was shaping up to be that sort of day. She started to go inside, then looked over her shoulder at him.

"You can use my bathroom if you want," she offered. "It's just right inside here. And take your time."

He peeked inside the cottage which gave her the opportunity to hustle off with the goods. She wasn't surprised by how heavy the sword was, but she had to admit she was a little baffled that something of such obvious vintage quality was being carried around by a guy who couldn't seem to keep hold of his keys.

She took her time stashing his sword under her bed, then went back outside and gave not eavesdropping the old college try. It had been hard to avoid hearing the initial squawk of surprise coming from the bathroom, followed by the current sounds of water running from every possible fixture, but maybe it was just better not to speculate.

She tucked the bags with Jackson's costume and what had apparently been his supper the night before inside the door, then jumped a little when she saw him coming back through her living room. He eased past her and went to stand with his back to her in the middle of her courtyard, occasionally rubbing the back of his neck as if he were trying to get hold of himself. She added *rustic bathroom conditions* to her ever-lengthening list of what he'd likely endured as a kid, then had to do a double-take when he turned to face her.

He was white as a ghost.

"Are you okay?" she asked in alarm.

"Faint from hunger, probably," he managed.

She would have complimented him on his bang-up American accent, but he honestly didn't look all that good. Maybe he needed something more substantial than cookies for breakfast. Since he'd done her the favor of keeping the ruffians at bay during the night, the least she could do was buy him lunch, no matter how much that might offend his sense of chivalry.

She pulled the door shut, locked it, and hung a *No Service Please* sign on the door. She supposed that was all she could do to keep his sword from terrifying the maids.

He reached around her and tried the door. It was apparently

locked enough to suit him because he stepped back and nodded toward the castle. "Key, then food."

She wasn't going to argue with that. She slung her bag over her shoulder and walked with him across the courtyard and toward the street. He caught her arm before they stepped onto the road.

"Things move very quickly here," he advised.

She realized she was growing increasingly accustomed to the way he mixed English and French. If it might take a few minutes to get truly comfortable with ignoring how desperately she wanted to open the lid of that gorgeous box walking next to her and have a peek, so be it. She was nothing if not committed to any and all vows made in vintage carpet.

She walked with him across the field that cozied up to the castle's bluff until he stopped in front of an enormous tarp in a shade of lime that made her teeth ache just from looking at it.

"Is this the spot?" she asked.

He nodded grimly.

"Maybe they're fixing a sewer line or digging for something of archeological significance."

He looked a little green, but that could have been the sun reflecting off the tarp. She left him to digesting whatever it was he was thinking and started looking around the edge of the plastic.

And for the second time in as many days, she saw something shiny half buried in the grass.

She dropped to her knees only to find that Jackson had done the same thing. She supposed the only reason they hadn't knocked each other out was that he possessed the uncanny ability of avoiding both elbows and determined former treasure hunters.

She realized immediately that they were both holding onto another coin. She waited for him to release it, but he seemed perfectly content to kneel there in a damp field and wait her out. Obviously she would have to make the first move.

She looked at the coin, then shrugged dismissively. "Worthless."

"Then release it."

"I couldn't," she said regretfully. "You know, because I found it first."

"Then why do I hold it also?"

She made herself comfortable. Unfortunately, Jackson had assumed her grandfather's favorite position of casually sitting back on his heel and propping his knee up to use as a place to rest his forearm. It had been Dwight Drummond's go-to way of putting fence-sitting sellers at ease, and it had never failed him. She was beginning to suspect that the current one was not Jackson's first rodeo. If she didn't end things decisively, she might run the risk of being there all day.

"Why don't we flip for it?" she asked pleasantly.

"Flip?"

She made sure she had a firm grasp on the goods, then dug around in her bag with her other hand for something else to use. She held up a quarter, then flipped it and caught it without looking. It was, as it happened, also not her first rodeo.

"Heads I win," she said, handing him the quarter, "tails you lose."

He took it and examined it, then looked at her suddenly in astonishment. "But then you would win either way."

"Just making sure you're awake," she muttered, and unfortunately he was. She put the quarter back in her bag, then looked at him. "What are we going to do then? Have a sword fight over it?"

"You have no sword."

"Neither do you."

He started to speak, then shut his mouth. He studied her for a moment or two. "You guard it first. We shall trade in an hour."

"Perfect," she said.

He looked at her pointedly, then deliberately released his hold on the coin. She stood up and pocketed the goods before he could change his mind.

"In a pair of hours, perhaps," he amended, getting to his feet. "To be fair."

"Whatever you say," she agreed. The rest of the day would, she was sure, take care of itself. "Do you want to keep looking for your key? We could look around the edges of the tarp, unless you live nearby and maybe you lost it near your house?"

"My home is too far." He dragged his hand through his hair and sighed. "Let us walk to the place of last eve's merriment and examine the ground there by daylight."

She'd heard worse ideas. She followed him as he made one final circle around that vile green tarp, then walked with him slowly across the field. The stage had been struck, but Jackson looked over the ground anyway. It occurred to her at one point that if anyone had found his key, Derrick probably would have dropped it off with her before he and Samantha had left for London that morning.

She wondered why Jackson was so stressed about something that hadn't looked as though it would fit any house or car she'd ever seen, but maybe he was some sort of super spy with secrets he couldn't share with her unclassified self.

"No luck?" she asked as he stopped in front of her.

"I fear I must search under that strange green cloth. Let us query the keep's guard as to its purpose."

She wasn't sure the castle still had any sort of guard, but what did she know? If nothing else, some castle employee might have thoughts on what was going on.

She walked with Jackson across that grassy field she hoped didn't belong to a local farmer, then up the path to the castle gates. She finally had to simply stop and take it all in. The only problem she had was trying to decide between gaping at the ocean or gawking at the castle. No wonder people had been writing about the spot she was standing on for decades.

She realized Jackson had stopped as well and was watching her as he leaned back against a fence obviously put there to keep people from pitching over the edge onto the dunes below. She smiled weakly.

"I've never seen a castle before," she admitted. "It's really old."

"Aye," he agreed. "Very."

She walked over to join him in his leaning. "Have you been here before?" she asked casually. "To Artane?"

"Aye."

She studied him. For all she knew, he'd had dozens of picnics down there on the beach, even if they had been *sans* chocolate.

"Are you from here?" she asked. "I mean, England."

He nodded solemnly.

"From around here?"

"Near here," he conceded.

She smiled. "You don't volunteer much information, do you?"

"That can be … dangerous."

And she was definitely beginning to suspect that whatever he might say, English was not his first language. Maybe there was a pocket of Kilchurns in the area who were committed to keeping Gaelic alive. Maybe he'd been shipped off to France as a kid because he'd been such a troublemaker. Maybe his family was full of re-enactment aficionados who were determined to start some sort of living history museum and that sword she'd stashed under her bed was razor sharp to lend it an authentic air.

Of course she'd pulled it partway from the sheath just to look. She was certain that didn't affect any vow she'd made to leave any and all mysteries alone.

Jackson clasped his hands behind his back and looked at her. "Shall we go inside?"

She nodded, perfectly willing to trade the slight mystery walking next to her for the astonishing piece of history sitting in front of her. She walked with him up the road to the gates, trying not to look as giddy as she felt. She paused at the ticket booth and looked for the admission times and prices. She started to pull out her wallet, but Jackson stopped her and gestured toward the booth.

"What is this? And where are the guards?"

"I don't know about guards," she said carefully, "but this looks like where we have to pay to go inside."

He blinked. "Give them gold to enter?"

"It's probably how they keep the lights on. You know, tourists and stuff. Don't worry, I've got this one."

He pulled her behind him. "I shall see to us both."

She would have protested, but he'd already walked inside what she guessed had been a guardhouse at some point in the past. She followed him, her wallet in hand just in case, and watched him approach the granny behind the desk. The woman sized him up, then sighed lightly, as if she'd just seen too many strange things in her life to be surprised by one more.

"Good morrow to you, good woman," Jackson said politely. "Your name, if you please?"

"Mrs. Gladstone," the woman said, patting her hair into place. "And you, young man?"

"I am Jackson," he said smoothly. He rested his elbow on her counter and leaned in as if he had a secret that only they two should share. "I must enter the gates, Lady Gladstone, but alas, I am without funds."

"And you won't let your girlfriend pay for you?"

Olivia started to protest, then caught the wink Mrs. Gladstone sent her way.

"I could not," Jackson said seriously. "Very unchivalrous."

Mrs. Gladstone looked him over again. "I have boxes to move."

He stepped back and made her a low bow. "I am your servant." He started to turn away, then stopped. "That covering on the field below—"

"Tarp over a sinkhole," Mrs. Gladstone said without hesitation. "Happens twice a year without fail. One might think there was something mysterious there if one were interested in taking note of those kinds of unusual happenings."

Olivia wondered if it would be rude to just turn and run away. She half wished she'd brought along a rope of garlic to wear around her neck to ward off those who might be fascinated by things she was absolutely never going to get within spitting distance of again.

And since it wasn't ladylike to spit, she would be standing back and letting everyone else get involved in things they shouldn't. Aunt Philly would have approved.

"It's usually a fortnight before they roll up the tarp and put it away for the next time," Mrs. Gladstone continued with a shrug. "Funny how the ground always seemed to fill itself back in without help, isn't it?"

Jackson nodded, though he looked a little green. Given the lack of offensive sheeting in the area, Olivia suspected that might be because he needed either food or a nap. She watched him as she left the guardroom with him.

"Your key is probably under that tarp," she offered. "Can you go home without it?"

"Nay, I must have it."

She wanted to ask him just what he planned to do for the next couple of weeks, but it was really none of her business. For all she knew, he had family in the area he could stay with.

He gestured toward a bench that was quite conveniently sitting in some glorious sunshine.

"Sit," he suggested. "Rest."

She wasn't convinced she wouldn't end up napping, but it was a novel enough sensation to have someone offer to work off an entry fee for her that she thought she might manage to stay awake to enjoy it. If nothing else, Aunt Philly would appreciate the details.

Jackson emerged from the booth a while later, tickets and a guidebook in hand. He handed her a ticket and the book, then made her the same sort of bow he'd made Mrs. Gladstone.

"Your servant," he said politely.

She smiled. "How many boxes did you move?"

"The same one, many times."

She imagined he had and she also imagined Mrs. Gladstone had been watching him as he did so, no doubt assessing his potential for use in some brochure or other. She took her ticket and realized he was still holding out that hand to help her up.

The guy didn't need to be painted, he needed to be cloned.

She let him pull her to her feet, then put her ticket in her pocket. "Thank you." She held up the guidebook. "You don't want to look at this?"

He merely shook his head.

She decided that maybe there wasn't any mystery to the guy who was soon walking next to her, his hands clasped behind his back, looking at the castle with absolutely no expression on his face. If he were English, maybe seeing yet another castle wasn't all that exciting. If he lived in the area, he'd probably been to Artane more than once. She, however, was a Yank and by the time she made it across the courtyard to the medieval keep itself, she understood why Eugenie Kilchurn had been so in love with the place.

Jackson climbed the stairs to the great hall as if he had every right to do so, so she followed after him. He opened the door and stepped back.

"After you."

She walked inside and decided that however many times he'd had to move that one box from place to place for Mrs. Gladstone had been worth it. She turned in a circle, gaping at a ceiling she almost couldn't see and the rest of the place that looked so authentic, she wasn't sure she hadn't gone back in time hundreds of years.

A fire was burning in one of the massive hearths, but she wasn't sure that was going to make any difference. She wasn't above making use of it, though, so she followed Jackson over to it and stood with her back to it.

"Chilly for spring," he said, shivering.

"Spring? It's almost September."

He blinked, then simply nodded. "Of course."

She turned sideways in a metaphorical fashion and allowed that mystery to gallop right on past her, then settled for looking through the guidebook. It seemed the safest alternative.

"There is a chair there," Jackson said eventually.

"I'm fine," she said. "You go ahead."

He looked slightly uncomfortable with that, but she had the feeling it was another entry in the familial book of manners. She waved him on, then warmed up a bit while burying herself in details about the castle. She was surprised to learn that the castle was still owned by the same family who'd started the whole thing, but maybe that wasn't all that unusual.

She looked at Jackson to see if he had an opinion on that only to discover that he apparently felt safe enough to simply pass out. So much for a reliable castle buddy. She looked around but there didn't seem to be anyone ready to come kick them out for borrowing a family chair. She supposed he wouldn't fall out and crack his head open, so she left him to his slumber and reopened her book to the map of the castle and outbuildings.

There was, she noted almost immediately, an addition to the medieval keep that contained a few things she thought she might be interested in ogling.

She looked at Jackson and decided that he would probably be very happy right where he was for the time being. She pulled pen and notepad out of her bag—she really was going to have to beg another one of them to take with her—and wrote a single word on the top sheet.

Armory.

She had no idea if Jackson would either know what that was or where to find it, but he seemed like a resourceful guy. If he got stuck, he could go flirt with Mrs. Gladstone again and probably get a personal escort to a room that was surely filled with lots of drool-worthy pointy things. She tucked the note under the edge of his coat and abandoned him to his fate.

She left the great hall and followed the map into a more modern—and that was relative, to be sure—part of the castle. She walked past items of an Elizabethan era, then trotted down the circular stairs to the room below as if she'd been doing it her whole life. She walked out into a chamber with surprisingly high ceilings, a polished stone floor, and walls lined with easily a hundred swords and an equal number of daggers.

She had to take a moment to catch her breath and that hadn't been from running down the stairs.

She started with a robust collection of medieval weapons. She could have spent all her time there, but she forced herself to move around the room and thereby through centuries of weaponry. She wasn't sure if the family had always had plenty of money or they had just been very fond of keeping themselves alive, but they had obviously spared no expense on tools of the trade.

She finally found herself back where she'd started, staring up at a fanned-out collection of medieval broadswords. They were unadorned, which only left her wondering if there might be another part of the castle where the more valuable blades were kept. She couldn't imagine some lord of the keep or other hadn't plunked a gem or two in the hilt of his sword.

But since that was the case, maybe no one would notice if she got fairly friendly with a piece of metal that had been in existence for 800 years.

She settled for the sword directly in front of her. The hilt was at least three feet over her head, but she had a good reach and wasn't opposed to a quick jump or two to do what needed to be done. Unfortunately, she also had to navigate the rope that separated the rabble from the goods and that had probably been her first mistake, but she was, as she'd noted before, a bit obsessed.

What she hadn't counted on was the blade of the sword coming loose from its moorings, the hilt pulling away from the wall, and both starting down toward her head. She froze, torn between the knowledge that she needed to get out of the way before that heavy piece of sharpened steel cut her in two and genuine concern that if she let it fall on the stone, it might damage the blade and not only would she be financially responsible for that, she would possibly ruin a centuries-old artifact.

She did the only thing she could think of, which in hindsight probably hadn't been a very good idea.

EIGHT

FUTURE GELS AND SWORDS WERE a dangerous combination.

Jackson used the sword he'd pulled off the wall to catch the blade of a different sword that was on its way to cleaving Olivia Grace Drummond's beautiful head in twain, then flipped it up into the air. He caught it by the hilt on its way down, then took a step back and looked at the woman standing there with her hands over her head, obviously thinking she would save herself from that blade with her flesh and bones alone.

"Are you hurt?" he asked.

Her eyes were absolutely enormous. "I'm fine, thank you. You don't look like you woke up very well, though."

Nay, he hadn't woken well at all. First had come the unsettling sensation of having been in the right hall but the wrong year, followed by deciphering his companion's missive to understand where she'd gone, and ending with enduring several frantic moments of imagining all the dire things that could have befallen her in such a place.

"Headache?" she asked sympathetically.

"Aye," he managed, "but less than yours would have been."

"I just wanted to look."

He suspected she'd wanted far more than that. In fact, not only was she not looking nearly as repentant as she should have been considering how close she had just come to death, she was eyeing the swords he was holding with ill-concealed interest whilst completely ignoring him. He might have been offended by that if he hadn't been that sort of lad himself.

He sighed gustily, then handed her what he quickly identified as the duller-edged weapon.

"Very well, look. Quickly."

She looked. He wasn't unaccustomed to wenches with blades, so the sight didn't make him uneasy. His sister Rose was one of the most terrifying souls he knew and she never went anywhere without something sharp on her person. Whatever it was that Olivia Drummond did to fill her days, 'twas obvious she had a decent eye for steel. She studied the sword she held, then looked at him.

"1260," she said, "or maybe a bit later, wouldn't you agree?"

He managed a nod, but the sensation of looking at a sword that had potentially been made in his own future in the past was almost painful.

"This is very exciting," she said breathlessly.

"As is looking at swords from a distance."

She looked at him assessingly.

He blinked, then shook his head. "Nay."

She kicked her small rucksack out of her way, took several steps back, then pointed the sword at him. "*En guarde.*"

He felt his mouth fall open. "*Nay.*"

"It'll be fun."

Ah, another of Kendrick's well-used Future terms. *Fun* was, however, not a word most of Artane's guardsmen associated with devotion to the blade, though he had to admit he disagreed.

"Too dangerous," he said firmly.

"What could possibly go wrong?"

He hardly knew where to start, but he was saved from making that list by a throat clearing itself from behind him. He stepped forward to relieve Olivia of her sword almost without thinking, then turned to see who might have come to scold them.

He looked at the man standing a dozen paces away from him

and almost took a step back. He half wondered if he were seeing a ghost—if he believed in that sort of thing, which he most assuredly did not.

He decided he would consider the improbability of his own place and time when he was at his leisure, which moment was not the present one. He had his hands full presently with staring at a man who looked so much like a mixture of Rhys de Piaget, his own beloved grandsire, and Rhys's son Robin, his own impossible uncle, that he could scarce believe his eyes.

He felt Olivia start forward, so he put his arm out to keep her behind him. If there was trouble afoot, he would see to it himself.

The man standing there studied him for a moment or two, then held out his hand. It was comfortingly empty.

"Stephen de Piaget."

Jackson took both swords in one hand and shook hands as was polite. "Jackson Kilchurn," he said, inclining his head. He dredged up his best Future speech and hoped it would be enough. "I beg pardon, my lord. I was overcome by the awesome nature of your steel."

The man only lifted one eyebrow briefly in a fine imitation of Robin of Artane at his most unimpressed, then he stepped to the side and extended his hand to Olivia.

"Stephen de Piaget," he said. "A pleasure, Miss . . ?"

Jackson glanced at Olivia to find her looking at Lord Stephen as if he'd been King Henry V himself. He had no reason to frown, but he was hard-pressed to remember why he shouldn't. After all, he was the one who had kept her from having her head cleaved in twain, not that de Piaget lad there.

"Olivia Drummond," she said faintly. "And that was my fault. I was also overcome by the awesomeness of your steel."

"It happens more often than you might imagine," Lord Stephen said dryly.

But you are—" Olivia said breathlessly, "I mean … you seem to be, ah, the—"

"Earl of Artane?" Lord Stephen asked with a faint smile. "It's a recent thing, but yes, that does seem to be the case. It is a very great honor to take my turn guarding what Rhys de Piaget built over 800 years ago."

Jackson managed not to choke only because he was his father's son and knew very well how to maintain a neutral mien.

"I attended a play staring Richard Drummond a couple of nights ago," Stephen continued. "A relation perchance?"

"My first cousin once removed," Olivia said dutifully.

"Then you must know Samantha, who is a cousin to my sister-in-law Megan, which makes us family," Stephen said with a smile. "My beloved wife is off with our son visiting her sister in the south so I fear you're left with just me, but it would be my pleasure to offer you hospitality. Where are you staying?"

"In the village," Jackson said before he could stop himself. "By herself in an unguarded hall, which I find unsuitable."

Stephen seemed to consider those tidings. "And you met, how?"

"At my cousin's play," Olivia said. "Jackson lost his keys, so I came along today to help him look for them. We came up to the castle to visit, I followed the map to this amazing collection of swords you have, and he came to rescue me from myself."

Jackson found himself being observed by both of them, which left him feeling surprisingly unbalanced. Or perhaps that came from being reminded of what he had lost and how powerless he was to attempt to rectify that. What was he to do now that he couldn't even dig about under that foul cloth for another pair of se'nnights? The days stretched out before him, leaving him being a captive audience with, as his aunt Jennifer would have said, nothing to do but chill.

He realized he was scowling, but damnation his relatives had many things to answer for. 'Twas no wonder Sam and Theo had mastered the use of that bloody gate. They had likely learned the skill from their dam herself!

"Oh, that's too generous."

Jackson pulled himself back to the conversation at hand and realized that things had gotten away from him. "How is he being too generous?"

Stephen smiled pleasantly. "I suggested that perhaps you two might like to stay here at the keep. Separate chambers, of course."

Jackson drew himself up, a tart retort halfway out of his mouth before he realized that damned de Piaget spawn there had just winked at him. In that moment, he couldn't have looked any more like Robin.

"*Very* generous," Jackson said sourly.

Stephen smiled, then turned to Olivia. "I'll have someone go fetch your gear."

"Oh, that's too kind," Olivia said quickly. "I wouldn't want anyone to see all the stuff I've shoved under the bed."

Jackson had a quick wink from Olivia that time and decided that perhaps his best course of action would be to seek out that chair where he'd fallen asleep half an hour ago and resume his nap.

"Of course," Stephen said easily. "I'll let Mrs. Gladstone know you're here as guests, then. Stay as long as you like, of course."

"I have to leave on Saturday," Olivia said, "but I appreciate the offer."

"Then you'll have at least a pair of comfortable nights here," Stephen said pleasantly. "I'm away for the rest of the day today, but I'm sure you two can amuse yourselves. The scones in the tea shop are not to be missed. We'll have our grand tour tomorrow, if that suits."

Jackson couldn't help a small bit of curiosity at how things might have changed over the centuries, so he nodded his thanks.

Stephen leaned close to him. "You stay out of my swords, lad. Wouldn't want to have to use one on you."

Then he laughed and walked away. Jackson smothered a curse, then looked at Olivia who seemed to be stopping just short of hopping up and down with joy. He wanted to tell her that a night in his uncle's keep wasn't that awesome, but perhaps she might have a different opinion.

"Can we hurry?" she asked. "There are lots of things to look at, and I don't have much time."

He came back to himself with a start, then what she'd said finally sank in. "You will go on Saturday? To where?"

"London," she said. "I have a job interview next week."

He had no idea what a *job interview* entailed, but he was absolutely familiar with the perilous nature of London itself. "Who will guard you?"

She looked at him as if he'd clunked himself on the head with his own sword and rendered himself witless. "I'm sure I'll be fine on my own."

There were many things of which he was certain and the first was that if he had a fortnight of chilling to look forward to, he would most certainly not allow that lovely woman there to go to London on her own—even if that meant remaining in the Future a bit longer than he'd planned. He suspected he might have a bit of a battle on his hands over it, but he had a great amount of experience in carefully helping the women of his family see the superior nature of his thoughts concerning their safety.

It was likely not useful to revisit how often those same women had told him in less-than-ladylike terms what he could do with his thoughts.

"You're starting to frown."

"I am ahungered," he said, then he looked at her seriously. "Thank you for keeping what's in your bedchamber hidden."

"You saved me from dying," she said cheerfully, picking up her rucksack and pulling it over her shoulder. "Let's go find that tea shop. I'll buy."

"Nay," he said firmly. "I will see to our meal."

"Whatever," she said with a smile.

Well, *that* was a word he had used scores of times under his breath and in just such a fashion. He knew he was being dismissed, but no matter. He might permit Olivia to spend her gold initially, but he would find something to do for Lord Stephen to repay her.

He stepped over the fuzzy red rope that should have kept unwary shield maidens away, replaced the swords in their spots, then followed Olivia up from the armory and out into the flat light of noonday. She looked over her map, then pointed across the courtyard.

"I think that's it over there."

Jackson wasn't sure if he should have been amused or appalled that his next meal lay in what in his day had been the blacksmith's hut, but perhaps he would share that with his sire when next they met.

The small hall definitely smelled better than the smithy ever had, but everything inside was so fine and delicate that he half feared to sit, rest his elbows, or take one of the knives from his boots to use on anything given to him. Olivia seemed to find it nothing out of the ordinary, so he copied her with as much skill as he had.

He turned his attentions to the rest of the chamber at one point to make certain he hadn't overlooked any dining niceties. No one else seemed to find the scones with clotted cream as staggeringly delicious as he did, but perhaps they were accustomed to such superior fare.

The meal ended far too quickly, but perhaps there would be more to be had on the morrow. He sat back and sighed deeply. "Glorious, truly. Now, I must find a way to repay the cook for his efforts."

"Lord Stephen has already paid for it," she said in awe. "So generous."

Jackson would have said 'twas nothing he wouldn't have done in Lord Stephen's boots, but perhaps silence was the better choice.

He left the small hall with her, then paused out in what he could scarce believe was autumn, not spring sunshine. 'Twas no wonder that bloody gate had collapsed. The confusion over the seasons had likely been too much for it.

He paid his respects to Mrs. Gladstone on their way out the gates, promising her more moving of unnecessary items at his earliest opportunity, then tried not to dwell on the utter improbability of where—or *when*—he was. It was a bit easier than it had been the day before, but he was also wearing clothing appropriate to the day and he'd had a decent meal.

He forced himself to simply cease thinking about anything past putting one foot in front of the other until they were standing in front of the door of Olivia's small hall. She started to put her key into the lock, then frowned.

"I'm pretty sure I locked this when we left earlier—"

He took her by the elbow and carefully drew her away from the doorway. He pulled one of his knives free, then gave the door a firm push to open it. He didn't hear anything move, which eliminated lads with no patience or courage. He entered, then made a thorough search. The bathing chamber startled him less than it had earlier that morning, though he thought it might take a few days to accustom himself to seeing himself with such clarity. At least his visage wasn't altogether ugly and his form even in Future garb was acceptable.

"Jackson?"

He had a final look about her wee solar, then turned to find his companion standing on the threshold. He shrugged carefully. "The house is empty."

"I'm sure it was only the maid," she said. "I'll go grab my stuff."

He nodded, then walked outside to give her privacy to see to her affairs. He leaned back against the wall of the small house and looked at his uncle's keep sitting there on the hill. He could scarce believe that so many centuries had passed, yet the hall was still where Rhys de Piaget had built it and his descendants still possessed it.

Time was a very strange thing, indeed.

"Okay, I've got everything. I just have to take the key back."

He realized he was half-asleep on his feet without any sense of time having passed, so he shook his head to clear it and looked at Olivia. She was standing next to him, gazing at the castle with a soft autumn sunlight falling gently onto her upturned face.

He paused, then decided there was no harm in settling in for a study of a woman he had definitely noticed right away but hadn't had a chance to properly admire. Had he seen her at court, he absolutely would have encouraged any men nearby to continue on toward women who were perhaps more brittle and haughty. That would have left him with the very great pleasure of having to himself a woman he thought he might want to spend a substantial amount of time drawing in various lights until he'd satisfied himself that he had sketched her properly. Perhaps an emerald gown would suit her, to match that deep green of her eyes, a green that was surrounded by a soft brown—

"Jackson?"

He blinked and realized that he was simply standing there, watching her. He took a deep breath and stepped back. "My apologies."

"Maybe you need another nap."

"And leave you scampering about the castle, looking for steel?" he said. "I think not."

She smiled. "We'll stick to the safer parts, then. I have a map."

He was halfway to telling her that he didn't need a map when it occurred to him that, given the changes he'd already seen, he just might.

"I think you need more food."

Food was definitely not going to cure what ailed him, though Stephen's scones had been a good start. He took his own clothing and her wee trunk from her.

"I'll carry these if you can manage my sword." He shot her a look. "Do not use it."

"I wouldn't dare."

He imagined she would the moment his back was turned, so he waited whilst she returned the key to the innkeeper. She returned quickly, looking absolutely thrilled by the prospect of tromping about that massive pile of stones. He handed her his sword, crossed the street without incident, then glanced at her as they walked toward the keep.

"How do you care to pass the day?" he asked.

"Looking at as much of the castle as possible," she said without hesitation. "Think Lord Stephen would let me borrow something from the armory so we could go have a sword fight on the beach?"

The saints preserve him, the woman was tenacious. "We'll ask him tomorrow."

"Really?" she asked breathlessly.

He came as close to smiling as he ever did, which he supposed wasn't all that often. The thought of a bit of swordplay on the shore or a pair of days spent wandering aimlessly over the place where he'd spent so much of his life was more pleasant than he would have thought, especially when he had the chance to see it all through Olivia Drummond's eyes.

"Aye," he said. "With his dullest blades."

She didn't hop up and down again, but she came close. He smiled to himself and walked with her up to the guard chamber, prepared to move yet another box for the unyielding Mrs. Gladstone.

It was very late that evening when he left his chamber and paused in the passageway. He had waked Olivia to her door a pair of hours earlier, so he imagined she was safely tucked up in bed. 'Twas with hardly an effort that he had simply moved past the knowledge that she was sleeping in the place where he'd always had a bed when in his uncle's hall.

His life had become full of very strange things.

He'd been given temporary possession of their shared coin earlier and realized almost immediately that it had to have come from his fee for marrying Fulbert de Piaget and the irascible Fiona

MacLeod. He'd set it on the table near his bed and imagined any offended ghosts from that time wouldn't be able to abscond with it in the night.

He made his way down to the great hall, then wandered back to the kitchens, just as he'd done innumerable times over the years. He supposed he'd spent more than his share of time at Artane, but he had also spent a year squiring for his uncle so perhaps that wasn't so strange. He'd asked his father once why he hadn't been sent away to page in his youth then to squire with a different family entirely.

His sire had only looked at him blankly for a moment, then shrugged. "Robin is the best swordsman in England."

As a child, he'd thought that his parents simply hadn't wanted to let any of them go too far away because they loved them, which obviously had been true. As a man presently, he understood how great a trust had to be placed in another man to care for one's son. And, he had to admit, Robin of Artane was the best swordsman he'd ever met.

He walked into the kitchens to find them not substantially changed from his day. He could see additions in spouts and sinks and something enormous and gleaming in the corner, but the hearth was the same. He brought a modest fire back to life, found himself a chair, and sat down to contemplate his situation.

Obviously, the gate outside the keep was going to be out of reach for the next fortnight. He hardly dared think about how he might find another one, never mind having it work for him. If he'd had any idea where to start, he would have looked for those monsters Samuel and Theophilus de Piaget, but he could hardly believe they might find themselves in his present year.

Zachary Smith was a better choice, but the man had claimed to be from Scotland and Scotland was a very large place. Perhaps Edinburgh would have been a reasonable place to begin looking, but at what cost? Two weeks for searching for someone he might not manage to find?

Or he could spend a fortnight in the Future without the weight of responsibility and expectation on his shoulders …

He would have wondered how his father would have advised him at present, but he already knew. His father would have told him to live the hell out of every single moment he drew breath, no matter the time or circumstance.

It occurred to him that perhaps he should have commenced that sort of thing with the moment immediately before the one in which he realized he was not alone in the kitchens.

He stood up immediately, wishing he hadn't left his sword in his chamber, then saw that 'twas simply the lord of the hall. Stephen didn't have any weapons in his hands, so perhaps things would go better than they had with Derrick Cameron. Then again, he was looking at a man who could likely have him thrown in the dungeon without anyone's having been the wiser, so perhaps he wasn't entirely safe yet.

"Wine?" Stephen asked.

Jackson nodded, deciding that the less he said, the better.

Stephen brought a bottle, two goblets of glass, and another chair for himself. He poured, handed over a glass, then simply sat back and watched.

Jackson imagined he could wait his host out for most of night before speaking first—he was his father's son, after all—but that seemed impolite, so he lifted his glass.

"Many thanks for the hospitality, my lord," he said, finding the modern English coming more easily to him after an afternoon spent conversing with Olivia. "Your steward Humphreys said you made a loan of the clothing I found in my chamber."

"You're quite welcome," Stephen said. "We're about the same size, so hopefully things will fit. You don't mind if I join you here, do you?"

"Of course not, my lord. 'Tis your hall." He had sat in the kitchens countless times with not only family but his uncle's cook, so sitting with a different relative wasn't unsettling. He would make conversation or not, as it pleased his companion—

He froze. It occurred to him that what he had heard coming out of Lord Stephen's mouth hadn't been Future English but rather his own particular sort of French. He let out his breath slowly, then forced himself to simply nurse his wine as if nothing in the world could possibly trouble him.

Stephen, damn him to hell, only watched him with a slight smile on his face.

"What interesting sort of French you speak," he said finally, in that same tongue.

Stephen shrugged. "I taught medieval history and languages at Cambridge for years and it was a passion long before that." He lifted an eyebrow briefly. "Your accent is very good, from what I can tell."

"Thank you," Jackson said, managing not to choke on the words. "I've worked very hard to make it so."

Stephen smiled politely. "I imagine you have. One other thing, just so you're not surprised."

Jackson faced his doom straight on. "Aye?"

"My brother's wife Megan is a sister to your Aunt Jennifer."

Jackson spewed his wine into the fire. Irony was obviously determined to see him repaid for too many impertinent remarks at the expense of others who might or might not have been able to best him with a sword. He dragged his sleeve across his mouth, the reached out to kick a few embers back into their place. He wondered if it might be possible to bluster his way out of what the current lord of Artane thought he might know, then decided there was no point.

"Do you know who I am?" he asked.

"Jackson Alexander Kilchurn the Fifth, unless I'm missing a generation somewhere." Stephen smiled. "There's a painting of your family tucked away in a corner in our private gallery. A remarkable likeness, if I may say so."

Jackson had the feeling he knew exactly which portrait Stephen was referring to, but he left that alone. "When did you know?"

"When you gave me a start in the cellar."

"You didn't look startled."

"Lad, when you live here, you see all sorts of things."

"Lad," Jackson echoed with a snort. He studied his cousin. "You can't be much older than I am."

"Depends how you're counting, I imagine," Stephen said with a smile, "though I'd give myself more than a handful of years on you in any case. Feel free to consider me the elder statesman. As such, would it be too personal a thing to ask what happened?"

Jackson sighed. "I was pushed into a gate through the centuries by a pair of my wee cousins."

"I think I might know them. Blond, mischievous—"

Jackson held up his hand. "Say no more, I beg you. I fear the merest mention of their names will summon them like demons."

"Given that I've seen them in more places than I care to admit, I'd have to agree." Stephen smiled briefly. "I'm assuming that means your journey here wasn't your idea."

Jackson shook his head, but had no words for that. Perhaps there was nothing to be said.

"If you're curious, the portal that lies under the tarp will pull itself back together without aid, though it generally takes about a fortnight after it becomes unstable to do so." Stephen looked at him seriously. "If you want to go back immediately, there are other of your relatives I can ask—"

"Don't."

The word hung there in the kitchen, accompanied by the occasional snap and pop of the wood in the hearth. He watched the fire for a moment or two, then looked at the current lord of Artane, words of justification on the tip of his tongue only to realize there was no need.

"Anonymity isn't a bad thing," Stephen said quietly.

"You must think me a perfect bastard."

"I don't," Stephen said. "There's nothing wrong with pausing before fully shouldering your responsibilities. In this day we call it a gap year. It's very common."

A gap between his past and his future, a fortnight to do exactly what he wanted to with no guilt accompanying the same?

'Twas almost unthinkable.

"Did you take one of these gaps?" he asked finally.

"Not before college, though I likely should have. I made up for it in other ways afterward, so I wouldn't fault you for doing the same. When you're ready to go back, I'll find people to help you and you can sort things to your satisfaction."

Jackson closed his eyes briefly. Kindness and aid from unexpected places. Truly, he was very fortunate to have such a family.

"Thank you, my lord," he said quietly.

"You'll do it for someone else, I'm sure. Now, let's discuss your immediate future. Do you have a plan for the next fortnight?"

"Nothing past perhaps accompanying Olivia to London. I don't like the thought of her going alone."

"My wife and I have had this same conversation more than once," Stephen said with a smile, "and fortunately she humors me when it comes to security. I've no idea what Olivia will think, but I understand your feelings on it." He leaned back in his chair. "Will you tell her about yourself?"

"To what end? It isn't as if I came to the Future to look for a wife who must needs know my history."

He listened to those words come out of his mouth and had absolutely no idea where they'd come from.

"Famous last words," Stephen said lightly. "I suppose at the very least you can keep an eye on her while she negotiates London. Have you met her family?"

"Aye," Jackson said. "Including Derrick Cameron, over blades."

"It doesn't get any better with him, if you're curious," Stephen said. "I would take very good care of her."

"And keep her out of your armory?"

"I wasn't going to say as much," Stephen said with a smile, "but, perhaps."

Jackson sat back and studied his cousin. "Do you run, my lord?"

Stephen shifted uncomfortably. "Why do I worry what you'll leave of me if I say yes?"

"Why don't we meet at dawn and discover the truth of it?"

"If we must," Stephen said with a sigh. "If you leave me still breathing afterward, I'll attempt to answer any questions about the Future that you might have." He finished his wine, then stood. "I'll put away the glasses if you bank the fire."

Jackson nodded, then did the same thing he'd been doing for as much of his life as he could remember. He then followed the lord of the hall out of the kitchens, bid him a good night, then made his way to his borrowed bedchamber.

A gap of a fortnight.

So many things could happen in that time.

NINE

OLIVIA SAT ON THE EDGE of the bed in her extremely medieval-looking bedroom and smiled happily. It was one thing to open a B&B door and look up at a castle; it was another entirely to have slept inside that same castle. She understood why the illustrious Miss Kilchurn had loved the place so much, though she suspected most of the paranormal happenings the woman had reported on could be attributed to the draftiness of a medieval building.

At least she was fairly sure about that.

She grabbed her jacket just in case she had the chance to investigate chilly basement rooms containing sharp things and realized she'd never looked in the bag her innkeeper had given her the day before as she'd checked out. She peeked inside, hoping she might find a handful of note pads emblazoned with her favorite castle, but instead found a couple of cell phones and a note from Derrick.

Mobile for you with local number, plus one for your guardsman if he hasn't found his way back home yet. Text us when you get to London. —D

She wasn't sure Jackson was going to be any better at holding onto a phone than he was his keys, but he would probably appreciate the sentiment. She left everything in the sack, sent good thoughts Derrick's way, then opened the door to find a folded piece of paper pushed halfway into her room. She was fairly sure Lord

Stephen wasn't going to be giving her a bill already, so she retrieved it almost without flinching. She unfolded it and found a sketch of a man obviously running on the beach and the word, *shore.*

Well, that was more than she'd left him, so she couldn't blame him. He was also a remarkably good artist, which was something she was absolutely not going to investigate. She checked the clock on the nightstand to find that it was barely past nine, so who knew how long Jackson had been off running. She left the note on a chair, then pulled the door shut behind her and made her way down to the great hall.

She had no trouble imagining how it might have been to have done the same thing hundreds of years earlier with a sword in her hand and enemies up ahead. She jumped out into the hall and crouched, ready to defend the keep, but realized she wasn't alone. Fortunately, it was just Humphreys, who she'd met the day before. He looked up from where he'd been sitting in front of the fire, reading, and smiled. She suspected it wasn't the first time he'd indulged a guest with an overactive imagination.

He stood up and tucked his book under his arm. "I trust you slept well, Miss Drummond."

"Wonderfully, thank you," she said politely.

"Now, would you prefer breakfast straightway or a small stroll about the grounds and then a meal? The gentlemen have finished their healthful run along the shore and are, I believe, taking a bit of air on the greensward. Swords are involved."

She didn't need to hear that twice. "You don't mind if I wait for breakfast?"

"Of course not, Miss Drummond," he said, waving her on.

She hurried across the hall, then opened the front door and listened for the tell-tale ring of metal against metal. She couldn't see around the corner of the castle, but she could definitely hear business going on there that she thought she might be interested in. She tiptoed down the stairs and kept to the edge of the keep because she'd had prizes disappear into the sticky-fingered mitts of fellow treasure hunters before. No sense in alerting anyone in the area to her movements.

She was grateful for all the duck canvas and corduroy her family stuck to, because her current outfit allowed her to blend in to the foundations of the castle as she rounded the corner to find there was definitely something medieval-looking going on. She was a little surprised to find that Lord Stephen knew how to use a sword, but she was absolutely not surprised to see that Jackson Kilchurn did as well.

There wasn't much conversation to be eavesdropped on, but what there was seemed to be in that French that Jackson couldn't keep from occasionally using. She'd read in Artane's guidebook that Lord Stephen had been a professor at Cambridge, so maybe that was just something guys who liked swords tended to speak. She wondered if there was also a book of insults sitting somewhere inside the castle that the earl had access to because whatever he'd just said to Jackson had her castle buddy growling something that she had the feeling wasn't all that polite in return.

Then again, that could have been because Lord Stephen had somehow caught Jackson's sword and sent it flying.

She watched sunlight glint off it as it hung endlessly in the air, then continued to watch as it started down toward the earth. She supposed it might land fairly close—

She felt herself be jerked off her feet and out of the way of a sword that was now thoroughly impaled in the ground not a foot from where she'd been standing. She watched it rock back and forth for a bit and wondered why in the world Jackson had been using his own extremely sharp sword on the earl of Artane.

She also realized it was Jackson holding onto her when he turned her around and looked her over.

"Are you hurt?" he asked quickly.

"No, I'm fine," she croaked. "How did you get over here so fast?"

He closed his eyes briefly, then pulled her into his arms and hugged her even more briefly before he simply let her go, pulled his sword out of the gravel, and walked away as if he did that sort of thing every day. She leaned against the base of the castle because almost being cut in half was absolutely not the kind of thing *she* did every day.

She was starting to think that maybe there was more to the entire business of steel than she'd imagined.

She watched Jackson and Lord Stephen exchange a quiet word or two before the earl walked over and stopped in front of her.

"That was my fault," he said seriously, "and I apologize. I wasn't as careful as I should have been. Are you all right?"

"I'm the one who should have been paying more attention," she said weakly. "For as much as I love swords, I don't think I've ever thought about the reality of using them."

"I suppose there's an art to it," Lord Stephen agreed with a faint smile, "but I might not be the right one to offer an opinion. Why don't Jackson and I clean up, then we'll have breakfast before we head off to rummage about in less perilous pieces of history?"

She nodded, then realized Jackson was watching her with an assessing look.

"I promise to stay right here," she said, because she thought it needed to be said.

Jackson pursed his lips, then looked at their host. "Do you have others coming inside the gates today or will she be safe with your guards?"

"No tourists today, and you've seen my security detail."

Olivia found herself towed around the edge of the castle and up the steps. Jackson released her hand, pointed to the top step, then walked inside after Lord Stephen. She let out her breath only to find he had poked his head back outside.

"Sit," he suggested. "Wait for me."

"I was going to sit," she grumbled.

"Stay," he added. "I shall make haste."

She would have offered to babysit his sword while he was

making that haste, but she had the feeling he wasn't going to share. She sat on the top step, sighed a bit at the lovely feel of sunlight on her face, then realized after a moment that she was spending less time enjoying and more time scanning the courtyard for potential danger.

She sighed, then closed her eyes and soaked up what she knew from her own climate was fairly rare fall sunshine. She heard the door open behind her eventually, then felt someone sit down on the step next to her. She opened her eyes to find the man who had rescued her not once but twice from very sharp things sitting there, watching her.

"You have very beautiful eyes," she said, before she thought better of it.

He simply blinked several times as if he struggled to understand what she'd said, but his English was definitely that good. Then he shifted uncomfortably.

"I prefer yours," he said gruffly.

"Are you blushing?"

"I've no idea what you mean."

And then he smiled. It was the very smallest of smiles, but she felt her heart stop briefly at the sight of it.

She realized at that moment that she'd never seen him smile before, but maybe the stress over what he'd lost was too much for him to allow it. That smile was gone as quickly as it had come, but she suspected she wouldn't soon forget it.

He pushed himself to his feet and held down his hand. "The traditional English breakfast awaits," he said. "You should partake before the thought of my lovely eyes overwhelms you."

"Did I compliment you?" she asked, letting him pull her up. "What was I thinking?"

"You were thinking of swords and flattering me into sparring with you. Perhaps tomorrow, if the weather is fine."

She couldn't bring herself to point out that she wasn't going to be there the next day, so she didn't. All she could do was take the day and soak up as much of the past as humanly possible. For all she knew, she might manage to get back to Artane someday and take Jackson up on a proper sword fight then.

Stranger things had happened.

Several hours and two wonderful meals later, she found herself standing in the medieval section of a wing built in the 18th century by some enterprising de Piaget ancestor. The centuries leading back to that spot had been fascinating and Lord Stephen's running commentary worthy of any exclusive tour guide. His love for not only the past but those who had collected it and kept it safe was plain.

Jackson had also seemed very fond of history, discussing historical items of note and the state of the monarchy with the earl in whatever era they found themselves. It had taken her a couple of hours before she realized that one of the most interesting things about the tour had been listening to Jackson adjust his accent to Lord Stephen's in real time.

He had done the same sort of thing the day before in the tea shop, reading the room and modifying his mannerisms to match what others were doing while appearing *not* to be watching everything going on around him. She might not have noticed if she hadn't had her powers of observation honed by Phyllis Drummond herself. Her aunt could spot a big spender across the street and a shoplifter across town. Her own skills were less, but she had the feeling Jackson Kilchurn's weren't. The man was an absolute sponge, which left her with more questions than answers.

And she knew where *that* led.

"I understand from your cousin Richard, Miss Drummond," Lord Stephen said, "that your background is in art history. If you're interested, I'll show you some of our earliest pieces."

Olivia pulled herself back to the tour at hand and nodded, then stopped alongside him to look at several things of an easily identifiable medieval style. There were just as many that were an unusual blending of medieval setting and what seemed to be a rather modern sensibility, but she supposed that wasn't completely unheard-of. After all, new experiments were often what sent things in a new direction.

She took a step to the right to look at the next painting in the case, then felt time slow to a stop.

There was a portrait there of a family dressed in medieval clothing. She immediately identified the parents and made a guess at the order of the children. The wife was the most beautiful woman she'd ever seen, though her daughters were stunning as well. The sons were ridiculously handsome, obviously taking after their father. It was a very formal portrait yet somehow managed to convey a warmth of kinship that she had rarely seen in medieval art. But that wasn't the thing that struck her as so unusual.

It was that the oldest son couldn't have looked more like Jackson if he *had* been Jackson.

She read the tag under the painting to get the names right and blinked.

Jackson Alexander Kilchurn, IV, and family.

"That is my aunt, Amanda de Piaget," Lord Stephen said from beside her, "the usual number of generations removed, of course. Her husband was the first lord of Raventhorpe. I don't know if you're familiar with that keep or not."

She started to say she wasn't when it occurred to her that she'd read about that castle in Eugenie Kilchurn's book. She thought she might need a reread sooner rather than later, but maybe after she'd managed to stop shaking her head over how much the eldest son looked like his father.

And like the man standing on the other side of Lord Stephen, actually—

She put the brakes on her imagination before it ran away with her. Doppelgängers were common in family lines, something she knew very well thanks to the batches of antique photos Aunt Phyllis collected as palate cleansers from mid-century-modern everything else. Jackson was probably simply related to those Kilchurn men somewhere in the mists of time. He had certainly benefitted from their great genes.

"Lord Jackson was from all accounts an excellent artist," Lord Stephen remarked. "He painted that portrait of Lady Amanda there next to the one of the family. I've also seen his work in London, as it happens. Henry III was apparently quite a fan."

She looked at the family portrait a bit longer, then moved on to study the painting of the lady Amanda. The woman's eyes were a remarkable color of blue, almost turquoise, quite possibly the same color as Jackson's.

Now, *that* was definitely something for a genealogist to chew on. She wouldn't do it herself because she, as she had to remind herself not more than once a day, was out of the mystery business. She was, however, moving into the art business so maybe making an assessment of valuable medieval art was nothing but useful practice.

She first checked the dates and found that portrait of Lady Amanda had been done in 1227 and the family group in 1256. She wondered if the first painting had been done as a sort of medieval bridal package. She looked back at the family to see how the woman had changed over the years—her astonishing looks had definitely not suffered from the passage of time—then realized something unusual.

"Miss Drummond?"

She looked a bit closer at both paintings, then pulled back and tried to gather her thoughts. She didn't want to ruin the earl's labels, but she thought she might have stumbled upon … well, one of those things she could investigate because it had to do with art. She looked at Lord Stephen.

"This might sound a little crazy," she said gingerly, "but I don't think Lord Jackson painted this family portrait."

Lord Stephen frowned thoughtfully. "What do you mean?"

Too late to back away now, she supposed. "I think someone

painted everyone in the family except the oldest son," she said. "And the person who painted the eldest son is the same person who painted Lady Amanda in that blue gown."

Lord Stephen peered at the paintings. "So you're suggesting that maybe the eldest son painted his family, then his father did the honors of painting him in after the rest was finished?"

"I'm not sure who painted the family, though I suppose if the eldest son was painted in afterward, he could have been the artist. I would have to see something else he'd done to know for sure." She looked at Jackson who was standing behind her. "What do you think?"

He held up his hands. "I wouldn't presume to offer an opinion, though the father looks to be a better artist."

"A different point of view, maybe," she conceded, "but I think they were both pretty amazing. Whoever painted the family seems to have had an Italianate sensibility, so I wonder if he or she spent any time studying there." She looked at Lord Stephen. "Would that have been odd for them at the time, do you think?"

"The family traveled abroad a great deal, or so I understand. A pity we can't travel back in time and ask the good first lord of Raventhorpe." Lord Stephen looked at Jackson. "I don't suppose you have any family legends to supply at this point?"

"I daresay I don't," he said. "My apologies, my lord."

Lord Stephen only smiled briefly. "Then I suppose this will remain a mystery, but Olivia you've definitely given me something to think about. And with that, I believe you've seen most everything that isn't hiding under inches of dust in a couple of very chilly attics. I would happily let you two rummage through it all, but perhaps we should save that for another day."

"This has been amazing," Olivia said, hoping he knew how much she meant it. "I don't know how to thank you."

"It was genuinely my pleasure," Lord Stephen said. "I'm always happy to meet someone who shares my fondness for old things. Now, why don't we repair to the lord's solar and have refreshments?

We should also discuss your plans so the morning goes smoothly for you."

"Aye, we should," Jackson said, turning around abruptly. "If Lord Stephen will be kind enough to look for my key if the cloth is removed before I have returned, I will see to keeping you safe. The journey is long through dangerous countryside, so we'll want to make an early start of it and travel swiftly."

"Not so long these days," Lord Stephen said easily. "Five hours by train, six in a car."

Jackson looked at him with absolutely no expression on his face. "Six hours," he repeated. "In a car."

"Ninety leagues," Lord Stephen said. "Three hundred miles generally at sixty miles an hour on a motorway. More slowly on smaller roads, of course, but the distance is about the same." He shrugged. "You do the maths."

Olivia watched Jackson look off into the distance for a moment, no doubt doing those maths, before he turned back to Lord Stephen and nodded briskly.

"That will leave time enough to see Olivia properly settled in London before she embarks on her job interview. We'll need more of the current Elizabeth Reginas for the journey, but I have coins to trade for them. Can you help me with that?"

"It would be my pleasure."

"I'll fetch them, then come to your solar."

Olivia looked at Jackson as he paused next to her.

"Not *the* coin, of course," he murmured. "That remains ours."

"Whatever you say," she agreed faintly. She watched him stride purposefully away, then looked at Lord Stephen. "I'm not exactly sure what just happened here."

Lord Stephen smiled. "I believe you just acquired a cracking bodyguard. He comes from a family of thoroughly stubborn but exceptionally chivalrous men, so unless you're completely opposed to having him herd you, I don't think you'll be sorry you took him along."

She started to nod, then realized what he'd said. "I thought you'd never met him."

Lord Stephen hesitated, then sighed. "To be completely honest, I know a pair of his uncles. I suspect he's taking a bit of a breather from the family business and trying very hard to keep a low profile, which is why I haven't said anything." He smiled faintly. "It wasn't for any more nefarious motives, I assure you."

"And you think he's trustworthy?"

"I would trust my family to his care without hesitation," he said seriously. "I'm quite sure his uncles would echo that, also without giving it a second thought. You will be perfectly safe with him."

"Well, he does seem to know his way around a sword," she conceded.

Lord Stephen laughed uncomfortably. "And what you witnessed this morning was Jackson treating me like a toddler. I can guarantee you won't get mugged in London if he's there with you, but I'll leave it to him to reveal any more personal details if he feels so inclined."

Olivia nodded to herself. It was probably best to politely leave those details alone on the off chance Jackson found them uncomfortable. Given what she suspected about his upbringing, a few days of immersing himself in modern London would probably be a dream come true. If she had company in a new city for a day or two until she got her own life in order as a result, so much the better.

She made polite small talk with the earl of Artane while they made their way back to a very cozy room just off the great hall. She was invited to sit while Lord Stephen made a quick fire, then he took a seat across a coffee table from her just as a knock sounded on the door.

"Come in, lad," Lord Stephen called.

Olivia watched Jackson scowl at the earl before he shut the door and came to sit down next to her.

"I believe, my lord, that if you call me *lad* one more time, you'll regret it."

Olivia leaned closer to him. "I don't think you're supposed to talk that way to nobility."

Lord Stephen snorted. "He would be in more danger if we'd made more progress in restoring the dungeon from an unfortunate boarding up, but that's progress for you." He leaned forward and rubbed his hands together. "Let's see what you have there."

Olivia watched Jackson lay out a decent amount of change on the table. She almost fell out of her chair at the sight, but that was just how she rolled with vintage coins.

She realized immediately that the coins weren't simply vintage, they were medieval specimens that looked as if the silver had been pressed that morning. Jackson dug in a different pocket and pulled out a handful of Elizabethan shillings that he tossed onto the pile as well. She knelt down next to the table, trying not to drool over those beauties, then looked up at Jackson in shock.

"Are those real?"

He froze, then did that room-reading thing again. She wasn't about to help him out and Lord Stephen seemed only inclined to watch him.

"My father has a collection," he said finally.

She reached for one, then stopped. "May I?"

"Of course."

She picked up one of the coins and wasn't entirely certain she wasn't going to have an out-of-body experience. What she was sure of was that her grandfather would have arm-wrestled her for possession of even one of them.

Lord Stephen was frowning over them, separating them into piles as he did so.

"Henry, John … " He blinked, then picked up one of them. "Richard the Lionheart with the omega above the cross." He looked at Jackson. "Very rare and almost impossible to find in this condition. You have two of them."

Jackson shrugged. "They're well struck, true. What of the later coins?"

"Not as valuable as the others, but I think I can find a buyer for them. How many do you want to sell?"

Jackson considered, then picked up one of the Richard the Lionhearts and looked for somewhere to put it.

"Pocket," Olivia suggested. She refrained from suggesting he let her put it in hers, which she thought showed an amazing amount of restraint on her part.

Jackson made good use of one of his front pockets only after turning it out and looking for holes, then he nodded at the rest of the coins there on the table.

"How much for those?"

Olivia looked at Lord Stephen who was only watching Jackson with a faint smile.

"I'm guessing a thousand for the remaining Richard, three hundred a piece for the other medieval coins, and probably two hundred for the Elizabethan shillings." He shrugged. "You do the maths."

Olivia watched Jackson do just that, then look at her.

"Is six thousand, ah—"

"Pounds," Lord Stephen supplied.

Jackson shot him a look. "I knew that, of course. Olivia, is that enough for London?"

"Are you planning on eating your way through the entire city?" she managed faintly. "And I'm sure that's enough for you. I'll pay for—"

"Nay," he said simply. He pushed the coins toward Lord Stephen. "Thank you, my lord. This will be enough for us for a few days."

"A pleasure doing business with you, la—" Lord Stephen paused, then laughed. "I won't finish that. I also suppose I don't need to say that Richard will be remaining with me."

Olivia supposed she didn't need to mention that she would have arm-wrestled Lord Stephen for that coin in a heartbeat if she'd been able to. She was still holding onto a fantastically preserved

Elizabethan shilling herself, so she wasn't going to complain. She watched Lord Stephen leave his office, presumably to make a few phone calls and possibly get Jackson some cash, then realized Jackson was watching her.

"Mine," he reminded her.

"You wish," she said with a snort, "though we might want to make some progress in settling ownership once and for all."

"Ownership of that worthless coin?"

"Nice try," she said, pretending to suppress a yawn. "I suppose since it's that worthless, we could just do a thumb war."

He looked at her assessingly. "Lay out the battlefield, lady, and describe the weapons."

She showed him how to link fingers, explained the gist, then looked at him with a smile. "On the count of three. Do you want to practice or just leap right in?"

"I never practice." He paused. "That might not be as true as I'd like it to be, but since this doesn't involve swords, I have no worries."

"You'll regret it."

"I suspect I won't."

She shrugged, counted to the appropriate number, then pinned his thumb without any effort at all. He looked at her, open-mouthed.

She reached out and patted him with her free hand. "Better luck next time, cupcake."

His eyes narrowed. "We shall battle again tomorrow night where you will not catch me unawares."

She would have warned him that she was rarely vanquished in that sort of thing, but Lord Stephen kept her from it by walking back into his den. Jackson shot her a look of promise before he smiled very briefly, then turned and watched Lord Stephen put twenty and fifty pound notes into two piles.

"My friend is interested, so I'll front you the funds and settle with him later."

Jackson recounted what was in front of him, then looked at Lord Stephen. "Paper," he said in disbelief.

"Absurd, isn't it?"

Olivia listened to them discuss monetary habits over the centuries and wondered about them both. She was admittedly a big fan of history so maybe it shouldn't have been so strange to watch other people be just as excited about it as she was.

Lord Stephen excused himself eventually to confer with Humphreys about a light supper for that evening and travel plans for the morning, which left her looking at a man who she suspected had the same fondness for old things that she did.

"I didn't give you a choice about my accompanying you," he said slowly. "My apologies."

She managed a smile. "Does anyone ever tell you no?"

"More often than you might suspect," he admitted. He took a deep breath. "I vow I will keep you safe from ruffians and ne'er-do-wells."

Well, if there was anything a girl needed during a trip to London, it was protection from ruffians and ne'er-do-wells.

"Samantha and Derrick offered to let me stay at their house," she said, "but maybe they wouldn't mind if you stayed as well. I can call them in the morning and ask."

He looked at her blankly.

"You know, on the phone."

"Ah, on the phone," he said, nodding. "Of course. And if Lord Derrick approves, I will take my place with their garrison. If not, I will find a nearby inn."

She imagined that if Jackson called him *Lord*, Derrick might approve of quite a few things.

"If we have time before your parley with the master of your new guild," he added, "we might take in the sights. London is an exciting place."

She wondered how he knew that if he'd grown up on a farm, but maybe even medieval character actors had to make the occasional trips to civilization centers for important things like toothpaste and junk food. In his case, that apparently hadn't meant chocolate, but his family obviously had strict food rules.

Lord Stephen came back inside his office, and she listened with half an ear to his discussion with Jackson about the best way to get to London without getting robbed in the wilds of the south. The whole conversation seemed a little surreal, but what did she know of big English cities?

Well, what she knew was that she'd just traded a castle buddy for a London buddy. What could possibly go wrong?

Nothing, especially when that London buddy could probably keep her from getting mugged, had in his possession a very rare medieval coin in almost perfect condition, and was a terrible thumb warrior.

She deliberately shut the lid on that box she was sure contained all the reasons why a guy from the sticks would have an opinion on modern-day London because she was firmly committed to keeping her sanity, her vow, and her Single and Unavailable status.

She realized Jackson was watching her watch him. He opened his eyes wide, apparently to give her a better view of them, then smiled at her very briefly before he turned back to watching supper arrive.

She took a deep breath. She wasn't in trouble, no sir, not at all.

She almost regretted not having packed curlers and more makeup, but London was a big place and she could probably buy both there.

TEN

JACKSON WALKED DOWN THE STAIRS to the great hall, sword in hand, and couldn't help but notice how the stairs were grooved where they hadn't been in his day. The hall itself was lacking in both rushes and the bones from the previous night's supper—a vast improvement, to be sure—but it didn't seem that much else had changed. His cousin was standing at the lord's table, pouring over a map, which was something he would have found in his day as well.

The addition of a phone in his pocket and a hot shower and razor instead of lukewarm water and his knife were things that perhaps he could mull over later. He was acquiring an unwholesome crackle in his neck from shaking his head so often, so perhaps 'twas time to just accept that he would spend the next fortnight struggling not to gape at everything he saw.

He ruthlessly suppressed the wish that it could be just a bit longer—

"Sleep well?"

"Perfectly," he said automatically, finding himself standing next to Stephen without remembering quite how he'd gotten there, "whilst at the same time painfully for I know I've a lifetime ahead of me full of bedclothes that cannot possibly equal what I just enjoyed."

Stephen smiled. "The current day does have its share of luxuries, true."

Jackson set his sword down on the table, looked behind him to make certain Olivia wasn't there, then pulled the phone from his pocket. "How do I wield this? Olivia said 'tis loaned to me from Derrick Cameron."

"Generous of him," Stephen said. He took it and studied it. "It's a newer model than mine, but I can still help you. Here's where you turn it on. There's also this bit here that slides out to give you a keyboard."

Jackson took the phone back from his cousin, looked briefly over both shoulders to make sure Irony wasn't standing behind him ready to cuff him for all his previous derisive snorting directed at cousins speculating on such inventions, then pushed the spot Stephen had indicated.

Part of the box sprang to life with a brightness that startled him so, he almost dropped the damned thing.

"Steady," Stephen said.

Jackson looked at him sharply, only to have back a wink worthy of Robin de Piaget at his most amused.

"I am well," he said briskly.

"I'm sure you are," Stephen said. "The mechanics of it would take too long to explain now, though we might manage that another time. For now, let me have it so I can put in my number, then I'll show you how to make a call."

Jackson watched Stephen tap on the wee numbers and letters inscribed on the small buttons, then he took his phone back with a feeling of reverence he had generally reserved for a perfectly fashioned blade.

The Future was a wondrous place, to be sure.

Stephen pointed at the half where the light seemed to be contained. "My number is there along with the one for the keep and Humphreys' private line. Derrick has obviously put in Olivia's number and his already. Now, to use it, you type in the number next to those names, then push the green button to send the call. Give it a try."

Jackson felt a thrill of something rush through him at pressing numbers and having them appear on the little window. He pushed the button Stephen indicated, then heard a strange noise coming from Stephen's phone that didn't resemble any bell he was familiar with. He followed Stephen's example and put the mobile to his ear, then almost tossed it into the air in surprise when he heard Stephen's voice not only coming to him three paces away, but through the beast as well.

"By all the bloody saints," he managed faintly.

"That's one way to put it," Stephen agreed wryly. "Push the red button when you're finished with the conversation. You can also simply write a message and send the words if you'd rather. Call it a modern-day carrier pigeon."

Jackson cleared his throat. "I think I prefer quill and parchment."

"And I imagine you'll get used to this so quickly, you'll wonder how you ever lived without it. Have Olivia show you how to use the text message feature. Also, I'm sending along a duffle bag with more clothes for you and a satchel full of books I thought you might find interesting. I assume you left your medieval clothing upstairs?"

"If that isn't too much of an imposition." He took a deep breath and made his cousin a slight bow. "My thanks for the gear. I'm sorry I cannot repay you."

"I would be offended if you tried," Stephen said easily. "And just so you know, Derrick called this morning to extend an invitation for you to stay with Olivia in London and keep her safe."

"Very generous, truly."

"He also suggested that you remember your last conversation with him concerning her care."

Jackson looked at his cousin evenly.

Stephen held up his hands. "I'm just the messenger. You might be interested to know that he had a car delivered."

"A car?" Jackson felt an unexpected wave of exhilaration wash over him. "For me?"

"For Olivia," Stephen said dryly. "You, my friend, do not know how to drive. Ah, and here is Olivia looking well-rested and ready for the journey."

Jackson put his mobile into his pocket, then turned to see Olivia struggling to get herself and her wee rolling trunk out of the stairwell. He strode over and took her burden from her.

"Send word to me on my mobile phone next time," he said as casually as he could manage, "and I'll come fetch you."

She smiled as she took his arm, which he found a bit more pleasing than perhaps he should have, then walked with him over to greet the lord of the hall. He set her gear down, then opted for silence whilst Stephen related to her the conversation he'd had with Derrick that morning.

"Here are keys to their flat," Stephen said, handing her the same, "as well as directions, this map, and an invitation for Jackson to stay with you as long as he behaves himself and you're comfortable with it. Also, Derrick had a little runabout delivered, which he invited you to use for as long as you like."

"Oh," she said uncomfortably, "I could try to drive, but maybe Jackson—"

"Has no license," Stephen finished for her, "though I'm sure he'll be a fantastic navigator."

"I could get us there without a map, but—" Jackson decided it might be best to leave off the rest of what he'd planned to say which was that it wasn't all that difficult to find London. Perhaps that wasn't the case any longer, something he wasn't sure he wanted to know at the moment. He looked at Stephen. "Have you any suggestions, my lord, about routes?"

Stephen apparently had many thoughts he was happy to share. Jackson memorized what he'd been told, noted changes of road he would need to make near particular cities, and forced himself not to make noises of utter disbelief. Six hours, indeed. His family would have wept over the idea.

Well, perhaps not his father, but that was a discussion he would be having with the man in the lists sooner rather than later.

"Let's have a quick breakfast, then get you on your way," Stephen said. "I don't think the traffic will be particularly heavy, but you'll want enough time to rest on the way if you need to."

Jackson picked up his sword out of habit and followed Olivia and his cousin back to the kitchens. He had scarce sat down before Olivia's mobile sprang to life, almost sending him pitching into his traditional English breakfast. He watched her read something in the window of it, then look at him.

"That was Sam," she said. "She wished us a good trip and said they would catch up with us in a couple of days."

"Very generous," Jackson noted. "They can rest easy knowing I will look after you."

"Well, you do have a sword."

"I do," he agreed. He applied himself to his meal, then stopped with a forkful of a spectacular piece of sausage halfway to his mouth when he realized Olivia wasn't enjoying hers in the same manner. "What ails you?"

"It's the driving on the left thing," she admitted. "It makes me nervous."

"I realize in America you've somehow migrated to the wrong side of the road," Stephen said with a smile, "but I can assure you that your Drummond ancestors rode their horses on the proper side of any byway. You'll be surprised by how easily you'll accustom yourself to it."

She closed her eyes briefly. "We can hope. Do you mind if I make one last visit to the powder room so I can have hysterics in private?"

"Don't get lost," Jackson said before he thought better of it.

She nodded uneasily. He waited until she was out of sight before he looked at his cousin.

"America? Driving on the left? Hysterics?"

"Read through the books I'm sending with you to learn about the first two and don't expect me to touch the last one." Stephen smiled faintly. "I'm only sorry I can't take you on a tour of the twenty-first century for a few days. Feel free to ring me just the same if you need anything, and let me know when you're coming back this way. I'll keep you apprised about the condition of the gate."

Jackson shook his head slowly. "This is a very odd conversation."

"Couldn't agree more, actually, but I'm happy we've met to have it."

Jackson nodded, then concentrated on finishing his meal before he found himself weeping on Stephen de Piaget's shoulder over the thought of how a fortnight of Future marvels might leave him utterly ruined for the life that was his in a different century.

"And here is your lady looking perfectly capable of driving on the proper side of the road without any trouble at all," Stephen said eventually. "Let's fetch your bags and get you two on the road."

Jackson nodded, then rose and followed them from the kitchens. He was fairly certain he'd handed Olivia his sword, then gathered up her trunk and the large rucksacks Stephen had loaned him, but he honestly didn't remember exactly how he'd gotten himself to where he was simply standing in the middle of the great hall.

It could have been any other day where he would have been rushing off in a hurry to take his place in the lists to prove himself yet again, only it felt as if he might be taking the first step toward an entirely different life.

He heard a light step and realized he'd closed his eyes only because he'd had to open them to look at the woman standing in front of him, watching him as if she expected him to rush off and do something unpredictable.

"I am okay," he said. "Let us go match ourselves against this car and come away victorious."

She took a deep breath. "If I can keep from running us into anything, I think we'll be fine."

He exchanged a glance with the lord of the hall, then followed Olivia outside and down the stairs to the courtyard where he found a white … car. He continued to follow his companions because he was accustomed to continuing to move without haste or fear until his wits had caught up with his feet, but it wasn't easily done. He was actually rather grateful Olivia was holding onto his sword.

Stephen took the sword from her and walked around the beast, gesturing to things Jackson attempted to memorize. He forced himself not to flinch as the tail of the car suddenly raised itself into the air. He fully expected the bloody thing to belch out some collection of enemies he would need to slay, but nothing emerged from inside.

"I can drive a stick," Olivia said. "My grandfather thought I should know how."

"A wise man, your grandfather," Stephen said approvingly. "Let's stow your luggage in the boot and find a place for Jackson's sword."

Jackson accepted the maps and reminded himself that he'd been to numerous places over the course of his score-and-eight years and never once gotten himself or anyone else lost. He tucked Olivia into her spot inside the car, then found Stephen waiting for him behind it.

"You're doing a much better job than I did in your time."

Jackson started to thank him, then he realized what he'd just heard. He looked at his cousin in surprise. "When—"

"Let's just say that my wife was wearing boots your uncle Nicholas provided and we ate food those bloody twins had to buy for us."

Jackson shook his head, because words were beyond him.

"If the roads we've discussed are too busy," Stephen continued, "try something near the coast where the speed will be less. You'll have to judge as you go along. And ring me if you need aid."

He nodded, clasped his cousin's hand in a confident fashion, then faced off with the door. Stephen discreetly pointed to a silver strip that apparently served as an outer latch. Jackson pulled, then put himself inside the beast.

"You'd better buckle up," Olivia said.

He knew he was looking at her blankly, but everything was more overwhelming than he'd suspected it might be. He found Stephen handing him a belt of some kind that was intended to go into a buckle. It clicked together with the finality of a dungeon door closing, which he didn't much care for.

"Push on the red button to release it," Stephen advised.

Jackson did and found himself almost surprised that the belt released. He rebuckled it, sent his cousin a look he was certain amused the man greatly, and pulled the door closed.

He turned to Olivia to find her less pale than she had been a half hour before, but not by much.

"All will be well," he said confidently.

"I might need to drive around the village once or twice before we get on the real roads."

"Past any decent chippies?" he asked.

"Do you ever think about anything but food?"

"Swords," he said without hesitation. "The shore, hot fires, and beautiful women who master journeys to large cities in the south."

She smiled faintly. "I'll try not to run us into anything."

He held out his hand to seal the deal, as his aunt Abigail would have said—damn her to hell as well—and tried not to shiver as she put her hand in his.

There were strange and mysterious things going on in the Future, to be sure.

"I should probably try not to run over His Lordship, either," she added, putting the key where it was apparently intended to go. She took a deep breath, then turned it.

Jackson wasn't entirely certain he hadn't at least caught his breath, but he was damned certain he hadn't squeaked. He suspected he hadn't been as cavalier, however, about the noise that suddenly filled the car as if its very innards were screaming in agony.

"80s pop," Olivia said with a shudder, reaching for a black knob near the large wheel in front of her. "Let's find something a little better. What's your pleasure? Led Zeppelin? The Beatles? Rachmaninoff?"

He pulled his hands away from his ears and swallowed uncomfortably. "I'm very fond of them all," he said, hoping he wasn't dooming himself for lying with such abandon. "You choose."

"My granddad was a big fan of country and jazz, but I'm not sure we'll get that over here. Let's see if there's something classical."

He was prepared to suffer through almost anything to keep from having to listen to what had assaulted his ears initially, then he realized something astonishing. Olivia had settled on something he was almost certain he'd heard his Aunt Jennifer play.

"Very beautiful," he managed.

"I think that's Schubert, but it's been a while since that music class I took in college." She took a deep breath, then put her hands back on the wheel. "I think I can do this now."

He wanted to make note of how she was putting the car into motion, but he was too busy trying not to stop the bloody thing by sitting back as he might have on a horse. He exchanged a glance through the window with the current lord of Artane, had a quick smile for his trouble, then turned to face what was coming.

He didn't particularly care for being the one not in control, but things were what they were. Olivia was very competent in guiding the car and by the time they'd made a circle of the village a time or two, he had grown accustomed to the noise and the movement. After all, there were wagons in his day and horses that came close to flying if the terrain was suitable.

He wondered what Kendrick would have thought about automobiles. Likely nothing past how quickly he could take them apart to see how they worked, but his cousin was that sort of lad.

"Do they not have these sorts of cars in your village—ah, land?"

"They do," she said, "but we drive on the other side of the road. And the other side of the car, if you want the whole truth. But other than that, it's pretty much the same thing."

He contemplated the improbability of that for a bit whilst keeping his eye on the map. 'Twas difficult to calculate their location whilst traveling so quickly, but the notices on the side of the road made that a bit easier once he realized what they meant.

"We could take a less populated road," he offered, "if you like. These wee B-roads seem like they might be less ... "

"Terrifying?"

"I didn't chose that word."

She shot him a glare, then she laughed. He had to smile slightly, because she was, as he had noted before, enchanting.

"We could travel near the sea, if you like," he said. He'd done it countless times himself.

"That might be good," she said, "but let me pull over for a minute first. There's a gas station up there."

He considered. "Will they have food?"

"You could call it that, I guess." She glanced at him. "Ever had Cheetos?"

"The saints preserve me, nay," he said, then realized he'd said it in French. She only smiled, so he supposed that had been intelligible enough.

"Don't worry," she said. "I don't think they have them in England. It's American junk food."

Junk food was something he was absolutely certain he'd heard the wee twins whispering about with their brother, so perhaps that bore some investigation. As did the country of America, though he suspected he would need more than a map of England for that.

"How long have you been in England?" he asked as she pulled into the strange pillar-laden courtyard.

"I got here the day before the play," she said.

"So recently."

She nodded. "And you?"

"The same," he said.

She turned the car off and rested her head against the steering wheel for a moment. "Lucky thing we were both at that play, then."

He took a deep breath, then nodded, because he wasn't sure he could begin to think about how close he'd come to never having encountered her.

"Food?"

"Aye," he managed, grateful for the distraction. He looked to his left, trying to decide which of the little levers and knobs needed to be tugged on to allow him out. Olivia leaned over him and pulled on one of them, releasing the door. She also unbuckled his seatbelt, which he thought very polite.

Her hair brushed across his face as she did so, then caught on the edge of his coat. He untangled it very slowly and carefully because it behooved him to make certain there were no knots in those strands and she wasn't in any pain.

A gentleman to the last, in truth.

He glanced at her to find her simply watching him, not looking as if she were on the verge of losing her breakfast. He smiled briefly.

"Wait for me," he said.

She nodded.

He crawled out of the car and saved himself from scorching his fingers on the bonnet only because he could feel the heat coming off the metal. He had the feeling that wouldn't be the last thing that startled him, so perhaps he would be making a more serious study of Stephen de Piaget's texts than he'd suspected.

Olivia had arrived only the day before the frolic.

He couldn't bring himself to think on what sort of hand Fate must have had in the timing of that.

The journey to London passed like a dream, leaving behind nothing but a vague impression of events. By the time they reached the outskirts of London, he'd become almost numb to the impossible number of cars, inhabitants, and buildings they passed. Olivia followed his reading of Derrick Cameron's directions and stopped them finally next to a long row of astonishingly elegant white halls. Jackson shifted to look at Olivia simply sitting there with her head leaning back against the seat, breathing lightly. He covered her hand with his.

"You've done well," he said.

She let out a shaky breath. "I hope we're in the right place. I'm not sure I can drive anywhere else for a couple of days."

He'd already checked the numbers on the front of that hall to find they matched what they'd been given, so he supposed that was answer enough. At the moment, he wasn't sure Olivia would manage to walk anywhere else, never mind drive.

"I'll bring in our gear," he said, opening his door. "Then we should find a tavern and have some supper. Things will look better tomorrow."

"Will they?"

He paused and looked at her gravely. "They always do. You've done all the labor of getting us here. I'll see to the rest of the day."

"Thank you," she said wearily.

"Have you the key to the house?"

She pulled the car key free from its mooring and handed it to him. There was another on that ring which he assumed opened Derrick's hall. He unbuckled himself and Olivia as well, then fetched her out of the car and walked with her up to the door that he found was indeed the correct one. He handed her his sword, then unlocked the door cautiously. He caught her before she simply walked inside.

"I must make certain 'tis safe," he said slowly. He lit the passageway light, pulled her inside, then closed the door. "I'll check the chambers."

"I'm sure they're—"

He shot her a look and she sighed.

"All right."

He put his hand on her shoulder briefly, reached behind her and secured the door, then made his way through the house. He supposed he was fortunate that he'd seen at least a few modern amenities at Artane or he would have been utterly undone by Derrick Cameron's hall.

He forced himself to ignore the impossibly polished surfaces in the kitchens and the bathroom, the luxurious floor coverings in what seemed to serve as the great hall, and the lights that still startled him with their brightness.

He nodded to Olivia as he passed by her on his way up the

stairs. There were bedchambers above, which didn't surprise him, but there was nothing in them, which did. He had a vague memory of Olivia and Stephen discussing the rather austere nature of Derrick and Samantha's hall being due to their not having occupied it yet.

That didn't trouble him. He'd slept on much worse than a floor as clean as the one downstairs and there had been some sort of bench there in front of the hearth that Olivia could use quite comfortably. If that made her uneasy, he would take his rest in the garden.

He ran back down the stairs to find her leaning against the wall, half asleep on her feet.

"Find anything rotten in Denmark?" she asked with a yawn.

He looked at her and frowned. "Ah—"

"Too much Shakespeare this past week," she said with a weary smile. "Let me rephrase that. No bad guys for me to do in with your sword?"

He shook his head. "You're safe."

"Thank you."

"'Tis my honor to do so," he said with a small bow. "If you'll hold the door, I'll fetch our belongings from the car."

She patted her pockets, then frowned. "Do you have the keys?"

He held them up. "These keys?"

She smiled. "Don't drive off without me."

"I wouldn't," he assured her, though he certainly would have attempted a wee journey in a less populated place *with* her if he'd had the time.

He left her standing just inside the door and loped down the trio of stairs to the ground. He ignored the very strange feeling he had whilst opening the boot of the car with that Future key, as if he'd done it scores of times before.

He couldn't bring himself to wonder what his own key might have opened.

He brought their belongings into the gathering chamber, made use of yet another perfectly luxurious garderobe, then wandered back to the great hall. Olivia was sitting there on that padded bench, looking as if she might either weep or simply fall asleep. He wouldn't have blamed her for either.

He sat down next to her, then frowned thoughtfully at the low table there in front of them. There was a round globe suspended on a spit sitting there, something that he suspected might be a map of the current world. He leaned forward and found his own country, then identified the places he'd been on the continent. After that, he found himself rather lost. He looked over lands and seas and names for places he'd never imagined might exist.

He looked at Olivia, then rose and looked for something to use as a pillow. He arranged things to his satisfaction, then took her by the shoulders and carefully tipped her over. He took off her shoes, then removed his coat and draped it over her. She looked up at him solemnly.

"You are a very nice man."

He grunted. "You're half out of your head with weariness, obviously. Sleep for a bit, then we'll find supper."

"Thank you, Jackson."

"You're very welcome, Olivia."

She closed her eyes and was asleep within a handful of heartbeats. Jackson rose, found the satchel with the books Stephen had loaned him, then pulled them out and set them on the table with the representation of the current world. He glanced at Olivia to make certain she was warm and comfortable, then turned his mind to the things before him. It would take him a few minutes to accustom himself to the way the letters were drawn, but he would allow no more time than that for the matter.

He had eight hundred years of knowledge to catch up on.

Eleven

Olivia lay on a couch in a gorgeous townhouse in what appeared to be a very nice part of London and allowed herself to ignore her amazing surroundings in favor of a little more digesting of the recent trip south.

The whole experience of getting to London had been an adventure, though she considered herself to be a fairly good driver. Even just having the rear view mirror angled in a way she wasn't used to had been frustrating. If the pedals hadn't been in the same place, she might have been tempted to pass on the whole experience.

Or, maybe not. She allowed herself to sneak up on the thought that there was something very exciting about having an entire life in front of her that was full of things she had yet to experience. She wasn't quite ready to completely unmake her vow, but she thought she could engage in the occasional sideways glance at things that were Marginally Interesting.

Such as the man sitting on the couch at her feet, slowly spinning a globe sitting on the coffee table. Whatever else could be said about him, it was obvious Jackson Kilchurn was very good with a map. Not only that, he had expressed an acceptable level of enthusiasm for all historical structures of note they'd driven past. He'd also shown an uncanny knack for sensing when she'd needed a break, and he hadn't been shy about insisting she take several. Even her grandfather would have given him a nod over that.

She watched him move the globe aside and look at the books

spread out on the table. He'd brought a bag full of them south, so perhaps they were a gift from Stephen de Piaget. She watched him pick one up and examine not only the physical book itself, but the contents as if he'd never seen anything like it before. He finally shook his head slightly, restacked all the books neatly into a trio of piles, then glanced her way.

He became very still in that way he had, as if he needed a moment to process something unexpected. She couldn't believe he hadn't experienced every woman he'd ever encountered falling all over him, so maybe there was something going on with him that was mildly interesting without being at all mysterious.

He shifted and leaned back against the arm of the sofa. "Sleep well?" he asked politely.

"I honestly don't remember. Did I?"

"For about an hour. You needed it, I daresay." He reached for a bottle of water and held it out. "These were left in the kitchens along with instruction on their use."

She would have made an offhand comment about Derrick being a terrible tease, but she didn't know him well enough to judge. She sat up, managed to get her feet on the floor without joining them there, then accepted a bottle of water. She might have been a bit fuzzy around the edges, but she was very aware that Jackson was watching her twist the lid off her water before he did the same with his own. She ignored that realization with abandon, congratulating herself silently on her vast amounts of recently acquired self-control.

"Where is your home?" he asked.

She leaned forward and found the appropriate spot. "Here, near Seattle."

He only nodded thoughtfully. "And how did you come to England?"

"I flew British Airways," she said, "because it seemed fitting. I took a train from London north, then finally a bus to Artane." She looked at him. "I never asked you how you got to the play or where you're from."

"England, still," he said solemnly, "and I walked."

"But you speak French."

"And Latin," he said. "Keeps me awake in chapel."

"What else?"

He lifted his eyebrows briefly. "A handful of other things found on the Continent, though if you're truly curious, you'll need to flip the knowledge out of me."

She smiled, then made herself more comfortable on the couch. "You really aren't going to give me any more details in your vastly improved English?"

"There are things that perhaps I could tell you," he said slowly, "and perhaps others that I *should* tell you, but I would rather not today. Let us say only that my journey was unexpected and I am here for the fortnight until I can recover my key."

"Then you'll go back home."

He nodded. He didn't look particularly happy about that, but what did she know? Maybe the thought of leaving chocolate behind was just too much for him.

For herself, the thought of his trotting off into the sunset was a bit more distressing than she'd expected which was more ridiculous than she'd anticipated. She was in England to get a job and make a new life, not waste a single thought of even just dating a man that absurdly gorgeous who likely wouldn't consider dating her—

A man who was holding out his hand casually toward her.

"I would like to spend this time with you," he said carefully. "If you're willing."

"Well," she said, realizing she sounded a little breathless but unable to fix that on the fly, "you don't want to let that coin get away from you."

He smiled faintly. "I could chase you down for that, if that were all I cared about."

She looked at his hand for a moment or two, then put her hand in his. She suddenly understood how her aunt had gotten so twitterpated so quickly over a guy with a collection of vintage cocktail glassware and dreams of a driftwood bar.

"You look a bit faint," Jackson said suddenly. "Perhaps you need food."

"You mean *you* need food," she corrected.

"Always." He squeezed her hand briefly, then released her to reach for his backpack. He removed all his cash, separated out five twenty-pound notes, then stuck the rest inside the cover of a book he returned to the coffee table. He stood up and held out his hand again. "Supper first, then we'll make plans for the morrow."

It was definitely not how she'd been expecting to spend the stress-riddled days leading up to the start of her new life, but now she wondered how she could have possibly wished for a better distraction. Supper, a London buddy, and a great place to stay.

What a wonderful way to start her future.

Two hours and a hearty pub meal later, she was walking back toward Derrick and Samantha's house with a man who snorted at her offer to go Dutch and continually put himself between her and the street. That kind of gallantry was absolutely going to ruin her for anyone else. She looked for something innocuous to chat about and latched onto the first thing that came to mind.

"Have you been to London before?"

"Aye, many times," he said, "but both with my family and by myself."

"Who was your security detail?"

"A cousin or two, usually."

"What was your favorite part?" she asked.

"Not finding myself locked in the Tower."

She would have laughed, but she wasn't sure he wasn't serious. "I don't think they lock anyone in there these days. It's all just for show."

"I'm very fond of history," he said easily. "'Tis easy to forget what a modern time we live in."

'Twas also easy to forget that London was just slightly more dangerous than the Irma-controlled streets of Northern Crook, Washington. She realized she should have been more aware of her surroundings approximately five seconds after she found herself looking at a man who had simply stepped into their path. He opened his jacket to reveal the haft of a knife protruding from an inside pocket.

"In there," he said briskly, nodding toward the shadows of the alley to her left.

"As you will," Jackson said with a shrug.

Olivia felt her mouth working like a marooned fish, but no sound was coming out.

Jackson pulled her into the alley behind him and left her near the entrance. "Stay."

"What the hell else am I going to do?" she squeaked. She thought she might have already said that once in his company, which meant it was starting to become a habit. She wasn't quite sure how she felt about that, but she suspected Jackson wouldn't be interested in her thoughts because he had already turned to face their new friend.

She stood against the wall where he'd left her and forced herself to make a list of details about their attacker. Why was it that men who got in her way always wore trench coats and sunglasses at night? If she hadn't known better, she would have suspected that Irma was sending her nephews overseas to shake her down for any funds Aunt Philly might have managed to hold onto. The one thing she could say for sure was that none of Irma's scrawny helpers would have lasted three seconds against Jackson Kilchurn.

He disarmed the guy and had him on his knees with his hand behind his back at a very uncomfortable angle before she could do anything but wheeze.

"Apologize to my lady for the inconvenience," Jackson said coldly, "before I leave you unable to do so."

The man managed to get out a few curses before Jackson tsk-tsked him and applied a bit more pressure to his hand.

"Another attempt, if you please."

"Sorry," the would-be thug gasped.

"Behave properly from now on," Jackson said, releasing the guy who then leaped to his feet, turned, and took a swing at him.

Olivia watched Jackson duck as if he'd been expecting the same, pulling her out of the way as he did so, which left their new friend running not only his fist but his face—which he admittedly had a little help with—directly into the brick wall next to her. He slumped to the ground with a groan.

Jackson picked up the man's knife and sunglasses and tossed both into the nearest garbage can before he took her hand.

"Let's go home," he said pleasantly.

Olivia looked over her shoulder to see the results of her security detail's work. She didn't imagine the guy would be trotting after them any time soon, but Jackson didn't seem inclined to stick around and find out. She walked down the street with him at a good clip, trying to catch her breath.

"What in the *hell* was that?" she asked finally.

He smiled, maybe the first genuinely amused smile she'd had from him so far. "Lads need lessons in manners now and again."

"Where in the world did you learn to do all that?"

"Family."

And that was apparently all she was going to get. She watched him making mental notes of everything in front of and behind them until he finally stopped and nodded at a camera on a light post.

"What is that?"

"Closed circuit TV," she said. "You know, so the police can keep an eye on you."

He blinked, then nodded. "Of course."

She was starting to wonder with an enthusiasm that felt like desperation just where in the world Jackson Kilchurn had grown up.

Well, wherever it had been, he'd obviously been accustomed to taking care of security. She tried not to notice how his bad-guy antennae were operating in overdrive, but it was hard to miss. He was casual about it, but it was still very clear that he was watching the shadows around them as they walked, scanning people as they passed them, and keeping an eye peeled for cameras.

She was relieved ten minutes later to find the steps leading up to Samantha and Derrick's townhouse missing any extra things like ruffians and ne'er-do-wells. She was even happier to find the inside as empty as it had been when they'd left.

"I'll check the hall," Jackson said as he shut and locked the door.

She wasn't about to be left behind, so she kicked off her shoes and looked at him purposefully. "I'll come along."

Jackson looked at her feet, then took off his boots as well. He frowned thoughtfully at the two sheathed daggers he'd pulled from those boots.

"I'll hold them for you," she offered.

He handed her one. "To keep things fair."

She suspected that two for her and none for him would have been closer to fair, but she was momentarily distracted by what she was holding in her hands. She followed him absently to the stairs, pulling the dagger out as she walked. She started to test the edge of the blade only to find her thumb caught immediately between a different thumb and index finger.

"I wouldn't."

She looked up at him. "You wouldn't?"

"They're perilously sharp."

"Who *are* you?"

He took a deep breath. "Just don't touch the blade."

She resheathed the knife and followed him up the stairs and through the rooms there. She didn't want to do any thinking about what had just happened up the street or why Jackson needed knives that were sharp enough to probably slice through bricks or why he'd flinched the first couple of times she'd turned on the lights in each room before he'd taken over the job himself.

That wasn't strange at all.

By the time he'd finished his reconnaissance mission and led her back downstairs, she was finished as well. She stood in the middle of the living room and had the most ridiculous desire to just sit down and bawl. She wasn't a crier, but she thought she might have just had enough of things that didn't make sense.

Jackson brought her suitcase and his bags over from where they'd been sitting behind the couch and set them against the wall where they weren't visible from the front door. He glanced at her, then stopped and looked at her in surprise.

"You aren't afraid, surely," he said.

"Of course not," she said. She wasn't afraid, she was on the verge of one gigantic, post-interminable-drive, post-mugging meltdown. There might have been a hearty helping of jetlag stress in there somewhere as well, along with nerves about wanting so badly to ace her interview but fearing she might just blow it, which would leave her messing up her chance to stay in England.

She was a little surprised to find how much that bothered her.

Jackson walked over and stopped in front of her. He opened his arms, then hesitated. "May I?"

She nodded and found herself gathered into a ridiculously comforting embrace. She closed her eyes and concentrated on simply breathing in and out so she didn't have hysterics and terrify him.

He smoothed his hand over her hair a time or two, then cleared his throat. "I think," he said quietly, "that we should stay in this great hall together. You take that comfortable bench over there and I will sleep in front of the door."

She nodded. "All right."

"All will be well, Olivia."

She took a deep breath, then stepped away before she accustomed herself to something she might have to give up sooner rather than later. "Thank you," she said. "And thank you for before. That was frightening."

He shrugged lightly. "People comport themselves poorly from time to time, but you've no need to worry. For all you know, this is simply a clumsy plan to keep you and my coin close to me at all moments."

"I doubt that," she said with an attempt at a smile. She looked up at him and felt her smile fade. "Is this how you guard your family in London?"

He nodded. "My mother and sisters always slept in perfect peace and safety."

She thought about that portrait she'd seen in the 18th century wing of Artane and looked at him speculatively. "How many women are in your family?"

"One mother, more than one sister," he said. "Now, think you there are bedclothes anywhere?"

What she thought was that she was going to have to get up earlier in the morning to catch him off guard, though what she hoped to accomplish by that she couldn't have said. There was probably a very good explanation for everything that baffled her, but she was too tired at the moment to try to figure it out.

She was also unnerved enough to think that having a guy with those sorts of guarding skills keeping the wolves at bay was a very good thing. She looked around herself absently and noticed an unopened moving box she hadn't noticed before. She immediately decided it couldn't possibly be one of *those* kinds of unopened boxes which meant she could open it without problem.

It contained nothing more mysterious than an air mattress and a few blankets. She handed Jackson the blankets, found a plug and blew up the air bed, then wondered what kind of thumb war she would have to fight to win that as the prize. She glanced at Jackson to find him looking at the bed as if he'd never seen anything like it before.

"A marvelous bellows," he said, pointing to the pump she'd used.

His finger was shaking slightly, which for some strange reason made her feel better. Maybe he wasn't as invincible as he looked, which meant maybe she didn't need to be, either.

"It's pretty nifty," she agreed. "Do you want to flip for the bed?"

"Nay, I will sleep on the floor."

She thought he might have a change of heart at some point, but she wasn't going to argue. She handed him a couple of blankets and made her bed. There wasn't any way to make it look as if they hadn't simply taken over the living room if someone unthuggish happened to drop by for a visit, so she didn't try.

She also realized she had zero qualms about falling asleep in the same room as her cracking guardsman especially when the alternative was going upstairs to one of those dark, absolutely not-haunted bedrooms and wondering if hanging Eugenie Kilchurn's book over the window would be enough to keep out any unwholesome elements, disembodied or not.

She grabbed pajamas and a toothbrush, then found that Jackson had done the same. If he'd unpacked his duffle bag and backpack in the same way she had, that was just coincidence.

"I'm going to go brush my teeth," she announced.

He nodded absently.

She left him standing in the living room, squinting at the ingredients on a tube of toothpaste. She had stared at his dagger in exactly the same way so she couldn't fault him for it.

Ten minutes later she walked into the kitchen in her Drummond plaid pajamas only to find him investigating the cabinets. He had ears like a bat, that guy, because even though she considered herself fairly stealthy—it made it easier to sneak up on exclusive vintage finds that way—he looked over his shoulder the moment she reached the kitchen door.

"Find anything interesting?" she asked.

"Food for a month, at least." He gestured at a bright blue range. "Do you have these in your home?"

"It's an Aga," she said reverently, "and no, I've only seen them in magazines. I'm pretty sure wood goes in and hot food comes out, but it could also be electric. We should probably ask Derrick and Sam how to use it before we try it. The fridge, though, I can definitely manage."

She walked over to the refrigerator and looked inside. Jackson hadn't been exaggerating. There was a large selection of perishable food inside, which she supposed meant it had been left for them. She considered, then opened the freezer to find things that were definitely more interesting. She looked at Jackson.

"Ice cream?"

He only looked at her blankly, which told her all she needed to know about his upbringing. She picked the most chocolate-laced thing she could find and rifled through drawers until she found silverware. She handed Jackson a spoon and popped the lid off something that boasted chocolate from five different sources. She took a spoonful, then held the container out toward him.

It was marginally interesting how he copied her movements exactly, but what did she know? A lifetime of his parents hiding him away so he didn't leave the local female population in a perpetual faint probably took its toll.

She tasted, then almost had to sit down. Jackson had his own bite, then he backed up into the kitchen table and sat down abruptly into one of the chairs there.

"Merciful saints above," he breathed, "what miracle is this?"

He'd said it in French, which didn't surprise her. She joined him at the table and realized, given the way he had just wolfed down an enormous second spoonful, that she was going to need to walk him through the basics of the junk food experience.

"You can't inhale ice cream like that," she said, patting him on the shoulder while he clutched his head with his hands and made noises of agony. "It'll give you brain freeze."

He breathed lightly for several moments, then looked at her blearily. "I cannot decide if that food was created in Heaven or Hell."

She wasn't going to offer an opinion, though finishing what he'd left could be considered a good deed. She reached for the container only to find his hand in the way.

"I'll need more before I decide. Let us continue to share."

There were probably worse things to do than double-dip with a man who had saved her from a mugging, so she did so without hesitation.

"Would it be impolite," he said as they neared the end of the road on that particular batch, "to ask about the soul you've come to London to see?"

She would have told him where curiosity led, but maybe he already knew. She fought him briefly for a final and particularly substantial chunk of Belgian chocolate, surrendered because he had saved her earlier that evening, then shrugged.

"I don't have very many details to give. My aunt met her, they got to talking about her needing someone with a background in art history for her new business, and here I am in London."

"And you know the history of art?"

"I studied it in college." She set her spoon down on the kitchen table. "I like looking at things in the past through the eyes of people who saw it happening."

He choked.

Really, the guy was going to have to get hold of himself or she was going to be driving him to some sort of midnight clinic. She got him a glass of water, then whacked him on the back a few more times until he held up his hand and begged her to stop. She sat back down and waited for him to stop wheezing.

"So, does your guild mistress paint?" he managed, holding his glass gingerly and eyeing it as if he expected it to shatter at any moment.

"No, but I understand that she used to make jewelry."

He had another drink, then carefully set the glass down on the table. "An interesting thing for a woman to do all alone in a forge."

"She wasn't alone," Olivia said. "Or at least not initially. Apparently the guy who owned the business got sick a couple of years ago and left everything to her. I understand he intended to live out his last days in Greenland."

"The country covered in snow."

"Ironic, right?"

"Very," he agreed. "And did her liege lord manage to travel there?"

"No idea," she said. "She never could get in touch with him after he said goodbye, but she kept having dreams about the whole thing which led her to looking for the same book my aunt was hunting down."

"A book about dreams?"

She nodded. "My aunt had had some doozies about Drummond ancestors so she was looking for answers herself. The book they wanted was hard to find, so maybe it was less Fate and more desperation that had them trying to buy the same copy."

He leaned back in his chair and studied her. "But your aunt lives in America."

"They're Internet friends."

He nodded sagely. "Of course." He peered into the empty pint, then frowned. "Is there more of this in that silver box?"

"Not if you want to sleep. That was a lot of chocolate."

"I feel very refreshed," he said. "Marvelous stuff, that."

She suspected he might have a different opinion when it kept him awake all night, but she didn't have the heart to discourage him. She did, however, get up and follow him to the freezer just to be on hand to save him from himself if necessary.

"You know," she said after he'd opened the fourth carton and tasted, "if you eat all that tonight, you'll be sick."

"My form will not desert me in such a way," he said. He paused, then looked at her. "There is tomorrow, I suppose."

If his mother hadn't discouraged ice cream for breakfast, she wasn't going to start. She left him to perusing his options, stopped by the bathroom to rebrush her teeth, then wandered back into the living room. She wasn't sure if she felt cold or just nervous, which had nothing to do with the man who had saved her from a mugging and everything to do with her interview in two days.

Jackson walked into the living room in sweats and a t-shirt and joined her in front of the fireplace. "I'll find wood tomorrow," he promised. "Will you survive the night?"

"Under plenty of blankets, yes," she said. "You're sure you don't want the bed?"

"Nay, I will make good use of this luxurious floor tapestry here by the hearth. Go settle yourself, Olivia. The hall is secure and I have my sword. You may sleep in peace."

And if that wasn't something the knight in shining armor from down the street would have said, she didn't know what was. She nodded, then hesitated.

"Could I borrow one of your books? We could share the lamp, if you like."

"One of the wee torches," he said, nodding. "Those are very useful and pleasing."

It was better than a lantern, though she'd read by those often enough on the endless camping trips her grandfather had bribed her into going on. She moved one of the lamps, borrowed something on royalty through the ages, and put herself to bed. She watched Jackson make himself at home on the floor and start with what she could see was a condensed pictorial history of the world.

"You can move closer to the light," she offered. "I won't clunk you over the head with this book in the middle of the night."

He snorted, but rearranged his blankets and pillow so he could actually see what he was reading.

She only managed to skim the first chapter of her book before she had to stop. It was much more interesting to watch Jackson read. He shook his head a lot, which made her wonder just where in the world he'd grown up.

He finally closed up his book, then looked at her. "I believe I partook of too much ice cream."

"Told you so."

"So you did." He considered, then looked at her. "We should take tomorrow and indulge in distractions so you don't think overmuch about your upcoming battle. What do you care to see in London?"

"I'm a little short on cash," she admitted uncomfortably, "so I might have to do a lot of just walking."

"But you cannot imagine I would allow you to pay for anything."

She blinked. "Why wouldn't I think that?"

"Because you are a woman."

"And you don't have any pockets."

"I have them," he said archly, "I simply forget to use them. As for the other, I have enough of those paper pounds to see to us both for quite some time. If they run out, I've gold sewn into my boots."

It was hard to argue with that, not that she supposed she would get anywhere arguing with him anyway. She made herself comfortable, then shifted to look at him lying next to her bed, rolled in blankets and diving back into the unfolding of the world.

"Thank you for keeping me safe tonight," she said quietly.

"My pleasure."

"You're terrifying."

He smiled briefly. "Go to sleep, Olivia, lest the thought overwhelm you. You can heap praise upon my deserving head tomorrow over breakfast." He held out his hand toward her without looking at her. "Thumb war."

"You aren't paying attention."

"And yet I will win anyway."

She took his hand and realized he was absolutely paying attention, but that was what he seemed to do.

She wondered about him.

She also lost, but he didn't seem inclined to release her hand, that man who had calluses on his palms and rubbed his thumb over hers absently while turning pages with his free hand. There were strange things afoot in London and they weren't limited to sunglasses-wearing thugs.

It was a good thing she'd sworn off mysteries of all kinds or she might have been distracted from her purpose of getting her new life underway.

TWELVE

JACKSON PADDED QUIETLY THROUGH THE house on bare feet, looking for the woman he was supposed to be guarding. He'd woken immediately when she'd stirred, of course, then done the unthinkable and gone back to sleep when she'd suggested that she would be fine on her own for a few minutes.

He had unfortunately slept longer and more deeply than he'd intended, which said much about his weariness and the perils of an ice-cream stupor. Obviously that was not an indulgence he could allow himself unless there was someone else there to guard his back. Who would have thought he would miss his cousins at such a time?

He picked up a bottle of water from the table in the kitchens, helped himself casually to its contents, then replaced the top on the first attempt. He continued on to the back door, feeling altogether modern.

Olivia was sitting on the stoop there, so still that he half wondered if she had been slain whilst he slept. He leaned over to peer in her face only to have her look at him and smile.

He almost swayed into her lap.

She caught him by the arm which allowed him the time to step onto the grass and squat down in front of her where he could see her visage properly.

"I feared you had been felled by some vile London … thing," he said. Ruffians, chamber pot contents, the saints only knew what else found home in the present day.

"I was meditating."

He frowned. "You were what?"

"Meditating," she repeated. "You know, being still."

"Why the hell would you want to do that?" he asked, baffled.

"It's good for your chi," she said, though she looked a little baffled herself. "I'm making changes in my life and I understand this is a good place to start."

He wasn't opposed to anything that might aid a man in preparing for battle, so he wouldn't discourage her.

"I'll prepare food for when you're finished. I was restless in the wee hours and found the manuscript that declared how the Aga is to be used, so I have it well in hand." He paused. "We could also have something else from the ice cream larder, if you'd rather."

"For breakfast?" She laughed a little and closed her eyes. "Maybe. Why don't you come meditate with me first?"

"I fear for damage to my chi," he muttered, whatever the bloody hell that was. He imagined it had nothing to do with sword skill, but what did he know? He watched her gather stillness to her, then almost smiled when she opened one eye and glared at him.

"You're distracting me."

That didn't begin to address what she was doing to him, so he simply rose and touched the top of her head on his way back into the house. He paused in the kitchens, then decided no one would be the wiser if he had a small bite of something to ease his hunger. He helped himself to a modest portion of a frozen concoction made by Marks & Spencer—brothers, no doubt—that contained chocolate, cookies, and other things he didn't bother to try to pronounce. He waited for another bout of that terrifying brain freeze, but perhaps he'd learned his lesson the night before because none came to vex him.

Unfortunately, that also left him wondering how he would manage the rest of his life with porridge for breakfast and eel for dinner. He would endure fewer pains in his head and avoid sleeping whilst his charges went off on their own to attend to their chi, but that seemed a rather poor exchange.

He made his way back into the small hall and gathered up what he'd seen on the low table in passing the night before. He fetched one of his knives as well, then paused to make certain he was dressed properly. Stephen's loan of clothing consisted of several Future tunics along with two pairs of jeans and the soft hose he'd called sweats, which he was currently wearing. They seemed modest enough, he supposed, so he found a sweatshirt to don over his tunic and went back outside.

He made himself comfortable on Olivia's step, far enough away that he could see her properly but not so far that he would fall off onto the grass. He then began what he'd been thinking about from the moment he'd actually had a proper look at her. The tools were certainly far finer than anything he had ever used before. The parchment was marvelous, the pencil lovely, and his subject glorious.

He sketched Olivia just as she was, wrapped in a blanket he was certain was covering a pair of scandalous … well, she had called them *yoga pants*, which he had immediately consigned to items she shouldn't wear in front of anyone she didn't want him to slay.

"You're swearing in French," she said calmly.

He grunted. "Yoga pants."

She only smiled and continued with her business. He continued with his, wishing absently that he'd had colors to use but perhaps those could be found later.

"I hear a knife," she said. "Should I be afraid to look?"

"Just keeping you safe." And other things, but perhaps that would be obvious later.

"You're very protective."

"Many wee cousins and siblings. Forgive me. I'll try not to smother you."

She opened her eyes and looked at him, then caught sight of his sheaf of Future parchment. He'd borrowed the book she'd been reading the night before to use in buttressing his sketching, though perhaps that had been badly done. 'Twas too late now to apologize for it.

She pointed at his drawing. "What is that?"

He wasn't sure anyone but his parents and siblings had ever seen anything he'd ever drawn and they'd all been sworn to secrecy. His father had taught him to render images properly, just as he'd taught all his children, though he supposed he might have been the only one to go to such lengths to depict on parchment all the glorious things he'd witnessed. A pair of his younger sisters could do the same, but they were the only ones who bothered. He was, however, absolutely certain no one else in his larger family knew what he could do.

Well, save Stephen de Piaget who had smirked at him mightily whilst Olivia had been admiring the family portrait he himself had painted, but Jackson was fairly certain the man could be quietly disposed of, if necessary. He was also sketching and not painting, so hopefully Olivia would think nothing of it.

He set his pride aside and turned his rendering so Olivia could see it.

She looked at it for so long, he wondered if she couldn't quite find words to tell him how dreadful it was, then she met his gaze.

There were tears in her eyes.

"You're … amazing."

He trotted out a few gruff noises and a curse or two, but that did absolutely nothing to stop the color that he was appalled to find creeping up his cheeks.

"Are you blushing again?"

"I'm hungry."

"That's your excuse for everything." She leaned over to peer at his work. "I'm trying to get past how beautiful you've made me look to the place where I am absolutely stunned by your abilities. Where in the world did you learn to do that and why didn't you say something before?"

He moved to sit closer to her. "Let's discuss instead what you called me," he said, shivering a little in the chill of the morning. "And lend me a bit of your covering whilst you repeat it for my edification."

She wrapped part of her blanket around his shoulders. "Do I get to keep that drawing?"

"Only if I might make another tomorrow for myself."

"Can you paint?"

"Who knows?" he asked, wincing a little at how close that came to lying.

She took his sketch of herself, then shook her head. "I just don't know what to think of you."

He knew exactly what to think of himself and that was that he was currently warm, remarkably content, and absolutely capable of leaning over and kissing her. He wasn't one to take liberties where they were not freely offered first, however, so he forbore.

"Breakfast?" she asked.

"If I can draw you again later," he said. "I'll prepare our meal as incentive."

"I won't argue," she said with a smile. "Let's go eat."

Lighting the cooking Aga was easily accomplished and the lower half of the ice cream larder provided all manner of remarkable foodstuffs. His mother's cook would have wept over the choices. He managed not to burn his fingers or the hall to cinders, though his eggs didn't fare as well as he would have liked. Olivia simply ate his offerings without complaint.

"Delicious," she said. "I'm guessing that stove takes a few days to get used to, but I'll happily eat your experiments."

He couldn't bring himself to think about how many days remained him in the Future.

Or how he wished there had been more of them.

He realized Olivia was watching him and hoped none of his thoughts had shown on his face. Not being very good at hiding them saved him time when it came to keeping his endless number of cousins in line, but that was perhaps not quite as useful in his present circumstances.

She smiled and rose. "You cooked; I'll clean."

He aided her in gathering up their trenchers and cups, then leaned his hip against the comfortably warm stove. He realized at one point that he was simply standing there, staring at nothing, but he was struggling too fiercely to rein in his emotions to do anything else. The thought of his own future, a future that would be in the past and not the present day, a future that would definitely not include that woman there who continually tucked her flyaway hair behind her ears and found his attempts at chivalry to be tolerable...

He could scarce imagine it.

Olivia put away the last cup, then turned to look at him. "You know," she said carefully, "you don't have to hang out with me if you don't want to."

Hang out sounded far too close to the sort of hanging that he had never wanted to get too familiar with, but he imagined that wasn't what she was getting at.

"You know," she added. "Spend the day together."

"But I do want to hang out with you," he assured her.

She studied him for a moment or two. "You seem unhappy. And life should be happy, don't you think?"

He suppressed the urge to turn and bolt out the back door. "Is that your chi speaking?"

"I'm not sure," she said with an uneasy laugh. "It might be."

He rarely stopped to consider whether he was happy or not because his life was full of devotion to the blade, keeping his cousins from tripping over and slaying themselves with the same, and making certain his family was safe. Perhaps 'twas time he changed that.

He reached out and tucked a lock of hair behind her ear. "I'm happy," he said, hoping Irony wouldn't come striding out of her hiding place and protest. "I am simply wishing I had more time here. What time I have, I would like to spend with you, unless you would rather hang out with someone else."

She looked at him then with a faint smile. "And miss out on our endless thumb wars? No way."

"You merely want me for my ability to keep you from slicing yourself open on whatever sword you've filched."

"Maybe," she agreed. She dried her hands. "Then where should we start today? I think those bus tours are really great, but they're pretty expensive."

"Whatever you want to do," he said, because he supposed *let us remain here for the day and I'll paint you half a dozen ways* was likely something better left for a different time.

"We could go to an art museum, then come home and take your sword out into the back garden."

He almost smiled. He suspected he might be a bit fonder of her than he should have been, but what could he say? She hadn't laughed at his attempts to draw her and she had an unwholesome fascination with sharp things.

"Aye," he agreed, "we assuredly could."

"Then let's go," she said, pushing past him. "The day's a wastin'."

Several hours later, he decided that he had almost satisfied his own unwholesome fascination with drinking in every last bit of the Future he possibly could.

They had started the day off by trapping themselves on a red bus and examining the more noteworthy sights in the city as they passed by them. Riding atop the beast and having it sway with every breath of wind had been, he could safely say, one of the more profoundly alarming things he'd ever experienced. That had been followed by a trip on what had been billed as the Eye, though the only eyes he had been interested in had been his own and covering them until he accustomed himself to looking down at his feet resting on what looked like nothing at all.

The view, however, had been breathtaking.

And then had come the art.

He had been prepared to exchange more of his paper pounds for entry into the enormous building only to find that wasn't necessary. He had purchased a guidebook, invited Olivia to take charge of digging through it, then simply taken her hand and prepared himself to watch history unfold before him.

It wasn't as if he hadn't seen similar things before, true. He had traveled extensively with both his family and occasionally just his sire and those journeys had always involved drinking in whatever art and music could be found. It was also true that his sire had earned a fairly exclusive list of important souls—both noble and royal—who were very fond of having their portraits done by a man with Jackson the Fourth's skills.

But at one point during the afternoon he had finally come to grips with just how much history he had leapt over to be where he was. Seeing that history through the eyes of those whose business it was to so faithfully note its passage had been more overwhelming than he'd anticipated it might be. He understood why Olivia had chosen that for her studies.

At present, he stood in front of a painting of flowers presented in such beautiful colors that he could scarce look at it for the fires of Hell that had apparently set up camp in his eyes. He attempted a few gruff and surly noises, but a quick look at his hanging-out gel only revealed someone who was merely watching him knowingly.

He took her hand and tucked it into the crook of his elbow as if he'd been doing it for years, then cleared his throat.

"Dust."

"I get a little worked up over Monet as well," she said quietly. "And I can't draw like you can."

He looked through his well-examined collection of Future terms, then understood what his uncle Nicholas had been getting at with what he'd occasionally muttered discreetly under his breath when faced with things of an impossible nature.

"These paintings are," he said slowly, "mind-blowing."

She smiled, looking a little blown about herself. "I agree. I've only seen pictures in books, so standing in front of them is a little more overwhelming than I thought it would be." She smiled. "Let's find an art store for you. I'll buy."

"Nay, you will not."

"In thanks for breakfast," she countered.

"A meal that I did not provide which leaves me in your cousin's debt, which I also cannot allow."

"You're extremely bossy."

He pursed his lips. "I am saving myself a very lengthy lecture on lack of chivalry from my sire who would be appalled did I permit a woman to pay for anything of mine."

"I don't like it," she said with a sigh, "but I won't argue."

"I would win."

"Says the guy who doesn't have possession of that Elizabethan shilling any longer."

"I was distracted by Rembrandt," he said.

"Well, if you have to be distracted, it might as well be by him," she agreed with a smile. She paused. "We don't have to go yet if you want to stay longer."

He closed his eyes briefly. If she only knew …

He took a deep breath, then nodded. "Perhaps one more tromp through English masters."

A pair of hours spent tromping through not only English landscapes but a nearby vendor of items for the creating of art left him simply past speech. He could scarce believe the things he'd seen that day, never mind the night before in the books Stephen had sent him. Automobiles, aeroplanes, televisions, telephones … the inventions were endless and, aye, mind-blowing.

As was London itself. The city was as startling to him in the present day as an adult as it had been the first time he'd come south in his youth. He wasn't entirely certain he cared for the modern method of traveling below ground, but those around him seemed to find nothing strange about it and 'twas less unsettling than those swaying double-decker buses. He held onto the bar above his head, glared at a lad who was making too close a study of Olivia, then looked to find her watching him. He lifted his eyebrows briefly.

"Guardsman."

"You're very good at it," she said, smiling faintly. "Where did you learn to do it?"

"First from my sire, then from my uncles."

"Interesting men."

"Very," he agreed. "Where to now?"

"You're changing the subject."

"'Tis less dangerous that way."

She didn't look convinced, but she also didn't seem inclined to press the matter. He realized she was tucking the thought away for future study only because he was so accustomed to watching his sire do the same thing. He suspected his parents might find the woman standing next to him quite to their liking, should they ever meet her.

"I wouldn't mind going by Ms. Cleary's office, if you wouldn't mind," Olivia said suddenly. "I think it's sort of on the way."

"The scene of the future skirmish," Jackson noted. "It will be wise to see what the terrain holds."

She smiled. "Is everything a battle for you?"

"I will admit life has seemed much like one to this point," he conceded slowly, "but I daresay the fault for that lies with me." He shrugged. "Not enough dessert, I imagine."

"Or a competitive family, maybe?"

"Is that how things are in your family?" he asked.

"You're not answering again."

He lifted an eyebrow briefly. "Aye," he said. "There's your answer to both, if you like."

"Are you the oldest boy cousin?"

He had to think about that for a moment or two, though he likely shouldn't have needed to. He shook his head.

"Nay, not the oldest, but definitely the most unpleasant of the lot."

She smiled. "I don't believe that. I think you're just very used to bossing everyone around."

Aye, because he could best every damn one of them with the sword with the possible exceptions of his own sweet sister Rose and his cousin Kendrick, though he imagined battles with several other of his cousins would have dragged on interminably. He was, as his uncle unbent enough to tell him on those rare occasions when Robin of Artane hadn't yawned his way through a morning in the lists with him, the only one who gave him any decent sport save Kendrick.

High praise, that.

"So many cousins to guide with my vast wisdom," he agreed, "and so few hours in each day to do so."

"I think I should be laughing at you, but I have the feeling you're serious about that." She looked up at the map above the windows. "Could we get off here and walk for a bit?"

He would have preferred a comfortable seat near a hot fire with supper on its way, but he supposed he could talk her into that later. He nodded and followed her off the Tube carriage and up the stairs to the street. He shook his head because he still hadn't managed to shake off the feeling that he was wandering about in some sort of dream.

He would have given much to have had an hour's speech with his sire.

He walked with her up to the street, contemplating all the questions he would like answers to, then stopped still. He looked at Olivia in surprise. "Forgive me," he stammered. "I didn't think."

She looked at him in surprise. "About what?"

"About bringing you to London without gaining your sire's

permission first." He took a step back and made her a small bow. "I will speak to him immediately and apologize for my actions."

"What actions?"

"Running off with you is enough," he said grimly. "I am honorable, though, so I daresay there would be no reason for him to put me to the sword."

"I don't know," she said slowly. "That thumb war last night was pretty vicious. And just so you know, my parents are … well, let's just say that my grandfather raised me, but he died a few years ago." She smiled. "You're safe unless you want to worry about my Aunt Phyllis. She can be pretty fierce with a vintage letter opener."

He took her hand in his. "I didn't mean to grieve you by bringing up painful memories."

"Oh, you haven't," she said with a smile. "My grandfather was a wonderful man. I've had a great life."

"And your siblings?"

She shook her head. "It's just me."

"No siblings," he said faintly. He could scarce imagine that kind of peace and quiet, nor was he sure he wanted to. He kept her hand in his and started to walk. "You have your cousin, though, here in London."

"Samantha, yes," she agreed. "I have a few other distant cousins, but we don't really see each other. What about you?"

"Too many cousins to count and a handful of siblings."

"Where are you in line?"

"Second," he said. "I have an older sister, but she has her own ke—house, I mean. And a husband." Rose also had her fingers in a few things that would have given their sire gray hairs did he know about them, which Jackson suspected he already did. His father was, as anyone would have said, a very discreet man. His sister was equally discreet, but she frightened even him from time to time.

"That sounds like that first Kilchurn family," she said thoughtfully.

He would have booted himself in the arse for letting his tongue run so freely, but he couldn't reach himself so he settled for a silent string of curses.

"Large families throughout the centuries, no doubt," he said, hoping that would be answer enough. "Where are we to go now?"

"It's here on the corner," she said. "I'm not sure what I expect, but maybe it would be good to just stand here for a minute or two."

He was happy to lean against a wall with her and consider the battlefield. He looked at the souls on both sides of the road out of habit, though he supposed there wasn't any danger until it was full dark. He leaned forward and looked around to the front door of the guild hall, but there didn't seem to be anything unusual about it.

Apart from the fact that it found itself in twenty-first century London, of course.

He shook his head out of habit, then continued to study the men and women within his sight. There was no reason to be uneasy, yet he couldn't shake the feeling that they were being watched.

That was, he realized with a start, because there was a man standing across the street watching Olivia more closely than he was happy with. He was tempted to walk across the road and offer a bit of instruction on the sort of good behavior a man should display, but he wasn't sure that would be welcome whilst the sun was still up. He settled for moving to stand in front of Olivia and glaring, but that didn't seem to inspire the man to do anything but pull his mobile phone out of his pocket and open it.

Olivia had told him images could be captured with the mobiles Derrick had loaned them—he'd verified that for himself earlier by photographing a painting he shouldn't have—but he had no way of knowing how modern that man's phone was.

That he was even speculating on the like was something he could scarce wrap his wits around—

"Jackson?"

He looked over his shoulder to find Olivia watching him with a look of concern. He would have attempted a reassuring expression, but feared it was beyond him.

"You're cursing," she said. "In French. Again."

He imagined he was. He had also just noticed that there wasn't a single man watching Olivia, there were two of them. Gaping, actually. Olivia was beautiful, true, but there was something about the situation that felt … off. Given where he was and what he'd experienced in the past se'nnight, that he could make that judgment might have satisfied even his ridiculously demanding uncle.

He pulled himself back to the present moment and looked around them. "What of those black cars I see everywhere?" he asked. "Are they merely for royalty or might the rabble ride in them?"

"The taxis?" she asked. "Anyone can, of course, but I think they're expensive."

"But an adventure," he said. He took her hand and pulled her toward the street, then motioned for one of the taxis to pause.

He watched surreptitiously as he climbed in after Olivia, holding her hand so he could pull her back out again if something went awry. He watched as the driver moved the car forward and was unpleasantly unsurprised to find the men from across the street attempting to secure their own taxi.

He listened to Olivia give the driver their address, then he shifted slightly on the seat so he could keep an eye on the cars behind them. He frowned at the utter impossibility of identifying who might or might not be following them, then leaned forward.

"My good man, would you find us a decent tavern near our, ah, house. I believe my lady needs supper."

The man looked at him in his small mirror, then nodded. Jackson didn't dare speculate on what he might be thinking. He was happy enough to pay the man, get out, then watch their taxi drive off. He looked at Olivia to find her watching him a bit more closely than he was comfortable with, but he wasn't sure how to apologize.

"Ruffians," he said with a shrug.

She didn't look convinced and he shared her sentiments. He got them inside the tavern without issue, however, and took a seat with her where he could keep an eye on the door. The common chamber was more like what he'd been accustomed to in the past, which he appreciated, and he could only hope the food was a bit better. He took a deep breath and looked at Olivia.

"Who were those men?" she asked bluntly.

"What men?"

She shot him a look that almost made him smile.

"I've no idea," he said honestly, "and I daresay I'm making more of it than I should. They were likely just bad-mannered louts with a decent eye for a beautiful woman, so they'll live to see another day. I will, however, teach them manners if I see them again."

"Who are *you*?" she managed.

"Your diligent guardsman who needs to provide you with supper. Then we'll haste ourselves home so you might go to sleep early. Very important, that, so you arrive on the field tomorrow refreshed and ready for battle."

She shivered. "I'm not sure I'll manage to sleep and that has nothing to do with weird guys looking at us. My whole life depends on tomorrow morning."

He put his arm around her shoulders in as much of an embrace as he thought the current location would allow. "A man who sleeps too soundly on the night before a battle tends to sleep *through* the battle, if you want my opinion."

"Do you think so?"

"I do. I also suspect a bit of ice cream would serve you well."

"That's absolutely not going to help," she said, but she seemed to relax a bit. She smiled. "It might be worth a try."

He patted her, then released her and went to procure them supper. He kept one eye on Olivia and the other on the door as he waited to give the tavern keeper his order, but saw no one enter who he recognized.

Surely there were many men in London who appreciated a lovely woman. Perhaps they had simply run afoul of a pair who had singled out Olivia to admire. It didn't mean she was in any danger.

Just the same, he would sleep lightly that night.

Thirteen

Olivia stood in front of the building containing her future and wondered if everyone in her situation had that same sense of the universe holding its breath, waiting for them to take that first step forward.

She looked for Jackson and found him standing a couple of steps behind her with his hands clasped behind his back.

"You are delivered safely," he said gravely.

She felt a little queasy. "I'm nervous."

"I find that a few vile curses tend to take the edge off that sort of thing."

She laughed in spite of herself. If she sounded every bit as unhinged as she felt, well, who was to know besides that man there who had held her hand in the cab and occasionally patted her when she'd started to wheeze?

She attempted a few salty things, which earned her a nod of approval from her guardsman.

"A fine effort," he said. "Now, off you go into the fray. I'll be here, waiting breathlessly for tidings of your triumph."

She nodded confidently before she opened the door and walked inside as if she'd done it hundreds of times before and would be doing it hundreds of times from that point on. She wasn't fazed by the elevator that looked like something from a Victorian murder mystery and her stomach wasn't contemplating rejecting her lunch of eggs that Jackson had cooked and definitely not burned an hour ago.

The ride up the single floor went by far too quickly and she was left with nothing to do be step out into the hallway and get her bearings. She followed the swanky-looking numbers down a too-short hallway to come face-to-face with her doom—er, her future.

She really had to get a hold of her imagination before it ran completely away with her, never to return. She made a frantic grasp for her recently tended chi, then looked at the brass tag on the door in front of her.

Dreams of Greenland

Well, that was definitely the place she was looking for. She started to knock when she realized there was something written in small black letters under that beautifully swirled company name.

Formerly Kilchurn, Ltd.

She opened her mouth to point out to any bekilted grandpas hanging around in the area that she might have run into just one too many Kilchurns during the previous couple of weeks, then decided that maybe it was best to just let sleeping genealogists lie. There was a mystery there, but she obviously didn't have time at the moment to even begin to avoid investigating it.

She raised her hand to knock on the door, but the door opened before she could. A middle-aged woman stood there, smiling pleasantly.

"Olivia? I'm Penelope Cleary. Come in, dear, and let's have ourselves a proper chat."

Olivia took a deep breath, shook Penelope Cleary's hand, and walked through a doorway she hoped led to her future.

An hour later, she floated out of the building into the overcast day and wondered if anyone else noticed how radiantly the sun was shining in spite of it. She didn't see anyone skipping along in time to the beating of her heart, but she did find her guardsman leaning against the side of the building, his foot propped up underneath him and his hands behind him, doing his usual thing of people watching. She managed to walk sedately over to him, but it took effort. He tilted his head and looked at her.

"And?"

She suppressed the urge to jump up and down, though she suspected by the way Jackson was watching her that he understood.

"It went well," he noted.

"It was amazing," she said, laughing in spite of herself. "You should see the jewelry she makes—and the jewelry her former boss used to make. I'm almost sorry I didn't learn to be a silversmith."

"You have time," he said. "So what happens next?"

"She has one more person to talk to today and then she'll make her decision."

"A celebratory feast of fish and chips now?"

"That sounds perfect. Let me just make sure I have her in my contacts before we go." She patted her pockets, then felt panic descend. "I think I forgot my phone upstairs."

Jackson pushed off from the wall. "I'll accompany you there."

She checked her bag to be sure she hadn't shoved her phone in there by accident, then nodded. "It won't take long, then I'll buy lunch."

He snorted at her and opened the door. "You won't, but you may lead the charge here."

She decided that was a battle that could be fought at the cash register later. She walked with him across the lobby, then hesitated.

"I know it's just one flight, but let's take the elevator."

"The what—" He closed his mouth around whatever else he intended to say and merely nodded briskly. "Of course."

She knew she was living on the edge with a second trip in that thing, especially considering the unwholesome noises it had made on her first turn inside its ancient self, but she didn't want to arrive all sweaty and gasping for breath from the stairs. She stepped inside, then stood in the middle of it where she wouldn't have to watch the mechanics she was fairly certain hadn't been changed in a hundred years.

Jackson wasn't white-knuckling it, though, so she concentrated on watching him press his face against the glass so he could get a better view of exactly what she didn't want to watch.

He glanced at her, then smiled a little sheepishly. "I like to see how things work."

She waved him on to his watching, then pretended not to notice how he jumped a little when the elevator stopped and the doors opened. He put his hand out to keep her behind him, then poked his head out into the hallway to apparently secure the area. He stepped out and waved her out as well.

"Safely delivered," he said.

She didn't want to think about how easy it would be to get used to that kind of chivalry, so maybe the best thing to do was enjoy it while it lasted. She nodded regally, had the faintest of smiles as her reward, and sailed down the hallway before she got herself into trouble.

She stopped in front of *Dreams of Greenland* and lifted her hand to knock. For the second time that day, the door opened before she could and Penelope Cleary stood there. The only difference was, this time she held the missing phone in her hand.

"Oh, Olivia, I was bringing you—"

Penelope looked at Jackson and her speaking came to an abrupt halt. Her mouth fell open and she took an awkward step backward. She teetered there for a moment or two, then her eyes rolled back in her head, and she fainted.

Olivia stood there with her hands outstretched and couldn't do anything but gape. She managed to look at Jackson, but he was a bit of a blur as he leaped forward and caught Penelope as she fell. He laid her gently on the ground, then put his finger to her neck.

"She is merely senseless," he said. "Olivia, find water if you can. She'll need it after we rouse her."

Olivia stepped over Penelope and grabbed one of the bottles of water she'd seen earlier on the sideboard. She hurried back to kneel down in the doorway next to her potential employer.

She looked at Jackson to see if he was panicking right along with her, but he was only checking Penelope's pulse.

"Was she this excitable with you?" he asked.

"No, this is new."

New and very strange. The only person she'd ever seen faint in real life had been one of her aunt's customers who had come face-to-face with an Eames chair in perfect condition, but that was understandable. The rest had been in movies and generally ghosts had been involved.

"She wakes," Jackson said. He put Penelope's hand in hers and stood. "I will go secure the stairs."

And with that, *he* was a ghost. Olivia knelt in the middle of events that seemed to be spiraling out of control and wondered just what in the world she'd gotten herself into.

Penelope sat up suddenly with a gasp. "Where did he go?"

"Ah—"

"I have to be hallucinating."

Olivia didn't want to offer an opinion on that, so she got to her feet and helped Penelope to hers. She would have suggested a sensible retreat to the sofa there in the reception area, but she was too busy being pushed out the front door.

"I need some time to think," Penelope said, wringing her hands.

Olivia blinked. "But you might need help—"

"It's been a long—" She took another deep breath. "I need to go lie down."

Olivia picked up her phone from the spot where Penelope had dropped it, then hesitated. "If you're sure you're okay."

"I'm fine."

Olivia backed out of the shop because she wasn't given any

choice, then watched her future disappear behind a door that was shut firmly in her face. The sound of the lock slamming home was almost deafening. She stood there for a moment or two because she suspected she might be in shock.

What the hell had just happened?

She didn't swear very much—*hell* and *damn* were, according to her aunt, spices not swear words—but she was tempted to saddle up a few of her grandfather's saltier sayings and take them out for some exercise.

She couldn't be angry with Jackson because it was hardly his fault he was so ridiculously gorgeous and apparently a dead ringer for quite a few other handsome men. She also couldn't be angry with Penelope Cleary because it was obvious that the woman had mistaken Jackson for someone she knew—quite possibly another in a long line of Kilchurn men and women who seemed to be popping up like daisies in a springtime meadow.

She also wasn't angry with Aunt Philly who probably hadn't wanted to insert herself in any more in an interview that had actually gone extremely well, or with herself because she'd been so damned determined not to do any of the normal investigations she would have done.

Vows were obviously more perilous than she'd suspected.

She took a deep breath, then turned and walked down the hall. Maybe Penelope was under stress and needed a good night's sleep to get her feet back under her.

For herself, probably the best thing she could do was take the rest of the day and fight Jackson for the rest of the ice cream in the freezer. The rest of her life would most likely sort itself in time.

Olivia trotted down the first half of those Victorian-era stairs to find Jackson loitering there on a charming, light-drenched landing. She almost stumbled at the sight of him, which likely explained why Penelope Cleary had taken refuge in a dead faint. He was almost hard to look at it.

He only watched her silently and offered her his arm. She took it and continued on with him the rest of the way down. It took until they reached the lobby before she thought she could attempt speech.

"Do you know her?" she asked, because that seemed like a reasonable place to start.

He looked as baffled as she felt. "I've never seen the woman before in my life."

"She seemed to think she knew you."

"I daresay she mistook me for someone else."

He was probably right. He also looked as if he might be enjoying a colossal headache later thanks to all the wheels she could see turning for him at the moment. He said nothing, but simply nodded toward the front doors.

She followed him, hoping that she wasn't leaving the building for the last time because her prospects had just gone up in smoke, then ran directly into Jackson's back. She looked around him to find a woman standing there in the doorway, gaping at him.

"Jake?" she gasped, then she took a step backward. "No, it can't be. Who are *you*?"

Well, if that wasn't the question of the day, Olivia didn't know what was. She stepped up beside Jackson and found him wearing absolutely no expression at all, which she knew from experience was a good indication of how much something was bothering him. And why not? He was batting a thousand so far when it came to mistaken identities.

"Are you some love child of my father's?" the woman demanded. She threw up her hands. "I *knew* it. Daddy's been trying to cheat me out of my inheritance for years!"

"I fear I know not you or your father," Jackson said quietly. "Please excuse us."

Olivia would have warned him that he was making more forays into French than usual, but she suspected her input wouldn't be appreciated.

"I'm Peggy Kilchurn and I'm not letting you go until you tell me exactly who your father is—"

"I've never met you or your father," Jackson repeated, in perfect English that time. "Again, my apologies. You must be mistaken."

Olivia found herself taken by the hand and pulled past a woman who continued to splutter as she followed them outside. Even thugs with her wallet on their minds would have been better than being tailed by a woman who was beginning to screech her accusations. The sight of the usual pair of guys lurking across the street was reassuring, but they didn't seem all that interested in coming over to offer a helping hand with the woman losing her composure right there on the sidewalk. Maybe there were thuggish lines they didn't cross.

Jackson put his arm around her shoulders and pulled her in the direction that led away from their admirers. She wasn't unused to occasionally having to outrun aggressive barn fowl, so she hoofed it right along with him and was happy to do so.

He flagged down a cab, then piled into the back with her. If he turned his back to the window to apparently hide not only his face but hers as well, she wasn't about to argue. He waited until they'd gone a couple of blocks past the office before he sat back and let out his breath.

He didn't make any comments or excuses, but she hadn't really expected him to. There was a big batch of crazy going on back there and she was as happy as he seemed to be to leave it behind.

"An early supper?" he suggested eventually.

"I'll come with you," she said, "but I'm not sure I'm up to food quite yet."

He only closed his eyes briefly and nodded. "Of course." He shifted to look at her. "What did Mistress Penelope Cleary say when she regained her senses?"

"Nothing," she said. "She just threw me out and shut the door in my face."

"Forgive me," he said quietly. "I fear I've created a situation of bollocks for you."

She smiled in spite of herself. "It wasn't your fault. Maybe you just look like someone both of those women know."

"Perhaps," he agreed.

She nodded, because that made her feel like she was actually accomplishing something besides watching helplessly as her plans unraveled around her.

"Maybe you're that Peggy Kilchurn woman's distant relative," she said hopefully. "And Penelope's shop might be called Dreams of Greenland now, but it was Kilchurn, Ltd. before then. There seem to be lots of you Kilchurns in England. Scotland too, I'm guessing."

"Very possible," he agreed.

She smiled, then turned to look out the window while she still had control over herself. She was beginning to wonder if she hadn't made an enormous mistake selling everything she owned and taking a chance on a completely different direction.

Maybe making big changes wasn't all it was cracked up to be.

"I will see to this."

She looked back at that profoundly chivalrous man sitting next to her and suppressed the urge to burst into tears. "It isn't your fault," she managed. "For all we know, those guys across the street you keep looking at are making trouble."

"I don't think they were eyeing me," he said seriously. "They were staring at you, no doubt stunned by your beauty."

She rolled her eyes. "You don't believe that."

"I'm stunned by it more often than not, so I absolutely do believe it." He reached out and took her hand. "You may weep, if you care to. I'll understand."

"I'll be fine," she said, squelching the urge to do just that. "Maybe I need to go hack at some weeds in Sam's back yard."

"I find that useful as well."

"You did promise I could use your sword."

He smiled briefly. "Very well. Let us see how much daylight

remains once we're back in the hall. You shall go do damage to your cousin's garden whilst I make supper."

He leaned forward and gave the cabbie their address. She was happy he had it memorized so she didn't have to look it up on that lone pad of paper with Artane emblazoned on it. She should have poached another one when she'd had the chance.

What they also should have poached was a faster cab driver. The day was admittedly dark and rainy, but an hour in traffic had left things gloomier than she was comfortable with. By the time they'd gotten back to the townhouse and Jackson had taken the keys from her shaking hands to open the door, the daylight was almost gone. Taking care of a few weeds in the garden would obviously have to wait for the morning.

Jackson locked the door behind them, then caught her by the hand. He turned her to him and looked at her seriously. "I am going to secure the hall—er, the home. I will find somewhere safe to put you, then I want you to stay there until I come fetch you."

She wasn't going to argue. It had been a very strange day that didn't look to be improving very quickly. She took up a place near the front door and accepted one of Jackson's knives.

"Use that on anyone but me."

She tried to give herself courage by repeating uplifting Gaelic axioms under her breath, but that didn't drown out the occasional creak of a floorboard upstairs. Hopefully that was just Jackson doing his thing, not a collection of ghosts warming up for an evening display.

She leaned her head back against the wall and sighed deeply. The day had been a perfect end to what she now realized was a month of incredible stress. That she had come so close to and now had potentially lost a great job was just a bit south of awful. Maybe she should have been more religious about sticking to her vow. Karma had obviously taken note of her *laisez-faire* attitude and rewarded her appropriately. Lesson learned there.

A knock at the front door almost had her jumping out of her

keds. She put her hand over her heart and was thankful she hadn't shrieked. It was probably Derrick or Samantha coming to check on them anyway.

"Jackson, there's someone here," she called, opening the door.

She heard someone jumping down at least three stairs at a shot, possibly tripping over one of them, only to roll right in front of her back up to his feet and haul whomever was standing outside inside and slam him up against the opposite wall. She didn't hear any wailing, though there was a grunt and then a very long moment of absolute silence.

"Friend, not foe," said a voice with a British accent.

"Olivia," Jackson said calmly, "please light the passageway torches."

She had to go turn on the lamp in the living room to even find the light switch, then she had to remind herself that they were backwards from what she was used to before she managed to get the hallway lights on. Then she leaned against the banister and watched Jackson casually shut the door with his foot. He needed to use his foot because his hands were busy pinning a man against the wall with a knife to his throat.

The other guy was standing impossibly still, simply watching Jackson with a look that said he'd definitely seen worse.

"Name," Jackson demanded.

"Oliver Phillips," the man said. "Samantha texted Miss Drummond to say I was coming."

Olivia was impressed the guy could get all those words out while on the verge of dying. She didn't remember having gotten any messages, but she'd been a little distracted. She pulled her phone out of her pocket only to realize that she'd never turned it back on after her interview. She remedied that quickly and discovered that her cousin had indeed texted her.

One of Derrick's lads, Oliver, is going to bring you groceries and some DVDs, so don't think he's a thug.

Olivia took a deep breath. "Sorry," she managed. "My phone was off. He is who he says he is."

Jackson took a step back, then shoved his knife into the sheath stuck down the back of his jeans. She wondered if it had been there under his coat all along or if she had been too distracted by the events of the afternoon to notice.

Jackson held out his hand. "Jackson Kilchurn."

"Oliver Phillips," the other man said, taking his hand and shaking it firmly, "still. Thankfully."

Jackson lifted an eyebrow, then held out another sheathed knife. "That was under your cloak, friend, so perhaps you would have fared well enough."

Oliver shrugged. "London can be a dodgy place."

Olivia felt her way over to the stairs and sat down. Oliver retrieved the goods from outside, shut the door with his elbow, then looked at her with a smile.

"Where would you like me to leave these, Miss Drummond?"

"I think you should stay here with them," she said honestly. "Jackson's probably going to yell at me after you go."

She wasn't sure who was more shocked: Oliver, who looked as if he might be reconsidering doing damage to Jackson; or Jackson, who looked as if she'd accused him of something truly unthinkable.

"A few vile curses, then," she amended.

"I'll admit to nothing that I might or might not have been willing to mutter perhaps not entirely under my breath," he said grimly, "but I wouldn't have shouted at you."

She lifted her chin. "I would have muttered them right back at *you*."

He closed his eyes briefly, then walked over and pulled her to her feet and into his arms. She wasn't sure which one of them was shaking harder, but she suspected it wasn't him.

"Sorry," she managed.

"*Stay* means *don't open any doors* and *don't invite in any ruffians*."

"I'm not a ruffian," Oliver protested.

Olivia felt Jackson run his hand briefly over her hair, then take her by the hand and turn to face Oliver.

"Many thanks to Lord Derrick."

"I'll let him know," Oliver said, setting his gifts down. He turned to leave, then stopped and turned back. "Step out and enjoy the night air with me for a moment, mate?"

Olivia wondered if Jackson might come back in with a black eye, but he didn't seem particularly worried. He did shoot her a very pointed look before he moved. She rolled her eyes, then sat back down on the step.

"Arf," she said crossly.

He smiled briefly, then went outside with Oliver. She listened, but didn't hear any noises of murder or mayhem so maybe the conversation was limited to a little male bonding. She found a bottle of water in one of the bags and decided that would have to do given that she'd lost Jackson's knife at some point during the excitement.

Jackson came back inside, then looked at the bottle in her hand. "Well done."

"I lost your knife."

"That could have been done better, perhaps," he said, shutting and locking the door behind him. He looked around, then picked his knife up from where it had come to rest near the front door. "You look terribly fierce just the same."

He walked over to hold out his hands for her, but she found she couldn't see him very well. Maybe she was in shock. Maybe having him pull her to her feet and back into his arms was one of the only decent things that had happened that afternoon.

"You are safe with me here," he said quietly.

Heaven help her, she was starting to believe that. She stood there feeling safe for quite a while before Jackson's stomach seemed to think she was safe enough.

"My apologies," he said with a sigh.

She pulled away, shook her head with a smile, then picked up one of the bags and walked with him back to the kitchen. She kept herself busy putting things in the fridge, then tried to distract herself by watching Jackson look everything else over as if he'd never seen anything quite like it before. She ruthlessly suppressed the question she desperately wanted to ask about just how primitive his farm might be and realized suddenly that she was standing in the middle of the kitchen, shaking. She thought she might have a bout of hysterics coming on, but maybe it was too soon to judge.

Jackson was leaning back against the counter, looking for all the world like a normal guy in Stephen's jeans and his *Parlez-vous Norman French?* t-shirt, but she knew better. He didn't say anything. He simply watched her as if he thought one false move might send her into some sort of frenzy.

"I don't want to know anything," she said unhappily. "And just so you know, I'm lying. I want to know many things, but not right now and not if they have to do with thugs. Or you. Or anything else that doesn't make sense to me right now."

He pushed off the counter, then took the two steps required to stand in front of her. He started to put his arms around her, then hesitated.

"May I?"

"Are you going to comfort me or tell me not to move again?" she asked, wishing she sounded annoyed instead of unnerved.

"Could I do both?"

"Ha," she said, shivering. "You're extremely bossy."

He put his arms around her, which was every bit as comforting as it had been both times in the hallway. There was just something about the guy that made her feel ridiculously protected.

He rested his cheek against her hair. "I believe we've run afoul of a pair of vexatious lads who want to make trouble for reasons yet unknown, but they will not prevail. We'll plan our strategy, then go about our business as we care to. London can be a marvelous place for an adventure."

"I could keep one of your knives handy."

"The saints preserve me," he blurted out in French.

She pulled back and glared at him only to find he was smiling slightly. "I understood that."

He hugged her tightly, then released her. "I'll make supper, you'll stay where I put you whilst I have a final look about the hall, then we'll enjoy whatever entertainments Master Oliver has brought us on those little silver trenchers. I'm not as familiar with them as I should be."

The guy's names for things were simultaneously very strange and absolutely adorable. She watched him begin to sort through things to use for supper. "Did you hurt yourself falling down the stairs?"

"I didn't fall," he said easily. He glanced at her over his shoulder. "I'll be complaining endlessly tomorrow about the bruises from my not falling, though, so you'd best enjoy the silence tonight. Sit, Olivia, and be at peace."

She'd heard worse ideas, so she sat and closed her eyes, listening to the soothing sounds of a very good chef humming as he chopped. She was relaxed enough that she hardly jumped at the sound of her phone ringing. She pulled it out of the jacket she realized she was still wearing and supposed Derrick was calling to scold her for almost killing his errand guy. She opened it and answered with a yawn.

"Hello?"

"Yes, erm, Olivia? This is Penelope Cleary."

Olivia almost dropped her phone. "Oh, Ms. Cleary, hello. I'm so sorry about—"

"Oh, no, dear," Penelope said quickly, "I'm the one to apologize. Your friend just startled me."

Olivia looked up to find said friend standing there, wooden spoon in hand, watching her.

"I was wondering if you two might want to come back in the morning and have a proper tour," Penelope continued. "We can chat a bit more about the position whilst you're here. Would ten be too early?"

"Would we like to come visit in the morning at ten," Olivia said, looking up at Jackson. "The two of us."

Jackson took a deep breath, then nodded.

"Of course," Olivia said. "We'll be there."

"Wonderful," Penelope said. "See you then."

Olivia hung up the phone, then looked at Jackson who had smiled at her before turning away to rescue his veggies from burning.

It was possible that Penelope Cleary had mistaken him for someone else. It was also possible that those strange men had also mistaken both of them, as well. Peggy Kilchurn was the wild card, but she hadn't seemed all that reasonable, so maybe she could be safely ignored.

Besides, Jackson had thought Oliver was a thug until he'd discovered the truth, hadn't he?

"Mint chip or double fudge for dessert?" Jackson asked, glancing over his shoulder at her. "Oliver apparently brought us new rations."

"How about both?"

He smiled, then turned back to the stove.

She let out a deep breath very slowly and made a grab for her good sense. The afternoon had most likely been a fluke, a crazy convergence of events that couldn't possibly be repeated. The best thing she could do was stop thinking, enjoy dinner, and distract herself with a movie. Everything would return to normal, she would get her job, and Jackson would maybe ask for her number before he went back home.

Stranger things had happened.

She pushed herself to her feet and went to look for things to use in setting the table.

Fourteen

JACKSON CRAWLED OUT OF THE back of the taxi as if he'd done nothing else for the whole of his life, made certain Olivia had exited behind him, then drew her over to shelter in the shadow of the building that had given him such a start the day before. He looked about them to make certain the two thugs across the street hadn't been joined by anyone else, then took a moment to ponder the improbability of a pair of things.

One was finding himself in current-day London where he was trying to keep his companion safely housed and properly fed, soaking up the sights and smells of a large city, and doing his damndest not to find himself robbed or slain. No matter the year, some things didn't change.

The other was having a woman faint at the sight of him, then finding himself called by his father's name by another woman he'd never seen before. He wasn't one to make leaps where no logic had been applied, but he was beginning to suspect that his present was coming face-to-face with his father's past—and whilst he was in the Future, no less.

He shook his head grimly. Irony. 'Twas his least favorite thing.

"Jackson?"

He looked at the woman standing next to him and felt his heart wrench a bit. She was lovely and fierce and endlessly tucking her flyaway hair behind her ears as she prepared to march into whatever fray lay before her. He didn't think, he simply pulled her into his arms and held her close for a moment or two.

"I apologize," he said quietly. "Lost in thought."

"You do that quite a bit lately."

"Too much ice cream, no doubt." He pulled away, then opened the door for her. "After you, my lady."

She ducked under his arm to go inside. He looked over his shoulder and glared at the ruffians standing across the road just so they would understand he knew they were there. At least if they came after Olivia in such close quarters indoors, he might render them blissfully senseless in a passageway instead of having to brawl with them in the middle of the street.

He followed Olivia into the elevator, wishing he didn't feel as if he were being trapped inside it. The journey was brief, though, and the upstairs passageway empty. Unfortunately, not knowing exactly what he was walking into made up for the relief of that. He could only hope his presence in a place that had once borne his family name wouldn't create more disaster for Olivia than it had the day before.

Penelope Cleary was waiting for them in the doorway. Jackson watched her shake Olivia's hand, then extend her hand toward him.

"I didn't catch your name yesterday."

Jackson took her hand and pretended not to notice how chilled it was. "Jackson Kilchurn, Mistress Penelope."

The woman looked as if she might faint again, so he carefully reached out and caught her by the elbow. She took a deep breath, then nodded carefully.

"Call me Penelope, the both of you. And I'm not sure how to say this, but Jackson, you look so much like my late employer that I … well, it gave me quite a turn yesterday." She looked at Olivia. "Jake Kilchurn was his name. Jackson Alexander Kilchurn, to be precise. Odd, isn't it?"

Jackson managed not to swear, but 'twas a near thing. He listened to Olivia make brightly accented conversation with Penelope that he couldn't have repeated had his life depended on it and tried not to indulge in a swoon himself. He wasn't given to weakness of any sort, but he had to admit his current straits were a bit unusual.

"I haven't fed him enough today," Olivia said. "Could I beg a bottle of water to keep him going?"

"I have some juice. Maybe this is the week for fainting over things, what?"

Jackson found himself pushed down onto a sofa and realized Olivia was peering into his face. He cleared his throat.

"I am well."

"You won't be once I get through with you," she whispered fiercely. "You have some major explaining to do."

He closed his eyes briefly, then he caught her hand. "I'm as surprised by this as you are."

"Surprised by—oh, thank you, Penelope. Jackson's fine. We've just been traveling a lot over the past few days. You know, stress of new places and all."

Jackson would have snorted, but he couldn't bring himself to. Instead, he concentrated on the glass full of deep-yellow liquid in one hand and the digestive biscuit he was soon holding in the other. He consumed both without comment because it gave him a moment or two to think. He watched Olivia and Penelope chat and felt the ground grow a bit steadier beneath him. He even began to idly speculate on which of his relatives he might want to slay first when next they met. His father, as it happened, came immediately to mind.

"I almost hesitate to show you this," Penelope said carefully, "but this is a picture of Jake and me."

Jackson imagined he would be thanking Olivia—perhaps with some sort of expensive gift—for saving his glass from tumbling to the floor. She set it aside, then sank down next to him on the sofa and looked at the photograph Penelope had handed him. He could hardly believe his eyes, but there was no denying it.

He was looking at his father.

The odd thing was, though, that his sire couldn't have been much older than he himself was at present.

"He'd just turned thirty the week before," Penelope added. "I'm a few years older than he is—or was, I mean." She took a deep breath. "He's gone now, of course."

Olivia looked up at her. "I once saw a series on modern-day people who are dead ringers for people who lived centuries ago. You've obviously got another entry for it with these two."

"Except for their eyes," Penelope agreed. "Your Jackson's are such an amazing shade of blue. I actually think I might have a stone in the vault that comes close. Would you like to see?"

"That would be fantastic," Olivia said. "Jackson, how are you doing?"

"I am well," he said promptly.

She shot him a meaningful glare, but he could do nothing but shrug helplessly. He wasn't sure there would ever be anything he could do to lessen her potentially unhappy reaction to the truth of his situation—if he dared tell her, which he suspected might not come down to being his choice.

He watched her walk away to join Penelope, then he had a final look at the photograph in his hands. The absolute improbability of it was coming close to pulling his soul apart, but there was nothing to be done about it. He set the photograph down on the table next to him, then heaved himself to his feet and followed after his companions.

Penelope led them through a trio of chambers connected to each other by passageways, then pushed open a heavy door.

"The inner sanctum," she said with a smile. "After you."

Jackson took off his boots because Olivia and Penelope had removed their shoes. Given that the floor covering was a snowy white, he supposed that was wise. He walked inside, then tried not to gape at the walls boasting strangely fashioned niches covered in glass and lit from within. He wasn't unaccustomed to being startled by some cousin or other hiding in such places—Sam and Theo were famous for it—but he *was* unaccustomed to seeing gems of such startling beauty and clarity fashioned into pieces that looked a damned sight more familiar than he was comfortable with.

"These are Jake's pieces on the right, while mine are on the left," Penelope said. "I'll never match his design skill, never mind his ability to find what he wanted in whatever part of the world visited." She laughed a little. "He was famous for making an offer, then simply waiting until the man on the other side of the table gave in to escape the silence. Diplomats could have learned a thing or two from him."

Jackson decided that admitting that he had been the recipient of that same long, unflappable stare more times than he wanted to think about was likely unnecessary. It was honestly all he could do to accept the truth that was staring him in the face:

He was standing in the middle of his father's life's work.

Penelope stopped finally in front of a small door set into the wall. "I'm not sure this will be interesting to you, Olivia, but your aunt said you liked mysteries."

"I do," Olivia said. "I keep trying to swear them off, but they keep popping up."

Penelope smiled. "I understand, believe me. Since that's the case, you might have an opinion on this. There's a safe of Jake's hidden here behind this door. I tried to have it unlocked after he left, but the locksmith told me it was designed to crush everything inside if anyone tried to break into it."

"Then how does it open?" Olivia asked.

"There's a particular sort of key that's required, but I think Jake may have taken it with him. I couldn't find it here in the shop."

Jackson felt himself sway. He didn't argue when Olivia casually stepped under his arm and put her arm around his waist. He listened to her make some excuse for him, but couldn't find any words to add to the fabrication. She and Penelope continued on with their discussion of things pertaining to his father's business, but he paid no heed to any of it. He was too busy facing the knowledge that he likely knew what key would open that Future strongbox.

He also had no idea where that bloody key was.

"And that's the end of the little tour," Penelope said. "Olivia, I think we can safely discuss your start date if you're still interested. If I do decide to move from London, we'll work that out as well."

"Oh, that's wonderful," Olivia said, sounding a little breathless.

"Then let's go look at a calendar."

Jackson realized they were waiting for him, so he nodded and followed them from the inner chamber, though that was not easily done. He wasn't overly emotional as a rule, but he was as close to weeping as he ever came. He knew Penelope and Olivia were discussing the details of their future business together, but all he could do was stare at what his father had created and feel torn between missing the man and being damned grateful he'd had the pleasure of his company for so long.

"Two weeks from today, then," Penelope said. "Jackson, you're welcome to come visit anytime you like."

Jackson listened to himself make polite leave-taking conversation, then found himself standing by the door without knowing how he'd managed to get his boots back on. He took Penelope's hand and bent over it as he would have any of his aunts', then realized how odd that had to have looked. He was honestly too off-balance to rectify it, so he simply pressed on, drawing Olivia out into the passageway—

And into a fight he hadn't anticipated, though he wondered why not.

'Twas the pair from across the street. He was slightly surprised to find they only had knives and not guns—that book of history Stephen had lent him had been highly illuminating—but he had definitely fought off worse. He pushed Olivia toward Penelope, vowing to apologize later, then turned back to seeing to the business before him.

The men weren't without both skill and determination and he

knew immediately that the current one was not their first skirmish. What they'd expected from him he couldn't have said, but he wasn't helpless even without his sword. That, and his boots were quite handy in ridding one fool of his knife and sending the other into a blissful slumber. He continued on with the first lad a bit longer, then decided that perhaps apologies for the ensuing broken arm might not be necessary. The ruffian was too senseless to have heard them anyway.

The second man sat up suddenly and pointed at Penelope.

"We'll have her and you," he slurred. "Boss says … waited long… enough for the both of ye."

Jackson decided he had heard enough, so he helped the man back into senselessness, then brushed off his hands and looked at Penelope.

"Do you know these two?" he asked.

She looked like she might be on the verge of another faint. "They're always outside," she said weakly. "I just assumed they were security for someone else in the building. I didn't think they were looking for me."

"Lock your shop, my lady, if you please," Jackson said. "We'll go before they wake."

He left Penelope to gather her things, then looked at Olivia. He closed his eyes briefly and pulled her into his arms.

"All will be well," he said confidently.

Whether she was trembling from fear, from his nearness, or from an intense desire to do damage to him, he couldn't have said and honestly wasn't sure he wanted to know. He waited until Penelope had shut and locked the door behind herself, then he escorted the ladies down the stairs, avoiding the enclosed space of that bloody elevator.

He exited the building first, then looked about to see if more ruffians might be loitering there. He was somehow unsurprised to look across the street and see the lad who'd pulled a knife on Olivia and him that first night.

"I think he was at the play," Olivia said faintly. "And he definitely looks like that guy in the alley, doesn't he?"

"Aye, I daresay," he agreed. He flagged down a taxi, then looked at Penelope. "Shall we accompany you?"

Her eyes were full of tears. "You're so much like him."

"Perhaps a distant relative," he said, because he could say nothing else. "Are your accommodations secure?"

She took a deep breath. "My flat has a doorman."

"Then please remain safely there until I can see to this business," Jackson said. "Olivia will contact you over your mobile phone when we've a plan in place." He handed her funds for her journey because that seemed the least he could do, then helped her into the back of the cab and shut the door. He patted the car as he might have a trusted steed, then turned to face his next battle.

He waved down another taxi, then kept an eye out over his shoulder for ruffians until Olivia was safely tucked inside and he'd pulled the door shut behind them. He didn't see the two men he'd rendered unconscious, but the third man was rushing inside the building.

What he needed, he decided abruptly, were walls. Impenetrable walls. Walls behind which he might sit and have a proper think. He looked at the woman sitting next to him.

"A visit to the Tower?"

She eyed him speculatively. "Am I going to want to lock you in one of the dungeons there?"

"You might," he said grimly.

"Can we look at the Crown Jewels before I decide?"

"Do they have them simply lying about—" He shut his mouth around the rest of that question and settled for a decisive nod. He gave the driver their desired destination, then sat back and closed his eyes until the motion of the taxi left him less soothed than ill.

He found himself uncomfortable with silence, for a change, so he opened his eyes and looked at his lady. "You have questions."

"Damn skippy I do," she said shortly, "and I can't tell you how much I *don't* want to ask them."

"You could leave them, then," he ventured, then decided that perhaps his opinion on the matter might not be welcome.

"Why does Penelope's boss look so much like you?" she asked. "He's not your brother, is he?"

Jackson managed to shake his head. "I don't have an older brother."

"He can't be your father because he couldn't have been much older than you are now when he left the business to Penelope three years ago." She paused and frowned. "I suppose that picture could have been Photoshopped."

"Photo … " he repeated slowly.

"Faked," she said. She looked quite suddenly as if she wished that could be the case. "She could have taken a picture of him as a young man and put it together with one of herself now and turned it into one photo."

"Entirely possible," he agreed. After all, he'd done that with the family portrait that resided behind glass in Artane, hadn't he? He had painted his family himself, then his sire had painted him into the scene.

Only he had every reason to believe the photograph he'd just seen hadn't been altered.

He put his hand down on the seat. He wouldn't have been surprised if Olivia had taken one of his knives and stabbed him with it, but she simply put her hand atop his. He looked at their hands together for a moment, then at her.

"Can you trust me?"

"Can I trust a man who made my potential employer pass out from surprise because he looks almost exactly like her former boss who is supposedly deceased?" she managed. "A man who sticks knives down his pants and boots, who speaks a version of French I don't really understand, and who fights me every damn night for a coin that I was the first one to grab?"

"I had it first—"

"You did not!"

He realized her eyes were very red and it occurred to him, with a flash of genuine alarm, that she might be on the verge of tears.

"Um," he began uneasily.

"I'm not going to cry," she said, dragging her sleeve across her eyes. "I am, however, seriously considering killing you."

"You would never manage it—"

"It wouldn't be for a lack of trying, believe me!"

He definitely suspected, in hindsight, that indulging in a brief chuckle had been a very bad idea, but as any of his female relations would have pointed out without hesitation, he could be a bit of a dolt from time to time. He was halfway to blurting out an apology when he realized she was staring at him in astonishment.

"You laughed."

He shook his head. "I did not."

"You did, and I refuse to believe that the possibility of my doing you in with your sword is that funny."

"'Twas nervous laughter," he said promptly. "Consider me properly cowed."

"I doubt that." She took a deep breath and leaned back against the seat, then glanced at him. "I made a vow, you know."

"To the veil?" he asked in astonishment.

"No, of course not—well, I did swear off men for a year, but that was just to get my life together."

"Swear off men," he repeated faintly. "What a thought."

"I'm rethinking it," she admitted. "The other vow was just a general sort of thing about not getting involved in any more mysteries. No more unopened boxes, buried treasures, or things made before the year 2000." She paused. "It seemed like a good idea at the time."

"But your labors for Mistress Penelope," he said carefully, deciding he could certainly ignore the last item on her list. "Aren't you looking at historic art?"

"That's different," she said. "I'm going to be looking at things and judging their age, not going on the hunt for them. There won't be much mystery to it. Not like, well, you know."

And then she simply looked at him.

He stared back, because he couldn't bring himself to say that if he told her the truth, she would think him daft and likely run the other way. The other thing was that after he'd seen her settled properly, he would need to find his key and go home to 1258 where he would likely spend every day of the rest of his life wishing he had told her the truth at that moment and asked her as bluntly as he knew how if she might not like to be a part of that life.

The saints pity him for it all.

"I will find answers," he said, hoping he might distract her with a vow of his own. "I will make certain you and Mistress Penelope will be safe, then I must return home."

There. That sounded perfectly reasonable.

Perfectly reasonable and perfectly horrible.

He just wasn't sure what else he could do.

Three hours later, he was sitting on a bench pushed up against a wall inside the Tower of London with not a one of Henry III's men in sight whilst wishing rather desperately for someone to guard his back. His sire, his uncle, hell, he would have been overjoyed to have had Rose standing there.

The foray into a part of the Tower he had happily never visited before provided him with a viewing of the Crown Jewels and a decent distraction. He'd exchanged several appalled looks with Olivia over the sparkling excess, but unfortunately all that time to think in peace had left him back where he'd started, which was considering what that second thug had gasped out on his way to senselessness. They had obviously been watching Penelope. He'd assumed they'd been keeping an eye on Olivia as well, but to learn they had been waiting for someone who looked like him …

Had they been looking for his father?

"All right," Olivia said suddenly, "what's wrong?"

He pulled himself away from that unsettling thought and looked at his companion. "I'm thinking on the tax monies that went to purchasing those sparkling rocks of the king's," he said, lying with an abandon that would have appalled his sire's priest.

"Queen's."

"Whatever." He took off his jacket and draped it over her. "You looked chilled."

"I'm not chilled, I'm unnerved, and you'll freeze without this."

He shifted a bit closer to her, didn't argue when she pulled his coat back over him a bit, and was fairly gratified when he felt her slip her hand into his. Her fingers were chilly, which he wasn't sure how to ease save taking both her hands in his own and trying to warm them. He applied himself to the task for several minutes until he realized it was going to take more than his efforts to manage it.

He also needed answers. In his day, the local alehouse would have been a good place to start, but London was so much bigger than what it had been before. They could return to his father's shop and see who else turned up, but that seemed a very inefficient way of going about things.

"I wonder if Derrick knows Penelope," Olivia mused. "He does have an antique business, after all. He might even know what happened to Penelope's boss."

Jackson felt time slow to a crawl in a way that usually indicated he was on the verge of doing something monumentally stupid. In the past that had generally included speaking words when he should have kept his bloody mouth shut and drawing his sword when he should have walked away from trouble, but he was in a different time with more unusual circumstances. He contemplated the possible outcomes of what he was considering, then pulled his mobile phone out of his pocket.

He'd paid attention to Stephen's instructions, true, but he hadn't had an opportunity to study anything on his own. He was appalled to find that when the moment for testing his mettle against the beast had come, he found himself pausing.

He glanced at Olivia to find her watching him. He was half tempted to blurt out everything right there inside walls he wouldn't have so easily escaped from 800 years earlier, but he found he could not. The thought of her fleeing was substantially more wrenching than he'd anticipated it might be.

"I'm composing a missive in my head," he stalled.

She only held out her hand. "I'll show you how to do it on your phone."

He watched, memorized, then turned the mobile off when she handed it back to him. He looked at her briefly.

"I must master this from the beginning," he said.

"I'm not judging you," she said with a shrug. "Well, I am when it comes to your unhealthy fascination with swords and how you kept muttering things I'm sure weren't complimentary about the Queen's jewelry while we were looking at it, but that's a different story. Makes you wonder what sort of spiders people had to crawl through to get those gems, doesn't it?"

"Spiders," he said with a shiver. "They have more legs than I'm comfortable with."

"Couldn't agree more."

He smiled at her, then turned his mobile on and took the appropriate measures to send his words out into the ether.

Contact me, if you would.

His phone rang a handful of moments later, which almost startled him into dropping it. The things he'd seen that would have given his father … He pulled back on that thought with a roughness he never would have used on a horse.

He was going to kill his father. Slowly. But only after extracting many, *many* details about which his sire should have been more forthcoming. He wondered just how many of those details Robin of Artane knew. His uncle had the kind of relationship with irony that Jackson understood and thoroughly approved of. Perhaps there was a good reason why.

He looked at Olivia. "I may say startling things."

"I have your coat and you have my coin," she said with a slight shrug. "Can't let you get away yet, can I?"

"Indeed you cannot, my lady."

She pulled his coat partway over him, then simply leaned her head back against the Tower's walls and closed her eyes. He put the phone to his ear.

"Aye?"

"What do you need, mate?"

He was unsurprised to hear a voice coming from that silver box which meant he'd obviously become too accustomed to the marvels of the current day. He took a deep breath and spoke into his phone.

"Besides the chance to thank you for the visit from your lad last evening and his standing post through the night?" he managed.

"Oliver found your knife to be sharp and your forbearance welcome. But so you and I are clear, if you've touched my cousin even once, you'll find that my forbearance is non-existent."

"I've been the soul of discretion and she is quite obviously above reproach." He thought it might be wise not to mention holding hands, sharing ice cream, or currently huddling together under a single cloak.

"Then you'll continue to breathe easily."

"I appreciate that."

"So, what do you need?"

"Information, but I'm not sure where to begin looking for it."

And that was the truth. The Future was a marvelous place, but there were more people than he'd ever dreamed might exist and he didn't have the weight of his father's name and his mother's connections to Artane to aid him.

"I'll help. Where are you?"

"Tower of London."

"Happy you'll be leaving it again?"

"Absolute—" Jackson stopped when he realized that at some point during that conversation, Derrick had switched from Gaelic to French—and not the modern-day version of either language.

"You still there, friend?"

He found his tongue. "What do you know?"

Derrick snorted. "What don't I know? I'll have a car by the ticket entrance in half an hour. Black Mercedes. Think you can find it?"

"Think you can keep yourself alive with a sword?" Jackson returned before he thought better of it.

"I'm a Scot, laddie. I can keep myself alive with whatever I have to hand. Oliver will be waiting by the car."

The phone ceased to carry Derrick's voice to him, so perhaps the man had tossed it over his walls in fear. He frowned thoughtfully at his own until Olivia took it out of his hands, pushed the red button, then handed it back. He looked at her only to find her studying the sky as if it held all the answers she sought. He cleared his throat.

"Derrick has invited us to come for a visit."

She nodded.

"A car is coming for us and Oliver will keep watch. Will you come?"

"Of course," she said gravely.

He stood up with her, put his phone into the pocket of his jeans as if he'd been doing it every day of his life, then settled his coat more comfortably around her shoulders. He took her hand and started for a gate he was happy to find was still open.

He felt a little odd, he had to admit, walking through those gates cluttered up with tourists holding cameras instead of guardsmen holding swords, but that was perhaps the least of what the Future had to show him that day.

He was on his way to ask questions about his sire's activities in the Future, a father who was currently in the past, while he himself should have been in the past but was currently loitering in the Future.

He could only hope it would be the last of the surprises Irony would be sending his way that day.

FIFTEEN

OLIVIA SAT AT THE TABLE in her cousin's kitchen and began to suspect that it hadn't just been the previous three generations of American Drummonds to take a flashlight in one hand and a magnifying glass in the other and gang unwarily into dangerous situations. It had likely begun back in the mists of time when some plucky Drummond clansman had gone out to hunt for supper and gotten distracted by the glint of something shiny in the distance.

Genes were apparently hard to deny.

She was currently making an effort, though, by distracting herself with an examination of her cousin's current house. It was full of antiques, true, but she was perfectly able to focus solely on the way the layout offered a sense of privacy between rooms. She didn't need to take any lengthy ganders at the furniture and sundry that each room contained.

She did notice the sundry sitting with her cousin's husband in the living room, but he was hard to miss. He and Derrick had been in there bonding over a laptop for the last fifteen minutes, but the conversation had seemed not only private but very intense so she hadn't interrupted. Maybe Derrick would have an opinion on the thugs Jackson had left very much worse for wear in the hallway in front of Dreams of Greenland.

Or Kilchurn, Ltd., rather.

Olivia realized Jackson had caught her staring. He sat back, flipped a coin up in the air—she was fairly certain she knew just which coin that was—caught it without looking, then lifted his eyebrows and smiled briefly before he turned back to his conversation.

"I think you're in trouble."

Olivia looked at her cousin. "I *know* I'm in trouble."

"He's very handsome."

"And *way* out of my league," Olivia said grimly. "Fortunately, there are too many unexplained things about him for my comfort level, so our lack of league-sharing isn't going to be a problem."

Samantha smiled. "Maybe that's just part of his actor mystique. You know how many quirks my father has."

Olivia did, though why Jackson would have to resort to that kind of thing, she didn't know. Just walking into any room with his medieval-knight-in-jeans-and-black-leather-jacket persona should have been enough to get him cast in anything he wanted to do.

She paused to give that some thought. It was odd, wasn't it, how after the show he hadn't seemed the slightest bit interested in acting? In fact, she honestly had no idea what he really did, her endless speculations about his family's business aside. She probably should have asked Lord Stephen about that while she'd had the chance.

"Want to make a list about what's bugging you?" Samantha asked, reaching for a pen. "Everything will seem more manageable if you can see it on paper."

The temptation to do so irresistible, especially with Samantha Drummond Cameron manning the pen. The woman's reputation for list-making was almost as legendary as her father's was for leaving everyone around him genuflecting when he passed. Besides, her grandfather had always said that out of all the extended relatives, Samantha was the least likely to blab, so maybe it was safe to do a little dishing.

"In order of appearance in my life," Olivia asked, "or in order of utter weirdness?"

"You choose."

Olivia took a deep breath and dove right into the deep end of the pool. "He's never had brain freeze."

Samantha shrugged. "So?"

"Well, haven't you had it?"

"Of course, but I grew up in the States where ice is a staple, not over here where it really isn't a thing. Maybe Jackson's parents were sticklers for keeping things at room temperature."

Olivia frowned. That was more easily explained than she'd been expecting, but she wasn't about to give up quite yet.

"I'm fairly sure English isn't his first language even though he says he's from England," she said. "He also tends to toss in a strange dialect of French I'm not familiar with. Or at least he used to. His English is now to the point where you can hardly tell it's not his first language, though it does have a sort of New-England-prep-school twang to it."

Samantha tapped her pencil against her chin. "I'll admit he does sound like New York old-money, but maybe he went to school in the States for a bit, or he has friends who are trust-funder ex-pats. It is a little unusual, though, so we'll put it on the list. What's next?"

"Last night he had Oliver inside, frisked for knives and up against the wall, ready to kill him, before I could even get the hallway light on. You have to admit that *that's* unusual."

"It's the UK," Samantha said with another shrug. "I know lots of guys who are into sharp things, especially if they have historical significance."

Olivia looked at her cousin evenly. "Are you helping?"

Samantha laughed a little. "Probably not. It's just that the men in Derrick's extended family are very committed to keeping their connection with history alive, so I might not be the best person to judge that kind of thing. I'm guessing this is just dancing around the edge of things, though. What's really bugging you?"

Olivia started to speak, then stopped. Even if she could have found the beginning of that trail of bread crumbs, she didn't want to follow it because she had the feeling it would lead her all the way back to Artane where she would find that painting of the first lord of Raventhorpe who looked like an older version of Penelope Cleary's boss.

That didn't even begin to address Jackson of Raventhorpe's son who looked exactly like—

She took a deep breath, then looked at her cousin. "Have you seen strange things here in England?"

"What do you mean by *strange*?" Samantha asked, taking a sip of water.

"You know," Olivia said, waving her hand in an all-encompassing, gather-all-the-weirdness-in-one-place sort of way. "Paranormally sorts of things, like modern-day people looking exactly like other people who lived in entirely different centuries."

Samantha froze, then set her glass down. Maybe she hadn't noticed how close she'd come to tipping it over, but Olivia certainly had. There was something fishy going on, she would have bet her favorite pair of Birkenstocks on it.

"What an interesting thought," Samantha said, sounding as though she were on the verge of choking on all that water she'd just imbibed. "What made you wonder about it?"

"Aunt Philly left me a vintage book full of speculations about paranormal things happening up by the border. There's even a chapter in the back about traveling through magical portals to other times and places." She attempted a carefree chuckle, but suspected she sounded like she was the one choking. "Ridiculous, right?"

Samantha blinked several times.

Olivia couldn't decide if her cousin had suddenly gone into early labor or she were trying to come to grips with the reality that drinking an entire pitcher of liquid in one sitting while very pregnant was probably a bad idea.

Except that she felt her nose twitch. She rubbed it a couple of times to remind it that she was out of the family business, but that didn't change the fact that her cousin was still sitting there looking as though she'd just been caught rifling through her mother's collection of Victorian reticules with the nefarious intention of selling one to buy a few pairs of 80s high-waisted, acid-washed jeans.

"You don't buy into all that haunted-castles and sprites-in-the-forest stuff," Olivia asked slowly. "Do you?"

"Oh, that seems a little fanciful, doesn't it?" Samantha asked, moving her hand in a way that looked less dismissive and more like a frantic wave for husbandly help. "But you know how it is when you live with things that have been around for centuries. Those ghost stories have to come from somewhere, right?"

Olivia didn't like how reasonable that sounded, but maybe Samantha had a point. Given how much history people lived with right in their back yards, it was probably normal to run into a few strange things.

Strange like a man who could draw like Rembrandt, for whom English was not a first language, and who hauled around a very sharp sword and two equally sharp knives as if he'd been attaching them to his lunch box since seventh grade?

She suspected it wasn't the right time to bring up Scottish grandfathers in airports.

She took a deep breath and got hold of herself. What she probably needed to do was just shove everything into a box labeled Mysteries That Shouldn't Be Solved, seal it up with industrial-strength packing tape, and then drop it off on Stephen de Piaget's doorstep to be hidden in one of his basements. It would fit right in, she was certain.

"I might be overthinking things," she said slowly.

"That's easy to do when you've made such a big life change. And who knows what sort of life changes you'll make in the future?"

Olivia rolled her eyes at her cousin's not-so-subtle nod toward the living room. "Jackson's not my type at all. He's too pretty, too chivalrous, and definitely too fascinated with pointy things that should probably be secured to walls with steel screws." She nodded as well, on the off chance she hadn't sounded completely convinced by a list that sounded fairly perfect.

"That's too bad," Samantha said airily. "He certainly seems to like you."

Olivia was just certain she didn't want to know, but she didn't want to be rude by not letting her cousin talk. "How can you tell?"

"Because he keeps looking at you when you're looking at me."

Olivia refused to blush. "He's probably afraid I'll go broadcast his presence and then he'll never be able to catch another cab for all the women who'll swarm him."

Samantha smiled. "I get the feeling that he would be ignoring them in favor of you."

Who knew that hiding behind a glass of water would be so effective? Olivia indulged in several lengthy sips of her own until she felt her cheeks stop burning and her good sense return. She might be willing to reconsider her treasure-hunting vow, but the dating vow was set in stone, even if it had been a casual sort of thing between herself and the inside of her pocket. It was the principle of the thing and she was nothing if not principled. Jackson Kilchurn was her guardsman, nothing more.

Besides, he was going to find his key, go home, then she would probably never see him again.

She looked at her cousin and hoped how unhappy that thought made her wasn't showing on her face.

Samantha pushed herself suddenly to her feet. "Too much water, sorry. I'll be back in a minute."

Olivia looked into the living room to find that the laptop had been shut and phones were being shoved into pockets. She sat back in her chair and watched Derrick and Jackson come into the kitchen.

She watched Derrick give Samantha a quick hug and a kiss on the forehead as he passed her. She looked at Jackson to find him watching them with a faint smile. He looked at her, lifted his eyebrows briefly, then turned away to talk to Derrick about dinner.

She realized they'd been speaking French when they'd come into the kitchen, but now they were back to English with the occasional bit of Gaelic for seasoning. They made themselves at home in the fridge and argued in a friendly fashion over who might make the better chef for supper. Duties were divided equitably, and she divided her time between watching Jackson prowl through Derrick and Samantha's cupboards with his usual focus and watching Samantha watch her husband after she'd returned from points unmentionable.

Olivia contented herself with speculating on just how wonderful it would be to have that sort of thing for herself in a year or so when she had her perfect life started and she could start looking for it. No sooner, no sir, and definitely not with a man who looked like Jackson Kilchurn. Too handsome. Too baffled by modern things. Too mesmerized by fancy spices and elegant-looking foods that were soon being placed on the kitchen table with a casualness that indicated that was the kind of thing he was accustomed to.

No wonder he had no idea what to do with modern junk food. He'd probably cut his teeth on things grown on an organic farm contained inside sky-high castle walls—

She almost tripped over the answer that was lying there right in front of her. What if his parents were not only re-enactment types, but extremely serious ones who ran a living history museum where they kept things completely authentic so tourists could come see how life might have been lived hundreds of years ago? A sort of English Colonial Williamsburg with swords and castles and absolutely no cell phones stuck down bodices or chocolate chips hidden in empty ale kegs?

She understood the thinking behind that in a business sense because that was a big part of what made her aunt so successful. Phyllis Drummond was a master at creating a shop full of the glamour of by-gone eras so just walking in the door was like stepping back in time. She herself had definitely spent her share of time ditching her grandfather and his fishing buddies to go hang out with her aunt at her high-end escape to a simpler era. Maybe Jackson's parents had had that same sort of spot lost somewhere in the mists of time—

"Olivia?"

She pulled herself back to the present, realizing only then how lost in the past she'd been, and looked at the three people sitting there. "What?"

Samantha smiled. "Don't you have a birthday coming up?"

"Oh," Olivia said uneasily. "That. Yes, tomorrow actually. A new job is a great present, isn't it?"

Derrick and Samantha exchanged a look, then Derrick slid a key across the table and left it next to her glass.

"Temporary housing solution," he said. "It's the company flat. Not terribly high-brow, but it's just around the corner from Kilchurn, Ltd. You're welcome to stay as long as you like."

Olivia looked at the key and wondered if the current moment would be a good one to burst into tears or if she should keep a stiff upper lip and save that for later.

"Many happy returns of the day," Samantha added, "as well as a proper welcome to England where we have lots of old things to investigate."

Olivia reached out without looking and slapped Jackson on the back a time or two until he stopped choking.

"I'm not sure how to begin to thank you both," she said sincerely. "I don't start for another couple of weeks, actually. Or that was until—"

She looked at Jackson to find him watching her with all the things she couldn't say written on his face. He cleared his throat, then looked at Samantha and Derrick.

"She will begin peacefully in a fortnight," he said firmly. "Thank you, my lady, for the excellent makings for supper, and to you, Lord Derrick, for sharing the pleasure of preparing the meal. I daresay Olivia and I should be wending our way homeward and leaving you two to your pleasant evening."

Derrick only nodded. "Let's talk in the morning. I'll have what answers I can find by then."

Olivia realized she was making her own bit of polite chitchat without really hearing any of it, but in her defense, she was a little distracted. She tended not to think about her birthday unless she had to, but twenty-seven was sort of a milestone when it came to her grandfather's will. She would have to call his former law student to talk about the details of whatever was waiting for her, but maybe after she was settled. She had money enough to last for a bit, especially now that she had the gift of a place to live for a while.

Kindness from unexpected sources, definitely.

Now, if only she could have gotten rid of the mysteries and kept the man who shepherded her out the front door and into the back seat of the same Mercedes that had picked them up at the Tower, her life would have been perfect.

Unfortunately, she had the feeling those mysteries weren't going anywhere any time soon.

Half an hour later, she was standing in the entryway of Derrick and Samantha's new home and wishing she and Jackson had stayed for a bit more after-dinner conversation. It was easy to forget the craziness of her situation when she had the distractions of a different place and people who weren't involved.

There was nothing to do presently except to try to ignore how Jackson was watching her as if he wasn't quite sure she wouldn't lose it right there at the bottom of the steps.

"Are you going to check the house?" she managed.

He nodded slowly. "The door behind you is locked."

"I won't open it."

"That would be easier," he agreed. "You should sit here on the steps and wait for me."

She looked at the staircase and almost didn't know what to do with it. Jackson led her over to it, helped her sit, then put his hand on her head briefly before he ran up the steps.

She sighed deeply, put her hands over her face, and decided that maybe it was just a different incarnation of post-antique-show letdown. She was accustomed to all the build-up, all the work, all the stresses of the show itself culminating in a massive post-show dip after all the energy had been expended. She just wasn't used to that happening in her everyday life.

Of course that letdown had nothing at all to do with looking into her future and realizing that things would seem just a bit less perfect if she didn't have a sword-wielding maniac securing the hall for her every night.

She heard Jackson come back down the stairs and stop, then opened her eyes to find him squatting down in front of her, watching her with not so much concern as understanding.

"It's been a long week," she managed.

He looked at her gravely. "Do you want to know what Derrick and I discussed?"

"I do and I don't, if that makes any sense."

"It makes a great deal of sense," he said quietly. "If it eases you any, we didn't find anything interesting on his small computer. I did, however, watch several brief movies of felines engaging in amusing antics."

She looked at him quickly to find that he was almost smiling.

"You're not funny," she managed. "And I'm very nervous about this all."

"I know." He reached out and covered her hand with his. "Derrick is going to make a few very careful inquiries tonight, then come over in the morning with the tidings from them. He will also see Mistress Penelope installed in a well-guarded inn until we can unravel this tangle."

"Really?" she asked in surprise. "Then I should call and tell him I'll pay for her hotel."

He looked as appalled as he generally did when she suggested using any of her money, which she found surprisingly reassuring.

"Nay, I have already made arrangements for it. As for the present moment, what say you to a fire and a DVD offering?"

"Do I get to choose the movie?"

"Aye, since it's your birthday on the morrow." He pushed himself to his feet and held down his hands for her. "I'm resigned to romantic dreck."

She smiled in spite of herself, then went to change into more comfortable clothes. Jackson only looked at her yoga pants and sighed on his way past her to use the bathroom. She double-checked the back door, then walked back to the living room to see what could be done about a fire. There was wood there that Jackson had unloaded out of the back of the car as they'd been dropped off, but she wasn't quite sure where to start with a fireplace that old.

"I'll see to it."

She stepped aside and let him have at it. He arranged the wood as if he'd done it a time or two before, made himself a pile of appropriate kindling, then pulled out one of his knives. She watched him drag his knife across the stone for a spark before she realized what he'd intended to do.

She opened a small box of wooden matches, then handed one to him. He looked at it as if he had no idea what to do with it.

"Same thing," she said, watching him closely and vowing to have a pointed conversation about modern marvels with his parents if she ever had the chance.

He frowned but scraped the match against the stone of the hearth just the same, then dropped it in surprise when it caught. He smothered the small flame with his knife, then took a deep breath and looked at her.

"Too much dessert."

She doubted that, but she wasn't going to embarrass him. She handed him another one. "All yours."

He took it and carefully dragged it across the stone, but he didn't drop it that time. He simply looked at it in that way he had, as if he were furiously assessing new information while maintaining an outward expression of absolute calm bordering on boredom.

She watched him create an admittedly lovely fire, then continued to watch him as he realized she was doing just that. He sat back on his heels.

"Please do not ask."

"Where in the world did you grow up that you don't know what a match is?"

"You asked."

"You baffle me."

He tilted his head and studied her. "Is that all?"

She scowled at him. "I'm not going to discuss what I'm sure you're aware are your considerable charms."

He sat down cross-legged there in front of the fireplace, patted the spot across from him, then smiled at her. "Come you here, Olivia, and enlighten me as to what those might be."

That was the other thing. She wasn't sure when he'd started smiling so often, but it was recently and it was very bad for the state of her heart. She sat, then watched him reach out and link one of his index fingers with hers. She looked at him quickly, wondering if he knew what he'd done only to find that he absolutely did.

"So," she said, looking desperately for something to talk about that might keep him from noticing the blush she could feel creeping up her cheeks, "you said your home is in Scotland?"

"I said England," he said, sliding her a look. "On the border."

"Remote?"

"Very. No mobile phones. No ice cream. I worked from dawn till dusk which left little time for anything else."

"Except drawing."

"Occasionally."

She looked down to find that he'd captured another couple of her fingers. She supposed she might not have noticed the slight bend in his right pinky if she hadn't been so accustomed to looking for the smallest of details to use in identifying things. Occupational hazard, probably.

"How did you break your little finger?" she asked.

"What?"

"Your pinky," she said. "On your right hand."

He let out his breath slowly. "You frighten me."

"I haven't begun to frighten you," she said honestly. "I'm also very good at mysteries, so save me the trouble and confess."

He pursed his lips. "If you must know, my sister Rose broke it."

"What were you doing to her?"

"How easily you assume I was the one at fault," he grumbled, then he shot her a brief smile. "Very well, she poached my favorite dagger, taunted me for allowing it to be so easily filched, then shut me out when I inquired politely if I might enter her chamber and have it back."

"I think you're still leaving out details."

"I might have inquired impolitely."

She smiled in spite of herself. "And then you put your hand inside her room just as impolitely and learned your lesson?"

"Mistress Penelope's future art acquisitions don't stand a chance against your ability to ferret out particulars that might rather remain comfortably hidden."

She almost smiled again, but somehow the thought of carrying on in London all on her own made the whole idea look slightly less sparkly than it had a week ago.

"I must fetch something," he said abruptly, releasing her hands and standing up. "I will return quickly, so there is no need to weep over my absence."

She gaped at up him.

He smiled, leaned over and kissed the top of her head, then walked off to points unknown. She shook her head and decided it was best to go with her earlier decision to stop overthinking things. She took a moment for a couple of deep breaths, then simply watched the fire until she heard the faintest hint of a footstep.

Jackson resumed his spot on the floor, then held out what turned out to be a bus ticket folded up into a little square and tied with a piece of dental floss. She looked at him in surprise.

"What's this?"

"A small gift for your birthday," he said. "How many years on the morrow, if I'm allowed to ask?"

"Twenty-seven." Her perfect year of new beginnings. She looked at him. "How old are you, if I'm allowed to ask?"

"I was a score-and-eight in, ah, April."

"Ancient."

"If you only knew," he said with feeling. He nodded toward what she was holding. "Nothing poisonous, I promise."

She unwrapped gingerly, then looked at a perfectly preserved, exceptionally rare King Richard the Lionheart medieval penny. The sight of it stunned her so, she felt her eyes well up with tears. Jackson made a few gruff noises.

"Good hell, woman, 'tis but a coin." He leaned forward to put his arms around her shoulders and rest his forehead against hers. "Remind me never to gift you steel."

She put her arms around him and hugged him, in spite of her vow and probably her good sense. Then she kissed him on the cheek and pulled away.

"Thank you."

He was so quiet that she had to see how he'd reacted to that. He was sitting there with his hand on his cheek, looking at her in astonishment.

"I want it noted when Derrick Cameron comes to slay me for taking any liberties with you," he said faintly, "that you kissed me first."

"That was just a friendly thank you."

He studied her for a moment or two, then reached out and tapped the coin. "That cross has an omega over it, as you can readily see, which might make it worthy of further thanks. I could turn the other cheek for your convenience, if you like."

She felt herself beginning to blush again. "Are you flirting with me?"

"Aye, but I'm terrible at it." He took her hand and kissed the back of it, then nodded toward the kitchen. "Go fetch your chick flick, woman. We'll roll ourselves in blankets here by the fire and stay warm."

"Where will I put Richard?" she asked, feeling a little breathless.

"Shall I keep him in my pocket with my Elizabethan shilling?" he asked politely.

"Given that you're going to lose *my* Elizabethan shilling during our next thumb war, probably not."

He snorted and turned to add to his fire, but he was smiling as he did so. She got up to go grab a movie, making a stop by her wallet so she could reverently put that medieval coin in the most secure part of it.

"We might need ice cream, as well," Jackson called after her. "Shall I come choose it?"

She smiled to herself. She had no idea what the future held, and she couldn't bring herself to think about what had already happened that past week, but maybe she would take things one day at a time and see what life brought her.

It's what her grandfather would have suggested, she was certain.

Sixteen

Jackson woke to the chirping of his mobile phone. He remained perfectly still, as was apparently his habit no matter the century, and assessed his situation.

The fingers on his right hand were numb, but that was likely because he'd fallen asleep with Olivia Drummond in his arms and at some point during the night their fingers had become intertwined. Waking with her having used him as a place to rest her head was perhaps one of the sweeter moments of his disciplined, unforgiving existence.

He would have liked to have said that it had been an oversight on his part to fall asleep next to her, but he had to be honest at least with himself. He'd happily stretched out in front of the fire with her, started a very long movie set in a time of top hats and flimsy women's gowns, then eventually faced the choice of moving and waking her or remaining where he was and allowing her to sleep on.

He had turned Mr. Darcy off in mid-speech, made certain Olivia was warmly covered, then fallen politely and chivalrously asleep with her. Knight of the realm to the very last, to be sure.

He realized he was feeling remarkably content, so content in fact that he was tempted to remain exactly where he was and let the Future sort itself for a bit longer. He would have if his damned mobile phone hadn't called to him again and left him no choice but to begin the day. He carefully untangled his fingers from Olivia's and sat up with a sigh. Perhaps there were some things about the

Future that could stand to be hurled over the walls for the sake of peace and quiet. His mobile might be one of them.

"No ice cream for breakfast," Olivia murmured.

He leaned over and kissed her cheek. "I absolutely will do."

She pulled the blanket over her shoulder. "It's your brain freeze, cupcake."

He smiled to himself, then took a moment to build up the fire before he paused and looked at the woman sleeping there. He wished for even half an hour to sketch her, but there was no time. He would memorize the scene and paint it from memory later, though the idea that his memory might be the only thing he would have to use—

He took a deep breath and walked away whilst he still could. He stopped in the kitchen to see what his mobile wanted of him. Ah, a pair of messages had been received. He pushed the appropriate buttons and found that the text missives were from Derrick Cameron, as expected.

Half an hour? followed a few minutes later by a curt, **You'd best not be anywhere near my cousin.**

He sent a brisk aye to the first, decided he was better off not responding to the second, then took the opportunity to shower and dress as easily as if he'd been doing the same for years. He boiled water in a marvelous machine that would have allowed even his beloved mother to fashion something not burned and made two mugs of tea. He saw the shadow at the back door before he heard the light tap, then set his offerings on the kitchen table on his way to let Derrick in.

He stood back and made the man a slight bow. "Welcome to your hall."

Derrick studied him. "Is Olivia still asleep?"

"Asleep and treated with the utmost chivalry."

"Then you live another day." He shrugged out of his coat and sat down at the table. "French or English?"

"French, if you don't mind," Jackson said, sitting down across from him. "I don't want to miss anything."

"Where do you want to start?"

There were several questions he wanted to ask, most notably how Derrick had first realized that traveling through time was possible, but perhaps that was too much for the present moment. He settled for the first thing that came to mind.

"When exactly did you know about me?"

Derrick snorted. "The moment I saw you in the play, of course. You gave me such a start that I almost forgot my lines."

"Was I so obvious, then?" Jackson asked unwillingly.

"Not at all. I'm just the one who helped your father exchange buckets of modern gold for medieval coins, and you look a great deal like him."

Jackson felt his mouth fall open. "You knew my father?"

"*Knew* is too strong a word," Derrick said with a faint smile. "I met him a time or two whilst we were about our business, but nothing more than that. In your case, I wasn't sure if you wanted to be recognized properly or not, so I left it alone. I would have said something, though, if I'd had any idea Olivia was intending to interview with Penelope Cleary."

"And I never would have gone with her if I'd known."

"It might be a blessing in disguise," Derrick said. "It's certainly forced your grandfather to reveal his hand where he might have preferred not to."

Jackson had a fortifying sip of his tea, refusing to wish it were something quite a bit stronger, then set it aside. Derrick had graciously skirted the issue of his father's unsavoury family connections the day before, but he supposed they could avoid it no longer.

"What did you uncover about him?"

"Less than I would have liked," Derrick admitted, "but he has excellent security and obviously makes a habit of removing anything from the public square that's less than flattering. It turns out, though, that he's the one who hired the men you left cluttering up Penelope's passageway."

Jackson shook his head in disbelief. "What could he possibly want from her?"

"That's really the question, isn't it? I regret not having paid more attention to the whole situation at the time, but I assumed your father had good reason for wanting a king's ransom in medieval coins." He smiled briefly. "Who knew he needed them to purchase a bride?"

Jackson smiled as well. "I daresay he thinks my mother worth the price."

"I'm sure he does," Derrick agreed. "As for what he left behind here, I'm guessing he's the one who gave Penelope the story that he'd become very ill and had decided to live out his last days in Greenland. The odd thing is, I remember hearing at the time that your grandfather was noising about a tale that your father had simply gone mad and disappeared to points unknown."

"Why would he say such a thing?"

"You would need to ask your father about their relationship to know for certain," Derrick said. "Personally, I would never do business with your grandfather. He has buckets of money, but no morals, sorry."

Jackson waved away his apology. "I've encountered that sort of man before. I wonder, though, what the rub was between the two of them."

"No idea, but you would think that after three years, he would have moved on. Perhaps he's afraid your father will return and make trouble for him again."

"There are worse reasons for spying on someone, I suppose," Jackson mused. "Olivia thinks the man who attacked us our first night here in London was also at your frolic. I didn't see him near Artane, but he was at my father's shop yesterday."

"If they were listening in on Penelope's phones," Derrick said, "they would have known when Olivia was set to arrive. Following her once she landed in England would have been easily done. I imagine all of Penelope's contacts have been followed, though, so Olivia shouldn't feel singled out." He paused, then looked at Jackson carefully. "I could dig a bit deeper, but you may not want me stirring up things that would be better left undisturbed."

Jackson toyed with his cup, giving himself time to gather his thoughts. "Is it that easy to find things in this day, even when those things would rather remain hidden?"

"Do you have anyone in mind?"

If he could find Maryanne and her bastard lover … now, that was a tempting thought.

"When I'm finished with this business," he said slowly, "aye, there may be a relative lingering in your time who I might want to see."

"When you're ready, send me a name," Derrick said. "Finding antiques is, after all, what I do."

Jackson glared at his companion and had a quick smile as his reward.

"I do have another suggestion," Derrick offered. "I happen to know your father's attorney, which might help you with a few details even I couldn't find for you. Would you be willing to travel north to meet him?"

"Aye, if Olivia will come with me," Jackson said. "I don't dare leave her here now."

He also didn't particularly *want* to leave her behind, but perhaps that didn't need to be said.

"She will likely be safer that way," Derrick agreed. He studied his mug for a moment or two, then shrugged. "I could be wrong, but I have to wonder if there isn't something inside your dad's shop that grandpa wants, something perhaps in a locked cabinet that he doesn't have the key to."

Jackson bowed his head and laughed. He could do nothing else.

"Oh, wait," Derrick said innocently, "didn't you lose a key?"

Jackson pursed his lips. "I should have slain you the other night."

"You wouldn't have managed it."

"You might be surprised."

"Actually, I imagine I wouldn't be," Derrick said with another smile. "And in the interest of continuing to keep family alive, I think I'll send Oliver and another of my lads with you when you go. You won't see them—actually, *you* probably will, but your grandfather's men won't. Oliver will let me know if he needs reinforcements. Just head north when you get out of London. I'll find you somewhere to stay, then contact the attorney for you."

Jackson took a deep breath. "My gratitude, truly. If I can repay you, I will."

"You never know." He reached in his pocket, then set a key down on the table. "This is to a more powerful car. Just leave the key to the current one here on the table." He rose, silently put his chair back in place, then paused. "Just out of curiosity, are you planning on telling Olivia about yourself?"

"I'm not sure there is a point."

Derrick looked at him gravely. "Going back?"

Jackson wished that question didn't exist. He was finding that the place between what he wanted to do and what he knew he should do was a vast chasm that was simply uncrossable.

"I have responsibilities there," he said quietly.

"Indeed, you do, my lord."

Jackson looked at him sharply, but there was nothing in Derrick's expression save pity. He inclined his head, then let himself out the back door. Jackson tidied up the kitchen, locked the door, then went back to the great room.

Olivia was sitting on the sofa, flipping through one of the books Stephen had loaned him. She looked up as he sat down next to her.

"Did Derrick have details for you?"

"Aye, a few. There is a lawyer he thinks I should speak to and apparently the man doesn't live in London. Perhaps we could make a journey north, speak with him, then take in a few sights before you begin your labors?"

She looked at him in surprise. "You want me to come with you on this trip?"

"I do," he said simply. "Will you?"

She took a deep breath. "I'd actually rather not stay here on my own, so yes, I'd love to."

He put his arms around her and leaned back against the ridiculous softness of the cushions behind him. That was definitely something he would miss. He couldn't bear to think about what else he might miss, so perhaps he would do well to keep that particular thing close to him as long as possible.

"You needn't worry," he said quietly. "I will rid us of these ruffians, then you'll go on to glory and riches with Mistress Penelope in perfect safety."

"My hero."

"Aye, well, you aren't wrong there."

She tilted her head back and scowled at him. He smoothed her hair back from her face, then leaned over and kissed her cheek. He absolutely didn't want to answer any of the questions he could see in her eyes, but he wasn't sure how he was going to avoid it much longer. He settled for a distraction.

"Many happy returns of the day," he said quietly.

She sighed, then leaned her head back against his shoulder. "Thank you."

"I'll see to a celebratory meal for you when we stop for the night. I'm certain frozen delicacies will be involved."

"I like your consistency."

He smiled and closed his eyes. Perhaps there would be no harm in sitting for a few minutes to enjoy the peace.

He wondered how long it might be possible to keep the facts of his own existence from ruining the same.

The journey north was easier than the previous one south, though he couldn't decide if it was because the car was more comfortable or because Olivia seemed to be more comfortable driving it. Derrick's directions, sent through a text to him an hour into their journey, had taken them on roads that decreased not only in other travelers, but in size. Having Derrick's guardsman Rufus leading the way in that black Mercedes also made the journey easier.

He supposed the fact that he soon recognized the landscape made it easier still.

"When are you going to start talking?"

He checked his phone for the time. She'd lasted six hours, which was five longer than he'd thought she would.

"About what?" he asked politely. "How I manage to win every battle for our wee coin?"

"You don't win every one, and you're avoiding the question."

He shifted to look at her. Her hands were more relaxed on the wheel than they had been on the way to London, but she was still wearing a bit of a frown. He reached out and slipped his hand under her hair to undo any possible tension.

"That won't work," she said with a shiver.

"I'm attempting to use what few charms I have to distract you from things I don't want to discuss."

"All right, so it might be working," she conceded. "But not very well."

He smiled.

"Stop *that,*" she managed.

"I'm only trying to help."

She shot him a warning look. "You're trying to stall. Don't think you're not going to be answering a few questions once we're out of the car."

"What of your vow to leave mysterious things alone?"

"I may be renegotiating it. You won't manage to run off before I make a final decision on that, believe me."

He would have assured her that he was very fast indeed when being chased, but his phone interrupted him with the arrival of another text missive. He managed to retrieve it with one hand, then read. He wasn't surprised to find it was from Derrick, but he was slightly puzzled by its contents.

I've asked the earl of Wyckham to house you for a bit.

Jackson wasn't unaccustomed to being polite enough to earn a meal and a bed, but where he would need to do the same was a bit curious. He glanced at Olivia. "Do you know anything about the earl of Wyckham?"

"Haven't got a clue."

Jackson considered, then wrote out his own message.

The earl's name?

He knows Alexander of Falconberg, your father's attorney.

That was assuredly not a proper answer. Jackson couldn't have said why, but he sensed there was something going on that he might not care for. He sent back a pointed question.

Wyckham's name?

Gotta run.

He gritted his teeth and avoided swearing only because he had full control over himself at all times—with the possible exception of when the woman next to him had first looked at him, or touched him, or leaned over a poor penny to kiss his cheek.

He was indeed in trouble where she was concerned.

"There's a castle sign up there," Olivia said, pointing to a spot down the way. "I think we might be close to Wyckham itself."

I know was almost out of his mouth before he caught himself. Aye, he did know because he'd traveled over the current countryside countless times in the past.

He watched Master Rufus continue on ahead past where they were turning aside and assumed the man would be about a goodly amount of scouting. He hadn't seen Oliver and Peter, but he had no reason to doubt Derrick's word that they were watching. He would be long in repaying the man for his aid.

Olivia continued down the well-maintained road, finally coming to a stop in front of the castle gates. She pulled up the brake, took the key out of the ignition, and simply stared at the castle in astonishment. He understood. His uncle Nicholas had turned Wyckham into a place that rivaled his keep in France for beauty and elegance. He'd hardly dared hope the place would have weathered the years so well, but apparently it had.

He hadn't had the courage to see what had become of his own home. The thought of what the centuries could have done there—

"This is stunning."

He took a deep breath and looked at her. "'Tis a pretty place, to be sure. We'll find shelter here tonight."

"You know, I don't need to come with you to talk to the attorney."

He studied her, trying to decide why she sounded hesitant. "Is that unpalatable?"

"I don't like to pry," she said with a shrug. "All my prying questions about you aside."

"I fear this business might be spilling over into yours, so perhaps a few details would be useful," he said, wondering if it might even be possible to discover what he needed to know without letting her know more about him than she could stomach. "At the very least, you should stay close to me for the next few days until we have things put back properly."

She shuddered. "Torture."

"Many wenches would consider it to be something far different," he said archly.

"I'll just bet they would." She leaned her head back against the seat and looked at him. "What now?"

"I will earn us supper and a bed, then we'll have a pleasant evening whilst we wait for Derrick to be about his arrangements." He opened his door and looked at her. "I'll come fetch you."

"Very chivalrous."

He thought it a poor exercise of the same, but he hardly had cause for trotting out any sword skill. Perhaps it would suffice for the moment.

He helped Olivia out of the car, offered her his arm, then walked with her through the gates and into the courtyard. He didn't expect any of his uncle's spawn to still be inhabiting the place, even if the title had survived the years, but stranger things had happened. He stopped as the door opened, patting himself figuratively for his manners so he might trot them out and not cause Derrick any embarrassment, then watched as a man stepped out onto the front stoop.

He felt his jaw slide south.

He patted himself in truth, just to make certain he was still residing in his generally reliable form instead of having fallen into a nightmare where ghosts of those he longed to slay had taken up residence in castles in which they had never lived. He felt his eyes narrow and was powerless to stop them.

He put his hand over Olivia's. "Please fetch me my sword from the automobile."

"What in the world for?"

I'm going to kill that whoreson there was almost out of his mouth before he thought better of it. He turned and made her a small bow. "That man absconded with my cousin, and I need to show him the error of his ways."

Her eyes were absolutely enormous. "And your sword's going to be useful with that?"

"When it ceases to be so," he conceded, "I'll finish my instruction with my fists."

He caught a movement out of the corner of his eye and noted that Zachary Smith had reopened his front door. Ah, so the coward was scampering off before retribution could be dealt out.

"Where are you going?" Jackson demanded.

"To fetch my blade," Zachary Smith said with a shrug. "Unless I don't get to have one this time, either."

"It won't save you."

Zachary Smith only smiled in a way that was so irritating, the temptation to fully end his ability to do so ever again was almost overwhelming. He paused with his hand on the door.

"Introductions before or after the bloodbath?" he asked politely.

Jackson swore at him, then turned and towed Olivia along with him to the front gates. By the time they reached the car, however, the holes she was boring into the side of his head with the force of her gaze alone had become somewhat painful. He took a deep breath, then turned and looked at her.

"This might be one of those things I need to tell you."

She pulled her hand away from his. "Are you a murderer?"

He had occasionally wondered, mostly during his yearly pilgrimage to chapel, what difficulties his attempts to tell the absolute truth at all times might cause him. It had never occurred to him that he might need to explain the less-palatable realities of his life to a woman who had likely never had to save a sibling from a ruffian or fight back-to-back with her sire in order to save herself.

It might be wise to leave border skirmishes blissfully buried.

"Nay," he said, and that was the truth. He had never once in his weary number of years deliberately marched out his father's gates with murder on his mind. "I have, however, unfortunately dealt out death to a handful of souls who would have otherwise slain my family. I have also hoisted my sword several times for king and country."

She was very pale, but she unlocked the car just the same. She stood back and wrapped her arms around herself.

"And now?"

He pulled his sword free of the car, imagined he didn't need the knives that were shoved under the seat, then shut the door and locked it for her. He handed her the keys.

"Just a bit of sport," he said lightly.

"But isn't that the Earl of Wyckham?"

"The saints preserve us if he is."

"Do you know him?" she asked uneasily.

"Unfortunately." He held out his hand for hers. "I must repay him for a terrible slight, no matter how he's styling himself at the moment. If he has treated my cousin badly—assuming he still has her captive in this hall that cannot possibly be his—I will perhaps beat him bloody. You might not want to watch, but I also don't want to leave you out here unprotected."

She was looking at him as though she'd never seen him before. "Is the earl dangerous?"

"Only to himself if he's in the vicinity of anything sharp."

"I feel better already."

She didn't look as if she felt better, but she deigned to put her hand in his and she did return with him into the courtyard, which saved him having to worry about her safety. He knew he would need to tell her things she wouldn't want to hear sooner rather than later, but the thought that she might not want to have anything else to do with him as a result bothered him.

Damnation, but traveling through time was more perilous a venture than he'd anticipated it might be.

Unfortunately for his peace of mind—and perhaps even for the state of his heart—he had business with that man coming down the steps from his Uncle Nicholas's family home, business that could not wait.

What he wasn't prepared for was to see his cousin following Zachary Smith out the front door. She was wearing a pair of those appallingly revealing jeans he couldn't seem to convince Olivia to give up and holding …

Holding a child.

He felt his mouth working, but no sound came out.

Maryanne only smiled beatifically. "Ours," she said loudly. "Her name is Anne, if you're curious."

Jackson closed his eyes briefly. Whilst there was great joy to be had in the happy occasion of his beloved cousin having had a child, there might be far less of the same when it came to Olivia's thoughts on the matter. He took a deep breath and turned to her.

"That is my cousin, Maryanne," he said, realizing too late that he was gesturing with his sword. "Maryanne, this is Olivia. Please keep her safe for me whilst I slay your bastard lover."

"Oh, Jackson," Maryanne said with a deep sigh. "Olivia, please come sit with me so we can be comfortable as they make spectacles of themselves."

Jackson shrugged out of his coat and draped it around Olivia before he saw her seated comfortably on the top step next to his cousin. He leaned over to quickly kiss Maryanne on the cheek, then trotted down the stairs and out into the middle of Wyckham's courtyard. He tossed away the scabbard of his sword and looked at the man who had caused him so much annoyance and a fair bit of embarrassment in a different time and place.

Zachary Smith rested his sheathed sword against his shoulder and looked at him calmly. "Really?"

"Aye," Jackson said shortly. "Fight me if you dare, now that you have a sword."

"Which you had made for me, so you know it's sharp."

Jackson ignored the pleasure of hearing his own tongue spoken so well and pressed on. "Afeared to use it?"

Zachary Smith sighed deeply, then tossed aside the scabbard of his own sword.

Jackson realized during the first moment of their blades crossing just how greatly he'd missed training with his uncle, his father, his brother, or any number of cousins. Zachary Smith was certainly not his uncle's equal by any measure, but it could be said that no one was. He would do for a moment's sport.

Or, perhaps a bit longer. Jackson fought with his cousin's, ah, well, whatever she wanted to call him that Jackson was certain he wouldn't agree with and had to concede that the fool had improved. Whatever else Zachary Smith had been doing—and *that* was definitely something he didn't want to think about—he hadn't neglected his swordplay.

That generous concession to his cousin's husband's skill lasted only for another quarter hour until he casually flicked Zachary Smith's sword out of his hands.

Damnation, he'd expected more.

What he hadn't expected was to watch Zachary Smith spin and let fly his foot. Jackson swore loudly and shook out his hand, trying to ease the brutal sting he was suffering thanks to having had his own sword removed from his grasp by a sturdy boot.

Zachary Smith looked at him and smiled ferally. "Even, again."

"You would like to believe so," he growled.

Zachary Smith only laughed briefly, which he would have found offensive if he hadn't been so busy trying not to, as his father had said on more than one occasion whilst fighting with him back-to-back, get his arse kicked.

He thought he might understand where his sire had come by the term.

Fortunately for him and perhaps unfortunately for his cousin's, er, whatever he was, he himself had learned well many unapproved tactics from his sire and honed them endlessly with his brother Thaddeus under the guise of never wanting to leave their mother or younger siblings undefended.

He didn't like to think about what Rose could have done to any of them, by herself or in concert with that motley band of demons she called guardsmen. He pitied her husband, truly he did.

It took quite a while, but he eventually found himself sprawled on the ground in front of the steps. Zachary Smith was equally vanquished and cursing him as he clutched his side, so perhaps balance had been restored.

Jackson looked at him. "You'd best have wed her."

"I did."

Jackson started to speak, then he sat up with a start. "But I saw you less than a fortnight ago. How is it you have a child?"

"We've been married for over two years," Zachary Smith said carefully.

"Impossible," Jackson said promptly, then he paused. "Undeniable, unfortunately, but we'll discuss later whether or not I'll allow the marriage to stand."

"Do you honestly think you'll have a say in it at this point?"

"How do I know my uncle granted you permission?"

"I have it in writing."

Which he would be verifying when he thought he could take a decent breath or even crawl to his feet and remain there successfully. There would be a price paid by that man for his cheek, 'twas certain.

Unfortunately, he suspected there was also going to be a price exacted for what Olivia had just witnessed and that price would be paid by him.

She was very pale, indeed.

He heaved himself to his feet and started toward her, but stumbled in spite of himself. He half wondered if Zachary Smith hadn't broken one of his ribs.

"I think I need a little walk," she said, popping up to her feet suddenly. "Thanks, Mary, for the chat."

Jackson caught the jacket she tossed his way, dropping his sword in the process, then watched her as she walked off toward the front gates. He scowled at his cousin. "Did you tell her?"

"Tell her what?"

"When I was born!"

Maryanne glared at him. "You're being rude."

"And you had to be honest?" he returned crisply.

"I'm making up for your lack."

He dragged his hand, bloodied knuckles and all, through his hair. "I was going to tell her," he muttered.

"When?" Maryanne asked with a snort. "After you'd wed her?"

Jackson imagined that was something that didn't require any comment from him. He climbed the pair of stairs necessary to lean over and kiss his cousin again on the cheek, hoping he hadn't left too much grime behind. He glanced at her daughter. "She's beautiful. Doesn't look a thing like your husband, though."

He jumped as Maryanne kicked him, but he was admittedly not at his best and she struck a spot that her bastard lover had already abused.

Her eyes were full of tears. She handed the wee lady Anne off to her husband, then stood up and put her arms around his neck. She hugged him so tightly, he feared he might have squeaked.

"I can't believe you're here," she said, pulling back to pat him rather too firmly on his cheeks. "Daft lad, what were you thinking?"

"Blame Sam and Theo," he said grimly. "Actually, blame me, for I feared that dolt over there might not reach you without a shove so I saw to the task myself."

"I'll thank you later. You'd best go after your lady now."

Unfortunately, she had that aright. Whether or not his lady would stop long enough in her bolting to speak to him was something he would worry about once she was in view.

He left his sword on the stairs, glared at Zachary Smith on principle, then limped off after Olivia. He wished his English had been better. He was fairly sure he would need it to understand all the slurs she was likely going to call him.

He sincerely hoped that would be the worst of it.

Seventeen

Olivia forced herself to walk through Wyckham's gates at a sedate pace when what she really wanted to do was hike up her metaphorical skirts and run for the hills.

She couldn't blame her unease on jetlag. She'd been in England for over a week which was plenty of time to get her days and nights straightened out. She'd also just had a fairly easy drive north, the sight of a spectacular castle, and a friendly chat with an honest-to-goodness countess, which had all been very pleasant and normal.

No, her desire to flee had everything to do with having watched Jackson take a perilously sharp, authentic-looking medieval broadsword in his hands and use it how it had obviously been meant to be used.

She continued to walk, not because she was running away from things she couldn't wrap her mind around but because it helped her clear her head. Given how much of that she needed to do, she suspected it might take her a couple of trips around the earl of Wyckham's entire estate to manage it.

And speaking of the earl of Wyckham, what was going on there? He had seemed like a normal sort of guy dressed in jeans and a sweatshirt, but he'd also had no trouble conversing in Jackson's version of French while keeping Jackson from using him as a pincushion. She'd wanted to raise her hand and get the attention of some cosmic hall monitor when swords had gone flying and the guys had moved on to martial-arts moves that hadn't looked all that fake to her, but she'd honestly been afraid that her London buddy was going to wind up in jail for assaulting a member of the British upper crust.

She was tempted to make a dash for that cute little cottage near Artane and lock herself safely inside until her life had gotten back to normal. Maybe she could pick up another couple of note pads with Artane on them while she was at it.

She took a deep breath and let it out slowly, trying to calm her rampaging imagination. Her life was just turning out to be a bit different from how she'd envisioned it. She had come to England expecting to start a new chapter full of art and swords and centuries-old castles full of history. If she'd wandered into a different sort of book entirely, full of thugs who watched buildings she needed to enter, men who couldn't use matches, and mysteries that felt too big and too dangerous for her small-town treasure-hunter self, what was she going to do about it?

She realized abruptly that she was simply standing in the middle of the road. Worse, she had no idea when she'd stopped walking. She wrapped her arms around herself and regretted not having kept Jackson's coat.

She would have wished for even five minutes with her grandfather to ask him what he thought she should do, but she already knew what he would say. The Drummond motto might have been *Gang Warily*, but his very best piece of advice had been much longer and perhaps more useful because of it.

Keep going, sweetheart. Lovelier days are ahead.

He'd said that to her the first night she'd spent at his house after her flakey parents had dropped her and her half-packed suitcase off so they could go find themselves in some child-free commune in the desert.

She'd learned to say it to herself over the years whenever she'd been faced with things she didn't think she could handle: high school drama or college exams or wondering what she would do with the rest of her life after her grandfather had passed away and she'd had to face adulthood on her own. Each time she'd run up against that sort of thing, she'd reminded herself that she sure as hell wasn't going to find those days if she sat down in the mud and cried.

She heard a footstep behind her and spun around, ready to fling keys at a possible thug, only to find a painfully handsome man standing there dressed in unremarkable jeans, a black t-shirt, and his own hand-made boots. His hair was still windswept and too long for corporate anything and his eyes were still that otherworldly color of turquoise she was sure only found home in some exclusive tropical bay.

Well, one of those eyes was looking like it might be sporting a helluva shiner come morning, but that was understandable.

Why he couldn't have been just the gorgeous but very ordinary boy next door who might want to ask her out on a simple, unremarkable date—

She took a deep breath, threw the keys at him, then turned and walked away while she still could.

She continued to walk until she'd walked all the way down the drive that led away from the castle, across the road that led back to London, and almost into one of those stacked rock walls that seemed to be everywhere. The flat stone on the top was warm, which she appreciated, and sturdy enough to lean against, which she suspected Jackson would appreciate. She knew he had come to a stop next to her not because she'd heard his footfall but because she could hear him breathing raggedly. Obviously the earl of Wyckham had dished out as much as he'd taken.

She looked out over that charming English countryside and took a few deep breaths until she thought she could speak calmly.

"I think," she said finally, "that I'm finished with impossible things today."

"Of course," he said quietly.

She looked down at the wall to see Jackson's hand resting on the stone next to hers, only it wasn't the hand with the break in his little finger that he'd earned from having his sister shut the door on it.

Did most sisters poach daggers? Did most ridiculously competitive brothers have daggers to poach? Had she fallen down some sort of vintage rabbit hole where knives and swords were the norm and frozen desserts were not?

She watched Jackson's undamaged pinky slide over and curl itself around hers.

"May I hold your hand?"

She nodded. She watched him take her hand in both his and couldn't deny how comforting it was. There was also no possible way to ignore the fact that he had calluses on both his hands in the same places. That probably came from all the sword-wielding he did for that family business he hadn't admitted to but she was just certain had to exist, because nothing else made sense.

Unless ...

She propped a metaphorical foot on top of that box to keep it closed, ignoring the small list of contents that had escaped and now hung temptingly over the side. She focused instead on the man standing next to her, holding her hand and wheezing.

"I think you need to sit," she said.

He nodded and turned to lean back against the wall, though he didn't release her. She perched next to him, partly because she needed a little rest herself and partly because she didn't particularly want to make it so he had to let go of her. She studied their hands for a moment or two, then looked at him.

"Are you ambidextrous?" she asked.

He looked at her blankly.

"It means you can use both hands equally."

He shifted uncomfortably. "How could you tell?"

"I watched you, ah, you know." She made a sword-poking motion with her free hand. "That."

"I don't like to admit it, but aye." He paused and smiled. "You were watching."

As if she would acknowledge anything when he was looking that smug. "But you're naturally left-handed—"

"Say nothing of it, I beg you," he said, looking genuinely alarmed, then he frowned. "I don't suppose we burn people for that any longer, do we?"

Damn it, would the torture never end? She almost threw in the towel right there, but she liked the way Jackson rubbed his thumb over the back of her hand. He was also listing a little to one side, breathing carefully and looking as if he might not be able to so easily scamper away from a few more casual questions. Maybe the time for towel-tossing hadn't come quite yet.

Ask him his birth date.

His cousin Mary's words floated back to her in a disembodied sort of way that probably couldn't be topped by a ghost who'd leaped directly from the pages of Eugenie Kilchurn's best work. She couldn't imagine why that would matter, but she'd been wrong before.

"Your cousin said to ask you when you were born," she said.

He looked heavenward briefly. "The fifteenth day of April."

Well, that was a letdown, but maybe she hadn't heard Mary correctly. After all, she had been slightly distracted by watching Mary's husband have a friendly skirmish with her guardsman who was now suffering the after-effects of that encounter.

"Should I go take care of the earl of Wyckham for you?" she asked.

"A woman fight my battles for me?" He attempted to stretch out his side, then shook his head. "'Tis unthinkable usually, but I might have a different opinion today. I fear what you might do to him, though, so perhaps we should allow him to enjoy his soft life for a bit longer." He pushed himself to his feet, then looked at her seriously. "Will you be okay?"

She wondered if she looked as shattered as she felt. "I'm trying."

He looked at their hands together for a long moment, then met her gaze. "What if you allowed your worries to be mine for today?"

"Are you going to think I'm a wimp if I agree?"

He smiled faintly. "I've no idea what that means, but I can guess. And nay, I will only think you very generous for allowing me to see to my knightly duty of caring for you."

It was hard to argue with that. She took a deep breath, then let it out slowly. "Well, if your chivalry demands it … "

"It does. Now, to seal the deal, might I hold you for a moment or two?"

She nodded, then closed her eyes as he gathered her close and wrapped his arms around her. She put her arms around his waist, wincing right along with him when she grazed his ribs, but he didn't release her and she couldn't bring herself to pull away.

Something washed over her that was so sweet, she couldn't help but catch her breath. It took her a moment to identify the feeling she had, but when she did, she lost that breath she'd so carefully taken.

It was as if she'd just walked into her grandfather's den to find that her seat by the fire was empty and waiting for her.

She felt as if she'd just come home.

She stood there in that safe haven for long enough that she realized she was becoming unsettlingly accustomed to how Jackson's arms felt around her and the way he occasionally ran his hand over her hair. She also discovered that if she turned her head just so, she could see a satisfactory amount of his ridiculously handsome face.

"I cannot feel my mouth," he remarked, "or I would be rewarding you for those lustful looks."

She snorted. "They aren't lustful."

"Lying is a sin."

She smiled and closed her eyes where she wouldn't be distracted by a man who definitely had the ability to inspire all kinds of looks. Aunt Phyllis would have been rifling through her nib collection on the off chance that inking invitations might be called for. Her grandfather would have been sitting in his chair, running his finger over his mouth as he'd tended to do when presented with something he found particularly delightful but didn't want to show it too much. She suspected he and Jackson had a bit in common there.

"Olivia?"

"Yes, Jackson."

"Don't go this eve."

She lifted her head and looked at him. "Maybe I should—"

"Nay, you should stay here with me."

"Tomorrow, then," she said, though that didn't sound all that great, either.

"We'll discuss tomorrow on the morrow."

"Are you bossing me around?"

"Trying to," he said. "'Tis surprising how often my sisters and gel cousins don't appreciate my efforts in that area."

She could only imagine. "I really should go find a hotel—"

"Of course you shouldn't," he said. "Zachary Smith is a useless whoreson, but he wouldn't think to send us off to find an inn."

"Do you always call him by his full name?"

"That was the least of all the things I could call him," he muttered. He winced and reached up to touch the corner of his mouth. "Damn him."

"I think he's probably saying the same thing about you," she offered.

"More than likely," he agreed. He looked at her for a long moment, then leaned forward and kissed her.

On the cheek.

"Let's go back to the keep," he said cheerfully.

"Hey," she said, digging her heels in when he pulled away. "What was that?"

He smiled, then put his arm around her shoulders and pulled her toward the castle. "I must find a bit of ice cream to repair the damage done to my mouth, but I will remember where this moment ended. Let us stable the car, then see what the frozen larder can supply."

She'd heard worse ideas. She was also grateful for the chance to deal with nothing more challenging than getting the car inside the gates and parked without hitting anything.

She walked with Jackson across the courtyard to the stairs that led up to the castle itself. His sword was lying there on one of the steps, as if he'd just set it down for a moment to run off and do something very ordinary while fully intending to pick it back up on his way inside.

A medieval broadsword.

"Would you carry that for me, my lady?"

She took her foot off the box she couldn't seem to get away from, tossed that unusual request inside, then shut the lid back up, picked up his sword, and followed him inside the castle.

Several hours later she was sitting in a lovely guest room with a book on Northumbrian paranormal happenings in hand and wondering if she should have left it in her granddad's haunted recliner.

The evening had started off in a reassuringly normal manner with a friendly little supper downstairs. The conversation had been interesting, the surroundings in that medieval-looking kitchen cozy, and the food cooked by a certain sword-wielding guy of her acquaintance absolutely spectacular. She'd opted for an early night only because it had been a fairly long week, she was tired, and Mary's excusing herself to put her daughter to bed had given her the perfect opportunity to have some quiet time to get her feet back under her again.

She had paced in her room for a bit until she'd seen Eugenie Kilchurn's *magnum opus* peeking up out of her bag. She had reluctantly pulled it out, promising herself that she would only read a page or two as a distraction because there was no way she was going to sit in a bedroom of a medieval castle and read about things that didn't just randomly go bump in the night, they went bump because they'd recently arrived from a different century and the furniture had been moved in the interim.

Talk about cosmic jetlag.

Unfortunately, once she'd gotten started, she'd had to finish. The final chapter had been chock full of hair-raising descriptions of all the time-travelers the authoress had encountered over the course of her life.

She got up and walked around her room only to almost trip—metaphorically speaking—over that equally metaphorical box containing all the mysterious things she'd encountered so far in England. She would have walked past it, but the thought of what it contained was too tantalizing to let it lie there, unopened and unexamined. Several generations of American Drummond ancestors would have agreed that she most certainly shouldn't, so she steadied herself with a decent breath and took the proverbial gander at things that unsettled her.

First was Jackson Kilchurn's chameleon-like ability to blend in so seamlessly to any given situation. She'd paid attention when he'd been stumbling initially over English while swearing in a version of French she was fairly sure they weren't using on the exhibit tags at the Louvre. His English had made exponential leaps into Dockers-and-penny-loafer territory in a way that would have left her scratching her head if she hadn't been so dazzled by watching him not only read a room like a pro, but adjust his language and mannerisms on the fly to fit into it.

Then there had been that business in the armory at Artane. She had extremely vivid memories of watching a sword coming down toward her face only to find it blocked by a different sword held by that same man. Then again, given what she'd witnessed that afternoon, she obviously shouldn't have been surprised.

His ability to reduce thugs to jelly in London had been interesting, but that had some pretty stiff competition from the way his mere presence had sent Penelope Cleary into a dead faint. Then again why not, when he looked so much like her boss that even Peggy Kilchurn had called him by the wrong name and accused him of being her father's love child?

There was also the fact that he'd tied a bow on her pre-birthday present with a Boy-Scout knot her grandfather would have approved of, but maybe that could be set aside as charming but unimportant in the grander scheme of things.

All of those things could have been safely tossed onto a pile of incredible and very mysterious coincidences, but there was one thing that she couldn't ignore, try as she might.

Why did he look so much like the son of the first lord of Raventhorpe who just happened to be named Jackson as well?

She realized she was standing next to her bed, looking at Eugenie Kilchurn's book and wondering why it got under her skin so much. The woman was already wandering in questionable territory with all her tales of things leaping out of the shadows and shouting *boo* before running off giggling down castle hallways, but at least ghosts were understandable. People who ditched the time period they were born in because they wanted to roll the dice in a far different century were not.

Was she really supposed to believe that some Elizabethan lord might decide that ruffs and codpieces were out and jeans and leather jackets were in? Or that an 18th-century dandy might find the quadrille simply too tedious for words, so he would reinvent himself as a modern-day, groupie-inspiring rocker?

Or that a medieval knight with a very sharp sword might mothball his mail and hop over seven or eight centuries to try out modern dairy products?

She attempted a dismissive noise, but that only resulted in choking. She took a deep breath and reminded herself that many modern-day people were dead ringers for their ancestors. Put them in a medieval outfit with authentic-looking hardware and things became all the more authentic. Trot out a little sword skill and a few antique phrases and the illusion was complete.

Her phone beeped at her, almost sending her jumping right out of her shoes. She took a deep breath, picked it up off the bed, and read the text.

The fire in the great hall is hot. Come sit with me? JAKV.

JAKV.

Jackson Kilchurn was a *fifth*?

She looked at those initials again and felt her mouth fall open. Just what in the world did *A* stand for anyway? Avoider? She rifled through a few less complimentary possibilities until she hit upon the one she wanted to entertain the least.

Alexander?

She tried Jackson's strategy of a few vile curses to take the edge off the panic that threatened to overwhelm her, but that didn't help at all. She was beginning to think that Karma had a whole host of very diligent note-takers who never let even the slightest murmur of a vow whispered behind a hand, under several layers of turtlenecks, or inside a hermetically sealed bank vault go un-noticed.

But what if she'd made a terrible mistake back in the cabin when she'd so cavalierly announced that she was giving up the family business? Were the cosmic penalties for unmaking a vow going to be less painful than leaving the mother of all mysteries sitting downstairs in front of the fire, signing his texts with initials that just begged to be investigated?

Her past, it seemed, had finally caught up with her. The box was open, her curiosity unbridled, her aunt's stitchery singing like a Siren from its hiding place in her jacket pocket. The time for thinking had obviously well and truly passed.

She drew another line in the carpet and without missing a beat took an extremely unwary hop right over it.

She waited for the world to end, but the only thing that happened was she could have sworn she heard a faint *finally!* coming from the hallway outside her door—and she didn't have to hear that twice. She ditched her phone on her bed, left her room in a panic, then bolted down the passageway at a dead run, ignoring what she wasn't entirely sure hadn't been the sight of a Scottish plaid in her peripheral vision.

The stairs were tricky, but she managed not to fall down them and make it out into the great hall before she came to a skidding halt.

Jackson's ears were obviously working better than the rest of him because he was halfway across the hall before she'd managed to stop sliding on that floor. He caught her by the arms and held her until she regained her balance. She leaned over to catch her breath, then squinted up at him.

"JAKV?"

"Aye, well, I'm learning that the wee button that sends the text missives off into the ether ofttimes acts without permission," he said, shifting uncomfortably. "What say you to a warm drink before the fire to celebrate the last few hours of your birthday?"

She heaved herself upright and pointed her finger at him. "Distracting me will not work."

He caught her finger and pulled her along with him. "I'll try just the same."

"I changed my mind."

He stopped and looked at her in surprise. "About what?"

"I'm considering rescinding my vow."

"Ah," he said, looking slightly relieved. "The one where you decided to swear off men for a year? I approve. Come enjoy the snacks I've prepared and tell me of it."

Olivia allowed herself to be towed across the great hall and wasn't surprised to find a small spread on a side table there. Maybe when one spent so much energy trying to kill one's host with a heavy piece of metal, one needed extra calories.

"I already did it," she said, watching Jackson make himself at home in one of the large, very medieval-looking chairs there. "I drew a line in the, ah, floor tapestry and jumped back over it. Giving up the family business is apparently not for me."

"What is that business? And know that I'm asking even though I fear the answer."

She suspected *afraid* was only going to be the beginning of the unease he was going to feel once she really got going.

"I'm not sure who started it—it might have been my great-grandmother—but we're treasure hunters. Both my granddad and my aunt had shops where they would sell what they found, but that isn't the important part." She reached into her pocket and pulled out the stitchery she had never put anywhere else. She handed it to him. "That's the family motto."

He read it, considered, then looked at her. "Unopened box?"

"That'd be you, cupcake."

He closed his eyes briefly, then took her by the hand and pulled her over to sit in the chair next to him. He handed her back her stitchery, then put his arm around her and pulled her close to him. "Is this too familiar?"

She started to answer, but was interrupted by an enthusiastic comment coming from approximately five feet away.

"What the *hell* is going on here?"

She looked up to find Zachary Smith—and she could hardly keep herself from using his full name as well—leaning on the back of the chair across from them, grinning. He winked at her.

"That was for Jackson, Olivia, not you. Well, you might want to reconsider dating that guy, but that's just my opinion."

Jackson looked at him coolly. "Your ability to continue to breathe freely is in peril."

"My daughter needs a father," Zachary said with a shrug, "and she might like other siblings."

Jackson shuddered. "Say no more, I beg you."

Zachary only laughed. "Olivia, I'll let you borrow my sword if you need to use it on him. Jackson, make sure she doesn't need to."

Olivia watched him walk across the hall and disappear into the stairwell before she managed to look at the man who had taken her hand in his, then settled back comfortably in his chair. He didn't look at all concerned about the thought of her potentially stabbing him with the earl's sword.

"I *will* solve you," she warned, putting her stitchery back in her pocket.

He looked at her, leaned forward, then looked at her again.

"May I?"

She nodded slowly.

He kissed her softly. She was fairly sure she heard an orchestra start up, along with angelic choirs and quite possibly a few butterflies in the vicinity of her stomach. Fortunately for her peace of mind, there were no Scottish grandpas shouting clan mottos or battle cries.

There was, however, a man who caught his breath and muttered what she was absolutely certain were not nice things about their host.

"I vow I will slay him the next time I see him," he managed.

"I'll help."

"I'll find you a decent sword, then." He shifted to make it easier for her to put her head on his shoulder, then took her hand again. "Let us leave everything difficult for another day, shall we?"

"Are you really the Fifth?"

"Perhaps I shall request a handful of kisses first thing on the morrow," he mused, "and more the day after. How many times would I need to kiss you to distract you from things I don't want to discuss?"

She lifted her head to glare at him only to find him watching her with a grave smile. "You're not funny."

"I'm very funny," he said. "Also, do you have my coin? I wouldn't want to make you run all the way upstairs to fetch it when I win our thumb battle again tonight."

"You didn't win last night."

"I was distracted by thoughts of kissing you."

Her dismissive noise went much better that time which was good because she suspected she would be using it quite a lot with a man who hedged like a professional gardener. "You're very good at avoiding what you don't want to answer."

He leaned forward and kissed her again, then sat back with a groan. "I vow I *will* kill him right after breakfast. 'Twill leave us the rest of the day for other things."

"That was French, buster," she said, "and I understood most of it."

He smiled, kissed her hair, then pointed toward the table. "Let us discuss the delights we have over there for your birthday dessert. I investigated the wrappings as I selected them, but there were several words written upon them that I didn't recognize as foodstuffs."

"There's a lot of chocolate on that tray."

"I did recognize *that*."

She couldn't help but smile as he reached over to drag the table closer. He was distracting and so were his dessert choices, so she decided that maybe a temporary retreat to regroup wasn't unthinkable. After all, if his parents were hardcore re-enactment performers, then maybe they'd tried to inspire him with an appropriate appendage to his name and keep him free from the influences of modern-food-scarfing, bodice-wearing babes who probably paid his parents for the privilege of hanging out in medieval times with him.

She wondered if any of them had seen him go at someone else with a medieval sword when he apparently meant it.

"Thumb war or a kiss?"

She pulled herself away from the mystery sitting right there with her and blinked. "Is this a new distraction tactic?"

"That depends on whether or not 'tis working, so to cover our bases, let's try both."

She gave up and tossed in the proverbial towel, but made a mental note about where it had landed. She was back in business and there wasn't a treasure she'd decided to hunt that hadn't given up and given in eventually.

The one who had just lost temporary possession of that Elizabethan shilling because she'd kissed him briefly on the count of three would be no exception.

Eighteen

JACKSON SAT AT THE TABLE in Wyckham's kitchens and entertained subversive thoughts.

It wasn't something he did very often. He liked events to proceed as he'd intended and the people around him to behave in ways he could anticipate. He'd been told more than once—generally by the women in his family—that he was tremendously annoying during his bouts of organizing everyone's lives to his satisfaction, but so be it. A man's life could best be lived as a battle and he had a fondness for winning.

That he was currently contemplating an entire day with nothing more to do than moon over the woman standing twenty paces from him, chatting amicably with his admittedly favorite cousin, was a surprisingly welcome departure from his usual method of conducting his life.

Of course, he'd started the day off very sensibly with a pair of hours in Wyckham's lists, trying not to kill the lord of the hall. Zachary Smith had shown relatively well and he had almost stopped yawning, so he considered the early morning hours a success.

He'd followed that up with a shower, garbing himself in jeans that boasted pockets and a t-shirt that wasn't the one sporting the words, *kiss me, I'm medieval*—someone would be paying for that, to be sure—then finishing his morning tasks with a rummage through the ice cream larder to identify potential candidates for dessert.

He'd also had a brief conversation with Derrick Cameron over the phone where he'd learned that Alexander of Falconberg was still on the Continent, no doubt lingering over one last glass of drinkable wine, but the man would be back on the proper side of the Channel the following day and hopefully available for a parley.

All of which had left him sitting in Wyckham's kitchens, trying not to think about the things he would miss about modern life, namely the food, the inventions, and the woman still standing with his cousin, smiling over something that apparently amused them both.

He propped his elbows up on the table and his chin on his fists and simply watched her. Perhaps he could worm his way into her plans and be about his excellent work of distracting her with kisses and avoiding answering things he didn't want to talk about.

"And there he goes," Zachary murmured. "Felled without a stroke."

Jackson glared at him, but it was half-hearted at best. He did worry that his feelings might be too obvious, though, which might frighten Olivia off. He stood up. "Let's go outside."

"Are you kidding me?" Zachary said with half a laugh, shifting his sleeping daughter carefully. "I already went outside with you this morning. I have other things to do today."

Mary dried her hands and walked across the kitchens to take Anne from him. "Be off with you both and take a healthful trot about the outside of the walls. I'm sure it will do much to settle your humors."

Jackson paused to briefly admire his cousin's command of modern English—a testament to not only her wit, but her time spent in the Future—then looked at her husband. "I don't want to leave them alone here. Have you no servants nor guardsmen?"

"Staff," Zachary corrected, "and security. Yes, we have both, but we gave the staff a couple of days off when Derrick let me know you were coming."

"You knew we were coming?"

"Of course," Zachary said. "It's why my sword was sitting just inside the door when you arrived. As for our security, the men are very discreet and accustomed to all sorts of possibilities. Our ladies will be safe enough inside and we'll definitely have company outside."

Jackson walked over and stood behind Olivia, not sure if he should embrace her or just pat her. She turned around slightly to look at him, perhaps a bit too assessingly for his comfort, so he settled for the latter.

"You'll be safe here," he announced.

"Thank you."

"I also realize I'm not."

She smiled and turned back to Maryanne. He exchanged an alarmed look with his cousin who only shooed him away and continued her conversation about the beauties of the English autumnal weather. He managed to get himself outside without wincing thanks to a decent night's sleep on a terribly comfortable Future bed and paused on the front stoop of his uncle's keep. He put his hands in his pockets, then looked at Maryanne's husband who was smiling.

"What?" he asked, preparing to be offended.

"Pockets," Zachary said. "A marvel that's sadly missing in medieval England, though I think they were invented during the Middle Ages."

Jackson had the feeling that might have happened long after he'd expired, so he didn't ask for any more details. He studied the man standing next to him and couldn't deny the solicitude with which he treated his wife and daughter, nor his generosity as a host, nor even the fact that he'd been willing to rise at an unearthly hour to tromp about the lists and do what real knights did.

He wasn't one to shy away from things that needed to be said, so he turned to face his cousin's, ah, he could scarce call him her lover so he settled for husband.

"I apologize."

Zachary looked at him in surprise. "For what?"

"I misjudged you."

Zachary smiled. "Forgiven."

"So easily?"

"Life's too short to hold onto the past." He nodded toward the front gates. "Let's go walk. I haven't had any reports of anything unusual, but we might want to have a look ourselves."

Jackson nodded and took the same path he'd used to follow Olivia the afternoon before. He walked all the way around the outside of the keep with Maryanne's husband, then found himself leaning once again against the same stone wall he'd occupied the day before.

He wondered how he would live the rest of his life without that sparkling woman who might have given any medieval lord's captain pause with her ability to ferret out details from an opponent, then carry on in spite of the dangers in front of her. He looked at his cousin's husband and suspected he might have the answer to the question he hardly dared ask for reasons he couldn't bring himself to consider. He was also no weak-kneed maid, so he walked into the middle of the battle and damned the consequences.

"Would you have stayed?"

Zachary Smith might have been many things—and Jackson would have been happy to make a list of all the viler items, if asked—but he was no fool. "Knives?"

Jackson pursed his lips. "Down my boots, though I daresay I can bear these tidings without killing you in my surprise."

"Had to check," Zachary said with a smile. He leaned against the wall and crossed his boots one over the other. "We don't discuss this outside the family, but since you're that, I'll be honest."

Jackson found, to his surprise, that he suffered hardly any desire to correct the man who had beguiled his cousin the saints only knew how into wedding with him. A cousin by marriage was, after all, still family.

"I might need to back up a bit, if you have the patience for it."

Jackson nodded and waved him on to whatever tale he wanted to tell.

"I was just a teenager living the good life in Seattle when my sister up and disappeared," Zachary said with a faint smile. "It turned out that she had fallen asleep on a park bench and woken up in medieval Scotland where she met and married a man named James MacLeod."

Jackson felt something slide down his spine. "He makes maps."

"He does," Zachary agreed. "I'm guessing you've seen one of them."

"In my uncle Nicholas's trunk," Jackson said faintly, "but 'twas simply a sketch of England and Scotland with several landmarks I wasn't familiar with. I thought it the scribblings of a madman, no matter what anyone else said."

"I'm sure you know better now," Zachary offered, "but to clarify, those landmarks are particular spots—fairy rings in the grass, doorways, gates—that lead from one time to another. You and I have both used the large one near Artane."

"A fortnight ago."

"Or almost two years ago, depending on your perspective."

"That's daft."

"Yet here you are."

Jackson shifted to look at him more fully. "How does Laird James know where those spots are? I'm assuming he and your sister are here in the Future."

"They are, yes, and he knows thanks initially to the adventures of various relatives. The rest he and I found because we spent over a decade tromping all over England and Scotland looking for them. I imagine I don't need to add that we used them all."

"How many … ah … "

Zachary shrugged. "Several score, at least. I stopped counting after a few years."

Jackson couldn't decide if he were more appalled by the fact that traveling through the centuries was possible or that Zachary had done it so often.

Or that he himself had been so oblivious to it all.

"The things you must have seen," he managed.

"Unforgettable, both the good and bad," Zachary agreed. "It's hard to go back to a normal life when you've seen what else it can hold."

Jackson could scarce entertain that thought. He stared at the castle in front of him, a place where he had first seen that appalling map eight hundred years in the past, then took a deep breath and looked at his cousin's husband. "Were you never tempted to remain in my time?"

"Very," Zachary answered without hesitation, "and I almost didn't have a choice. Traveling through time isn't as simple as walking through a doorway. There's always a risk that you won't get back home. I was very fortunate that the gate near Artane worked as I wanted it to or things might not have turned out as they did."

"My uncle and aunt are, I'm certain, very grateful Maryanne lives still."

"I wish it hadn't come at such a terrible a price for them," Zachary said, "but none of us could have changed that. About that gate, though, I'm not sure how much longer it will keep from collapsing in on itself. It's a very turbulent portal."

"But I must use it again," Jackson said slowly.

"I know."

"I cannot stay here," Jackson added, in case he hadn't sounded as convinced as he should have.

"I understand, believe me," Zachary said with feeling. "Jamie would give you an entire lecture on the perils of remaining in a time not your own. Unless you're replacing something that has gone missing from that place, you change things, much like adding or taking away a thread in a pattern of plaid. You might not notice it right away, but the farther along you get—" He took a deep breath. "Please stab me right now before I say anything else."

Jackson would have smiled, but he actually felt quite ill. Of course he couldn't remain in the present day, so thinking on how he might affect future events shouldn't have troubled him.

Yet somehow it did.

"In my case, I didn't dare change the past by inserting myself in your time," Zachary continued. "That was made substantially worse by knowing that I also couldn't do anything to change Mary's destiny."

"Yet you intervened."

"What else was I to do? I love her. When I failed to save her in your time and I knew her only hope was to come to the Future, I brought her here and damned Jamie's endless yapping about threads and patterns." He shrugged uncomfortably. "I'll have an accounting with Father Time at some point, I imagine."

Jackson felt a little of the tension ease out of him. "I think you'll be forgiven just the same."

Zachary smiled. "One can hope." He paused for several moments, then spoke very carefully. "Your situation is different, if you want my opinion."

Jackson snorted in spite of himself. "I don't see how. I'm nothing but a peasant here in your day, though I do have a bit of gold still sewn into my boots."

"I understand how you feel," Zachary said with a quick smile, "but I wasn't talking about money. Your father left a hole here that you *could* fill if you wanted to stay, but you have complications in the past that I didn't have in the future. There, *I* was the peasant, not heir to a powerful family dynasty."

When had the day become so unsettled? Jackson tugged on the neck of his modern tunic. He was parched and feverish and chilled beyond measure all at once.

"I would have complications here as well," he managed, "far beyond feeding myself and Olivia."

"With your father's family?" Zachary asked. "I don't know them, but I understand they're not a great bunch. My brother knows them, though, and could probably tell you which ones to avoid."

"You have a brother?"

"Several," Zachary said. "What's a bit ironic is that I found out after I came back from the past that my brother Alex was your father's attorney here in the future."

Jackson looked at Zachary incredulously. "Your brother is the earl of Falconberg?"

"How do you—" Zachary held up his hand. "Never mind. Derrick must have said something."

"How do you know *him*?"

"We're cousins by marriage." He smiled. "The branches of that family tree are loaded with time-travelers, but yours are as well, aren't they?"

"To my continued surprise," Jackson said uneasily. "And aye, Derrick told me, but he neglected to mention Alexander was your kin—which I'm beginning to suspect was deliberate. He's arranging a parley for us with him, though I feel a little foolish now knowing your connection to the man."

"I don't get involved in Alex's lawyering," Zachary said with a shudder. "He's terrifying."

"I'll be sure and bring a sword."

"He probably will as well, so you two will get along fantastically," Zachary said dryly. "So, are you going to tell Olivia about yourself today so you can take her with you tomorrow, or do you want us to keep her here?"

"I thought I would put it off until tomorrow," Jackson said reluctantly. "I will take her with me, though, so she'll see that the tangle is successfully resolved. It will give her confidence that she might safely begin her labors in London."

And then he would go, because he had no choice.

"What can I do to help?"

He looked at Zachary in surprise. "You would?"

"Family, remember?" Zachary pushed off the wall. "You're

going to need to score massive points with Olivia today if you're going to spring this on her tomorrow. Let me know if you need wooing ideas or apology chocolate."

Jackson couldn't deny that Maryanne looked very content so perhaps the offer of aid shouldn't be too quickly dismissed. There was also much to be said for plying a goodly amount of romance on Olivia that afternoon so she might be less likely to look at him as if he'd lost all his wits, then bolt the other way on the morrow.

Would that he could have wooed her far into their old age—

He took a deep breath and turned his mind to things he could control. The list was unfortunately very short, but perhaps a few answers weren't unthinkable.

"If Derrick Cameron knows you, does he know about Maryanne?"

Zachary shot him a look.

"And yet he said nothing," he said, then realized that perhaps that wasn't entirely true. Derrick had told him that he was able to find many people, he just hadn't divulged any names. Perhaps there was good reason for that.

"We try not to volunteer information to time-traveling relatives who might want to nip in and out of other centuries without being marked," Zachary said with a nod. "What Derrick knows and doesn't reveal would probably keep you up at night, so don't think about it."

Jackson didn't doubt it. "I hesitate to ask this, but have you seen Sam and Theo?"

Zachary shuddered delicately. "Unfortunately, yes. They showed up in my kitchen as teenagers a couple of years ago, which was as alarming as you'd expect it to be. We fed them all the junk food they could eat, then Stephen and I shoved them back through the gate near Artane while they were distracted with upset stomachs. I'm not sure you'll want to know anything else that I may or may not have seen since then."

"Then Stephen knows about you—" He shook his head.

"Never mind." He shot Zachary a look. "You're a discreet group, aren't you?"

Zachary smiled. "For a variety of reasons I don't need to explain to you."

Jackson nodded, then enjoyed a companionable bit of silence with his cousin's husband as they walked back up to the keep. He considered all the questions he could ask of the man walking next to him, but set them all aside as too painful to discuss. He did have one thing pertinent to his plans for the morrow, though.

"I thought to take Olivia to Raventhorpe," he said, pausing on the steps with the lord of the keep. "For the conversation we must have."

"The keep hasn't weathered the centuries well, but the chapel is still there on the hill outside the gates."

"I think I won't look in the graveyard."

Zachary smiled in understanding. "Can't blame you. You're welcome to use one of my cars tomorrow so you and Olivia have a bit of anonymity."

"Thank you," Jackson said seriously. "Derrick informed me this morning that Master Rufus had led my grandfather's men on a merry chase back to London, but I suspect that peace won't last long." He paused. "I'm not sure how to repay you, which is something I find myself continuing to say."

"I said the same thing to Robin several times," Zachary said. "You'll do it for someone else, I'm sure. Besides, I think you're going to have a difficult afternoon avoiding things you don't want to talk about, so watching that will probably be repayment enough."

Jackson would have given that comment the salty reply it deserved, but he was too overcome by the fact that in another fortnight he would likely be walking in the same place only hundreds of years out of the current time.

Without Olivia.

He took a deep breath, then continued on into the hall with his cousin's husband. It took a moment for his eyes to adjust to the comforting gloom only to find Maryanne chasing her wee daughter about the floor. They were both laughing, the sound of which caught him tightly about in the heart.

He was starting to feel broody, which he decided abruptly he would share with no one. He couldn't imagine a single cousin who wouldn't have laughed themselves sick over the thought.

He stopped next to his cousin. "Where is Olivia?"

"In the library," she said, catching her daughter up into her arms and smiling at the messy kiss she was given. "'Tis in the wee chamber next to the lord's solar that Auntie Jen used for Sam and Theo's bedchamber. Your lady spoke of her love for swords, and I thought Zachary's books on metal smithing might interest her."

Jackson felt something very unpleasant rush through him that he refused to call fear. He could only imagine what else Olivia Drummond, hunter of treasures and unraveler of mysteries, might find with all that free rein.

"My apologies," he said. "I'd best go supervise her choices."

He gave his cousin a hasty embrace, then bolted for the chamber that had a long and illustrious history of housing all manner of untoward things.

The door was open, which aided him in his rushing. He came to a skidding halt on one of those damned floor tapestries, sending it sliding right along with himself and almost plowing into Olivia as she stood near a wall of books.

She reached out and steadied him, looking at him as if she'd never seen him before. "What's wrong?"

"Ah," he said, scrambling for something that wouldn't leave him sounding as mad as he knew he looked. "I didn't want you to become lost. The castle is very big."

She eyed him skeptically. "I think I'm okay."

"I'm okay, too," he said. He straightened something his aunt Jennifer would have slain anyone for putting on the floor, then moved to lean against the back of a sturdy chair. "What interesting thing are you reading?"

She held up a book with a sword emblazoned on its cover. "This."

"The saints be praised."

She looked at him in a way that left him realizing that he had relaxed too soon.

"Is there something I shouldn't be reading?" She reached for something on a small table next to her. "Like this?"

He peered at it to find it was a history of Artane and its inhabitants. He shrugged lightly. "Quite a boring lot, those lads there."

"They have other books on various places," she said, setting that book down. She picked up another one. "This one is about Raventhorpe—"

"Not that one." He pushed away from the chair. "Not today, please."

She leaned back against the collection of books and looked at him seriously. "I think you have some 'splaining to do, my friend."

He grasped desperately for words that sounded casual. "Friend? I have obviously been less diligent about distracting you during our thumb wars than I should have been if that's how you think of me."

She was seemingly unimpressed. "You know, my aunt Philly sent me to England with a book written by a Miss Eugenie Kilchurn."

"A relative, perhaps—"

"It was published in 1910," she said, as if she hadn't heard him. "It's all about ghosts and other strange, paranormally happenings up here in the north of England. She was very fond of Artane, apparently. I think she might have been related somehow to the owners."

"'Tis entirely possible—"

"Her favorite place, though, was her family's ancestral castle."

Jackson only waited, because he had the distinct feeling the time for outrunning not only his demons but those terrible questions that woman there had for him had run out. He jammed his hands in his pockets and braced for what was coming, but Olivia only stood there, watching him silently.

"Raventhorpe?" he said finally, because he suspected she would never speak again if he didn't volunteer the information.

"You're not surprised."

"It has been home to the Kilchurn family for quite some time," he said, attempting a light tone. The saints only knew how long, but the last thing he wanted her to do was dig through Zachary's library and find a list of Raventhorpe's lords through the ages. He glanced at her then sighed. "I might have that 'splaining to do, but I beg you not today."

"You have some sitcoms to catch up on, my—"

He stepped forward, pulled her into his arms, and looked at her seriously. "I am not overfond of that word."

"What one would you prefer that I use?" she managed.

"I'll make a list in a moment, if you might be amenable to a small display of affection first."

She looked up at him solemnly. "You talk an awful lot."

"I can stop."

She smiled. "You're very charming, you know."

And she was very generous regarding his failings, so he did his damndest to make up for it with that handful of kisses he'd been contemplating since breakfast.

The saints pity him for it.

He lifted his head eventually. "Swords or a walk on the roof?"

She looked at him blearily. "You don't fight fair."

"I do," he said. "I just always win."

"Do you?"

"Unless my mother, my sisters, and a decent array of gel cousins are on the other side of the field, then things become more difficult to arrange to my satisfaction."

"Poor you."

"Let us go walk on the roof and you can feel sorry for me a bit more."

"I have to go put the books back," she said, pulling away from him.

He made a mental note of where those manuscripts had come from because he liked to know what lay on the battlefield, then took his lady's hand and left the chamber. He had to admit to feeling as if he'd left things behind that perhaps he should have read.

Then again, perhaps he was more like Zachary Smith than he wanted to admit, for there was a part of him that desperately wanted to change history and beg Father Time to make his reckoning later.

He walked into the great hall with Olivia to find his cousin holding her daughter whilst concurrently enjoying a fond but thankfully chaste embrace from her husband.

The saints preserve them all.

He stopped in front of them, took a steadying breath, then looked at Zachary. "We're going for a walk on the roof, then we'll take a turn in the lists. Have you any blades?"

"I'll go fetch a pair." Zachary kissed his wife. "I'll be back. Maybe a nap then?"

"Good hell," Jackson said faintly. "Can you two not cease with this endless mooning? Olivia, let us be away whilst I still have my breakfast residing where it should."

Zachary only winked at him and walked away. Jackson looked at his cousin and could scarce believe she was there, holding a child, and she was now somehow *older* than he was. He hugged her briefly, then took Olivia's hand and walked with her through the castle. Again, a very long conversation with Father Time about quite a few things.

He led Olivia up the stairs, finding himself watching the turns of those stairs as he'd done either in his own home or in his uncle's hall for as long as he could remember. The difference was, he was holding the hand of a woman he cared for.

He could scarce bear the thought of missing that in the future.

He set that aside as something to be mourned later and continued up the stairs, along a passageway, then up a different set of stairs to the guard tower he knew would open onto the parapet wall.

"Did I tell you what the last chapter of Eugenie Kilchurn's book was about?"

He opened the far door of the tower chamber and led his lady out into the autumn sunshine. "Nay, you did not."

"It was about all the time-travelers she'd met."

He almost fell over the wall, truth be told. He caught himself and hoped Olivia hadn't noticed. She had hold of the back of his shirt, so perhaps she had.

"What absolute rubbish," he managed.

He glanced at her to see if he'd sounded convincing enough, but she was only watching him speculatively.

"It seems like it should be, doesn't it?"

"What might I offer you so we needn't discuss this any longer?" he asked without hesitation. "I could let you best me with the sword when we descend to the lists."

He realized as he said it that most modern lads probably wouldn't have used that as a wooing tactic. 'Twas out there, though, and there was no calling it back.

"Very generous."

He shifted uncomfortably. "Aye, well, I don't want you putting me to the sword whilst there are kisses to be had later. We'll use those blades Zachary is fetching for us. I'm certain they'll be very dull in deference to his skill."

"You're down to calling him by only his first name."

"I believe we came to an unspoken understanding," he said with a sigh. "He also has a very well-stocked frozen larder, so being the self-serving lad I am, I decided 'twas best not to have him cluttering up my path to it." He held out his hand. "A moment here to enjoy the view before we repair to the lists?"

She took his hand, but the speculative look on her beautiful visage didn't fade. He kept her hand in his as he leaned against the wall with her, very happy to put off difficult things for a bit longer.

"Stephen said you were taking a bit of a breather from the family business," she said carefully. "He wasn't gossiping, just trying to reassure me that you weren't a ruffian or a ne'er-do-well."

He nodded slowly, assuming that was the same sort of thing as a gap. "He has that aright. I'm just taking a … breather."

She turned to look at him, though he was gratified to note that she didn't release his hand. "Then how do you want to spend your breather, since it's only going to last for the rest of the day before I really get going with my investigations?"

He smiled in spite of himself. "An afternoon in the lists, then an evening in front of the fire where I'm allowed to draw you."

"And tomorrow you'll answer everything I ask?"

He took a deep breath, then nodded. "Everything, so don't scamper off in the night."

"You have my coin," she said with a shrug. "Don't *you* scamper off during the night."

"I won't," he said quietly, "and I don't give a damn about that coin."

She blinked, then muttered what he was sure were rather uncomplimentary things about him under her breath as she walked into his embrace. He rested his cheek against her hair and stared off over that lovely English countryside that in all honesty hadn't changed all that much from his day.

There was a part of him that wished someone had destroyed that bloody gate near Artane.

He just couldn't bring himself to admit upon which side he would have wanted to find himself.

Nineteen

Olivia opened the front door to the great hall and walked outside. She was fairly sure she'd had breakfast, but she hadn't tasted any of it. Jackson had packed up food for the road and told her he would cool his heels for a bit if she needed a moment to run upstairs and get her rampaging imagination under control before she flat-out accused him of missing his spot in Eugenie Kilchurn's final chapter.

Actually, he'd told her he would wait for her outside, but she was fairly sure he would have said the rest if he'd had any idea what she was thinking.

She walked down the stairs to find one of Zachary's cars waiting there with the man she was suspecting of all kinds of paranormal activity leaning against the side of it.

"I moved the car to this spot," he said casually. "In case you were curious."

"How'd it go?"

"Easily managed, of course."

She smiled and held out her hand. That earned her a light sigh, the keys, and the pleasure of being tucked into the car with great care. She watched him buckle himself in as though he'd been doing it his entire life and tried to rein in the bolting horse that was carrying her thoughts right along with it.

A time traveler? That man there?

She realized he was watching her and shook herself back to

the reasonable side of her line which was no mean feat considering she was on the unreasonable side of the car. She looked it over to get her bearings, sent Zachary and Mary a quick mental thanks for giving them a chance to sight-see with a little anonymity, and concentrated on getting them out of the gates.

There was no Rufus waiting for them at the end of the drive, though there was a car pulled over to the side of the road in the distance to the south. She reminded herself that it was a public road, so anyone was free to drive on it.

"Oliver and his companion Peter are in that automobile there," Jackson said quietly. "I don't imagine we'll see them any closer than they are at the moment, though they will help keep us safe."

"Did you bring your sword?"

He looked at her in surprise, and she held up her hand.

"I know," she said. "I've lost it. Where are we going and should we have brought Lord Stephen's map?"

"North, and nay, I know the way."

Of course he did. If he lived close enough to Artane to be able to walk there to act in her uncle Richard's play, he obviously knew the area. That he hadn't gone home right away was still a little odd, but maybe misplacing that key was a bigger deal than he wanted to admit.

She followed his directions north until a turnoff to the right appeared and he nodded for her to take it. That lasted about an hour along a tiny B-road that didn't do all that much for her nerves before they reached a small village. She drove through it without taking off any side mirrors along the way, then came to the point where she couldn't go forward any longer. She paused and looked at him.

"Go left, if you would," he said quietly.

She suspected there were lots of beaches in that direction, and she was definitely a fan of the ocean. The closer they got to the coast, though, the quieter Jackson got—and he hadn't been exactly chatty to that point. She glanced at him occasionally to find him watching their surroundings with a look of seriousness she'd never seen on his face before.

"'Tis that way," he said eventually, pointing very carefully in front of her nose toward the east.

She followed that very small gravel road until it terminated in front of a remarkably well-preserved, obviously medieval church. She parked outside the low stone wall that enclosed it, then turned off the car.

Jackson opened his door. "I'll come fetch you."

She wouldn't have expected anything else. She watched him get out and walk around the front of the car. She folded her hands over the steering wheel and rested her chin there, allowing herself a moment to just watch him while he was watching something else. Rural farm boy or medieval knight on vacation?

She honestly didn't know what to think.

Jackson turned away from his study of that church, then obviously realized she'd been watching him. He closed his eyes briefly, then came and opened her door for her. She accepted his hand out and found herself pulled into his arms.

She understood. She wasn't sure which one of them was shivering, but maybe it didn't matter. There was definitely some sort of storm coming their way.

"I believe there is a blanket in the hind seat," he said. "We might wish for it later."

She watched him get it, retrieve the keys from the ignition and lock the car without incident, then hand them to her.

"You don't want them?"

"I do," he said with a grave smile, "but my history with them isn't terribly good." He took her hand and laced his fingers with hers. "Shall we?"

She nodded, then walked with him toward the ocean. She had seen the ruins of the castle as they'd driven up the road, but she almost didn't recognize it as the same place that Eugenie Kilchurn had sketched. She'd expected it to be a little weathered, but she hadn't expected it to be a shell of its former self. She looked at Jackson quickly, but he was only studying it gravely.

"The ravages of time," he observed.

"Do you want to go look anyway?"

He nodded. She wasn't unhappy to have him holding her hand because she was starting to feel like she was floating. She made it about twenty feet from the car before she looked down at the ground under her feet and realized she was standing in the middle of a ring of what had likely been pretty wildflowers in the summer. The only thing missing was a yard sign advertising a one-way trip to a different time, quite possibly not one of her choosing.

"Jackson, there's something weird about this place—"

She squeaked, but that might have been because Jackson had hauled her into his arms and away from that spot so quickly, she was fairly sure her feet had left the ground. She was not at all surprised to find herself behind him as he studied the ground there in front of them. He stepped aside, pulling her with him, and gave the place a wide berth.

"Let us avoid that place."

She couldn't have agreed more. She walked with him along the path to that castle that was balanced on the edge of a bluff with only a little beach to one side of it. It would take not only courage but the right kind of shoes to attempt that trail, but Jackson didn't seem to have that in mind. He wasn't speaking, which didn't surprise her, but he seemed to be growing more serious with every moment that passed, which did. After all, it was just a castle.

Surely.

The front gates were missing and there wasn't all that much left of the rest of it. Some of the outer walls, the foundations of the great hall, parts of other things she thought she might need a book to identify. She stopped next to Jackson as he studied the stairs that led up to a parapet, then followed him up them when he apparently found them safe enough for use. He tested a section of wall, then leaned against it gingerly and put his arm around her. She looked out over the sea and caught her breath.

She realized he was watching her, and she smiled reflexively. "Spectacular."

"As lovely as Artane?"

"Different," she said. "Artane is stunning and the beach in front of it wonderful, but this is something else entirely." She put her hands on the weather-worn rock and shook her head. "I wonder what it looked like when it was whole."

"It was glorious."

She took a deep breath and braced herself for a conversation about things that would be different from how she'd imagined they might be. She realized that she'd been doing that on some level since … well, since the moment she'd looked at that man there in medieval clothes, carrying a medieval sword, and surveying the backstage area of a play as if he'd been assessing a battlefield where he might stride out and announce his medieval presence.

It also might have been because at some point during the middle of the previous night she had come to grips with the fact that Eugenie Kilchurn had been doing less speculating and more taking notes.

"Are you going to faint?"

She came back to herself and attempted a glare. Jackson only looked at her gravely as he tucked the ends of the scarf she'd borrowed from Mary inside her coat.

"We should find shelter away from the wind. We'll still be able to hear the sea."

"You would know?"

He hesitated, then nodded.

She was starting to think maybe there were definitely more things in heaven and earth than were found in her cobbled-together philosophy inspired by too many 50s and 60s sitcoms.

Jackson eased past her carefully, then reached back for her hand. She followed him down stairs that were substantially more alarming to descend than to climb up, mostly because they were completely open to the inside of the castle. He seemed to be particularly concerned that she not take a header off the side of them, which she appreciated.

He led her across the courtyard, picking up the blanket he'd left on what remained of a wall, then sat down next to her on a sheltered bit of weathered stone.

"Do you want me to hold you and keep you warm," he asked carefully, "or shall we speak from a distance?"

"We'd better stick together," she said. "We could huddle under that blanket until I feel the need to get up and run away."

He smiled very briefly, then leaned back against the wall and pulled the blanket over them both. He took one of her hands between both his own, then let out his breath slowly. "I will answer anything you ask."

There was the smallest part of her that wondered if she might be opening a box that should have remained closed, but she suspected she'd been waiting for the current moment since approximately five minutes after she'd met the man next to her. She wasn't about to walk away while she had him captive and willing to confess.

"Who are you?" she asked without hesitation.

"Jackson Alexander Kilchurn the Fifth."

She'd already known that which made it a bit less startling than it might have been otherwise, but she was just getting started. "Who is your father?"

"Jackson Alexander Kilchurn the Fourth."

She was also not terribly surprised to hear that given what she'd seen in Stephen de Piaget's case full of medieval paintings. "Jackson IV who was the first earl of Raventhorpe?"

He took a deep breath, then nodded.

"In ... 1257?"

"He took the title in 1227," Jackson said, "but aye, he was lord of the keep in that year. He still was when I left in 1258."

1258. That was certainly a number one didn't encounter all that often in the current day. She felt a buzzing start in her ears, but maybe that was from too much chocolate for breakfast. "Then you were born on the fifteen of April in what year?"

He glanced heavenward, then looked at her seriously. "1231."

Ah, more numbers. She listened to them come out of his mouth and recognized them as such because she'd encountered numbers before and knew what they sounded like. She'd scoffed at quite a few of them during tense negotiations with sellers of vintage barn items and occasionally with sharp-eyed grannies scoping out Aunt Philly's 1950s Christmas brooch collection, but she wasn't sure she'd ever heard numbers like that apply themselves to anyone's birthday.

1231. She was tempted to shake her head, but she suspected that if she started she would never manage to stop.

"I feel funny," she managed.

Jackson pulled away, took off his coat, then made her a pillow with it. She realized he'd caught her as she tipped over only because she hadn't cracked her head open on any of that medieval stone.

"Drummonds don't faint from shock," she said hoarsely.

"Of course they don't." He smoothed her hair back from her face. "Keys?"

She fumbled for them, then dropped them when she tried to hand them to him. "You aren't going to leave me here, are you?"

"Nay, I'm going to fetch you water," he said. He picked up the keys, then paused. "We would be warmer in the car."

"No," she croaked. "I like it here. I just need a minute to breathe."

She felt his lips on her forehead briefly, then heard him tell her to stay. For some reason, that was reassuring. She closed her eyes and listened to the roar of the sea, grateful for a moment or two to regroup.

There were strange things afoot in the world, of course, like ghosts, ungroomed manlike creatures in Pacific Northwestern forests, and vintage monsters in Scottish lochs. She could also accept that maybe doppelgängers weren't cosmic coincidences and all those cheesy tabloid stories that promised pictorial evidence of time travelers weren't completely fake. For all she knew, a few of those re-enactment types were the real deal hiding in plain sight.

But it was one thing to have a comfortable distance between one's self and all those paranormal happenings; it was another thing entirely to be watching one of those paranormal somethings jogging across the grass of the courtyard, not looking at his feet while not missing a step.

Jackson knelt down and looked at her with an expression of such genuine concern that she had to smile.

"I'm fine." She started to sit up, then realized that had been a bad idea.

The next thing she knew, Jackson was sitting next to her with his arms around her and she wasn't quite sure how he'd gotten there. She concentrated on breathing for a bit longer, then managed to focus on a bottle of water she didn't remember having accepted.

"Hold," he instructed.

She watched him twist off the cap as if he'd been doing it forever. Then again, she'd also watched him once look at a bottle of water as if he'd had no idea how to get it open. There were a dozen other items she could put on a list of things he'd been momentarily stymied by, but all that could be explained by the man having grown up in a very sheltered and possibly quite remote home.

Or in a far different time.

She sipped, allowing her head time to clear, then sat up as Jackson put his coat back on. For some reason, that was such a normal thing to do that she wondered if she might have been hearing things. She looked at his face to find that he was watching her carefully.

"Your chi has been buffeted," he said cautiously. "Perhaps we should both meditate for a moment or two so you might recover fully."

She probably shouldn't have smiled, but she was in the process of having her mind blown so what else was she going to do? She let him gather her back into his arms, then pulled the blanket up over the both of them. She leaned her head against his shoulder and managed to note that his hand holding hers felt like a normal hand—if normal included wielding a sword and painting masterpieces.

"That portrait in Artane is of your family, isn't it?" she asked finally.

"Aye."

"But you painted it and your father painted you into it after the fact."

"That depends upon whether or not you thought it was rubbish."

She smiled. "You're brilliant, which you know."

"I just dabble," he said modestly. "My father is the far superior artist."

She shifted a little so she could see his face. "He's very good, but so are you and this is the truth, isn't it?"

He closed his eyes briefly, then nodded.

"Have you ever lied?"

"Must I admit it?"

"Yes, and it better not have been just now, buster."

He smiled briefly. "Nay, 'twas in my youth."

She made herself more comfortable. "Then go ahead and confess. You'll feel better if you do and I'll have a minute to pull myself back together. What whopper did you tell?"

"I cannot believe this is what you want to know."

"I want to know all kinds of things, but I'm off-balance and I want you there with me." She lifted her head and smiled at him. "Don't make me flip it out of you."

He snorted and gathered her close again. "Very well, I will humor you until your chi is restored. If you must know, on the day I turned ten-and-two, I found a key in the passageway in front of my father's solar—ah, his private chamber, er—"

"I get the picture." His dad's, er, solar probably had a floor tapestry and no snacks, but the reason why was definitely clearer than it had been half an hour ago. "Carry on."

"I picked it up," he continued, "then shoved it down the side of my boot and never admitted to having seen it."

"You have a thing about keys, don't you?"

"I seem to."

"It's a good thing that wasn't a key to—" She froze, then sat up straight and looked at him in astonishment. "Wait a minute. It wasn't *the* key, was it? The one to the safe in Penelope's shop?"

He looked at her helplessly. "Daft as it sounds, I suspect it might be."

She looked into his otherworldly turquoise eyes and couldn't decide if she should laugh or get up and bolt. "But how is that possible? I mean, it's not like your father was Penelope's boss, because Penelope's boss was here and you and your father were there. Even if he were here before he went there, he couldn't be much older than you are now. Here, not there."

She realized she was babbling, but it had been that kind of morning so far. Jackson didn't look much better than she felt, so maybe he wouldn't notice.

"Unless that photograph is deceiving us," he said carefully, "'tis a certainty that Mistress Penelope did labor with my father, for that is indeed his likeness. The jewels we saw in the shop are very like what he has created during my lifetime. But 'tis also true that he has been in my day for the past thirty years."

"That's very strange."

"I agree. Then again, I saw Zachary and Maryanne but a fortnight ago in the past, yet two years have gone by for them in this day."

"Then how did you get here?" she asked, because that seemed easier to contemplate. "From, ah, 1258 to 2008, I mean."

"You aren't going to faint again, are you?"

"I didn't faint before," she said with a scowl. "My chi was under assault from numbers I couldn't wrap my mind around." She took a few more restorative breaths, then looked at that medieval knight in jeans and a leather jacket who was still watching her as if he thought she might do something terrifying. "I'm braced."

He smiled faintly. "Then come you here and hold onto me, for now I find that I'm the one feeling a bit faint."

"You don't look faint."

"I might be exaggerating my condition for slightly self-serving reasons."

She smiled because it was either that or run off shrieking through the front gates that were no longer there and honestly, she didn't want to do that. She made herself comfortable with her head on his shoulder and happily allowed him to pull her arm over his waist.

"The easy answer is that a doorway opened between the centuries and a pair of my wee cousins pushed me through it."

"So, a doorway out in the middle of a field?"

"Aye, exactly so. This particular doorway finds itself in the field just outside Artane under that vile green cloth. I shudder to think how many people have simply walked over it and landed where they hadn't intended to go."

She imagined Eugenie Kilchurn might have had an opinion on that, but perhaps that could be left for a different discussion.

"How often does it do its thing and open up?" she asked.

"I've no idea. I haven't dared ask Zachary for the particulars. I assumed there was no point in thinking about it until the covering was gone and the ground had repaired itself."

She understood why he hadn't gone home yet. Even if he'd found his key, he wouldn't have had a way to *get* home.

But that would change once the tarp was gone.

She tilted her head back to look at him and saw in his eyes that he was thinking the same thing. He pulled her close and wrapped his arms more tightly around her.

"Let us speak of anything but that," he said quietly. "Not today."

She couldn't have agreed more, so she took a deep breath and dug around in her shopkeeper's arsenal for a cheerful tone.

"So, you were out doing knightly things, one of these doorways randomly opened up there in front of you, and a couple of your cousins gave you a shove through it?"

He nodded. "I suppose the opening of it wasn't random, though I've no idea how any of it works. Zachary was standing there in my day, looking across the centuries to where Maryanne was waiting in your day, and it looked to me as if he might not reach her."

"So you gave him a nudge?"

"A gentle one, of course."

She smiled. "Very romantic of you."

"A moment of madness, to be sure."

"Why was Zachary even there in the first place? I realize this means Mary is also from, ah, well, you know."

"Her father Robin is brother to my mother, Amanda," he agreed.

"And Robin is?"

"The second lord of Artane."

Of course he was. She was beginning to think she should have followed that McKinnon clansman's lead in the airport and picked up a book on genealogy at some point.

"As for why Zachary found himself in my day, I've no idea and his opinions on the matter are better relegated to one of your chick flicks. All I know is that he arrived unannounced at my uncle's hall where my poor cousin had the terrible misfortune of being wooed by him. Now, not only is she wed to him, but blessed with a babe I refuse to believe was sired by someone so unskilled with a sword."

She smiled, because she half suspected he might actually think that. "It's obvious he loves her very much."

"And she him, unfortunately," he said grimly, "which means my attempts to get her to see reason will no doubt go unheeded."

"I'm starting to see a pattern with you." She studied him for a moment or two. "Do you think Lord Stephen knows her? Does he know about *you*?"

He sighed deeply. "I assume he knows about her, and aye, he recognized me from the portrait. He seems to know about the, ah—"

"Time traveling?"

He looked a little green. "'Tis complete bollocks, isn't it?"

"'Tis," she agreed, "but hard to deny when you're sitting here. No wonder you were surprised when we had to pay to get into Artane—and you knew your way around there!"

"The armory was new," he said promptly. "And the tea shop is where the blacksmith hut was in my day."

She would have put her hands on her hips and glared at him, but he was smiling at her, medieval hedger that he was, which made him hard to resist.

"Are you really that annoyed with him?" she asked. "Zachary, I mean. He really seems to get under your skin."

He winced. "Must I tell you that, as well? It paints me in a terrible light."

"I need another breather from my new reality," she said, shifting a bit so she could lean her head against the stone wall and watch him. "Paint away."

"If you must have the truth," he said, keeping her hand in his, "I thought he was becoming a bit too familiar with my cousin—at a time when I still believed I could do anything about it—so I went at him when I had a sword and he did not. What I hadn't expected was for him to disarm me, then pin me face-down in the dirt. I managed a few vile threats, but that didn't diminish the humiliation."

"Just desserts, I'd say."

"True," he agreed. "So, you can imagine my surprise when I found him walking out of my uncle's hall at Wyckham. Derrick said nothing of it to me, though I know he knows."

"Perhaps he thought it would be a nice surprise," she said solemnly.

He snorted. "Aye, I daresay. Who knows how much those two gossip like giddy maids? I suspect Derrick Cameron knows far more than he tells, which leaves me wondering about him as well. We might have to pin him in a corner of the lists someday and have a few answers from him."

She tried to ignore how lovely it was to be included in his plans and how much she didn't want to think about the moment when she would no longer be in those same plans.

She took a deep breath and latched onto the first thing that came to mind. "Tell me more about how it works. You stepped through one of these doorways and it took you right from 1258 to 2008?"

"Nay, not at first," he said. "I found myself briefly in some year of Elizabeth I's reign, though still near Artane. Once I recovered from my shock over the appalling manner they had of garbing themselves, I disguised myself as a priest, wed one of my relatives—I'll need to apologize for that at some point—then I tried the gate again. That is when I arrived in this time where I wound up joining the band of players and finding myself stuck with tiny bits of steel by a woman who I'm not sure can sew."

She scowled. "I was helping Sam out."

"I was willing to endure many punctures to have the pleasure of watching you," he said with a smile, "though I'll admit I didn't look as lingeringly as I would have liked. I was half afraid I would kill someone in the frolic by accident."

"Your sword is very sharp."

"Did you test it when I asked you to put it inside your small hall?" he asked politely.

"What do you think?"

"I think, my lady, that you need more lessons in swordplay and perhaps a stern lecture on the perils of steel. Even my father's men have listened to that on more than one occasion from him."

She would have shaken her head, but she'd done it too much already that morning. "It sounds like your dad is happy with his choice."

"He adores my mother, and they have lived very happily together these past three decades." He paused. "Though I suppose now—"

"Don't think about it," she said quickly.

He blew out his breath. "I saw them but a fortnight ago."

"I'm sure they're still there waiting."

He closed his eyes briefly, then nodded. "Bid me speak of anything else, before I unman myself in front of you."

She patted him, realizing only then how useful it was. "Lovelier days are ahead. That's what my granddad always told me, and he was right."

She would have said more, but she was rescued by his phone. He kept his arm around her and slid the keyboard of his phone down with one hand. He glanced at her.

"We don't have these in my day."

"I would never have known."

He smiled briefly. "I'm showing off. Put your arms back around me, woman, and keep me together whilst I attend to this business."

She did, then closed her eyes and let his vintage French wash over her without trying to understand it. She could hear Derrick speaking it on the other end, but she didn't even start down the path toward wondering where he'd learned it. Maybe there had been a good reason for Samantha to have looked so unsettled when their conversation had veered toward castles slathered with history. Just how much history was Samantha Drummond familiar with?

She listened to Jackson close his phone and felt him put it back in his pocket as easily as if he'd done it every day of his adult life.

"Medieval Norman French?" she asked lightly.

"Aye."

She lifted her head and looked at him. "I don't know how you did any of this so well. I think I might need a meltdown later over just thinking about it."

"I might indulge in one with you. Did I mention that the lawyer we're meeting with aided my father three years ago?"

She glared at him, had a quick smile in return, then put her head back on his shoulder. "No, you did not, which you already know."

"Aye, I know," he said. "Why don't we simply sit here in this unusual sunshine and listen to the ocean for a bit longer? Derrick has arranged for us to meet with Lord Alexander at Seakirk in a pair of hours, so we've time yet."

That was one way to put it. She closed her eyes, felt him take her hand again, and could hardly believe what she'd heard. Stranger still, she couldn't *not* believe it because it answered everything about Jackson that she'd found mysterious.

What were the odds of having arrived in England only to meet a man who, against a different set of odds, had traveled 800 years out of his day to end up accompanying her to the shop his father had once owned?

She didn't want to think about what sorts of bets Fate might or might not have made with her bridge club over whether or not she herself would take one look at that man, fall uncomfortably hard for him, then do everything in her power not to think about where he might be in a couple of weeks.

Or *when*, rather.

She felt Jackson tighten his arm around her and decided that maybe not thinking for a bit might be best. They would meet with his father's attorney and that would leave them one step closer to having the situation solved.

It was also one step closer to Jackson going home.

For some reason, she found that a very terrible place to be.

TWENTY

JACKSON WATCHED SEAKIRK RISE UP before them as they drove through the village and suppressed a shudder. He had seen it several times in the past, to be sure, but never dared venture inside. Why Alexander of Falconberg had chosen it as a meeting place was baffling.

"Have you been here before?" Olivia asked suddenly.

"Never. The lady of the hall was rumored to be a witch, so we always gave the place a wide berth. Who knows what goes on inside in this current day?"

"It is on Britain's Most Haunted list," she said with a shiver, "but it only came in at Number Seven."

"Somehow, I'm not reassured," he said grimly. "Paranormal oddities make me uneasy."

"Is that really something you should be saying?" she asked, sending him a quick smile. "You know, given your background and all."

He pursed his lips. "Hopping across centuries isn't nearly as weird as being a ghost."

"I'm not sure you should be trying to make that distinction," she said with a snort. "You with your *I'm from England* and *I worked from dawn till dusk*. What a load of horse pucky."

He smiled. "But 'tis the truth."

"Technically, maybe, but it was still a catastrophic bit of hedging." She looked at him assessingly. "I'm going to be making an entirely different list of nosey questions for you, you know."

He imagined she would and vowed silently to answer each to her satisfaction. The more time he had her within reach, the better.

"So, while we're on the subject of nosey questions," she said, as they continued on through the village, "what else do you know about this lawyer?"

"He's Zachary Smith's brother."

She looked at him in surprise. "That's a pretty unusual coincidence, isn't it?"

"Very," he agreed, though he had the feeling it wouldn't be the last of those. "Derrick said he might have tidings regarding my father's father that will serve us, so I was willing to ignore quite a few things for the chance to question him."

"Tidings regarding your modern grandfather."

"Aye, if you can fathom that."

"It definitely makes for an interesting family tree." She paused to allow a quartet of grandfatherly types to cross the road, then drove on. "Did you never wonder where your dad was from?"

"More often that I'll own, though the whole idea seemed daft," he admitted. "Maryanne's older brother, Kendrick, was convinced my sire had come from a different time, though I thought him daft as well. It was he who had learned your future English and insisted that a select few of us should learn it as well. I refused to participate because I am a man of maturity and good sense."

"So you eavesdropped like a fiend?" she asked with a smile.

"I refuse to admit anything."

"Which answers that question, because I'm guessing you learned it because you like to be prepared for contingencies."

"That does make it easier to boss my loved ones about," he agreed.

"I'll just bet it does." She glanced at him briefly. "Is this what you were talking to Derrick about at their house?"

"Aye, for the most part."

"I understand why you didn't want to say anything, though I wouldn't have freaked out."

"I feared to take that chance," he admitted. "Hence the thought of wooing you with a medieval penny before you learned the truth, lest you think me a madman and go running off into the night."

"It was a lovely gift, and Richard does seem to enjoy having that Elizabethan shilling nearby, so keep that in mind as well." She nodded up the way. "Should I stop outside the castle gates, do you think?"

He would have answered her, but the gates opened as they approached. He looked for guards manning the same, but saw none. He wasn't one given to unease at the first sight of trouble, but their current straits were a bit unusual.

"Ah—" he began.

"Couldn't agree more," she said uneasily, bringing the car to a full stop. "What should we do?"

He didn't have his sword, but his knives were down his boots so perhaps that would be enough. "Let us continue on," he said, hoping he didn't sound as unnerved as he suddenly felt. "I'll attend to whatever comes our way in time."

Olivia nodded, then guided the car through gates that remained open until they had driven past them, then they swung closed silently.

"I'm surprised it's only seventh on that list," she said with a shiver.

Jackson had to agree. He looked at their surroundings, wondering just how in the hell they would flee if they found themselves facing a ghostly garrison. Olivia placed the car near the keep in a way that would leave them able to drive off without trouble, which he appreciated.

"I will see to us easily," he said, "now that you've made it so we might easily escape."

"You noticed," she said, "but you always notice."

"I noticed more than your stabling of the automobile," he said with a shrug, "but you are very distracting."

She looked at him in surprise. "Are you flirting with me?"

"Trying to." He smiled for good measure. "Is it working?"

She smiled, seemingly in spite of herself. "How can you possibly flirt with me and pay attention to battle strategy at the same time?"

He shrugged. "I'm ambidextrous."

"All right," she said with a bit of a laugh, "you're a little funny, but I'm too unsettled to really enjoy it. I keep expecting a ghost to come roaring around the corner and terrify us."

"I'm certain 'tis but a rumor," he said confidently. He took her hand, kissed her palm, then let himself out. "I'll come fetch you."

"Jackson?"

He leaned over to look back into the car. "Aye?"

"Try the other later."

"The other?"

"Not the battle strategy."

He bowed his head and almost laughed, then he shot her a quick smile and nodded before he shut the door. He took a deep breath to stop what he was fairly certain might have been a discreet blush, then walked around the car to fetch his lady.

He glanced up at the keep as he opened her door and shivered in spite of himself. Seakirk had been a place teeming with supernatural happenings in his day, so the saints only knew what lurked inside at present. He didn't see anything vile lurking in the courtyard, but who knew how long that would last.

He helped Olivia out of the car, then shut the door and took her hand. "We'll make this a brief visit," he said, trying not to shiver.

"Is it too late to run?" she asked.

He would have answered her, but he was distracted by the sight of a trio of lads exiting the hall and coming to stand on the bottom rung of the steps leading up to the keep.

"I fear so," he murmured. "Let's make ourselves known and see if those three are corporeal or not."

She walked with him readily enough until they were standing a few paces away from the obvious vanguard of the castle. They were lads of perhaps eleven summers, but that wasn't what was so startling. There were three of them—triplet demons, as it happened—which left him almost backing up onto Olivia's foot. He made her a quick apology before he turned back to their present trouble.

He wasn't quite certain what to say because those looked like de Piaget lads if he'd ever clapped eyes on one. They regarded him unblinkingly for a moment or two, then one of them, perhaps the eldest spawn, stepped forward and folded his arms over his chest in a gesture that was so reminiscent of Robin de Piaget, Jackson almost flinched.

"Welcome to Seakirk," the lad said, his voice not quite yet that of a man. "Your names, if you please?"

Jackson supposed the boy was the son of the earl, so he would accord him the respect due him.

"Jackson Kilchurn, my young lordling," he said inclining his head. "This is my lady, Olivia Drummond. If I might be so bold as to ask your name as well?"

"Lads, don't vex the guests—"

Jackson looked up as a man came trotting around the corner of the keep proper, then skidded to a halt. He supposed he was fortunate that Olivia was decently sturdy or he would have swayed into her and taken her down to the ground with him. He didn't argue when he felt her arm go around his back, keeping him upright.

Because he was looking at his Uncle Robin.

Or … perhaps not.

"Jack?"

Jackson felt his mouth working, but no sound issued forth. He watched the lads be swept aside in the incoming wave that was …

"Kendrick?" he managed weakly.

Kendrick laughed and threw his arms around him. Jackson

felt Olivia's hand leave his back which he would have chided her for, but he was too busy finding himself enveloped in a manly hug whilst simultaneously having the breath pounded out of him.

Kendrick released him, then stepped away with both hands still on his shoulders. "What in the *hell* are you doing here?"

"I've come to meet Alexander of Falconberg," Jackson said weakly. "What are *you* doing here?"

Kendrick only lifted his eyebrows briefly and shrugged. "Fate," he said, then he turned his admittedly tremendously charming smile on Olivia and extended his hand. "And who might this very lovely woman be?"

Jackson slapped his cousin's hand away. Kendrick only smirked at him in the same way he'd been smirking for as long as Jackson could remember, then held out his hand again.

"I am Kendrick of Seakirk," he said politely. "Husband, father, and quite possibly the only one who can damage the man next to you."

"Olivia Drummond," she said faintly. "Do I want to know the details?"

"How much do you know already?"

"Enough that I generally want to look for somewhere to sit down."

Kendrick laughed. "That answers most everything right there. I'll fill in the gaps in a moment or two, but first allow me to present my eldest children." He gestured for the lads to come closer. "Robin, Phillip, and Jason."

The one who had spoken before sidled up to his father. "Another cousin?" he said in French.

Jackson looked at the lads and suspected they might know enough to want to sit down as well.

"Jackson of Raventhorpe," Kendrick said with a nod. "Auntie Amanda's eldest son."

Jackson found himself being assessed by three smaller-sized versions of their sire.

"The only one who can stand against Grandfather Robin?" one of them asked. "Besides you, Father, of course."

"He manages it for a moment or two," Kendrick agreed. "Lads, run ahead and make certain the hall is secure. We'll follow momentarily."

Jackson had half a dozen questions springing immediately to mind, though he wasn't sure he wanted answers to anything save how Kendrick had come to be lord of Seakirk, never mind being the same in the twenty-first century. He supposed he made polite conversation, though he remembered none of it. He felt Olivia's hand slip under his elbow and he made a note to thank her properly when his mind was once again clear.

"We've just recently told the triplets about my upbringing," Kendrick was saying. "Our younger ones don't know."

Jackson refrained from pointing out that Kendrick's oldest children were as likely to keep those sorts of enticing details to themselves as Kendrick had been in his youth, which was not at all.

"Does Maryanne know you're here?" Jackson asked, then he bit his tongue. "Forgive me for speaking out of turn—"

Kendrick waved away his words. "Oh, I know she's here. There's more to it, of course, but for now let's just say that I almost killed Zachary Smith before I permitted him to so much as date her. Father sent along his blessing so I couldn't stop the wedding, though that wasn't for a lack of trying."

"I'll sleep better tonight knowing that," Jackson said, nodding. He studied his cousin standing there looking perfectly comfortable in his modern gear and wondered if he might venture a casual question or two. "And what of you? Anything interesting to relate?"

"Apart from endless days full of glory, riches, and everyone in the area being too terrified to present themselves at my gates without a damned good reason?" Kendrick shrugged. "Just the usual business of life, I daresay."

"So," Olivia said gingerly, "if it wouldn't be rude to ask about your, er, journey here? Did you, ah … "

"Travel through time?" Kendrick finished. He shook his head. "Too pedestrian. I was murdered downstairs in the cellar in 1260, haunted the keep as a ghost for several centuries, then my beloved wife broke a curse and here we are."

Jackson put his arm around Olivia as she swayed. Or that might have been because he'd swayed. He looked at her.

"We should sit."

"Couldn't agree more."

He turned to his cousin who had only been a pair of years older than he was not more than a fortnight earlier but was now obviously galloping toward the middle of his life span. Kendrick was watching him with a faint smile, as if he understood. He walked up the stairs and held open his front door.

"Come inside, Mistress Olivia, and bring your servant with you. Perhaps something strengthening to drink in front of the fire?"

Jackson followed his lady into the hall and imagined there would be time later to slay his cousin for his cheek.

"My wife Genevieve has taken our youngest three to the village for an outing, but she will return this afternoon. I fear you're limited to me and my shadows there for now, but we'll do our best to entertain you. Warm yourselves by the fire whilst I go see what's to be had from the kitchens."

Jackson watched his cousin walk away, followed by his eldest three children, then walked over with Olivia to stand in front of a blazing fire. He wouldn't have thought anything of her pleasant expression if he hadn't spent so much time with her under such trying circumstances.

"I'm fine," she said, before he could ask.

He sighed and took her hand. "Drummonds usually are, or so I'm given to understand."

"Do you think it's true?" she whispered.

"He doesn't lie, though the tale seems fantastical, doesn't it?"

"Was he alive, ah … "

"Aye, he was off on the Continent a fortnight ago, wreaking havoc in every tourney possible."

She considered, then looked up at him. "Jousting?"

"Aye, undefeated." His cousin was, as any of them would have admitted without hesitation, truly terrifying with any number of different weapons in his hands.

"Do *you* joust?" She looked at him in astonishment, then shook her head. "Sorry. These aren't normally questions I ask."

"I understand, believe me," he said. "And aye, I have jousted countless times, though I don't particularly care for it. I would much rather humiliate someone with the sword than knock them off the back of a horse."

"Jackson, I think Drummonds faint more than once a day."

He swept her up into his arms just to be safe, then looked around himself for a place to sit. 'Twas then that he noticed the mailed knight standing right there in front of him where he certainly hadn't been the moment before.

"My lord Jackson," the man said politely. "My lord Kendrick instructed me to see if perhaps our lady might enjoy a small rest upstairs."

Jackson looked at Olivia, had a careful nod as a result, and suspected a moment or two of peace and quiet might be the best thing for her. He started to follow the guardsman across the hall only to almost go sprawling over the chair that he realized their guide had just walked through. He caught himself, then let Olivia slide down to her feet. He put his arm around her shoulders and hoped he wasn't leaning too much on her.

Perhaps Kendrick—the saints pity them all if it were true—hadn't been the only ghost to haunt Seakirk over the centuries.

"What have we done?" Olivia whispered, looking thoroughly alarmed.

He would have answered, but he was interrupted by the arrival of a white-haired gentleman who was currently shooing away the guardsman. The man turned to them and inclined his head politely.

"I am Worthington," he said, "His Lordship's steward. A guest chamber has indeed been prepared for our lady's comfort, if that suits."

Jackson considered the elderly gentleman in front of them for a moment or two, then reached out and poked him firmly in the shoulder.

Worthington only sighed, as if he'd experienced that more than once.

"I would love a chance to catch my breath," Olivia said politely. "Thank you, Mr. Worthington."

The man smiled, then turned and started toward the stairs. Jackson kept hold of Olivia's hand and trusted that Kendrick's steward wouldn't lead them astray.

Worthington led them, as it turned out, to what obviously served as a guest chamber. He pointed out its finer features, invited Olivia to make herself at home, then left them with another polite bow.

Jackson waited until the man had disappeared back into the stairwell before he turned to his lady. "I would like for you to stay right here in the doorway."

"And just what are you going to do?"

"Make certain there are no gates through time or stray specters inside this chamber."

"I wish that weren't funny," she said uneasily. "You don't want help?"

He took her hand again. "I suppose we're safer together. Don't let go of me, though, if we find something unsettling."

"All right."

He wandered about the chamber with her, peering into corners and clothing closets, then led her back over to the doorway. He didn't think, he simply pulled her into his arms and held her close. He wasn't entirely sure what he intended by the embrace, but he found he couldn't release her.

"You will be safe here," he said finally, "and I'll be downstairs."

"I'm not worried."

He held her for a moment or two longer, then released her carefully. "Lock the door just the same."

"Of course, my lord."

He snorted. "The first display of deference and I didn't even get a brief embrace—"

He stopped speaking. A man did that, he supposed, when the woman he was inordinately fond of leaned up and kissed him. He caught her before she pulled away and drew her back into his arms.

"Let's revisit that, shall we?" he asked politely. "I think I might prefer a display of affection over any lordly title any time it pleases you."

She put her arms around his neck and hugged him so tightly, he wasn't sure he would manage a decent breath for quite some time to come. That was probably just as well, for anything he would have said would have been overly maudlin. She kissed him again, a bit less quickly that time, then pulled away.

"Thank you for the breather," she said gravely.

"I would take it with you if my cousin wouldn't come and shout at me for not giving you a bit of peace," he said. "If I'm not napping in front of the fire in the hall, find a sword and come rescue me in the lists."

"I'll come find you wherever you've gone."

He could only hope so.

He nodded and walked out into the passageway, then waited outside her door until he heard the bolt slide home. He stood there for a moment or two, wishing he'd just bolted himself inside that bedchamber with her, then he sighed and made his way back down to the great hall.

He found his cousin waiting for him on the front stoop, which left him feeling as if he were not quite where he was supposed to be whilst standing next to someone he'd spent enough time with to call a brother.

"She's beautiful," Kendrick noted. "And obviously full of a goodly amount of courage."

"She is," Jackson agreed. "I daresay she was just giving us a chance to speak privately."

"I thought as much. Lovely gel, that one. Perhaps when my Gen comes home, they can discuss our flaws and pass the rest of the afternoon pleasantly until Alexander of Falconberg arrives."

"Your poor wife," he said, shaking his head. "Six children?"

"And still she hasn't booted me out the front gates," Kendrick said with a shrug. "You should be so fortunate. When did you tell your Olivia about yourself?"

"This morning."

"Poor gel."

Jackson agreed, but he did so silently. He turned abruptly to his cousin. "I don't remember you coming to Seakirk."

"Why would you? 'Tis still in your future, isn't it?"

Jackson had to concede that was the case, though he supposed the reverse was most definitely not. Kendrick might have lost his life in 1260, but he would assuredly remember the events that preceded it.

Events such as perhaps having visited Raventhorpe at any point leading up to his murder, which would have allowed him to note any and all who were living there at the time.

"Knowing the future isn't necessarily a good thing."

Jackson looked at him then, that cousin who had led him on countless adventures that had left him squawking with indignation and a fair bit of terror. Kendrick had also taught him the exhilaration of leaping before looking which had left him learning to rely on all sorts of unsavoury tactics to get himself out of whatever disaster he'd followed his cousin into.

"Did you know the truth about my sire?" he asked, because that seemed the safest of all topics to discuss.

The look of disgust Kendrick sent his way almost left him smiling.

"Didn't I tell you that learning Future English would serve you well?"

"I practiced it," Jackson muttered. "On my own. I was very busy doing other things, such as perfecting my skill with steel."

Kendrick smiled. "'Tis a pity you aren't staying. I could roll out of bed before noon tomorrow and see if your swordplay has suffered over the past—how long have you been here?"

"Almost a fortnight."

Kendrick leaned back against the doorway of his keep and looked at him in a way that was far too shrewd for Jackson's taste, but his cousin was like that.

"Can't bring yourself to count the days?"

"How has it been watching every century unfold without being able to sally forth and conquer your enemies?" Jackson returned.

"Who said I couldn't sally forth? Shades can be damned terrifying under the right circumstances." Kendrick watched him with half a smile. "I still won't answer your questions."

"I wouldn't ask them."

"No matter how desperately you want to?"

"Have I told you recently how deeply I loathe you?"

"*Merde*," he said cheerfully. "You have worshipped me from the time you could toddle after me, begging me to be sensible. If you hadn't had me, you would likely be huddled in a corner of the lists, fretting over your next move."

"I'm wildly adventurous," Jackson said through gritted teeth. "It simply wars with my good sense and overwhelming desire to keep everyone around me safe."

Kendrick smiled. "Aye, I know. After all, you obviously came here, so perhaps you're more adventurous than I give you credit for being."

"It wasn't planned," Jackson managed. "I pushed Zachary Smith into your sister's arms, then stumbled after them."

He imagined he didn't need to admit to his cousin how often he'd wished he'd could simply leap into the Future and see its wonders for himself. Unfortunately, he could tell by Kendrick's expression that he already knew.

"Forgive me, Jack," Kendrick said quietly. "I didn't have a choice in my path, which allowed me the luxury of loving where I willed and leaping into my future with abandon. You have responsibilities I didn't, and you're honorable enough to see to them."

He nodded, because there was nothing to be said. The silence that then fell was companionable, but he would have been the first to admit it was fraught with things he wasn't going to say and he knew Kendrick wouldn't pursue. Aye, he did have a keep and a legacy awaiting him in the past, and he did know exactly how much responsibility the same placed upon shoulders that had been marked from birth to bear it.

And nay, he wouldn't shirk his responsibilities, no matter how much he might want something else.

"Sometimes 'tis best to mind your own business," Kendrick offered.

"I know that," Jackson muttered. He shot his cousin a look. "Very well, I'm learning that."

Kendrick rubbed his hands together. "Fancy a go in the lists to pass the time?"

"Would your lady wife object?"

"Nay, she wouldn't. She's an angel."

"She would have to be, to be wed to you."

"Did you bring a sword, lad?" Kendrick asked politely.

"I don't imagine I'll need one with you."

"You know, Jack, I've lost none of my skill and I've had several centuries to reflect on all the times you insulted me."

"I never insulted you," Jackson said with a snort. "Pointed out your flaws, aye, but that was always to your edification."

"Which I would repay you for, but look who is here well ahead of the appointed hour. I suppose you're safe from my superior swordplay for at least another hour or so."

Jackson looked at the sleek black car coming through the gates. "Alexander of Falconberg?"

"The very same. If you're curious, I think he even frightens his younger brother."

"I like him already."

Kendrick smiled. "I thought you might. Very well, business first, swords later if we've the time."

Time. Jackson was beginning to dislike the very word, but he was no coward. He nodded and walked down the front stairs with his cousin to wait for the man who might have answers he would need. He shoved his hands in his pockets, ruthlessly squelching the thought that he would miss them in the future, and watched Alexander of Falconberg exit what looked to be an extremely expensive automobile. He sized the man up immediately and was pleased to note that he carried himself as if he weren't intimidated easily.

Alexander stopped in front of them and greeted Kendrick with a familiarity that bespoke previous encounters. He waited, then shook Alexander's hand when his turn came.

"Lord Alexander," he said politely.

"Call me Alex and wow, do you ever look like your dad."

"Do I?" Jackson asked, then he started in surprise. "You speak my tongue?"

"Learned it from my wife," Alexander said easily, "which might be a story for a different day. I understand from Derrick Cameron that you've been scampering around London, stirring up trouble."

Jackson was half-tempted to be offended by that, but 'twas obvious that Alexander was trying very hard not to smirk. The saints preserve him, was he doomed to be vexed by cousins, half-cousins, and cousins-by-marriage no matter the century?

"Unwittingly," he managed, "but that does indeed seem to be the case."

Alexander propped his boot up against the bottom step of Kendrick's stairs. "Polite chitchat or right down to business?"

Jackson didn't see the point in not walking directly onto the field of battle. "Business first, if you don't mind."

Alexander tilted his head slightly toward Kendrick. "Do you want this one here to listen or should we banish him to the kiddie table?"

"I know where your lists are, friend," Kendrick said mildly, "so tread carefully."

"I'm appropriately terrified," Alexander said dryly. "Jackson?"

"He may stay," Jackson said, "if he cares to hear the madness."

Alexander nodded. "Walk or sit?"

"I think better when I run," Jackson said slowly, "but in deference to Kendrick's advanced years … "

He stepped aside to miss his cousin's elbow, which he supposed had been wisely done considering how much abuse his ribs had taken already in the past pair of days.

"Let's walk then," Alexander said, "in deference to your cousin's ancient knees."

"One thing, though," Jackson said. "I daresay Olivia should hear these tidings as well." He paused. "Olivia is my, ah … "

Both Kendrick and Alexander looked at him expectantly. He wasn't entirely certain they hadn't tilted their heads in exactly the same direction, damn them both.

He glared at them. "She is my, er—"

Kendrick looked at Alexander. "Girlfriend."

"Does she know she's his girlfriend?"

"I daresay not. We might need to offer him some wooing ideas later. He's very bad at it, if memory serves."

"I am not," Jackson said through gritted teeth as he patted himself for a non-existent sword.

Alexander laughed a little, then nodded toward what seemed to serve as the castle's lists. "I'll take your word for it. Let's go dance around the edges of the details for a bit, then. Kendrick, try to keep up."

Jackson caught up with Zachary's brother and elbowed his

cousin out of the way in one smooth motion. He glared at that cousin who had indeed led him into innumerable perils, then prepared to listen to things he was likely better prepared to hear thanks to Kendrick dragging him places perhaps he definitely shouldn't have gone.

"So, do you want me to start before or after your grandfather had your father declared dead and tried to steal all his stuff?"

Jackson took a deep breath, waved Alexander on to wherever it was he wanted to begin, and suspected that even a walk around the lists wasn't going to be enough to help him digest what was no doubt coming his way.

TWENTY-ONE

OLIVIA STOOD IN THE STAIRWELL and looked out into Seakirk's great hall. The castle was beautiful, blending a very medieval aesthetic with an unmistakable touch of modern convenience. She'd noticed something similar at Wyckham, though knowing what she knew at present, she suspected Zachary had kept the more modern traces behind tapestries in deference to his wife.

There was a woman standing near the fireplace, discussing things with Mr. Worthington, so it was probably safe to assume that was the mistress of the castle. Olivia wondered if it would be rude to tell her that she might want to check her house for mice because the sound of them skittering along the walls was a bit obvious.

Olivia considered, then shifted slightly and looked over her shoulder to see just what sorts of frolicking rodents Seakirk actually boasted.

There were six of them, all perching on separate ascending steps of that circular stairway. Well, the youngest, a little girl of perhaps five, was actually having a piggy-back ride on one of the triplets who himself was standing on the step directly behind her, but the number of children was still the same.

That brother inclined his head politely. "We've been charged with keeping you safe, Miss Drummond."

The other five nodded in unison.

Olivia smiled and leaned back against the wall. "By whom, if I might ask?"

The youngest wiggled down out of her brother's arms, then came to take her hand.

"By Jackson," she said enthusiastically. "He's brilliant!"

"And named after me," said another of the younger boys.

One of the other brothers scooted past his siblings to jump down onto the floor next to her. "We encountered him several times outside as we were securing the area," he said seriously.

She could only imagine. There were some first-class snoops right there.

"He curses in French like Father—"

"Chris! We're not supposed to talk about French."

Olivia looked at that brother, zipped her lips, and threw away the key.

There was a collective sigh of relief, then she found herself swarmed and escorted out into the great hall by a handful of kids who seemed to have various levels of knowledge about things that she suspected didn't make up the reality of most British schoolchildren.

"We could go out to the lists," one of the eldest said, nodding hypnotically. "If you cared to visit them."

"Can't imagine anything I'd love more," she said.

"We'll wait to escort you there. Lads—and Addy—make sure all gear is accounted for."

Olivia found herself deposited next to the obvious lady of the hall before the children huddled up to inspect each other for heaven only knew what. Even that little girl had her own wooden sword.

"We frisk them before we let them out the front gates," the woman said with a smile as she held out her hand. "Genevieve de Piaget."

"Olivia Drummond—wait, you're American?"

"From San Francisco, actually," Genevieve said. "I saw Jackson briefly on my way in and he mentioned you were from Seattle, so we have our foggy days in common. Jason, it's your turn to make sure Addy doesn't give herself splinters."

One of the triplets sighed lightly and put his hand on his sister's shoulder. "We'll keep her safe as we continue to patrol the area. Onward, lads. And Addy."

Olivia watched them go, then couldn't help but wonder just what she'd gotten into. Children who were obviously in touch with their father's medieval side, her own brush with a medieval lord, thugs potentially lying in wait outside the gates? Oh, and a guardsman who had looked substantial enough earlier until he'd walked his ghostly self right though a chair?

"Too much paranormal activity?" Genevieve asked sympathetically.

"Is it that obvious?"

"I recognize the look," Genevieve said dryly. "It gets easier, though it is a bit of a shock the first time you run up against it." She paused. "It might take a few times before it stops being a shock."

Olivia felt her mouth working, but words weren't making their way out.

Genevieve laughed a little. "I understand, believe me. How about a walk outside where we can watch the carnage? Kendrick was thrilled to have Jackson show up for reasons I probably don't need to explain. Alex Smith is out there as well, but I don't think that will stop them from showing off."

Olivia nodded, then decided she probably didn't need to point out that most people didn't talk about their husbands dragging out swords to use on their guests, mostly because she suspected Genevieve de Piaget already knew that.

She walked with her hostess outside, not unhappy for a bit of chilly fall air to help her clear her head, and was somehow unsurprised to walk around the side of the castle and find a large space that looked as if it hosted all kinds of knightly activities. Less surprising still was the sight of the castle's lord and her medieval

London buddy in that field, hacking at each other with what she imagined were very sharp swords.

A third man was simply standing there with his hands in his pockets, offering what she assumed were insults. She supposed that had to be Alexander Smith, Zachary's brother and the earl of Falconberg. He looked their way, nodded, then went back to harassing the combatants.

She looked at the metaphorical towel in her hand and didn't bother to reconsider before she tossed it into the usual pile and surrendered. Her life had veered so far into uncharted territory that she wasn't sure she would ever get it back on track.

Then again, maybe she didn't want to. She listened to Kendrick say something she suspected might be very rude to his cousin. Jackson stopped, deliberately changed his sword over to his left hand, then replied with something she was certain was equally rude. Kendrick only laughed heartily and threw himself back into the fray.

Olivia looked at Genevieve to find her watching her, not the guys out there trying to kill each other.

"Do I look like I just tossed in the towel?" she asked with a light sigh.

Genevieve laughed in a friendly fashion. "Actually, you do. It's hard to deny what they are when you see them like this, isn't it?"

"Very." She watched the men for another moment or two, then looked at her new friend. "Think they know we're here?"

"Absolutely. It's that medieval radar thing they do."

"I've watched Jackson do it. I wouldn't want to be a thug."

"Or a misbehaving eleven-year-old boy," Genevieve agreed. "Our kids don't get away with much."

Olivia looked at the lady of the castle and wondered about her. There were things she could believe—big caches of doubloons hiding in back yards and Caribbean lagoons—but other things she had more difficulty with, say, ghosts and time travelers and things that weren't found in musty old barns or hidden between pristine copies of National Geographic magazines. Ghosts and mortals falling in love didn't even make any list she'd been keeping.

Genevieve leaned back against the footings of the castle and smiled. "So you don't have to ask, yes, whatever Kendrick told you about us is absolutely true."

"I bet that wasn't what you were expecting when you got on that plane," Olivia managed.

Genevieve laughed a little. "I'd expected maybe a few spiders and some avocado-green appliances, but definitely nothing more otherworldly. Kendrick was a bit of a shock, but we managed to pull off the impossible and wind up in the same place together. We live with some interesting quirks now, but I wouldn't trade any of it. A husband with medieval sensibilities is pretty terrific."

"I can see how that would be true."

Genevieve smiled. "You're handling this all very well, by the way. It's a lot to take in."

"Are you kidding?" Olivia said faintly. "I'm completely freaked out. I'm also tempted to ask you to make a list of medieval swear words so I won't be completely in the dark, though I'm not sure it matters. I mean, it's not like Jackson and I are, um, well, you know." She had to take a deep breath. "Dating. Or anything like that."

"I don't know about that," Genevieve said thoughtfully. "He seemed to be pretty concerned that you be properly looked after. Besides, he's what, pushing thirty? He's probably dated half the population of both England and France. I'm guessing he knows what he wants."

Olivia attempted a smile. "I'm a big fan of happy endings, but he has his life there and I have mine here."

What she couldn't bring herself to say was how much she wished it could have been different. She could see the movie tag line hanging in the air in front of her: *Medieval boy meets modern girl after Fate drops something shiny between the centuries.*

"Makes you wonder why some time gate let him through then, doesn't it?" Genevieve mused.

"I think he got shoved by a couple of teenagers and didn't have a choice."

"Maybe," Genevieve conceded. "But wouldn't it be interesting if you two were supposed to be together and those two teenagers had given Fate a helping hand?"

"Pfft," Olivia managed, though she supposed she sounded less like she was good-naturedly dismissing the idea and more like she was choking on denying it. She was, however, beginning to understand why her aunt was so good at that noise, though admittedly she hadn't made it all that often after setting eyes on Randy of the tie-dye t-shirts and vintage love beads. Maybe love changed all kinds of things.

Genevieve smiled. "Feel free to ignore me," she said easily. "I'm a hopeless romantic and the fairy-tale castle surroundings don't help."

"Oh, I don't mind," Olivia said, imagining that she didn't need to admit how many hours she'd spent carefully plowing through her aunt's entire collection of Barbara Cartland novels. "I love the idea of a knight in shining armor rescuing a damsel in distress. I'm just not sure how it works out when the knight is the real deal with a pretty substantial inheritance in medieval England."

"He does have a younger brother, you know."

Olivia started to say that she'd had no idea, though that wasn't exactly true. She'd seen his brother in that painting, but it hadn't occurred to her what that might mean.

Then again, if Jackson didn't start paying less attention to his cousin heckling him and more attention to his sword wielding, he wasn't going to be inheriting anything. She watched as he slipped, then gasped as Kendrick's sword went through him.

Or, maybe not. No wonder he'd managed to avoid knocking her out as they'd been diving for the same coin. He was obviously used to getting out of the way of things.

Jackson looked at the gaping slash in his t-shirt, then shrugged. "It belongs to Zachary."

Olivia leaned back against the castle and looked at Genevieve. "Does this ever get any easier?"

"Not much," Genevieve said with a smile. "I think they might be finished for today, though. Those swords are too sharp for the escort you're about to have out onto the field. I've got to round up some boys for homework, but why don't we exchange numbers after you're finished talking to Alex? It never hurts to have friends in a foreign land."

"I'd love that."

She watched Genevieve go gather up her three eldest and shepherd them back inside, then looked to her left to find the three youngest de Piaget children standing there watching her. There were half a dozen mailed knights standing behind them, though she supposed those guys weren't exactly, ah, corporeal.

Adelaide de Piaget shook off a brother's restraining hand and came forward to look at her. "I have my sword," she announced. "Let's see to our business."

Olivia nodded with what she hoped was the appropriate amount of solemnity, then followed Addy and her entourage over to where Jackson stood with his cousin and Zachary's brother. She found her hand taken by a kindergartner with a sword and decided that was indicative of the day she was having. Jackson smiled at her briefly, then squatted down in front of Adelaide.

"I see you have a very large garrison at your disposal, Lady Adelaide."

"Ghosts," Addy said blandly. "Very terrifying."

"Indeed they are," he agreed solemnly. "I shall entrust my lady to your care, then. Your garrison and your brothers will follow your instructions, I'm sure."

"They tend to," Addy agreed.

Olivia watched Jackson stand, then turn and make her a small bow.

"I'll find something else to wear."

"Well, you wouldn't want me coming after you with straight pins."

"You might be surprised." He stepped back and indicated the man standing next to him. "This is Alexander of Falconberg. Alex, this is Olivia. I will return as quickly as I may, but don't hesitate to speak freely until that time."

Olivia watched him walk away with Kendrick, then found herself standing with Zachary's brother, watching as her guardsmen—and Addy—deserted her to apparently make the rounds.

"I don't know what's gone on," Alexander said with a smile, "but I'm sure it's Zach's fault."

"I think he's been on his best behavior," she said, smiling in return. "So, you're American, too?"

He nodded. "My sister started it and we all followed like lemmings. Should we go have a seat on the steps and wait for your boyfriend? I'll save the juicy details for when he gets back, but I'm happy to answer other things, if you like."

Boyfriend? Pfft. She refrained from attempting to say the same, though, and simply followed Alex over to the steps leading up to the front doors. It wasn't as if she hadn't had a thoroughly satisfying meltdown in the privacy of a guest room, but she also wasn't going to pass up the chance to have a little rest in a castle courtyard.

She took a deep breath, then looked at Zachary's brother. "I'm not sure where to start. This whole experience has been a little surreal."

"Trust me, I understand. I once walked into a fairy ring in modern-day Scotland and stepped out into medieval England."

She looked at him in surprise. "Really?"

He nodded. "It happens more often than you might think, which my brother-in-law Jamie would be the first to admit."

"What happened when you landed?"

"After I recovered from the indignity of face-planting into a bunch of flowers, I had a good look at the lady of the castle nearby and found I couldn't live without her. We ended up deciding that the future was the best place for us both." He shrugged easily. "Maybe there's something in the water over here."

"Your brother would probably agree."

"Are you kidding?" he said with a snort. "He's lucky Mary looked at him twice. But you're right about the rest of it. He and Jamie need a frequent flier program for all the trips they've taken to various times and places. It figures that the accidental journey is the one that had him meeting the love of his life." He smiled. "Funny how that works, isn't it?"

"It is very interesting," she managed.

"You mean *unsettling*," Alexander said, "which I also understand. Your guy's father is a good example, actually. I know for a fact that Jake hadn't planned on heading back to the past and meeting his future wife, but life has a way of giving you things you didn't realize you needed, if you let it."

She had to take a deep breath. "I'm beginning to think that might be the case."

"How's Jackson been doing here in our little corner of the cosmic calendar?" he asked politely.

"Outside of regular brain freeze and being subjected to too many chick flicks, I think he's been okay—"

"I've been okay, how?"

She looked up to find Jackson trotting down the stairs on the other side of Alexander and stopping on the courtyard floor. He glared at Alexander briefly, had a snort as his reward, then clasped his hands behind him and smiled at her.

She couldn't do anything but blush. Jackson looked at Alexander with a frown.

"What did you say to her?"

"I was regaling her with time-traveling success stories," Alexander said easily. "It's a pretty spicy topic, though, so maybe we'd better move on. Shall I get you both up to speed?"

Olivia noted the new t-shirt Jackson had probably borrowed from his cousin. The illustration of a mailed knight on horseback holding a jousting pole was, she suspected, chosen with care. She looked at him only to have him hold up his hands in surrender, then shoot her a quick smile before he turned back to his father's attorney.

"Tell us whatever you think we should know."

"The facts are fairly straight-forward," Alexander began. "Jake rolled his car off the road and himself into medieval England, Jackson III—your modern-day grandfather, Jackson—had him declared dead, and Jake popped back up inconveniently while his father was rifling through his wallet. Jake hired me to make that stop, so I gathered a carefully curated selection of things guaranteed to make Jackson III rethink his plans and we presented those at a meeting chock-full of his business associates."

"I imagine my sire enjoyed that."

"Actually, I think he was mostly concerned with getting back to the past so he could marry your mother, but *I* enjoyed the hell out of it. Jake went on his merry way, leaving me to just transfer a few remaining assets to Penelope Cleary. I brought copies of all the pertinent legal documents so you can look them over. You never know when they might come in handy."

Olivia couldn't help a brief wish that there would be no need, but it was probably too late for that.

"Has he vexed Mistress Penelope this entire time?" Jackson asked.

"Kept watch, rather," Alexander said, "which surprises me. I figured he might rage for a bit, then let it all go. There was nothing left in the shop for him to take past what Penelope had received, and that definitely wasn't enough to make any difference to him." He shrugged. "Maybe he just doesn't like to lose."

"Three years is a long time to nurse his wounded pride," Jackson said grimly, "though I've seen worse."

"Unfortunately, so have I. Your uncles have been making noises about Jackson III suffering cognitive decline, but I'm guessing that's an excuse to try to gain some control over him. It's also an uphill battle, because he seems pretty *compos mentis* to me."

"What of attempting to shame him so thoroughly in the public square that he decides to cry peace and exit the field?"

Alexander shook his head. "We've already tried that. He has top-shelf security instantly cleaning up anything negative that shows up about him." He considered, then looked up at Jackson. "I hate to say it, but I think the only person who's going to be able to tell you what you need to know is your dad."

"Do you mean go back in time?" Olivia asked in surprise.

"I think it's the only solution, though it's obviously not without its perils."

"Your brother-in-law James MacLeod seems to indulge quite regularly," Jackson said evenly. "Never mind Zachary."

"Jamie is formidable," Alexander said with a shrug, "and Zach has a few stories he probably wouldn't tell you unless you'd spent quality time together with one of the kegs in his cellar. As for your particular tangle, I don't think your grandfather will stop until he has no choice. Your father is really the only one who will know how best to make that happen."

Olivia listened to them discuss other things, but she honestly couldn't hear them. She wondered when exactly that sort of thing had become part of her reality. Jackson might have to go back through some magical gate into a land that couldn't possibly exist on the other side of it in order to save her from a future of craziness that was neither her fault nor his?

She jumped a little at the ringing of Jackson's phone, then watched him excuse himself and answer it.

"This is a lot to process," Alexander said quietly.

She took a deep breath and nodded.

"I understand Jackson has a reputation for being ferociously tenacious about having his way," Alexander added, "so I'd put money on Grandpa not standing a chance."

"But none of this will stop until his grandfather gives up, will it?"

Alexander shook his head. "I'm sorry, Olivia."

She nodded, then watched Jackson put his phone back in his pocket and return to stand in front of them.

"That was Derrick, phoning to find out where we were. He thought it might be wise for us to begin our journey again whilst there is still daylight."

Alexander pushed himself to his feet. "I'll go grab those documents plus the thumb drives I made as backups." He paused, then looked at them both seriously. "Sometimes the best way out is through, to quote Frost. It's also been my experience that there's *always* a way through, even if the path is a little thorny in places." He shrugged and smiled gravely. "Just a thought."

Olivia watched him go, then found herself pulled to her feet and drawn into an embrace that she was becoming hopelessly addicted to.

"If we make haste," Jackson said quietly, "we might manage a brief walk on the shore before supper."

"You don't want to stay here a bit longer with Kendrick?"

"I've humiliated him enough for the day. Let me give Alex something for his trouble, we'll collect these things he has for us, then we'll be off. Is the driving too much?"

She shook her head. "It's still daylight."

"Then let us make haste while that lasts."

An hour later, she was looking forward to having her driving duty done for the day. The waning light wasn't quite as lovely when she was watching it from the vantage point of what felt like a getaway car instead of a cozy spot beside a toasty fire. She would have tried to look a bit more confident, but she suspected she'd left all her composure back at Raventhorpe that morning.

It also didn't help that there was a car behind them that she was fairly sure didn't belong to Oliver.

"Jackson?"

"Aye, love."

"I think there's someone strange behind us."

Jackson's phone rang suddenly. He looked at her, then answered it. "Aye?"

She could hear Derrick on the other end of the phone, but he was speaking in French, which didn't help her at all. Jackson was fortunately limiting himself to one-word questions and answers, which helped quite a bit. He hung up, then looked at her.

"Derrick has spoken to Oliver who is following that unknown automobile behind us," he said carefully. "He suggests that we make for the coast, just to see whether or not they're following us deliberately. Even if we must go north for a bit, we can turn for Artane once we've reached the main road there."

She nodded and continued to drive, but the silence in the car didn't last as long as she would have liked. Jackson answered his phone again, spoke briefly, then hung up and looked at her.

"I fear my grandfather has added to his guardsmen," he said carefully. "We might need to make a different choice."

She glanced at him in alarm. "What sort of different choice?"

"I'm not sure yet." He dialed, then spoke. "Zachary."

Olivia wasn't entirely sure what Jackson expected his cousin-in-law to do about the current situation, but what did she know? She was too busy trying to keep them on the road to wonder why her time-traveling London buddy might want to chat with a man who probably knew too much about the popping back and forth through the centuries.

Unfortunately for her peace of mind, Jackson had somehow put his phone on speaker and she could hear Zachary perfectly well. He frowned at his phone, then glanced at her.

"Will this unnerve you?"

"Less than not knowing," she said. She also wasn't going to pull off the road to show him how to fix it, so she gripped the wheel and eavesdropped with abandon.

"Is there a gate close to my home?" Jackson asked.

"Are you going to tell me why you want to know?"

Jackson swore. "Your brother suggested I go home and speak with my father about the madness his sire is causing, and I agree."

"As much as I hate to admit it, Alex is generally right. And yes, there's a gate in front of the church." He paused. "Sometimes."

"By the saints, who designed these things?"

Zachary laughed uneasily. "Don't blame me. I just use them. It's a very small gate, though, so if thugs try to follow you through at least you'll only face one of them at a time. Where are you now?"

"On the road home."

"Are Derrick's men with you?"

"Behind us, and there will be more waiting at Raventhorpe to distract the enemy whilst I use the gate. Derrick has already instructed Oliver and his companion to take Olivia and ferry her safely away to Artane."

"We'll take care of her for you there, so don't worry."

She knew they were still discussing things, but she couldn't hear them any longer for the blood pounding in her ears. The guy behind her had apparently decided a little tailgating would be a great way to pass the time and she was too busy trying to stay on the road to make sense of phone calls about paranormal possibilities.

She was a treasure hunter, damn it, not a superspy. Her skillset included ducking under large arachnids, eluding angry roosters, and dodging small and terrifying garden snakes. Keeping thugs from rear-ending her was just a little bit beyond what she could handle.

Maybe panic had given her a lead foot or maybe she'd grown

accustomed to driving on the left, but she realized she was pulling up to that little chapel near Raventhorpe far sooner than she'd expected. She parked the car, then grabbed her bag and got out before Jackson could get to her door. She looked at that grassy spot five feet away that had given her the shivers earlier in the day only to find a doorway shimmering there.

It was without a doubt the most paranormal thing she had ever seen in her life—and considering what she'd been through in the past two weeks, that was saying something.

She could hear shouting going on behind her, but it didn't seem very important. Maybe she'd become too accustomed to having people around her to protect her. She hauled her bag over her shoulder, then looked at Jackson.

"I guess you'd better go."

He took a deep breath, then nodded at a spot behind her. "Oliver is here, so you will be safe."

She looked over her shoulder to find that was indeed the case. Oliver held out his hand and she tossed him the keys gratefully. If they were going to make a clean getaway, she was more than happy to let him be the one driving. She looked back at Jackson.

"So, I guess this is goodbye," she managed. "For a bit?"

He nodded, took a deep breath, then stepped onto the threshold of that doorway. He stood there with his back to her for an endless moment, then turned around suddenly.

"Come with me."

She looked at him in surprise. "What?"

He thrust out his hand. "Come with me."

"But the gate's too small and I probably shouldn't—"

He reached out and took her by the hand. "For a few days. I promise I will keep you safe."

Something rushed through her that she immediately identified as terror mixed with the tiniest bit of … curiosity.

And she knew where that led.

She looked at Oliver who only shrugged.

"I've seen it all and done a bit of it myself. Off you go, lassie. Mind the gap."

She watched the doorway begin to close and heard the words she'd said not all that long ago echo in her head.

I, Olivia Grace Drummond, am making a change . . .

She closed her eyes and leaped.

Twenty-Two

Jackson lay on the ground with Olivia sprawled over him and closed his eyes for a moment whilst he caught his breath and assessed the situation.

He could hear the ocean roaring from its proper place which was useful, though he had to admit it had done him an ill century-hopping turn before so perhaps he shouldn't relax quite yet. He didn't hear Oliver shouting that the gate had failed them, which was reassuring. He was without his sword, which was less reassuring but perhaps solvable with a bit of luck.

First things first, though, and that was to have a look around and see where—and possibly when—they were. He opened his eyes and looked up.

Robin of Artane was standing there, watching him with what could have charitably been called a smirk.

Olivia crawled off him only far enough to kneel next to him. He realized she was groping for a dagger from his boot and thought he just might love her in truth.

"Never fear, lady," Robin said, with a small bow. "I am friend, not foe. Robin of Artane, your servant."

Olivia stopped groping and simply stared at Robin in astonishment. Jackson was certain she understood him because the good lord of Artane was speaking in perfect modern English. He looked at his uncle and wondered if it were possible to put into his expression a happy mixture of fury, disgust, and resignation. The only way he might improve on that would be to top it off with a dollop of rich and creamy irony.

'Twas possible he needed to stop eating so much dessert.

He sat up, then heaved himself to his feet and helped his lady to hers. He had to lean over for a bit until the stars stopped swirling around his head, but it had been that sort of day so far.

"I see you've met my nephew, Jackson," Robin said politely. "Has he behaved himself, or should I beat manners into him now?"

"Oh, no, my lord," Olivia said, "he's been very chivalrous."

"Perhaps you'll give me the details of those moments so I might see if I approve. Jackson, bring my horse."

Jackson straightened and watched his uncle make off with his—well, he wasn't quite sure what to call her. Girlfriend? Time-traveling companion? He briefly considered something far more serious, but the thought of it almost brought him to his knees. To find a woman he thought he might want to spend the rest of his life with in the last place he suspected he would ever look?

He took a deep breath and caught up the reins of his uncle's horse, then followed along after his lady and his uncle toward the keep. It didn't take many steps before Robin was pausing and holding out his hand casually. Jackson took the cloak his uncle had draped over his saddle and handed it over as if he'd been helping hide Future souls from the moment he could toddle off across the floor. Robin settled it around Olivia's shoulders, shot him a look of amusement mixed with something Jackson couldn't quite identify, then carried on with her.

It took him almost to his sire's gates before he understood the look. It was affection mixed with a bit of sorrow.

Jackson told himself that his uncle likely grieved over the notion that instead of booting a nephew into a different time, he might be hosting Jackson in his kitchens far into the future, but perhaps not.

He looked up at the massive outer walls of his home as they approached and permitted himself a brief moment of admiring it. Raventhorpe wasn't as large as Artane, true, but his father had made many improvements over the years to create a formidable and rather lovely fortress. It was also home, and he was surprised to find how much he'd missed it. He should have purchased a camera in London to use—

He stopped himself, shook his head, then continued to walk.

One of his father's stable lads came running out of the gates and took Robin's horse from him which left him with nothing to do but subsequently run directly into his younger brother because he'd been watching Olivia instead of where he was going.

Thad gaped at him, then took off his cloak and handed it over. Jackson swung it around his shoulders as if he had also been hiding his own Future-gear-wearing self for as long as he could remember, then found himself having the life half choked from him by his brother's manly embrace.

"Enough," he gasped finally, pulling away. "I am well."

Thad's eyes were very wide. "I have questions."

"I'm certain you do. I will answer them all after I slay Father."

"I'll help." Thad embraced him once more, then looked at Olivia with more interest than was good for his ability to continue to breathe easily. "Who is that?"

"My lady, who will not be at all interested in you."

Thad lifted his eyebrows briefly. "We'll see."

He caught his brother's arm before he walked away. "What's the date?"

Thad shot him a look that he had no trouble interpreting. They had, as it happened, never discussed frankly any of the unusual things swirling around them, though they had certainly exchanged the same sort of look his brother was giving him at present more than a few times.

"You've been gone five months," Thad said. "Journeying in the south, or so we've claimed. That has satisfied all but those who were in the field near Artane. You can imagine what they thought." He pulled his arm away. "Your lady looks as if Uncle might be boring her with talk of swords and the weather. I will execute a rescue."

Jackson made another grab for his brother only to find himself holding onto naught but air. He watched Thad introduce himself to Olivia, discover she was a Drummond, then begin to converse with her in Gaelic. He listened to that language come out of her mouth with ease and realized he was gaping at her. She looked at him, shrugged with a faint smile, then accepted his brother's arm.

"You're in trouble."

He glared at his uncle. "One of these days, someone will stab you for sneaking up on them that way, you know."

"Your sire has threatened to do so many times over the years," Robin said, stretching lazily, "but I'm still alive as you can plainly see. I'm guessing being overcome by the fairness of your lady's visage is the reason you never thought to ask her what tongues she spoke?"

"Actually, I was too busy trying not to slay your son-in-law, listening to your daughter speak Future English, and admiring your wee granddaughter, Anne."

"Did you bring a photograph?"

He wondered if the day would come when he might be past surprise. "Are we actually having this conversation?"

Robin smiled. "I fear we are. You'd best go see to your lady before Thad makes off with her. I'll have the details later."

He scowled at his uncle on principle, then walked over to execute his own rescue. He arrived in time to save his lady from his brother's best smile.

"Mine," he said, pushing Thad out of the way.

His brother looked at Olivia. "Are you?"

"Ah, I think so."

"You sound uncertain," Thad said politely. "Why don't we discuss your other possibilities—"

Jackson gave his brother a shove, then took Olivia's hand. If she was having any doubts about things, then his work was obviously not done. He smiled at her so she would know where his thoughts lay, then realized that her returning smile was rather strained. He suspected he might have looked equally pale after the first time he'd seen himself in her bathroom polished glass, so he understood. He glanced at his brother and uncle who were discreetly watching the sky, then put his arm around her shoulders to pull her close.

"Let's consider this a breather from our troubles in a different day," he said quietly. "You will be very welcome here, and I won't leave you alone unless I must kill a select number of my relatives in the lists. That won't take long."

His uncle snorted, but Olivia smiled more easily.

"All right," she said. "Thank you."

"'Tis an honor and a privilege," he said seriously. He took her hand, then led her through the gates of his home.

He felt as if no time had passed, but the chill in the air told a different tale. Five months? Obviously Zachary would need to be consulted as to the particulars, but perhaps he wouldn't know, either. James MacLeod might have an idea. It occurred to him in passing that he had married a certain Fiona MacLeod to one of his relatives in a far different time, but surely the two couldn't have been related in any fashion.

He was halfway across the courtyard before he saw his father coming down the stairs from the hall itself. The late afternoon shadows were as deep as they ever were, but he had no trouble marking his sire's expression or noting that his sire had immediately taken note of Olivia and her hand in his. She tugged, but he only smiled briefly.

"All will be well," he promised. "Permit me to introduce you to my father."

"I'll probably recognize him."

"Very likely, damn him to hell."

He continued on with her across the courtyard until they were standing a pair of steps away from the man who had not only sired him, but taught him all he knew about being honorable and courageous. The absolute improbability of standing there facing his Future-born father wearing medieval clothing whilst he himself was marching through the past in a pair of Zachary Smith's most comfortable jeans was almost more than he could bear.

He was beginning to understand why his uncle Robin shook his head so often.

He made his father a low bow, then straightened and looked at him gravely. "Father, if I might present my lady, Olivia Drummond," he said quietly in Future English. "Olivia, my father, Jackson of Raventhorpe."

His father, unsurprisingly, didn't bat an eye. He only continued down the stairs and reached for Olivia's hand to hold it between both his own, just as he would have done with his own daughters. He smiled easily. "You're very welcome here, Olivia. I hope the journey was pleasant?"

"Very, my lord," she said weakly.

"I also assume my son has been chivalrous?" the good lord of the hall continued in his own modern English.

"Always, my lord."

Jackson found himself the recipient of a look of approval, so perhaps a discussion of the beauties of comporting himself as a proper knight wouldn't be necessary that night.

"We'll talk in my solar after we find more discreet clothes for the two of you. We'll also need to be careful about what we speak in front of others."

"Would Gaelic work?" Olivia asked.

Jackson looked at his uncle and sighed. Robin only shrugged and leaned his elbow on Thad's shoulder, looking as if he might be settling in for a long evening of more things to shake his head over. He himself was the recipient of a brief embrace from his father, a quick smile, then the opportunity to watch his sire offer Olivia his arm and lead her up the stairs and into the great hall.

He followed after them and found himself suddenly assailed by the feeling he'd had the first time he'd walked into the Artane of the Future, that of being torn in two from knowing he was in the right place but the wrong time. It was foolishness, of course, so he shrugged it off without hesitation. He was back in his proper sphere, so there was no reason for anything but relief over being home.

He also refused to break down and weep like a bairn at the sight of his mother rushing across the hall toward him with tears streaming down her face.

"I am well, Mama," he said, holding her tightly for a moment or two, then submitting to her checking him over for injuries just as she'd done after every skirmish he'd been involved in. He smiled. "Safe and whole."

Amanda of Raventhorpe dabbed at her eyes with her sleeve, put her shoulders back, then turned to look at Olivia. Jackson watched her closely, not quite sure how to proceed. He had spent his share of time in the company of beautiful women in various places, true, but he had never introduced any of them formally to his parents. He took a deep breath and reached for Olivia's hand to pull her over to stand next to him.

"Mother, may I present Olivia Grace Drummond," he said politely. "Olivia, my mother, Amanda of Raventhorpe."

He realized he'd said it in French, so he tried again in Gaelic. His mother only smiled briefly at him before she turned back to Olivia.

"I'm Amanda," she said in modern English. "Welcome to our home, Olivia. I'm so happy you've come."

"Thank you, Lady Amanda," Olivia said with a slight curtsey.

Jackson watched his mother laugh a little, then put her arms around Olivia and hug her briefly.

"You're very sweet," she said, "but no deference needed. Let's find you something more comfortable to wear, shall we? And perhaps we should speak Gaelic before others, though you and I can converse in your tongue in private as much as you like."

"Whatever you think best, Lady Amanda," Olivia said faintly.

Jackson watched his mother link arms with his lady and walk off with her. Olivia only glanced briefly over her shoulder at him, but he imagined his sigh of resignation said it all. He smiled encouragingly at her until she disappeared with his mother into the stairwell, then took a moment to wonder how it was he'd been so oblivious to what had been going on inside his own family. His mother's command of a language that would be spoken hundreds of years in the future was nothing short of startling.

He looked around himself to see what else might leave him unbalanced only to find his father, his uncle, and his younger brother all watching him as if they'd never seen him before.

"What?" he demanded.

His father only smiled faintly. "Just watching you think."

Jackson sent his father a look of promise the man couldn't have helped but understand, then scowled. "I believe I shall change my clothing as well."

"Where's your sword, lad?" Robin asked.

I left it at your daughter's hall so I could go visit your second son was rolling around in his empty head long enough that he managed not to say it before it occurred to him that perhaps Robin had no idea what would happen to Kendrick in a pair of years. After all, why would he?

It was in his future.

"I lost it," he said, because that was the simplest explanation. "I'll find another on the morrow."

"I imagine you will," Robin said easily. "Jake, what's for supper? I'm famished."

Jackson left them to it and made his way to his bedchamber. Surely there was something in his trunk that might be clean.

He was somewhat unsurprised to find his three younger siblings waiting outside the door. He didn't need to look behind him for Thad, because his younger brother was pushing him inside and shutting the door behind him. Jackson opened his mouth to demand some privacy only to realize that no one was interested in anything he had to say.

His sisters swarmed him as if he'd been a wagon full of desserts and they children with an invitation to make free with the goods.

"Did you bring chocolate?" one of his sisters asked, frisking him expertly.

He suspected he should have stuffed his pockets with something besides his phone which was now in the possession of a sister who glanced at him, then turned it on as if she'd been doing it the whole of her life.

He looked at her in astonishment for a moment or two, then reached out and relieved her of something she shouldn't have been fussing with.

"I'll answer questions tomorrow," he said, herding them out of his bedchamber. "Do not vex Olivia or I'll answer nothing."

"But—"

He shut the door, bolted it, then quickly exchanged his clothes for fashions appropriate to the current year. He locked everything including his phone in his trunk, then turned to find his brother leaning back against his door. Obviously, there was no hope of an easy escape quite yet.

"Well?" he asked, resigning himself to his fate. "Are you going to ask?"

Thad smiled. "Since you don't have a sword, I suppose I might manage a few impertinent questions."

"I have my knives."

"There is that. Are you going to tell me everything anyway?"

Jackson wondered if he might look as ill as he felt. "I'm not sure I can bring myself to."

"She's very lovely—"

"And, again, mine."

Thad lifted an eyebrow. "Does she think she's yours?"

Jackson was halfway across his bedchamber with his hands outstretched before he realized his brother was teasing him. He rubbed his hands over his arms.

"Chilly today."

Thad only smiled. "Jack, you need a very long run with your beloved younger brother for company."

"I'm not sure I have the time," Jackson said, realizing as the words were out just how bleak they sounded. "There is a situation in Olivia's day that I must sort to free her from perils she didn't create."

"And you're going to return to do so?"

Jackson nodded slowly. "I must."

"Then you will, and you'll see it put to rights," Thad said without hesitation. "Tell me of it or not, as it suits you. But I am curious about Zachary Smith and Mary. Did that end well?"

"It did, though they apparently married two years ago in the Future, if you can fathom that. They now have a girl child named Anne."

"Weird," Thad said uneasily.

Jackson looked at his brother, then bowed his head and laughed. "Very," he agreed, then he pushed his brother out of the way. "Let's go find a hot fire. I'll tell you whatever you want to know tomorrow. I don't want to leave Olivia alone now, though I'm sure Mother will care for her well."

"And if not, I will happily take on the task myself."

Jackson swore at his brother on principle alone, then left the chamber before he left his brother unable to walk down the stairs.

Half an hour later, he was standing in the great hall with his back to the fire, torn between worrying about his lady and wondering when supper might be forthcoming.

He was, in truth, a simple man.

He heard the sound of light laughter coming from within the stairwell before he saw the flash of a gown. He supposed he should have been accustomed to the beauty of his mother and younger sisters, for he'd seen them dressed in their normal, era-appropriate clothing for the whole of his life.

What he hadn't expected was to be rendered mute by the sight of Mistress Olivia Drummond as a medieval noblewoman.

"He's truly in trouble now."

"Can you blame him?"

Jackson looked at his father and uncle standing next to him and glared them into silence. Well, he glared at them. They only looked at him dismissively and elbowed their collective way past him to welcome Olivia into their midst.

If he had been a lad to get a little maudlin, he would have indulged at that moment. He watched his family draw Olivia into their circle, listened to his uncle announce loudly enough for any inquisitive servant to hear that he'd been fortunate enough to encounter Lady Olivia as she'd been abandoned by her retinue whilst traveling along the border. Her courage and bravery in outmaneuvering ruffians and sundry had been the stuff of legends.

Jackson thought he might have to offer to polish his uncle's boots for quite some time to come in return for that tale.

He managed to get himself next to his lady without having to flatten any relatives, which he considered a success, then tucked her hand into the crook of his elbow and retreated with her back over to the fire where at least the illusion of privacy was possible.

"I didn't catch any of that," she whispered. "Did I just become medieval nobility?"

Jackson smiled, partly because she looked almost as thrilled over that prospect as she had a visit to the armory at Artane and partly because her hands were icy cold yet she gave no outward sign of being afraid.

"Aye, you did, Lady Olivia," he agreed with a smile. "And apparently you eluded thugs along the border after your guardsmen were vanquished and arrived here unscathed and unruffled."

"It sounds like I'm pretty impressive."

"I might be biased," he admitted, "but I think so."

She looked up at him and attempted a smile. "I don't feel formidable," she said. "Maybe I shouldn't have come."

He took her hand and kissed the back of it. "I find, my lady, that any moment I have you in my poor life is a lovely one, no matter the year, so I'm very glad you came."

She looked at him as if she'd never seen him before.

He attempted a scowl, but her expression caught him too tightly about the heart to manage it. "Have I been so uncharming to this point?"

"You haven't. I'm just not sure what to do here."

"Stay close to me at all times."

She took a deep breath. "Okay."

"Very close."

She smiled. "All right."

"Not torture?"

She squeezed his hand. "It wasn't torture any of the other times, Jackson. I was just messing with you."

He would have given that the response it deserved, but they were called to table. He was happy to find himself sitting next to Olivia, though less pleased that his brother was on her far side. At least he and Olivia would be sharing a trencher which would definitely save Thad a lengthy stay in the lists on the morrow.

He could scarce believe he was home where that would take up his morning.

He remembered little about supper save that 'twas spectacular, as usual. He did find himself eventually simply sitting back in his chair, nursing his wine, and watching his lady as she made polite conversation in Gaelic with his brother. She glanced at him occasionally and smiled each time, which he found promising. She finally leaned close.

"You should stop looking at me that way," she whispered.

"Which way is that? As if you were a pint of double-chocolate ice cream with ribbons of fudge running through it?"

She smiled a bit more easily than before. "Flirting again, my lord?"

"Trying." He smiled. "I'll attempt the same in Gaelic at some point."

"That might be interesting."

He pursed his lips. "Were you going to tell me eventually?"

"Eventually, if you flipped it out of me."

He reached around her and flicked his brother between the eyes, then smiled at his lady. "We'll take a walk on the beach tomorrow and you can give me the entire tale. I'm certain the day will be lovely."

She took a deep breath, then nodded.

He puzzled over her reaction to that through the rest of supper, then a bit more whilst his family gathered in their usual fashion in his father's solar. He found himself surprisingly grateful at their willingness to speak Gaelic in deference to his lady and more than a bit amused by how his younger siblings were watching her if they'd never seen anything so marvelous.

Except Thad, who was going to die as soon as he could stir himself to take the wee fool out to the lists and enlighten him as to the meaning of *mine.*

"All children to bed," his sire announced at one point. "Except Jackson, of course."

"When did Jack become an adult?" Thad asked in surprise.

Jackson watched his father send Thad that same sort of level stare that Jackson had seen coming his way more than once. Thad broke first, which wasn't a surprise.

"My apologies, Father," he said humbly. He stood and made Olivia a bow. "My apologies, Lady Olivia. Should you require an escort on the morrow, please consider me your servant."

Jackson shot his brother a look of warning as he ushered their younger sisters out the door, but he suspected it would go unheeded. The door shut and his father rubbed his hands together.

"We probably didn't need to do that," Jackson IV said with a smile, "but I like to remind them who's boss. So, Olivia, tell us about yourself."

Jackson listened to his father, mother, and uncle speak in modern English and wondered if his soul would split in twain in truth right there in his father's solar, a place where he had almost never considered that things might be different from what they appeared to be.

Almost.

"Where did you two meet?" his mother asked with a smile.

"Jackson became part of a play where I was backstage sewing up costumes—"

"Very skillfully, of course," Jackson interjected.

Olivia smiled briefly, then turned back to his mother. "He's being kind because I stuck him with more little pins than I want to admit to. He very chivalrously guarded my door that night, then we were invited to stay at Artane for a day or two before I went to London."

"Is Stephen keeping the place from crumbling to the ground?" Robin asked politely.

Jackson put his hand over his eyes because he simply couldn't shake his head any longer. He was half-tempted to simply laugh, but he wasn't sure he would be able to stop. He finally managed to look at his uncle.

"Your hall still stands," Jackson assured him, "and I did all within my power to properly intimidate your grandson. His swordplay could use a bit of work, but there was only so much I could do in a pair of days."

Robin smiled, then turned back to Olivia. "I may have to attend to it myself at some point, but I hope he housed you well. Can I assume my nephew escorted you to that nest of ruffians in the south?"

Jackson leaned back in his chair and tried not to smile as Olivia related the details about their journey and the reason for it. He did shift slightly to watch his father as Olivia supplied the name of Mistress Penelope's shop.

"Dreams of Greenland?" Jake echoed. "What an interesting name."

"It was previously called Kilchurn, Ltd.," Jackson said, because he couldn't help himself.

His father looked to be fighting a smile. "Was it?"

"Damned skippy, it was," Jackson muttered.

Jackson watched his father sigh lightly. "Did Jackson come along with you to the shop?"

Olivia nodded.

"What did Pen do when she saw him?"

"She fainted."

"Why am I starting to get the impression that this might not be a random visit?"

Jackson looked at his father. "Because you, my lord, have some 'splaining to do."

His father bowed his head and laughed a little, then he smiled at Olivia. "He hasn't stabbed me in my own solar yet, so there's that. Jack, did you bring your phone?"

He looked at his father evenly. "Are my ears deceiving me?"

"They aren't, but still let me see your phone. You didn't follow any baseball while you were there, did you?"

"Father, do we still have lists?"

"Aye, son, we do."

"I believe we should make a visit first thing."

His sire only winked at him, then turned back to the conversation at hand.

Jackson accepted a bit more wine in his cup courtesy of his uncle, then sat back and simply watched as a very pleasant visit unfolded in his sire's solar between people he loved.

There. He'd admitted it.

The saints pity him, he just wasn't sure what he was going to do about it.

He caught the quick smile his mother sent him and hoped he

wouldn't unman himself by displaying any of those maudlin feelings he was fighting.

Olivia seemed to grow more comfortable as the conversation continued, which he found encouraging. If she sent him the occasional look of disbelief, he could scarce blame her. If their places had been reversed, he would have been favoring her with just such looks, he was certain.

"Olivia, love, you look weary," his mother said finally. "Let Jackson see you to your chamber, then we'll pass the day together tomorrow."

"Thank you, Lady Amanda," Olivia said with a smile.

Jackson rose, bid his family goodnight whilst Olivia did the same, then took his lady by the hand and led her from the solar. He walked with her up the stairs and to the chamber he was certain she would have been offered. He inspected it for rogue siblings, then stepped back into the passageway and smiled.

"All safe."

She looked at him. "I don't suppose you can sleep just inside my doorway, can you?"

"If I tried, my father would slay me, then my mother would dig up my sorry self and do me in a second time," he said honestly, "though I would otherwise, certainly. I would tell you to send me a text missive if you become uneasy, but I don't suppose our mobiles will work here, will they?"

"They won't, and I'm guessing you should save your battery anyway for your father."

He leaned against the doorway and smiled. "I keep finding myself in the midst of very strange conversations."

She smiled, then her smile faded. "I don't know how you managed it all so well."

"I had a Future gel to impress. That sort of thing inspires all manner of heroic behavior." He supposed reaching out and casually lacing his fingers with hers could have been considered that sort of thing as well. "I will need to visit the lists in the morning, but I will send someone to watch over you until I can be there myself."

She nodded, then let go of his hand and put her arms around his waist. He gathered her close and rested his cheek against her hair.

"One day at a time?" she asked quietly.

"One lovely day at a time," he agreed, just as quietly.

She pulled away, smiled at him, then leaned up and kissed him quickly. "See you tomorrow."

"Wait—"

She smiled and shut the door.

"But our thumb war," he protested.

She opened the door and held out her hand. "Make it quick."

He didn't win, but he had another quick kiss and a smile for his trouble, so he supposed his loss hadn't been great. He waited until she'd shut her door and he'd heard the bolt slide home before he smiled to himself, then retreated to the great hall. There was no sense in not having a final look about before he sought his own repose.

He stepped down the last step to the floor, then stopped abruptly. His parents were standing by the fire, wrapped in each other's arms. It wasn't the first time he'd walked in on them embracing—though he'd fortunately had the good sense to knock and thereby avoid anything more embarrassing—but it was the first time he'd simply stopped dead in his tracks and had the scene pierce him through the heart.

He wanted that.

And he wanted that with Olivia Grace Drummond.

Let's push him into the arms of a beautiful woman …

By the very saints of heaven, had he wished himself into the Future for a marriage to be arranged … for himself?

He took a deep breath and set that aside to think about when he wasn't feeling so close to shedding a manly tear or two. Events would sort themselves as they needed to, with perhaps a bit of a push from him.

However and whenever that might be.

TWENTY-THREE

OLIVIA STOOD AT THE WINDOW of her medieval—her *extremely* medieval—guest room and looked out over the ocean to find it full of the same sort of water she was accustomed to seeing. She probably wouldn't have thought anything had happened to her if she hadn't been standing in a fully functional castle after a rather rustic toilette while freezing in a particularly medieval sort of way.

And the saints preserve her, it was probably not quite nine.

She'd already been awake before the light tap on her door had almost sent her clinging to the gorgeous wooden canopy over her bed. Since it hadn't been the sort of pounding she was sure was used by thugs, she'd crawled out of bed and opened the door to find a teenager who identified herself as a servant in a charming mixture of medieval French and what apparently was also medieval Gaelic.

Warm water for washing up had been provided as well as more clothes from fabrics her aunt would have lost her mind over. She had already stashed her modern gear in Jackson's dad's solar the night before, so she'd immersed herself in the 1258 experience and gone with the flow.

That had been half an hour ago. She'd spent the subsequent thirty minutes overthinking her entire life, especially the dating part of her current life. That had led to angsting over things she was just sure wouldn't make any difference in the end, though there was one thing in particular she couldn't get past.

Just when had she lost her mind over a guy who was not just a lot out of her league but centuries out of her time zone?

She stepped away from the window, closed the shutters, then turned to face the door. The best thing she could do was take Jackson's suggestion about putting difficult things on hold for a bit and just enjoy a little down time in medieval England.

She opened the door to find the youngest Kilchurn sister leaning against the far wall, accompanied by what looked to be a guardsman. She ventured out into the passageway and faced an adorable medieval miss who she guesstimated might be about ten years old, then put on her most polite smile.

"Good morning," she said carefully in Gaelic, "I'm—"

"Olivia, and I'm Penelope," the girl said, popping across the hallway and sidling up to her. "You might have forgotten our names, so I'm reminding you. Why don't you speak French? Are you from England? France? Somewhere else entirely?"

"Pen," the guardsman said sternly.

Olivia realized that she wasn't looking at a twenty-something man, she was looking at a woman of about that same age who was quite possibly related to the younger sister who had abandoned Gaelic in favor of the language *du jour*. She spared a brief wish that she'd tried to learn more of it the twenty-four hours—give or take a few centuries—since she'd realized it was something Jackson could teach her.

"Are you going to faint?"

Olivia looked at the older sister in surprise. The sound of perfect modern English coming from a girl who was obviously from a far different time was extremely odd. "Ah—"

"This is a variant of the peasant's tongue that my sire speaks in private," the girl said easily. "Or so 'tis rumored."

Olivia just bet it was.

"I'm Gwendolyn," the girl said, holding out her hand. "We should perhaps speak Scots so we don't draw undue attention to ourselves."

Penelope cut in front of her sister. "Do you care to go watch my brother in the lists, Olivia? Do you have a blade?"

"Not at the moment," Olivia began, then realized her input might not be necessary.

"I'm very fond of swords, but my family continues to tell me I'm too young to know my own mind. That's annoying, don't you agree? I can find you a blade, if you like. Let us do so after we watch Jackson decimate the garrison. "

Olivia exchanged a look with Jackson's other sister who was dressed not at all like a medieval lady and had the feeling Penelope wasn't the only one who knew where swords were to be found.

"Pen, you know that Father doesn't want you in the armory," Gwendolyn said with a warning look.

"But you visit it often."

"Aye, but I am almost ten years older than you are, and I have earned the right to do so."

"I will be that old someday."

"I'm quite certain you will."

Olivia was equally certain that the present moment was not the first time those two had had the current conversation, but she didn't want to offer an opinion. She pulled her door shut behind her, then walked with Jackson's sisters down to the great hall.

It was only marginally warmer than her bedroom had been, but that was soon taken care of by something hot to drink and a warm cloak that had been left for her by Jackson. She acquired a third sister along the way, then found herself heading out to the lists as if she'd never done anything else with her mornings.

That training ground lay inside walls that she was absolutely certain hadn't survived the centuries. She had a vague memory of having seen the archway she walked under to get to them walled up in the twenty-first century, but thought it might be wise not to speculate. The area beyond it was far larger than she would have suspected and it was definitely filled with medieval guys working away at their day jobs.

She saw Jackson immediately, though he and his uncle Robin were hard to miss. She didn't argue when Penelope took her hand because that gave her the chance to continue to watch the action without having to watch where she was going. She sat when invited, found herself joined by medieval misses who were obviously accustomed to huddling together for warmth, then took a deep breath and allowed herself to watch the show.

The first thing she realized was that Jackson had been toying with Zachary Smith, though Mary's husband was absolutely no slouch in the defense department.

"Jackson is the only one who gives my uncle any decent sport save his second son Kendrick," Penelope whispered.

Olivia made a noise of agreement, happy to leave Kendrick safely tucked in 2008. She was also beginning to wonder how it was she had so badly misjudged what Jackson Alexander Kilchurn the Fifth was able to do with steel.

"I have asked my uncle repeatedly to train me."

Olivia looked at Penelope in surprise. "Have you?"

"Repeatedly," Gwendolyn said with a long-suffering sigh.

Olivia smiled at Jackson's youngest sister. "What did he say?"

"He says he will when I can rid him of his sword on the field."

"And have you?"

"Not yet," she admitted, "but I shall."

Olivia had the feeling it was just a matter of time. She was half afraid to ask Gwendolyn anything, but she could see the hilts of knives sticking up from her boots, so maybe the question wouldn't be unwelcome.

"Would it be impolite to inquire about you?" she asked.

Gwendolyn lifted one of her eyebrows. "Once."

"What happened then?"

"He had a sword made for me," Gwendolyn said solemnly. "Five years ago."

"I have time," Penelope put in. "Ginny says she doesn't want one, though."

"I never said that," the last sister said. "I said I have other things to attend to at the moment before I turn my mind to steel."

Olivia looked around Penelope to find the elusive last sister there. She looked to be somewhere in age between Gwendolyn and Penelope, but that was just a guess. That sister realized she was being observed, then smiled and held out her hand.

"Eugenie of Raventhorpe," she said politely. "Forgive me for not introducing myself sooner."

Olivia was saved from choking only because she was already having a sort of out-of-body morning, so hearing that name didn't faze her. She considered, then mentally shook her head. Obviously that sister couldn't be the same Victorian miss she was acquainted with, though she was tempted to tell Penelope that there would apparently be a long line of Kilchurn women who definitely *had* gotten what they wanted when it came to swords.

She listened to Penelope and Eugenie with half an ear as she watched what was going on in front of her and came to a few conclusions about it. The truth was, if she'd seen Robin of Artane coming at her with a sword, she would have tossed in that towel she'd left in Seakirk's courtyard and bolted for the hills.

She would have fainted if Jackson had been doing the same.

She leaned closer to Gwendolyn. "Is Jackson showing off?"

"Nay, I suspect he fears to upset your humors, so he is much less ferocious than he might otherwise be." She looked at her assessingly. "You aren't overwhelmed, are you?"

Olivia decided abruptly that discussing her potentially lustful—er, platonic and entirely casual feelings for the girl's eldest brother was probably not appropriate medieval-lists chitchat, so she shook her head and hoped that would be answer enough.

Penelope reached over and patted her hand. "It's all right," she whispered. "You might watch him all you like."

Olivia smiled at Jackson's youngest sister, then supposed there was no reason not to give the man a polite gander since she was already there and so was he.

He was taller than his uncle by a couple of inches, but that height seemed to run in the family. She realized with a start that he was wearing chain mail, though how she had missed that she didn't know. For all she knew, he was afraid Lord Robin would stab him. His uncle had to be mid-fifties, but he moved like a man half his age and he was absolutely merciless.

Robin did smile occasionally, though, and laughed once or twice at something Jackson's father said to him from where he stood just outside the circle of crazy. She wished she'd gotten those swear words out of Genevieve de Piaget because she had the feeling they were being used liberally.

Jackson seemed to ignore anything being said, but he was single-minded like that. She wondered how she had ever thought him to be anything but what he was: fearless, skilled, and so damned beautiful she could hardly look at him.

She glanced at his sisters to find them all watching her speculatively.

"Do you like him?" Eugenie asked.

Olivia decided it was probably too late to deny anything, so she simply nodded.

"A great deal?" Penelope asked breathlessly.

Olivia took a deep breath, then nodded to that as well.

Gwendolyn elbowed her. "Ah, but look you now how my uncle now begins to fight with his left, which perhaps makes him a demon but no one would say as much to his face. This change allows Jack to finish him decisively, though my brother has bested him several times in the past to much acclaim. This is for your benefit, I daresay, that you might see how well he fights. Are you impressed?"

Olivia swallowed with difficulty. "I was impressed before, actually."

Gwendolyn smiled, then rubbed her hands together suddenly and blew on them before she flexed her fingers. "They're finished. Is my hair hidden well enough under my cap, gels?"

Olivia watched Jackson's youngest sisters tuck and smooth and pronounce their sister fit for the lists, then Gwendolyn stood, made them a quick bow, then walked out onto the field. Robin only nodded briskly at her.

Olivia leaned close to Penelope. "Is she going to fight *him* now?"

"That is the bargain he made with her," Penelope said with a shrug. "He will not break his word, which is why I must go see to my swordplay. Ginny, will you help me?"

"I'm working on my manuscript—"

"A quarter hour?" Penelope asked. She clasped her hands together and dropped to her knees right there in the dirt. "Please?"

Eugenie sighed. "Very well. Let's greet Jackson, see Olivia safely back to the hall, then we'll go see what Father has hidden away in the armory."

Olivia watched Jackson make his uncle a low bow which she supposed passed for a high-five in the current day, then turn and walk over to where she was trying to recover from what she'd just watched. He stopped in front of her and made her a similar bow.

"We're going to the armory," Penelope said brightly before he could speak. "Olivia might like to come along."

"The saints preserve me," he blurted out.

Olivia would have glared at him, but damn him if he didn't wink at her. He gingerly took her hand and bowed low over it, then straightened and looked at her.

"Leave the sharp things alone."

"You're bossy."

"But she thinks you're fairly perfect," Eugenie said helpfully. "She didn't say as much, but I could tell."

Olivia looked at Jackson and shrugged. There was no point in denying it.

"We'll continue this intriguing conversation in a bit," Jackson said with a faint smile. "Girls, keep her safe for me. I will make myself presentable and return quickly."

Olivia watched him go, then turned to find herself being observed by the remaining two sisters.

"Are you going to wed him?" Penelope asked, looking at her closely.

She blushed. "Oh, I don't think he—"

"Oh, I think he does," Eugenie said mildly. "Have you ever seen him smile at a woman before, Pen?"

Penelope shook her head, her eyes very wide.

Eugenie lifted what Olivia realized was a feather into the air as if it had been a sword. "Onward, ladies, to blades and then something to drink. Then I must make note of what I've witnessed here. 'Twas rather romantic, I daresay."

Olivia was saved from speculating on Eugenie's observations by finding herself swept up in the energy of two girls with mischief on their minds. She made a quick vow to keep her hands away from anything sharp and walked with Jackson's youngest sisters across the lists.

An hour later, she was strolling along a small stretch of beach to the south of the castle with a different Kilchurn and contemplating the utter improbability of her situation.

The hike down to the sand had been a little unnerving, but Jackson had gone first and kept her from sliding down the path. The ocean breeze was chilly in a normal, fallish sort of way, and she was bundled up in something that could have passed in a pinch for a 1950s swing coat. She was tempted to do a little beach-combing, but restrained herself on the off chance that swiping a couple of shells might upset the balance between centuries.

Then again, she was probably doing that just by being in a year when the castle up there on the bluff was in one piece and the gorgeous guy in line to inherit it was walking next to her, but she couldn't change that. Besides, Jackson's hand was warm and she still liked the way he occasionally rubbed his thumb over hers as they walked, as if she were his personal worry stone that he didn't particularly want to overstress. Maybe the balance of the world would survive for a bit longer.

She looked at him to find him watching her with a very faint smile. "What?"

"I'm watching you think. Actually, I might be just watching you, but I didn't want to sound creepy."

She couldn't help a smile of her own. "Where did you learn that word?"

"From some cousin or other," he said. "The saints only know many things will find themselves inserted where they were never meant to be. I blame a trio of my aunts for it."

"More people from the future?" she asked.

He shrugged. "I suspect so. My uncles aren't completely without sword skill, and they're tolerable to look at, so perhaps they were worth the sacrifice. They would need to be, I suppose, to inspire a woman to give up chocolate and ice cream."

The man had a very interesting relationship with desserts, but he probably knew that already. She nodded and continued to walk with him until there was no more beach, then found herself wishing for an Artane-level amount of it in front of her. There was a very long list of things they probably should have been talking about, but she couldn't make herself bring up anything that might ruin such a lovely afternoon.

Jackson bent, picked up something, then handed it to her. She looked at that perfect whelk shell, then at him.

"Do I dare keep this?"

"I don't think the world will end if you hold onto it for a bit."

She looked for somewhere to put it, then tried not to smile. "I don't seem to have any pockets."

"Now you begin to see why their use escaped my notice for so long," he said with a knowing nod. "Let me put it in what passes for them in my day, and I'll return it to you later."

She watched him put the shell in a little bag attached to his belt, then looked at him in surprise. "Wait, those coins you sold to Lord Stephen were yours," she said. "I mean, I know they were, but they really were from now."

"Ordinary coins from my purse which is useful but not nearly as useful as pockets."

"Then do you—"

"Nay, I do not."

She scowled. "How do you know what I'm about to ask?"

"You want to know if I want Richard back," he said politely, "and I do not, for he was your birthday gift. I daresay the world will also survive his taking up residence in your purse. If you want a bit more truth, I suspect our Elizabethan shilling is part of what I was paid for marrying my cousin during Elizabeth's day."

"I'm not just handing that one over," she said without hesitation. "Ill-gotten gains make it fair game."

"My Latin was excellent," he said archly, "so the gains were fairly earned. My authority to wed them might be in question, admittedly."

She smiled. "That's probably something you don't want to think about too much."

"Likely not," he agreed. "Fortunately for the happy couple, a pair of my cousins were there to put things to rights."

"You do have a lot of cousins."

"I would say I have too many, but I am rather fond of them." He shrugged. "What some of them know should likely terrify us."

She could only imagine. "Since we're on the subject of frightening people, that was very nice of your uncle to make up such a great story about me."

"You Drummonds are very fierce in battle," he agreed, "or so I understand."

"Vanquishing ruffians wherever I go apparently," she said lightly.

"Vanquishing ruffians, leaving my cousins and brother swooning," he said with a faint smile. "What will you do next?"

She smiled in return, but it cost her a bit. "I'm not sure."

He studied her for a moment or two, then took her hand. "Let us walk a bit more, shall we?"

She nodded because that seemed preferable to running away, not that she had anywhere to run to because she was hundreds of years away from her own time. Then again, her time wasn't all that great either because it was full of things she hadn't expected like revenge-crazed grandpas and time-traveling extended relatives.

If that had been the what really bothered her, it would have been enough, but that wasn't the worst of it. The truth was, it didn't matter what time she found herself in, the man she was walking with wasn't just an ordinary boy next door who might want to date her. He was a medieval lord's son, a nobleman in his own right, and she was about ready to take another stroll down the lane that led back to a very sensible, unremarkable life where he wasn't a part of it.

Damn it, anyway.

"Olivia?"

She took a deep breath, then put on a smile and looked at him. "What?"

"The plot is thickening in a way that makes me uneasy," he said, frowning slightly, "and considering how many chick flicks I have watched, I know of what I speak."

"You've only seen two."

"Which told me all I need to know. What troubles you?"

"Not a thing," she said, hoping she sounded more convinced than she felt. "I'm probably just thinking too much."

He made a non-committal noise and continued walking with her. She lasted another ten feet before she couldn't take it any longer. She wasn't quite sure what she intended to say, if anything at all, but she wasn't good at faking things for longer than a four-hour shift at her aunt's shop.

She stopped and turned to Jackson suddenly, only to realize

he'd done the same thing. She dug without much success for her best five-minutes-before-closing smile.

"You go first."

"Nay, you."

She looked up at him helplessly, but couldn't force herself to ask him for his thoughts on anything because she was fairly sure she wouldn't want to hear them. There was only one way their little non-love story could end and it wasn't going to be something fit for the quill of Miss Eugenie Kilchurn, no matter in which century she found herself—

"What do you think of chocolate?"

She blinked and realized Jackson was talking to her. "What?"

"Chocolate," he repeated. "What do you think of it?"

What she thought was that he'd probably had too much of it and it had affected his brain, but maybe that wasn't the right thing to say at the moment.

"Well, I have some in my bag," she said slowly. "That's in your dad's solar, though."

He seemed to be chewing on his words. "He doesn't usually keep that sort of thing there."

"I imagine he doesn't," she agreed.

He looked down at their fingers laced together for a moment, then at her. "Does that bother you?"

He didn't look unwell, but she was beginning to think maybe the morning in the lists had been more taxing than he wanted to let on. "Does it matter what bothers me?"

He nodded solemnly.

She was on the verge of asking him what difference that could possibly make when she glanced to her right and saw a trio of men jogging toward them. She ducked behind him without much effort because he had stepped in front of her.

At least some things were consistent, no matter the year.

"Where's your sword?" she wheezed, leaning up to look over his shoulder.

"I don't need my sword."

She suspected a worshipful glance might not be unwelcome, so she stepped around him where she could throw herself into that sort of thing with enthusiasm. He blinked, then smiled.

"Stop."

"I'm terrified."

He lifted his eyebrows briefly. "Why? You're intimidating enough."

"Well, I did take a free self-defense class with my Aunt Phyllis," she conceded. "I could poke you in the eye, then run away before you could catch me."

"Do you think so?"

She shivered. "At the moment, I don't think I could outrun Aunt Philly."

He put his arm around her shoulders and pulled her close. "Those are sons of my uncle Nicholas, so don't worry."

She let out a breath that wasn't all that steady. "More cousins?"

"I find them everywhere, like vermin. Just be forewarned that they may know more than they should."

She nodded and watched the trio of cousins that approached. She realized with a bit of a start that Jackson's sisters were following after them, so maybe there would be more plotting and scheming going on than Jackson would likely be comfortable with. The whole crew stopped a couple of feet away and made her a unified, flourishy bow.

"My cousins Connor, Samuel, and Theophilus," Jackson said, indicating each in turn. "Lads, this is my lady, Olivia Drummond."

"*Your* lady?" Connor asked, scratching his head. "I think Thad has a different opinion."

"Which won't be his opinion for very long," Gwendolyn said wisely, "if Jack has anything to say about it."

Olivia shook Connor's hand, spared a moment to wonder if every man in the family was too handsome for his own good, then watched one of the younger teenagers ease over to stand next to Jackson.

"We heard you were journeying in London, cousin."

His twin brother placed himself between her and Jackson and looked at his cousin. "'Twas a very *long* journey, was it not?"

"Started, it would seem," Jackson said with a snort, "thanks to your hands placed quite firmly in my back."

Olivia watched the twins exchange knowing glances with each other before they abandoned their cousin and turned to her with purposeful looks.

"Lady Olivia," one said, making her a low bow. "'Tis our very great honor to meet you, isn't it, Theo?"

"Aye, Sam, it is," the other said, also making her a deferential bow. "It would also be the greatest of privileges to query you about several things that intrigue us."

"Or it might not be," Jackson said, taking them both by the backs of their coats and pulling them away. "Begone, blights. Don't vex my lady."

"But crisps," Sam said. "We must know about them."

"And pizza," added Theo. "This is intelligence we are desperate to have, cousin!"

Jackson gave them a nudge toward his sisters. "I might tell you what you want to know if you go away. Olivia might be prevailed upon to do the same if you go away *now*."

Olivia watched the twins gather up Jackson's sisters and move a few feet away, but no farther. She considered, then leaned in where she could whisper but be heard over the roar of the ocean.

"You know who they remind me of?" she said from behind her hand.

"The six children of someone who married far above himself?" he murmured.

She nodded and had a quick smile in return. Jackson put his arms around her, then wrapped his cloak around her for good measure. She turned her head so she could watch his family and listen to him converse with Connor. They were speaking in French, which she didn't mind mostly because it gave her a moment to simply stand and breathe. It was odd enough to think about where she was—*when*, actually—but looking at people who actually belonged to that time was almost more strangeness than she could wrap her mind around.

"I wasn't speaking of chocolate."

She realized Jackson was talking to her. She lifted her head and looked at him. "What?"

"A few moments ago," he clarified.

She pulled back a bit so she could see his face. He looked more uncomfortable than in pain, so maybe there was something besides junk-food withdrawal going on.

"What in the world are you talking about?" she asked.

He looked at her for another moment or two, then took a deep breath. "I wanted to discover what your thoughts were on desserts. And the like. It is an important matter and I wanted to determine if you might possibly be amenable to, ah … "

He stopped talking and looked at her.

She wondered if she looked as baffled as she felt. She was still searching for something useful to say when she caught a movement out of the corner of her eye and found that Connor had come to stand next to them. He put one hand lightly on her shoulder and the other on Jackson's, then looked at Jackson seriously.

"Either ask her to stay," he said in perfect English, "or kiss her and convince her she should at least think about it. Please do one or the other soon so I can go back to the keep and find something very strong to drink."

Jackson shot his cousin a look of promise. "I'm at the beginning of my wooing and do not need your aid."

Olivia found herself rather grateful that the air was so damned cold or she would have been blushing.

"Olivia?"

She looked at Connor. "Yes?"

"He wasn't talking about chocolate."

"Thank you, Connor."

He smiled and walked away. She watched him gather up the cousins, then looked at the man who had put his arms back around her. He cleared his throat.

"I wasn't speaking of food, though you know my fondness for it." He paused. "I'm fond of several things, actually, and are you blushing?"

"I'm freezing," she said, because that was partly true.

He smiled, kissed her softly, then put his arm around her shoulders and nodded toward the keep. "Let's go warm up by the fire. I believe we might have other things to discuss after you're not freezing and I'm not an idiot."

She smiled to herself as she walked with him back up the beach. He hadn't been talking about food? She was fairly sure there weren't too many moments in Jackson Kilchurn's life when he wasn't thinking about food.

Though apparently she'd just experienced one of those.

She closed her eyes briefly and let that thought go. Jackson wouldn't ask her to stay because there wasn't any way that she could, no matter how many ruffians she had apparently vanquished just over the border. Drummonds were, as any of her ancestors could probably have verified, extremely fierce and possibly usefully wary in battle. She suspected, however, that they weren't time travelers.

But as she walked back up the hill with a medieval lord, she wondered if it might be time for that to change.

She'd come to England wanting just a fresh start.

She just hadn't realized how fresh a start that might possibly entail.

Twenty-Four

Jackson walked down the passageway, then jogged down the stairs to the great hall, his borrowed sword in his hand and his usual knives stuck down the sides of his boots. He'd brought his cloak as well, because one never knew when a brief foray into the lists or perhaps a lengthy walk on the shore might be called for.

His knightly duties had been attended to that morning, and he'd even managed a quick visit to the kitchens before retreating to his chamber to prepare for the day. He didn't hold out any hope that he would have located his good sense in his trunk, because that had apparently deserted him on the shore the day before.

He had queried his lady about foodstuffs.

He had already been thoroughly mocked for it in the lists by not only his brother, but his cousins who should have known better. He vowed to repay them after he had found Olivia and attempted speech with her that didn't include Future snacks.

He strode out into the hall to find a collection of family members standing in front of the hearth, keeping warm. The sight caught him about the heart so fiercely that he came close to stumbling. He was spared that indignity by his youngest sister running across the hall to throw her arms around him.

"Uncle Robin is going to take us to the armory!"

Not if he had anything to say about it. He took Penelope by the hand, almost surprised she still allowed it, and pulled her with him to go investigate whatever madness had been combined whilst he'd been detained by his grooming.

He parted the group of cousins gathered there and found that his lady was dressed in hose and a tunic and flanked by his uncle and Gwendolyn. The twins were standing to one side, looking like trouble, and Eugenie was circling them all like a carrion bird.

Keeping his family safe was like herding felines, in truth.

He exchanged a look with Connor, one they'd perfected over the years. It was a look full of resignation and, it had to be said, a decent amount of fondness for those they had charge of. If Connor smiled at him as if he expected Jackson himself to burst into maudlin sniffles at any moment, well, the man could be repaid in the lists later.

"We're off to make trouble," Sam said, his eyes bright with excitement.

"Nay," Gwendolyn corrected, "we're off to show Olivia the armory, as she's very fond of steel. You, Samuel, will not be making any trouble."

"I'll guard you out in the lists, Olivia," Penelope said, rushing over to push Theo out of the way and take Olivia's hand. "I'm young, but very useful in this—Eugenie, don't poke me with your quill again!"

Jackson realized immediately that his opinion on anything was not going to be required. Olivia smiled at him happily before she was swept up and carried off in a flurry of sisters and cousins. Thad, at least, had the good sense to make him a low bow, then nod briskly before he strode after that gaggle of troublemakers.

"We'll see if she has a good eye for a blade."

Jackson looked at his uncle who was watching him with a faint smile. "Please keep her safe."

"I would be offended," Robin said mildly, "if I wouldn't feel the same way about entrusting my love to another man. I suspect, nephew, that you might wish never to vex her after what I'll teach her this morning."

"She will enjoy it all, I'm sure," Jackson managed.

His uncle only smiled and walked away. Jackson took a moment to warm his hands by the fire, then made his way across the hall and out the door. He would have preferred to have kept watch over his lady, but he suspected he needed to speak with his sire sooner rather than later. Fortunately for him, he found his sire standing on the front stoop, watching the goings on inside his keep with a faint smile.

He took the opportunity to do the same thing. Now that he knew what to look for, he could see what his father had done to bring as much of the Future into the place as possible whilst avoiding having anyone burned at the stake for the same.

What a fine line that had to have been.

"Do you want to take a walk?"

He nodded. He had, as it happened, taken innumerable walks with his sire in countless locales, scouting for decent inns, walking through foreign towns, looking at things that interested them both. He had learned, as he'd matured, to trust his sire on those same rambling strolls with thoughts he didn't share with others. He had never been disappointed in his sire's ability to brush away the unimportant to uncover the heart of the matter.

That was likely why he'd been so unsurprised by the pieces of his sire's jewelry he'd seen in Mistress Penelope's shop. His father was a master at revealing the beauty of what lay under the surface of things, a skill he'd obviously possessed for decades.

He walked with his father down to the strand and along the water until they had gone as far as the tide would allow. Jackson IV considered the ocean for a moment or two, then looked at him.

"What answers will you have?"

Jackson hardly knew where to begin, but he was at least past patting himself purposefully for a blade to use on the man standing in front of him. He settled for the first thing that came to mind.

"Did you know about the gate below Artane?"

His father looked at him with yet another in one of his long, even stares.

Jackson smiled and shrugged. "'Tis a reasonable question."

"Did *you* know?" Jake asked mildly.

He sent his sire a pointed look of his own, had a brief laugh as his reward, then regretted having left his sword in his bedchamber.

"All right," Jake said with a smile, "so we both knew. So you don't have to ask, we aren't the only ones who do. What else do you want to know?"

"How they work," Jackson said. "I pushed that damned Zachary Smith through the doorway, yet when I saw him again a se'nnight later, two years had passed for him with Maryanne in the Future. Now five months have passed here, though I was only gone a fortnight."

"Well, don't look at me for that sort of answer," Jake said, holding up his hands. "You're already far beyond my experience with any of this. I just got lucky a couple of times with that big one near Artane."

"No passage of time you couldn't account for?"

Jake shook his head. "Fortunately not, or I would have been in trouble. You would have to find someone with more experience than I have to ask about the mechanics of it all."

"Zachary Smith?" Jackson asked grimly.

Jake smiled. "Probably, given his background. I will say that the little doorway up the hill is from all reports a bit more reliable than the one near Artane, but I'm not sure how many more trips anyone will make through either of them."

"From all reports," Jackson echoed with a snort. "I can scarce bring myself to ask who might be the source for those."

"Well, there are quite a few souls here who know things they shouldn't," Jake agreed with a smile. "I've thought about trying to cover that spot up with a boulder, but I'm not sure it would make any difference. Sam and Theo would find a way to push it off and be on their merry ways to make trouble in some other century just the same."

"They frighten me."

"They also sent you off on *your* merry way which seems to have put you in the path of a very lovely woman, so you might not want to complain too much. I'm interested to hear about your trip and how you met Olivia, if you want to give me the details."

Jackson clasped his hands behind his back and turned to walk again with his father back the way they'd come. "I hardly know where to start," he admitted, then he glanced at his father. "That I'm beginning anywhere with this makes me feel daft."

His father smiled dryly. "I understand, believe me, but go ahead and give me the whole story."

Jackson set aside his own questions and settled for what details he thought his sire might find interesting.

"After I dashed my head against a rock," he began, "I woke in Elizabeth I's time where I disguised myself as a priest and officiated at a marriage."

His father looked at him blankly for a moment or two, then laughed. "You?"

"Trust me, I found it absurd as well," Jackson said with a sigh, "though you'll be pleased to know my negotiating skills did not fail me in the critical moment. Sam and Theo vowed to see the actual marrying put to rights."

"Well, thank heavens for—" Jake stopped and looked at him in surprise. "Wait, the twins were there? In Renaissance England?"

"Aye, but as grown men, not lads."

Jake considered, then shook his head and walked on. "Spooky."

"Very."

"You didn't ask them details?"

"I was too busy trying not to be slain after the proper priest roused himself from his drunken stupor and identified me as an impostor."

"Fair enough," Jake said with a smile. "Lucky you that they were there, then. I'm assuming you made a successful get-away."

"I did," Jackson agreed. "The lads aided me in getting to the gate which was again visible, I stepped backward into it, then it spat me out into Olivia's day." He glanced at his father. "The year 2008."

His father lifted his eyebrows briefly, but said nothing.

"From there, it is as Olivia related. I encountered her at a frolic, decided she needed her doorway guarded, then I escorted her to Artane so she could see the castle. We encountered Stephen, the current lord, then traveled to London so she could attend an interview with Penelope Cleary. You might be interested to know that Olivia is cousin-by-marriage to Derrick Cameron."

"It's a small world," Jake said, shaking his head. "Derrick helped me buy a small fortune in medieval coins."

"So said he. He was very helpful to us on our journey various places, most notably back to Wyckham where I found that Zachary Smith had become the lord of that hall."

"Did you two shake hands like gentlemen?"

"After I tried to slay him? Aye, for Maryanne's sake." He decided that perhaps 'twas best to leave Kendrick safely where he was, though it made him slightly uncomfortable not to give his sire the entire tale.

"What then?"

He took a deep breath. "I spoke to your lawyer, Alexander, who suggested that you would know best how to see to your sire. I had intended to leave Olivia in safety at Artane whilst I returned here to speak with you, but we were waylaid."

"By whom?"

Jackson supposed there was no reason not to be truthful in that, at least. "I fear they were your father's men. They've been watching your shop apparently for the past three years there."

Jake blew out his breath, then nodded. "We'll discuss that in a minute. Keep going with your trip here for now. You were waylaid, then what?"

"I rang Zachary who gave us the very useful suggestion to use the gate up the way, so we made use of it in great haste. I honestly hadn't intended to bring Olivia with me—Derrick's men were there and could have taken her to Artane—but I couldn't leave her behind."

"I imagine you didn't want to leave her behind," Jake said with a smile. "She's very lovely—and courageous. Traveling through time is not easy."

Jackson nodded and spared a brief wish for a larger stretch of ocean to pace along. Then again, he suspected he could have walked with his father to London and back and still not have had enough time for having all the answers he wanted. They would just have to pace back and forth until the tide drove them back up the bluff.

He looked at his father. "Speaking of traveling through time, my lord, now that my adventures are properly divulged, perhaps there are things you would care to admit?"

Jake laughed a little uncomfortably. "Yes, well, I suppose it's past time you knew everything. Where do you want me to start?"

"Where were you born?"

"In Manhattan," he said, "which is in New York—"

Jackson stopped still and looked at his father in astonishment. "You're a Yank?"

Jake slid him a look. "And so, my son, are you—half, at least—so you'd better memorize the national anthem to make your girlfriend feel more comfortable."

Jackson decided that if he started shaking his head so early in the conversation, he would never stop, so he settled for a nod and walked on.

"It was a fairly unremarkable upbringing in America until I annoyed my father too much at thirteen and he sent me to boarding school here in England. That's a bit like going off to squire," he clarified, "only no real swords are involved."

"What a terrible thought," Jackson managed.

"Well, there were plenty of other weapons available," Jake said with a shrug, "but I suspect you would have been bored stiff. I hadn't really intended to stay here, but I found I liked driving on the wrong side of the road and living with all the history. One of my father's companies was based in London so I had more than enough opportunities to run into my family."

"I met your sister in London," Jackson ventured.

"What did she say when she saw you?"

"She accused me of being your father's bastard son, then of trying to steal her inheritance. We encountered her after I'd sent Mistress Penelope into a faint, so it was the perfect end to a rather uncomfortable morning." He paused. "Father, I think you married into a better family."

Jake laughed briefly. "That's truer than you know. I hope Peggy wasn't there to harass Penelope."

"I've no idea why she'd come, and Mistress Penelope said nothing when we met her the following day. Perhaps she was simply there to make certain that you hadn't returned." He paused, then looked at his father. "There are many of your pieces still in the shop."

"I would have thought Pen would have sold them," Jake said lightly. "Maybe not."

"They were spectacular."

His sire only smiled. "No, I will not give you an extra share of my gold for that, but I am deeply flattered that you think so. I don't suppose you met your uncles, did you?"

Jackson nodded. "I didn't."

"Well, you have three of them, but you didn't miss anything there. I wish I had better news about any of it, but it is what it is. I'm very grateful for the family I have here."

Jackson nodded and continued to walk. He glanced at his father, but the man only seemed to be waiting for him to speak. He supposed if he were going to have answers, he might as well have as many as he wanted.

"How exactly did you come, ah … "

"To medieval England?" Jake finished. "Well, it wasn't planned, if that's what you're asking. I had actually been on my way to deliver something for my father to Artane and some terrible weather left me seeking shelter at Seakirk."

"And you met Seakirk's lord?" Jackson asked carefully.

Jake snorted. "Of course, and no, I haven't said anything to anyone, not even your mother. I will tell Robin at the right time so he doesn't pull the keep down around Matilda's ears."

Jackson smiled in spite of himself. "Did Kendrick ever tell you what had happened to you, ah, in your future ... "

"Which was in his past?" Jake asked. "What do you think?"

"I think there's a reason you are so ferocious with him in the lists."

"There is," Jackson agreed. "And to answer your question properly, no, he didn't say anything to me about *my* future. I'm assuming he didn't say anything to you, either."

"He didn't." Jackson glanced at his father. "I didn't ask, actually."

"That's also wise," Jake said carefully. "There's something to be said for knowing how and when to keep your mouth shut."

Jackson couldn't deny that. His father and uncles were, to a man, absolute vaults. Then again, he wasn't much for mindless chatter, either, so perhaps it ran in the family.

"I should clarify that on my first stay at Seakirk, I didn't meet Kendrick," Jake continued. "Worthington was good enough to give me a bed for the night while Kendrick and Genevieve were away. I set off in the morning, rolled my very lovely and expensive Jag, and wound up in Robin's solar." He paused. "I'll draw the Jaguar for you, if you like."

Jackson nodded. "I would. And then?"

Jake shrugged. "I saw your mother, decided that maybe I could bluff my way past your grandfather Rhys—"

"Father," he warned.

Jake smiled. "All right, I spent many, *many* hours with anyone who would train me so I might possibly stand against my future father-in-law for more than five minutes, then I used the gate near Artane to go back to the future to round up my assets and buy some medieval coins. Unfortunately, I was delayed a bit thanks to my father locking me up and pumping me full of poison. I'm still a little amazed that didn't kill me, but it must have been all that clean living I'd done until then."

"No ice cream?"

"Junk food'll kill you, son."

"So will bad eel."

Jake smiled. "You're not wrong there. After I made my escape, Alex Smith helped me put some pressure on my father to give me back my gold, I got out of the Future as quickly as I could, and came back home here." He nodded. "Being with your mother was, after all, the most important part."

Jackson nodded. It was, to be sure.

"Did Alex give you any ideas about what's been happening since I left?"

Jackson shook his head. "Nothing beyond your sire's men keeping watching on your shop in London. Alex suspects your father thought you might return and make trouble."

"There are some people in the world who really don't like it when they can't control you."

"Enough to want you dead?"

"Yes." Jake shot him a look. "Just so you know, I am nothing like him."

"Father, I never would have thought anything else."

Jake smiled briefly. "Just thought it needed to be said."

Jackson stopped and looked at his father. "I cannot leave Olivia or Mistress Penelope in these straits, though, no matter how unhappy he is. Is there no point where the entire enterprise becomes too perilous for his taste?"

"I think I could dig through my memories and come up with

a few things that would send him to jail if they were revealed," Jake said carefully. "That might be enough to inspire him to behave."

"Alex did send papers with us that he thought you might find interesting. Perhaps there is something there we could use as well."

His father looked at him and shook his head. "This is not a conversation I ever thought I would be having with you."

"Father, if I had a pound coin for every time I'd thought the same thing over the past fortnight, I would be a rich man."

"Jackson, you are a rich man," Jake said dryly. "But I understand what you're getting at." He sighed deeply. "I'll look over what Alex sent and see what else comes to mind. I'll make you a list. I think if you took that to Alex and had him arrange things, my father might decide it was enough to walk away."

"And if not?"

Jake shrugged helplessly. "Short of my showing back up and dying right in front of him? I don't think anything else will stop him."

Jackson felt silence descend. He looked out over the endlessly rolling waves for a bit, then turned to his father. "That is a thought."

His father stared at him for several minutes in silence, then nodded carefully. "You look enough like me that you'd be believable. You could also change your eye color courtesy of little pieces of plastic you would wear in them. Not entirely painless, but very effective."

"Would that work?" Jackson asked. "The feigning death part, I mean, not shoving things into my eyes."

Jake considered for another long moment or two. "It is something to consider," he said slowly. "Then again, my father has some pretty damning skeletons in his closet, which he knows I know, which is also why he wanted me dead. The money was just a bonus."

"Alexander said your brothers have been trying to have him declared unfit to rule."

"They can try that all they want, but it will be extremely time-consuming. I don't think you'll have the luxury of time. Is Penelope safe at the moment?"

Jackson nodded. "We saw her installed in an inn with guards." He paused. "She misses you, I daresay."

"She was a good friend," Jake said. "We might need to set her up with someone—"

Jackson rolled his eyes. "Father, I beg you to cease."

"You haven't seen any ghosts, have you?"

Jackson looked at his sire evenly.

"Just asking," Jake said with an easy smile. "I met a few in Kendrick's study, and I'm pretty sure they're not the only ones. You should do some investigating."

Jackson supposed that in the past, he might have shouted at his sire for that. Now, all he could do was smile.

"All right," he said with a light sigh. "I'll consider it."

Jake studied him. "You've changed."

"In a fortnight?"

"Apparently."

Jackson shrugged. "The Future is a marvelous place, my lord. It left its mark upon me."

"I imagine that was Olivia, but it was well done on her part."

Jackson nodded, because he couldn't deny it. He continued with his sire back toward the path that led back home, then hesitated. "I suppose I do have one last question, but I won't ask it in front of my mother."

"You shouldn't," Jake said mildly, "but you absolutely could because the answer wouldn't change. I would do it exactly the same way as many times as necessary because I love your mother more than life itself."

Jackson didn't doubt it. "You must, for I've seen what you gave up."

"You didn't see my '67 Jag."

"Draw it for me, then."

Jake smiled. "I will later. Let's go rescue your lady now from your uncle and siblings, then find something hot to drink. I'll take a look at what Alex sent and see if anything else occurs to me."

Jackson nodded and climbed the path back up to the keep. He'd done it so many times over the course of his life that he imagined he couldn't begin to put a number to it. The castle rose up into the sky with its usual starkness, which had been an endless source of comfort to him over those same years.

He walked until he realized that he had stopped, though he couldn't have said when that had happened. He found himself simply standing twenty paces outside his father's keep, looking at those gates he'd walked through innumerable times on his way to a hall that his sire had sacrificed so much to have …

He felt something inside him shift, then fall into a place that he realized in that moment had been waiting for him to be standing just where he was, looking at his father's gates, having traveled to a different place he had only dreamed about.

And he knew.

It almost sent him down to his knees.

He hardly dared look at his father, but a coward he was not. He took a moment to steady himself, then he turned to face the man who had given him so much.

And he found what he could scarce bring himself to say already written in his father's expression.

"Father … "

Jake shook his head. "It's okay, Jackson."

"Please don't blame Olivia," he said very quietly. "This is my doing."

"Jack, why do you think I stayed here?" Jake said gravely. "It sure as hell wasn't for the food." He put a hand on Jackson's shoulder. "If you want to look at it this way, I left an empire and gained a family I adore, including the love of my life. There's no reason you can't do the same thing."

Jackson cleared his throat roughly. "I refuse to weep."

"Well, you don't think I'm going to, do you?" Jake took a deep breath. "We might have to make a visit to the cellar after everyone's put to bed. I'll find some excuse to account for what we'll manage to drink."

"You must think me so ungrateful," Jackson managed.

Jake only looked at him with the same calm, measured look he always used, only this time it was full of understanding.

Jackson closed his eyes briefly, then looked at his father. "Thank you."

Jake only shook his head and smiled very faintly. "What else would I do, Jack?"

"I thought you might be … "

"Angry?"

Jackson looked at his father unflinchingly. "Disappointed."

Jake closed his eyes briefly, then swore. Jackson found himself pulled into a rather unforgiving embrace, complete with hearty slaps on the back and perhaps even a noise or two that might have resembled on their worst days a manly sob.

His father pulled away first and dragged his sleeve across his eyes. "Daft lad."

"Thank you, Father," Jackson said dryly.

"Oh, I'm not saying I'm not an idiot, too, but that's never been in dispute."

"Oh, I don't know," Jackson said seriously. "I've always thought you were the best man I knew, all my uncles and sundry relatives included."

Jake cleared his throat roughly. "I'll go weep some more over that later. Unless you're going to change your mind."

Jackson only looked at his father steadily.

"Just wanted to make sure."

"In truth, Father," he said very quietly, "though I hesitate to ask—"

Jake shook his head and smiled. "Son, I wouldn't change a single thing save the loss of two children. Anything else? It was worth it for every single moment I've had with my love, my children, and the family that I gained here in a time and place that I absolutely chose to live in."

"It is a good time," Jackson agreed.

Jake clapped him on the shoulder. "Let's go find your lady and make sure she's warm and comfortable, then we'll have a look at those papers."

"Father—"

Jake shook his head. "Your lady's safety first. We'll sort the rest of it out later."

"I don't know if she'll wed me."

His father stopped short. "Haven't you asked her yet?"

"I haven't dared ask directly, though she did seem to indicate that she might be willing to give up chocolate." He looked at his father helplessly. "'Tis promising, don't you think?"

Jake looked at him in astonishment for a moment or two, then bowed his head and laughed. "Jack, have you even *tried* to woo her?"

"I gave her a penny with King Richard's image on it that she seemed to find pleasing."

"Son, do we need to have a talk about the birds and the bees?"

Jackson looked at his father evenly only to have the man laugh at him again, then turn and walk away. He caught up with his sire, refrained from cursing him because he was a dutiful son, then smiled in spite of himself.

"I will woo her properly."

"I'm sure you will."

"Might I root about in your coffers for a few more coins?"

His father rolled his eyes and walked away.

Jackson followed him, smiling in spite of the burning in his eyes and the breaking of his heart.

He suspected his father would understand.

Twenty-Five

If she had ever wondered what it might feel like to have a medieval lord plastered to her like a gooey band aid, Olivia supposed she need wonder no more. She walked out the front gates of Raventhorpe with said sticky nobleman and reviewed the events of the day so far.

She'd woken after a relatively decent night's sleep to find herself still in the wrong century but the right time zone which had gotten the day off to a fairly promising start. She'd gotten ready with the usual help of her teenage maid, Joan, who had used a charming mix of Gaelic and French to discuss the weather and the state of her dating pool. Joan's, not hers, which was something she was happy to gang right on by as quickly as possible.

She had been pronounced fit for public viewing by Jackson's sisters who had arrived to offer their opinions, then exited her bedchamber to find that same handsome medieval lord she couldn't seem to get out of her mind leaning against the far wall of the passageway, waiting for her. He'd obviously had some sort of agenda, but she'd been too distracted by the butterflies fluttering in her midsection to ask for details.

He had made certain she was comfortable outside before he spent an hour showing off for her in the lists followed by inviting her to rest in front of the fire in the great hall while he cleaned up. She had listened to his sisters discuss his sword skill, but the only conclusion she'd come to was that she'd been damned lucky to have such a grossly overqualified guy for her guardsman in London.

That had been half an hour ago. Currently, she found herself walking away from Raventhorpe toward the beach, enjoying a bit of fall sunshine and wondering just what was up with the guy walking next to her. If Aunt Philly had been commenting on his behavior, she would have said that he seemed as nervous a cat on a porch full of rocking chairs. She couldn't imagine why that might be unless he'd heard things from his dad that he might think were too much for her.

She made it down that perilous path to the sand before she finally stopped and looked at him. "All right," she said bluntly, "spill it."

He looked at her in surprise. "Spill what?"

"Why are you so nervous?"

"I am never nervous."

She was tempted to throw up her hands in exasperation, but he was tucking her cloak up around her chin and looking at her gravely. She would have argued that he was distracting her from things she might want to know, but she imagined he knew that already.

She'd almost gotten used to his startling face and his beautiful eyes and the rest of him that obviously had benefitted from many, many hours in what passed for a medieval gym. She generally suffered only a momentary impulse to swoon when he caught her by the hand and linked just a couple of fingers with hers, or tucked a bit of her hair behind her ears before he did the same with his own, or stepped in front of her if there seemed to be the slightest hint of danger.

What she wasn't sure she would ever get used to, though, was that slightest softening of his usual expression of seriousness that indicated something had either amused him or touched him.

She might never be ready to talk about how her heart reacted to the sound of his laugh.

He smiled very faintly, then took her hand.

"Let us walk, aye?"

Since it was either that or escape back up the way to that time gate to avoid any difficult conversations—never mind what awaited them on the other side of *that* doorway—she nodded and walked with him down toward the water.

"Are you going to tell me what your Dad said?" she asked, because of all the topics on the table, it seemed the easiest to discuss.

He sighed. "That his father is mad, his brothers worthless, and his wee sister terrifying."

"She did seem a little unhinged."

"But apparently not dangerous, though I half feared she might draw a dagger from her purse and stab me."

Olivia looked at him quickly to find he wasn't serious. "Still not funny."

He smiled briefly. "I'm making sport of her, but I think we can dismiss her easily enough. My sire is looking over what you so cleverly brought along in your satchel to see if anything else occurs to him, but we did discuss my changing my eye color and dying in front of my grandfather."

"Jackson," she said, faintly horrified. "What a terrible idea."

He shrugged helplessly. "I would only feign death, of course, but I fear he won't leave Penelope—or you, for that matter—alone unless he's convinced my sire is gone." He paused. "He did also suggest digging up some unsavory details to have on hand if necessary."

"A dead-man's switch? That's an interesting idea."

"A what?" he asked carefully.

"It's where you have incriminating evidence collected in several places and ready to send out everywhere," she said with a nod. "That sending only happens if you get murdered, which I understand tends to leave the bad guys wanting you to stay alive."

He was looking at her as if he'd never seen her before. "How do you know that?"

"I watched a lot of movies with my granddad."

"Apparently," he said uneasily. "I believe that was what my sire was suggesting. I would rather see the matter put to rest decisively, but we'll see what other suggestions my sire might have to offer. I won't leave you outside for those discussions, just so you know."

"Thank you," she said, "but I haven't felt abandoned." She looked up at him. "You've made my time here very easy."

"And you made my time there much easier."

She ignored how much it felt as if they were inching toward a conversation she didn't want to have. He would stay and she would go. There really wasn't any middle ground there.

"I was afraid you'd get mugged by a bunch of fangirls if I didn't protect you," she said with an attempt at lightness.

"Fangirls?"

"Women who would take one look at you, decide you were the most gorgeous man they'd ever seen, then follow you endlessly to take your picture and ask you to marry them."

He smiled. She wasn't entirely sure he hadn't come close to purring. "Sadly, they would have departed disappointed."

"Too many women chasing you here in the current day?" she asked, managing not to grit her teeth because she was extremely disciplined.

He shook his head. "Nay, that isn't the reason."

She wasn't sure she wanted to hear the reason why because it didn't matter how many women were chasing him in either day if she couldn't be one of them—which she couldn't be. He would come back to the future with her, do what needed to be done, then return to the past where he would inherit the castle behind them, marry a medieval noblewoman, and live his life herding and protecting and managing the people he loved.

She would have made an attempt to dredge up a few salty curses, but she found herself turned and pulled into his arms before she could. She wasn't about to protest his wrapping his arms more tightly around her and holding her while she did a great deal more of that not-thinking thing.

There were many things she could say about Jackson Alexander Kilchurn V, but maybe first on that list had to be that the man knew how to hold a woman so she knew she'd been properly embraced. She felt him occasionally skim his hand over her hair, but for the most part, he simply held her close to him.

She stood there, perfectly content and safe, for as long as she could bear it, then she took a deep breath and stepped away from him.

"I need to walk," she managed.

"Of course." He held out his hand. "Shall we?"

She took his hand, because he was a gentleman and she didn't want to discourage him. She walked with him for quite a while before she thought she could speak without choking on the words.

"So, we'll go back," she said.

"Aye."

"And you'll do what you have to."

"Aye."

She would have danced around that one for a while, but she could hear Aunt Philly's voice floating across the centuries with a pithy, *fish or cut bait, Livvy*. It was sound advice, even in the present moment. Easier to know ahead of time what Jackson had planned so her heart was just a little bruised, not completely broken.

"And you'll stay just a couple of days?" she asked finally.

He stopped. She stopped alongside him, but she couldn't look at him, not because he wasn't a fantastic sight, but because she had the ocean right there and she was a big fan of the ocean. No wonder Aunt Philly had decamped for Belize. She would have to visit her soon.

Jackson was apparently just as big a fan of the water because he wasn't moving either. She snuck a glance at him, fully expecting him to be enjoying the view as well, but he wasn't.

He was watching her.

"What?" she managed. "You're going to stay fewer than a couple of days?"

He looked at her for so long, she was tempted to just start babbling to break the silence that was somehow still full of the sound of waves and seagulls and the distant noise of castle life.

And then he shook his head.

"What's less than fewer?" she asked, though the question almost killed her.

He considered. "More?"

She was tempted to punch him. "That's not less and what do you mean by more? A couple more days? A week?"

He only looked at her, silent and grave.

She opened her mouth to tell him just how annoying it was to be the only one talking at such an uncomfortable time when she realized what he'd just said.

"More?" she said, wishing she sounded less like a squeaky toy and more like a sultry 40s actress at her most disinterested and aloof.

He nodded.

She decided immediately that he couldn't possibly be intending that to mean he would be spending all that extra time with her, so she pasted a smile on her face. "What an interesting idea. I'm sure you'll have a great time."

She realized after a moment or two that he wasn't agreeing with her, which was maybe for the best. She wasn't sure she wanted to hear anything he might have to say on the off chance it included detailed plans for all the things he might or might not do in the Future that … well, the thought of his being in a time where he wasn't the future lord of Raventhorpe was one she couldn't entertain. She hugged herself, because that seemed like a decent way to keep from falling apart.

Jackson closed his eyes briefly, then stepped forward until his boots weren't quite touching the hem of her glorious medieval gown. She knew that because she was, her medieval reputation aside, a complete coward when it came to getting her heart ripped into pieces, which she suspected might be happening in the next two minutes. She absolutely refused to be looking at his face while he was dumping her, not that there was anything to be dumped from. It wasn't as if they were even dating, never mind that he'd just taken both her hands in both of his in that way he had that left her feeling cherished and protected, damn him anyway.

"Olivia."

She looked up at him, because she suspected it might be rude not to.

And then time slowed, and stopped, because she saw in his face just what *more* meant.

She knew she would never in her lifetime forget that moment, the precise point in time when she looked into his eyes and realized that he wasn't going to stay in the past.

He was going to come to the future and *stay* in the future.

She shook her head. That didn't help the way her eyes were burning as if she'd just sneezed into a jar full of pepper. His eyes were a little red as well, so maybe there was something a little zesty in the medieval air around them.

"You can't mean it," she whispered.

He nodded slowly.

She let that sink in for approximately ten seconds before reality stood up and demanded her attention. The truth was, he might mean it, but that didn't mean anything was going to happen with her.

And why would it? He was an insanely attractive medieval knight who no doubt left entire ballrooms breaking out into brawls over him every time he entered. Yesterday's Treasures would probably take out full-page pictorials featuring him just to boost their circulation.

"Well, there are lots of great gals there in the future," she said.

He shrugged. "Perhaps."

"You'll probably want to date a lot," she said, trying not to grit her teeth. "Have you dated a lot here?"

He blinked. "Have I what?"

"Dated," she said crisply. "You know, where you go out with women? Dinner, a movie—well, not a movie for you. A play. Dancing. Hobnobbing with royalty."

He looked at her with a faint smile that had probably sent more than one potential date into a medieval sort of swoon.

"What are you trying to say?" he asked politely.

"You should date," she said, pulling her hands away from his and wrapping her arms around herself. "In the future."

"Why the hell would I want to do that?"

"Because you don't know what's available there," she said primly.

"Olivia, I have traveled the world," he said, looking faintly exasperated, "and perhaps familiarized myself with more of its offerings than I care to admit."

"Still, you should date," she said. "There."

"I refuse."

She spluttered. "You can't refuse."

"Of course I can." He looked at her. "I want you."

She felt her eyes narrow without permission. "You can't have me until you date. At least one time. And who said you could have me at all? You aren't—"

In my plans had been what she was going to say, but somehow she lost her train of thought somewhere between that medieval lord pulling her into his arms and then smiling at her sweetly before he kissed her.

And then she just stopped thinking for a bit.

It seemed wise.

He finally lifted his head and smiled at her again. "I want you," he said simply.

She gave up trying to keep her tears in her eyes where they belonged. "But how do you make this work?" she asked, pained. "Your family will be devastated."

He smoothed her hair out of her eyes. "They will be overjoyed that I was fortunate enough to find a woman who could tolerate me."

She didn't bother trying to muster up a dismissive noise. It was all she could do not to weep.

"Besides, is it so difficult to believe that our chis brought us together?"

"I'm not sure that's what that means," she managed.

"Fate, then."

Or a couple of Scottish grandpas and quite possibly her Aunt Philly, but maybe that didn't need to be said. She had also cut her teenage teeth on all those romance novels where the titled guy plucked the regular girl out of her life of obscurity and made her his duchess, so she was probably not the right one to offer an opinion.

"We could handfast, if that might be more palatable."

She dragged herself back to the romance in progress. "Handfast?"

"'Tis like being wed save you would have a year and day to decide if you wanted to keep me."

"I know what it mean—wait, is this a *proposal*?"

He looked behind him at his metaphorical tail and cast a pair of sideways glances at the rockers that flanked him. "You could consider it such."

She normally had an excellent poker face, but she was under a fair bit of duress at the moment. "I could consider it such?" she repeated incredulously.

He shrugged helplessly. "I don't want to presume. Besides, this way you would have all the benefits of a husband without having me underfoot for more than a year, cluttering up your bathing chamber."

She made a valiant effort to keep her jaw where it belonged instead of losing it down there on the sand. Handfasting? All the benefits of a husband without years of battling over the proper way to squeeze toothpaste?

"I guess I wouldn't have to fight you for the coin any longer," she muttered.

"Or for the last, best bites of ice cream."

"That'd be just grand," she said, realizing she sounded very grumpy and not at all just-proposed-to, but she was having a hell of a day so far.

She glared up at him only to have him laugh a little, then pull her into his arms and hold her close. She closed her eyes and tried to come to grips with what she'd just heard. It was made a bit easier when she was standing in the embrace of a medieval guy who didn't seem to want to let her go.

"What say you?" he asked, pulling away only far enough to look at her gravely.

"A year and a day?"

He nodded.

"Do *you* need a year and a day?"

He smiled, a very small smile that almost finished what was left of her knees. "I do not. Do you?"

"Well," she said slowly, "I guess I'm not all that opposed to a cluttered-up bathing chamber."

He smiled, bent his head, and kissed her with the same attention to doing a thorough job of it that he seemed to apply to everything in his life.

Heaven help her.

She wasn't unhappy to have him just hold her after a bit so she could catch her breath. She stood in his arms and looked out over the sea for a few minutes before she could ask any more questions about his plans.

"Are you going to take your father's place?"

"Aye."

"You're really giving up a lot here to go there." She looked at him and couldn't bring herself to finish the thought, but it included the words *for* and *me*.

"I think I am gaining far more," he said easily, "but perhaps I have spoken too soon and assumed interest where there is none."

"Perhaps you talk too much."

He smiled. "You know I don't."

"I know," she said, feeling her eyes burn again. "But, Jackson…"

He pulled her close again. "Handfast with me, Olivia," he said quietly. "We'll solve our problems, then you can decide if you want me or not. Just know that the only woman I will date will be you."

Well, if he was going to put it that way, she wasn't going to discourage him.

He pulled away, then held out his hand. "Shall we go look for a threshold?"

She put her hand in his and decided that walking was better than swooning, though she was tempted to do the latter. She stole looks at him as they walked back up the hill and to the castle gates, but he was only watching her with a faint smile.

"I would stay here," she said, because she thought it needed to be said.

He took a deep breath. "You must be very fond of me, indeed."

"I just might be."

He squeezed her hand gently. "We'll find a century that suits us both and live our lives blissfully together."

She nodded, though she imagined where he was going to need to be in a time where the world might possibly manage to keep up with him.

She walked with him through his father's courtyard, across the same stones she'd crossed with him eight centuries in the future, and tried not to shiver. Those they passed bowed deferentially to him—and to her, it had to be said. Vanquishing ruffians along the border was apparently a one-way ticket to all kinds of medieval respect.

Jackson stopped in front of a small stone building and looked at her. "This is my family's private chapel where there happens to be a very useful threshold."

She took a deep breath. "Do you want me to stand there with you?"

"Aye, Olivia," he said seriously, "I want you to stand here with me."

She put her hand in his and let him pull her up onto that step. "But we don't have rings or anything."

"Where is our coin?" he asked. "I'll cut it in half—"

"Oh, you can't," she said quickly. "It's old."

"I'm older."

She smiled in spite of herself. "Well, you do have a point there."

He looked at her. "Will you have me?"

She took a deep breath because she thought that might keep her from tearing up again. "Yes." She hesitated. "Do I ask you if you want me now?"

"You may if you like," he said with a grave smile, "and I do."

She smiled and thought she might have found the one thing in her life that left her a bit giddier than the thought of a perfectly preserved medieval sword. Jackson smiled in the same way, so she suspected he understood.

He pulled her into his arms, bent his head, then froze at the sound of a throat clearing imperiously.

Olivia looked to her right to find an entire collection of family members standing there. His parents were standing to one side, their arms around each other, smiling. She suspected the lady Amanda might not know tears were running down her cheeks, but she realized she was having the same issue, so maybe they were in the same boat.

Jackson's sisters were clustered near his parents, smiling as well, and Connor's younger brothers were gaping at them with all the enthusiasm of sixteen-year-old boys watching a romantic event they thought might make them want to howl with terror. Connor, Thaddeus, and Lord Robin were standing in a separate group, watching with wry smiles.

There was a man standing directly in front of them, however, who wasn't smiling at all.

"Lord Jackson," he said crisply, "what do you here without alerting me to your intentions? You shall not handfast with a noblewoman of such quality! A wedding must be arranged and I will see to the particulars." He looked over his shoulder. "With your permission, Lord Jackson, Lady Amanda."

Olivia watched Jackson's dad wave the priest on to his business. She listened to him begin to organize things in a way that probably should have left Jackson thinking he had some work to do in that area, then she leaned close to her, er, whatever he was.

"I think you're in trouble," Olivia whispered.

"I *know* I'm in trouble," he said, wincing. "This is going to be very expensive." He shot her a quick smile. "Do you mind wedding first and dating later?"

"We definitely wouldn't have to fight over the coin any longer."

"We wouldn't."

"But Richard's still mine."

He smiled and kissed her. "He's still yours, love—oh, aye, Master Galfrid, I will absolutely have a look at the state of your coffers without your having to ask, of course."

"Very generous, my lord."

"A small matter when compared to your attending to my wedding, good sir."

Olivia had to admire Jackson's ability to evade a pointed question or two about his spotty attendance record, then shove his brother and cousin in front of him to be a buffer while he pulled her with him through the cluster of people there. She wasn't sure quite what to expect when she came face-to-face with his parents, but apparently there had been no need for worry.

Amanda hugged her, then kissed her on both cheeks and smiled without a trace of unhappiness. "This is as it should be," she said softly.

"My lady, I'm—"

"Perfect for him," she said. "Olivia, take my blessing and live happily with my son."

Olivia blinked rapidly and nodded, promising herself a good cry when no one would have to watch.

"Am I *finally* allowed one standing up?"

Olivia watched Jackson turn and look at his uncle.

"Aye, if you intend to cross blades with me after supper," he said coolly.

"A skirmish in the great hall?" Robin asked, rubbing his hands together. "I will settle for that."

"Be silent, you fool," Amanda said shortly, "for you'll not manage it this time, either. Come with me, Olivia, and the girls and I will see you garbed pleasingly. Ignore my brother. We all do with great success."

Olivia found herself gathered up and hustled away toward the great hall. She managed a look over her shoulder to find Jackson simply standing there, his cousins and brother bouncing around him like a pack of puppies, his father and uncle looking as if they might be moving their discussion to the lists. He, however, was simply watching her with a slight smile on his face.

She waved. Jackson waved briefly in return, then surrendered to the enthusiasm of his cousins.

She took a deep breath, then turned and walked with her yet-to-be-made mother-in-law up the stairs to her medieval home.

Several hours later, she was being ushered inside her bedchamber by a different Kilchurn. She watched Jackson shut the door then lean back against it. He looked at her as if he weren't quite sure what she might do.

"I'm not going to run," she said dryly. "Or faint."

He smiled at her fondly. "What would you say then, wife, to having this be our first date?"

She couldn't help but smile back at him. "All right."

He pushed off from the door and walked over to put his arms around her. "What does one do on a first date?"

"Well, we've already had a moonlight stroll."

"From the great hall to the chapel where we were married," he agreed. "What else?"

She shifted so she could rest her head against his shoulder and watch the fire that some thoughtful someone had obviously built for them. "We've already had dinner, but a movie is probably out." She looked at him. "Cards?"

"Is that more or less involved than a thumb war?"

"Much more involved."

"Lay out the battlefield then," he said with a smile, "and we'll see how I fare."

She imagined he would fare very well, but that was just what he did, that assuring himself that everyone around him was happy and safe before he attended to his own situation. She'd watched him do it unthinkingly with his family over the course of the afternoon, then realized he was doing the same thing with her. She knew she shouldn't have been surprised, because he'd done it from the very moment they'd met.

She was, she realized, an extremely lucky gal, in whatever century she found herself with him.

"Texas Hold 'Em," she said, dragging herself back to the present moment and looking at her husband with a smile. "We'll have to wager something besides money, though. I don't have any, and I gave all my digestive biscuits to your sisters."

He considered. "Kisses?"

He was definitely her kind of guy.

She nodded, had a brief sample of potential winnings for her trouble, then went to dig around in her bag for her cards.

She sincerely hoped he wouldn't notice if she deliberately lost as many hands as possible.

Twenty-Six

Jackson leaned back against the wall and watched the morning sunlight that streamed through the windows and fell upon the woman he loved. She was dressed in a glorious emerald green gown, remarkably like the one he'd once envisioned her wearing, and sitting in front of the fire whilst her maid attended to her hair.

He was currently distracting himself by trying to decide which male relative he would slay first. He had reason, he supposed, given that there were just so many to choose from.

The banging on his door had begun just after dawn. He had stumbled to that door partially dressed because he'd fallen asleep with his wife in his arms, perhaps with both of them a bit more undressed than that, then found none other than his uncle and younger brother standing in the passageway, looking at him with wide-eyed innocence.

They had informed him with barely suppressed grins that they had been beside themselves with worry that the newly made couple might not have had anything to use in keeping up their strength in the early hours.

He'd taken a bottle from one of them, a basket from the other, then slammed the door so he didn't have to listen to their giggles.

There wasn't a shred of dignity in that lot, to be sure.

He'd hardly had time to wish his wife a proper good-morrow before another knock had sounded. It had been a discreet tap, though, which had left him merely opening the door and looking instead of ripping the door open and snarling. Joan, the daughter of his mother's personal attendant, had arrived bearing that same lovely green gown and instructions to see Lady Olivia garbed properly.

He had sighed and retreated to the corner with half a loaf of bread and a cup of ale to wait out his lady's toilette.

He'd also taken a quick moment to see to his own grooming whilst his wife and her maid had retired discreetly behind a screen to attend to whatever matters needed attention, then retreated back to his comfortable spot, wondering if he might manage an hour in the lists before events got completely away from him.

He considered the possibilities, then he'd realized something else entirely. It couldn't have been clearer to him if some relative or other had burst into the chamber and announced what had to happen that day.

He and Olivia needed to return to the Future.

He came back to himself as Olivia escorted Joan across the bedchamber and out the door. She turned to lean back against the door and smiled at him.

"Has it been a year and a day yet?"

He put his cup down on a table as he walked around the bed, then reached out to pull her into his arms. "Somewhere, surely."

She put her arms around his neck and held onto him tightly. "Yesterday was a lovely day, thank you."

"I believe you allowed me several wins during our dating foray into the holding of Texas."

She pulled back and smiled at him. "I might have."

He kissed her softly. "Thank you for wedding me."

"Thank you for asking me to." She blushed a little. "You're a very lovely man."

He knew exactly what she was getting at, so he shrugged lightly. "I thought I would at least date you a few times before we, ah, marched fully onto the field, so to speak."

"I get the picture," she said, blushing furiously. "Very chivalrous."

He considered. "Would stirring up the fire count as another date, do you suppose?"

"I think you should definitely try it and see."

He did, then spent a respectable amount of time trying to properly date his lady whilst not ruining her coiffure. He had almost decided—admittedly with her permission—that she could be remade for the day, when he heard the very unwelcome sound of pounding on the door.

"Someone's knocking," Olivia said faintly.

"I'm going to kill whomever is there."

"What if it's a sister?"

"'Tis a cousin-like knock," he said grimly, "but who knows? I will investigate, then return."

He walked over to the door and opened it to find not only sisters but twins standing there.

"Breakfast," Sam offered politely.

"Delicious," Theo agreed, nodding encouragingly.

"Death," Jackson said crisply.

The twins grinned and bolted. Jackson looked at his sisters who only held up their hands in surrender and followed after them.

"We tried," Eugenie tossed over her shoulder as she walked away. "Am I excused from meeting you in the lists?"

"But not me," Penelope called. "I'll meet you there!"

Jackson shut the door calmly, bolted it, then went to take his seat by the fire. He invited his lady wife to sit on his lap, then looked up at her pleasantly. He would have pointed out to her that he had too much family, but he realized before the words came out of his mouth that such would have been the wrong thing to say. He reached up and tucked a stray lock of hair behind her ear, then simply looked at her.

"I'm not looking forward to today," she said honestly.

"This is my choice," he said, "but I understand."

She didn't ask him if he were certain about it, though he suspected that was what she was thinking. He held her for a bit longer, then looked at her.

"We should go break our fast," he said, "then I must speak to my sire, then we'll go. And don't apologize, Olivia. My path is of my choosing. I am merely grateful you're willing to walk it with me."

She attempted a dismissive noise, but didn't argue when he put his arms back around her and held her close.

He couldn't say he remembered much of the morning, though the meal had been spectacular and his family had obviously been going out of their way to leave things seeming as ordinary as possible. He was grateful for it and knew Olivia was as well.

He wanted to reassure her that he had spent an inordinate amount of time at Artane, or traveling by himself, or journeying with his family where he roamed the outsides of inns and halls to make sure everyone was safe, and his family was thereby accustomed to his absences, but he imagined those were things he could tell her later.

His family was also used to having him underfoot, but hopefully he had tormented them enough with his presence that they wouldn't miss him overmuch when he wasn't there.

He sighed. The things he told himself to spare his tender heart from being pained were truly legion.

He watched his mother and sisters gather Olivia up and make off with her to points unknown whilst his uncle collected the rest of the rabble, leaving him trailing after his sire to his solar. He sat down and looked at the man who had given him so much and found himself without a single useful thing to say.

"This is new," his sire said with a smile.

Jackson attempted an answering smile, but he feared it had gone rather badly. "I apologize."

"For what?"

"For ... " Jackson took a deep breath. "Honestly, Father, I can't begin to make that list, though it includes my leaving even though I know I must."

"Son, why do you think I left you that key?"

Jackson nodded, then pulled up short when his sire's words arranged themselves into something he understood. He felt his mouth fall open. "You did not."

"I absolutely did."

"I blame you for this, then."

Jake snorted. "You can try."

"That bloody key almost ruined my life," Jackson said in astonishment. "I was forever wondering what it fit to, where it would lead."

"I imagine it led you to rooting around in your uncle Nicholas' trunk with Kendrick and quite probably those monstrous little cousins of yours."

"It was Connor, I'm sure he had nightmares for months, and what lock does it fit to?"

His father only looked at him blandly. "It ruined your life. Why would I tell you anything else?"

Jackson was tempted to invite that man there out to the lists, but he imagined it would go badly for him at the moment. He settled for a glare, but that was half-hearted at best.

"You truly aren't going to tell me?"

Jake only smiled easily. "You probably already have your suspicions. I would hate to ruin a good treasure hunt for you."

Jackson rubbed his hands over his face, flexed his fingers a time or two just to see if they might be equal to doing damage to anyone else who might be lounging about uselessly in his vicinity, then stared at his sire and tried not to swear at him.

And then it occurred to him just what Jackson Alexander Kilchurn IV had done to him.

His father had given him exactly what he needed.

"Would it be rude," he asked after he'd caught his breath, "to damn you to hell for it?"

"Very. Don't make me take you out to the lists. I'm not Robin, but I think I could stir myself to beat a little respect into you just the same."

Jackson smiled, because his father was a man without peer and there was no one, not even his uncle, who he would have rather had guarding his back.

"Is there anything else you care to tell me?" he asked, because he had apparently become a lad of ten-and-two who was still trying to digest the gift of a mystery. "About your place there?"

"The place you'll basically assume?" Jake paused and seemed to consider his words carefully. "Have you met James MacLeod?"

"I haven't, but I suspect I should."

"You should," Jake agreed. "He is, as you'll find out, an inveterate time traveler. I'm guessing he could give you a very long list of reasons why certain souls might be destined to live in a time not their own."

"What rot," Jackson managed.

"Well, you go ahead and have that conversation with Jamie, then enjoy the subsequent trip to his lists." He shook his head and his smile faded. "I don't know if Fate had a trade of you for me in mind, but who knows? Let's just say that from the moment you could walk, you were flinging yourself into places you could reach and complaining about what you couldn't."

"I blame Kendrick."

"Kendrick was just your excuse to go off and make trouble." He shook his head, then smiled faintly. "I just had a feeling that that key might give you something to think about. I hope I wasn't wrong."

"You weren't," Jackson said slowly. He looked into the fire in his father's hearth until he thought he could speak without weeping. "How do I leave, in truth?"

"I don't know," Jake said quietly. "I won't say I won't miss you more terribly than I want to admit. I don't think I can talk about how your mother will grieve."

"Will she forgive me?"

"She will. The key was her idea, if you want the entire truth of it."

"Why?"

"Because she loves you with a mother's love and wants nothing for you but what you want for yourself."

Jackson looked at his father and smiled. "And you don't?"

"Oh, I'm fairly fond of you as well, but I've only ever wanted you to do what I tell you to do without arguing."

"You taught me how to argue," Jackson pointed out.

"My mistake."

Jackson felt his eyes burn in spite of his legendary self-control. "I will miss you."

"For all you know," Jake said, clearing his throat roughly, "I'll arrive on your doorstep in a few years, you mother and all the little ducklings in tow, and expect to be fêted in glorious Future style. I'd say you'd best make certain you've earned buckets of money before we arrive."

Jackson took a deep breath and nodded. "Olivia and I will have a place for you."

"I'm certain you will. Now, why don't we talk a little about your battle plan? I'll tell you what I know, though I've written it down as well so you won't have to remember all the details."

Jackson nodded and tried to listen to his father, but he found himself with the unsettling sensation of being in two places at the same time. It was the same feeling he'd had in Artane when he'd woken to find himself in the right keep but definitely not the right year.

Or so he'd thought.

"He's distracted."

He came back to himself to find that they'd been joined by his uncle Robin. He looked at his uncle and father, made note of their faint looks of amusement, then shrugged.

"I am," he agreed.

"Don't blame me," Robin said, holding up his hands in surrender. "I brought you food this morning—oh, did we knock at an inappropriate time?"

Jackson looked at his sire. "He does this on purpose, doesn't he?"

"He's been endlessly denied a standing up," Jake said dryly. "Thank you for continuing the tradition."

"Kendrick is my last hope for my own brood," Robin said cheerfully. "I won't fail there."

"I'm sure he'll appreciate your efforts," Jake said easily. "Let's go find lunch before you give that too much thought."

Jackson rose, then held the door open for them. He caught his father's eye on his way by and had a brief lifting of an eyebrow for his trouble.

He followed his elder relatives from the solar and had to shake his head briefly. Kendrick had it aright, to be sure. Knowing the future wasn't necessarily a blessing.

Far better to wrench it to his purposes, which he fully intended to do after he managed to survive another meal, then face what he was certain would be difficult goodbyes.

He was somewhat surprised to find, a pair of hours later, that those farewells hadn't been as painful as he'd feared, which left him thinking quite seriously that perhaps he wouldn't be going anywhere after all.

He stood with his sire on the steps of the hall, watching his family clustered in the courtyard with Olivia in their midst and gathered his thoughts. He was wearing his usual clothing from the present day, with Zachary's gear and all the appropriate papers he needed stowed quite safely in a rucksack. Olivia was garbed in that green gown that was almost equal to her beauty, though Thad was carrying her gear for her. Jackson almost shouted to his brother to enjoy his last few moments of breathing, but decided that he could let the moment of his brother gazing at her adoringly go.

She was, after all, wed to him.

He took a deep breath and looked at his father. "I think we must go."

Jake nodded. "I think so, too. I can think up a story for you, but I'll only say what you want me to say."

"And you'll say my goodbyes to those I cannot?" he asked, though the words almost stuck in his throat.

"Of course."

"And you'll come," Jackson said, because *those* words were already half out of his mouth before he considered the advisability of them. "At some point."

"Heaven help me if we're the same age when we manage it," his sire said with an uncomfortable laugh. "But yes, we'll try. And just so you know, I can't say that I haven't imagined this moment more often than I'll admit, but this is the right choice for you. You need to be there, hunting for things that are hidden, living your life with a woman you adore." He smiled faintly. "I might be biased."

"I'll try to have a grandchild or two for you to dote on," Jackson said. "When you come."

"You'd damn well better."

Jackson couldn't see his father any longer, but he supposed his sire didn't expect anything else. After all, the man had held him as he'd puked his guts out, then wept after his first battle, and slapped him companionably on the back after his first heartbreak. Perhaps 'twas only fitting that his sire be the one to push him into the future that he so desperately wanted.

He dragged his sleeve across his face, then looked at his father in surprise. "You weren't the one who pushed me into that gate, were you?"

Jake shook his head. "Stuck my foot out and tripped you, but you can thank Sam and Theo for the push, the little demons."

Jackson smiled in spite of himself. "Thank you, Father."

"I'll see you in a bit, son." Jake stretched. "Or I might see you tonight if the gate doesn't work. Either way, we'll have a drink together and worry about tomorrow when it comes."

"And do you—"

"Yes," Jake said simply. "I like her very much. You might actually be able to keep up with that one."

Jackson would have called his sire a vile name, but it was his father after all and his heart was so ripped to shreds over the beauty of his life to that point and the wonder that awaited him that he could hardly breathe.

"Let's go, son. You'll want to get home before dark, I imagine."

Jackson nodded, then walked down the stairs with his sire. He found himself embraced by his family, each in turn, and lost count of the endearments he blurted out and the manly tears he shed. He held his mother last of all and was almost surprised that he had more tears on his cheeks than she did.

"I love you, Mama," he said quietly. "I worry about your feelings for me, though."

She laughed and hugged him tightly. "Daft lad," she said, sinking back down to her heels and looking up at him. "I love you dearly, which you know, and I want you to be happy, which you should know if you don't." She took a deep breath, then smiled. "Go with that lovely gel of yours, make beautiful children between the two of you, and we will meet again."

He nodded, because he couldn't say anything more than that. He kissed his mother's cheek, kissed his sisters, avoided kissing his uncle, then slapped his brother and Connor on their backs in a friendly fashion. He glared at the wee twin demons and decided that assuring them he would see them in a different locale might lead them to contemplating things they shouldn't.

Which they would likely do anyway, but that wasn't his worry.

In the end, he took his lady's hand and left through the front gates with her, followed by his sire and his uncle. He listened to his mother and siblings make a commotion in the courtyard which he hoped would allow them to get away mostly unseen, but he would need to leave it to his sire to, as Sam and Theo had once said in a different era, clean up the details.

He glanced at his sire as they walked up the path toward that portal he could actually see shimmering there in the distance.

"Father?"

"Aye, son."

"I should tell you one more thing."

"Son, I know you love me."

Jackson smiled grimly. "I do. I also lost your key."

Jake pulled up short. "You what?"

"Somewhere between here and there," Jackson admitted. "There was a vile green cloth over the gate area in the Future, so perhaps it lurks there. What was in the safe?"

His father only laughed at him and gave him a nudge out of the way to offer Olivia his arm. "He dislikes unsolved mysteries, daughter," he said cheerfully. "Keep that in mind."

"I will, my lord."

Jackson followed after them with his uncle, then glanced to see how Robin was taking those tidings. His uncle was, unsurprisingly, simply watching him with a dry smile.

"I didn't *mean* to lose it," he muttered.

Robin only snorted and walked on with him.

He stopped in front of that shimmering doorway, then embraced his father and his uncle. He reached for his lady's hand, then looked at the two men there.

"Advice?"

"If you can't replay in your wee head everything I've ever said to you," Jake said with a snort, "then there's no hope for you. Do good. Live the hell out of each moment you're given. Never let that woman there forget that you know you're lucky to have her."

Jackson nodded, watched his father and uncle embrace his wife, then he took her hand again and faced the gate. He took a deep breath, then pushed it open.

He was almost surprised when it revealed naught but the kirk that lay on the other spot of that patch of ground in his day—

Or, perhaps not.

He stared in astonishment at the church on the other side of that gate that most definitely didn't find itself in the current day. He stepped through the gate, keeping Olivia's hand securely in his own. He made certain she was safely with him in the same century, then he stood on the threshold and looked behind him to give his sire a final wave.

That might have been, in hindsight, a mistake.

"Jackson!"

That was Zachary Smith's voice. He turned back toward the Future and understood in a blinding fashion just why things that didn't go according to how he'd designed them bothered him so much.

He pushed Olivia into Zachary's arms and watched him pull her behind a row of men who included not only Zachary, but Derrick Cameron, and perhaps Kendrick as well, disguised as he was by a deep hood. He would have tried to put names to the three men standing to his right, but he found himself far too busy trying to fend off a white-haired man holding a weapon in his hand.

He made the mistake of stepping backward over the threshold of the gate and understood why Zachary had been vexed so thoroughly by the one near Artane. Unfortunately, that unsettled patch of ground seemed to pose no problem for the old man coming at him with what he could see was a needle attached to some sort of hilt. He managed to keep from being stabbed with it only because he'd had a lifetime's experience of getting out of the way of tools of death.

He grasped the old man's hand, swearing sharply as the metal scratched his palm in the process, but that was at least just annoying and not fatal.

"Damn you, Jake," the old man snarled, "I'll kill you this time!"

Ah, Jackson III rushing out to battle, obviously. It went against every word of his knightly code to be so ungracious to someone of advanced years, but he knew he had no choice. He had to keep his Future grandfather out of medieval England whilst at the same time away from Olivia. He spun his father's father around and encouraged him with a sharp shove to take his deadly intentions in a different direction.

His grandfather stumbled toward the three men Jackson had to assume were his Future uncles. He shook his head sharply to clear it from the buzzing that suddenly assailed him, but that didn't help him make sense of the English his grandfather was snarling at his sons. He leaned over with his hands on his thighs and tried to catch his breath.

"Dad, you really need to get a grip—"

"Shut up, you idiot," Jackson III shouted. "He's supposed to be dead, but here he is again like some damned ghost. I am *not* going to be embarrassed again!"

Jackson watched his grandfather spew out increasingly unpleasant things about his sire and would have protested, but he could hardly see for the fog that swirled in front of him. He had lived on the edge of the sea for the entirety of his life, to be sure, but he had never seen such a dense mist.

That came, surely, from standing in the midst of a portal through time, which he would need to address the moment he thought he could move his feet. He was half afraid to move lest he find himself plunged into a century devoid of both his family and his newly made wife.

"I swear I'll finish him this time."

"Dad, watch out for that rock—"

Jackson watched his grandfather stumble, trip, then fall.

Directly onto his weapon of death.

Jackson would have offered aid, but there was no stopping his grandfather's tumble. He, too, felt himself begin to make that same sort of slide toward the ground.

He looked blearily for Olivia and found her standing there, her hands outstretched, Zachary and Derrick holding her back. Jackson looked down at his hand and saw nothing more than a thin cut. He shook his head, but that only came close to unbalancing him.

What he needed was just a brief rest, then he would move again. Derrick and Zachary would take care of Olivia until his head had cleared. With any luck, that third lad was indeed Kendrick and he was absolutely terrifying when angry. Disguising himself had been wise, though, for it wouldn't have done for his father to have seen him in the Future.

He looked at Olivia who was trying to shake off the hands of those men holding onto her. He shook his head sharply, which he immediately regretted as it sent the entire world spinning around him.

"Tomorrow," he said hoarsely. "I will find you tomorrow."

He felt himself falling backward. He would have caught himself on the edges of that doorway, but it wasn't a proper doorway at all. He clutched at naught but the stuff of dreams, stepped backward, then fell into an endless void.

He closed his eyes and surrendered to the darkness.

TWENTY-SEVEN

OLIVIA WATCHED THE GATE CLOSE. The world was filled with the roar of the ocean, the occasional call of a sea bird, and an autumn breeze that carried with it the faint smell of the sea. She couldn't feel the chill, though. She hardly felt the hands on her arms, pulling her behind a trio of men dressed in modern clothing.

She realized she had been handed off to Oliver who had apparently taken over the duties of holding her upright. She supposed that shouldn't have surprised her. He was always where he needed to be when trouble was afoot. He and Jackson would probably be very good friends.

She remained where she was, hiding behind Kendrick, Zachary, and Derrick. Jackson would have made some sort of tart remark about being endlessly surrounded by cousins, though she imagined he wouldn't have complained about the barrier they made between her and his unhinged grandfather who had just fallen onto a syringe of something she suspected might be deadly.

"I think you're not going to have time for an ambulance," Zachary said carefully. "Not this far out. Better get him to a hospital yourselves."

"But we saw—

"Mist," Kendrick said crisply. "That, and the spot here is actually rather haunted."

"How would you know?"

"Because I am the earl of Seakirk," Kendrick said, 750 years of disdain dripping from his tone, "and I live in a haunted castle. Look it up."

Olivia shifted slightly so she could look around Kendrick's shoulder to watch the three men standing twenty feet away, discussing the events of the day with increasingly poor language. She almost regretted not having asked Jackson IV about his family, but in her defense, she'd been a little busy marrying his son.

That son who she had watched slip to the ground on the other side of a doorway that had simply vanished into thin air.

She forced herself to focus on Jackson's uncles arguing while their father lay wheezing on the ground in front of them.

"Who are these guys anyway?" one of them said, gesturing angrily to Kendrick and his companions.

"And how did they show up here so quickly?"

"Does it matter?" said a third uncle, one who sounded a bit more reasonable than the other two. "Do you really want to explain to the local authorities why Dad was running around trying to stab people?"

"We can blame it on them," one of his brothers bluffed.

Oliver smiled at her. "Excuse me, pet." He stepped around her and moved to stand next to Kendrick, then held up a video camera. "Instant upload to a dozen private servers," he said politely. "Fancy a copy, would you?"

One of the uncles pointed a shaking finger at Oliver. "You were here a few days ago. When Jake and that woman behind you disappeared."

"Don't remember it," Oliver said. "But twilight on the coast's tricky. People run off roads."

"I understand some people run *other* people off roads," Kendrick said with a yawn. "That sort of thing is a bit bothersome, wouldn't you agree?"

"You three really should get your father to a hospital," Zachary repeated firmly. "He's not breathing very well."

Olivia supposed that might have been because grandpa had fallen directly on the syringe of poison he'd been trying to inject into others, but what did she know? She listened to the brothers bicker as they hauled their father up with a decided lack of care and trudged off to their car. She watched them get inside, but she could hardly make any sense of it. The sound of the motor faded into the distance eventually, leaving her with just Jackson's family and Oliver.

She watched as Zachary went over to examine the spot where the gate had been. He considered, then returned and looked at her.

"I think it's closed for business for the day at least," he said gently. "Why don't we go back to Artane for a bit?"

"I'll stay and keep watch," Oliver said.

"I'll go find supper for you," Derrick said quietly, "then have a look around as well."

Olivia looked at Kendrick who was standing in front of her. "What am I going to do?"

"Come home to Artane with us, as Zachary suggests," he said seriously. "Tomorrow will take care of itself."

She didn't want to have another look at the spot where the gate should have been, but she couldn't help herself. She walked over to it and stepped on it, but that produced nothing for her but an intense desire to sit down and weep.

"Olivia?"

She looked up at Kendrick and nodded, then walked with him to a car. She watched him open the door for her, but wasn't sure she could make the commitment of getting inside quite yet. She looked at him. "I met your father."

"Did you?"

"You're a lot like him."

He nodded gravely. "I daresay I am."

She got inside then, because there was nothing else to do. She closed her eyes and enjoyed the feeling of having someone else taking care of her security, but she'd become accustomed to that.

She opened her eyes and watched the scenery go by for a while before she looked at Jackson's cousin.

"Do you know?"

Kendrick concentrated on the road for quite a while until Artane came into view, then he glanced at her. "I never answer anyone's questions."

"Does that mean you won't answer mine?"

He sighed, then continued to drive. The gates were opened for him by corporeal employees, which she found somewhat reassuring. He also seemed to have an assigned parking spot, which almost made her smile. The beauties of twenty-first century castle life.

He turned the car off, considered, then looked at her. "I think," he said carefully, "that you should just move ahead with whatever plans you have for your future and let the days go by as they will. I'll come get your door."

She nodded, though the only door she was interested in was the one that had recently separated her from the man she loved.

She managed to get herself inside the castle where she found several people gathered by one of the massive fireplaces. She greeted the people she knew, was introduced to and immediately forgot the names of the ones she didn't, then didn't argue when Mary and Samantha made excuses for her and walked with her upstairs.

They put her in her usual bedroom, which she appreciated because it gave her something that felt familiar. She took a shower, found her own clothes waiting for her—Mary had obviously brought them for her from Wyckham—then sat on the edge of her bed and examined her options.

One was to go to bed and pull the covers up over her head. That was tempting, but impossible. She was a Drummond and Drummonds who vanquished ruffians along the Scottish border in medieval England didn't hide out under duvets.

She tried to make a list of other ways she could keep herself busy, but she wasn't a list maker. She was too weary to go find Sam to do it for her, and she could hardly bring herself to open her bag and see if she might have her treasured notepad with Artane adorning the top of every page. She briefly thought about opening her bag to see if she'd forgotten to take out that shell Jackson had given her from his purse the night before, but that also seemed too taxing.

What she did know was that she wasn't going to ask anyone for a genealogical tome that might show her the names of the lords of Raventhorpe through the ages.

Not yet.

She decided that maybe the only thing she could do was get up and get on with at least looking as though she weren't on the verge of losing it. It had gotten dark outside without her noticing which was unsettling, but that also meant that someone might be thinking about dinner. She would carry on Jackson's tradition of offering to work off a meal and see if that wouldn't be a decent distraction for the evening.

She walked downstairs to the great hall without encountering any ghosts, then attempted another round of meeting Jackson's modern-day relatives. She was fairly sure she'd met at least one time-traveling uncle in that bunch, but she didn't have the heart to pin anyone down for details.

She finally made herself at home in the kitchen, perching on a stool next to the fire in true Cinderella fashion. The kitchen remained full through supper, though no one bothered her except to bring her food and drink. She was enormously grateful for the compassion of people who offered a stranger kindness.

In time, she found herself sitting in front of that enormous fireplace with just Zachary and Mary.

"Medieval poisons are terrible," Mary said, "but that was a modern creation."

"But it only grazed Jackson's hand," Zachary said quietly. "I'm guessing it will just knock him out for a couple of days, then he'll be back on his feet."

Olivia looked up and realized they were watching her gravely.

She took a deep breath to tell them she was all right, but other words came out of her mouth instead.

"We got married yesterday."

Mary caught her breath, then leaned over and hugged her. "He's very fortunate to have you. I'll remind him of that often when he gets here."

Olivia nodded, because she couldn't do anything else. She let their conversation wash over her until she thought she could sleep, then she accepted the offer of their company on her way back to her room.

"He's a canny lad," Mary said seriously. "He'll come for you."

Olivia nodded and tried to smile. She imagined she wasn't all that successful, but neither Mary nor Zachary seemed to expect anything else.

She went inside her room, locked the door, and put herself to bed.

She didn't sleep a wink.

She went back to the gate every day for a week.

It hadn't been so bad the first day or even the second day. It had rained on the third day, but it was England and it was autumn, so she hadn't really expected anything else.

She had quickly made friends with the priest she found cheerfully watching over the village church that Jackson IV had built so his people might gather together and worship. She hadn't dared go inside that church on the hill mostly because her memories of crowding into a much smaller chapel down the way were still fresh and she didn't want to replace them with anything else.

The priest hadn't asked any questions and she hadn't volunteered any answers. He had simply greeted her each day over the small wooden gate and promised to bring her hot tea if she needed it.

She had spent the days either pacing around the church walls, walking to the ruins of the castle and back, or occasionally venturing to the beach. They had been enjoyable walks, but they hadn't produced much past a case of sniffles that she had to admit hadn't come entirely from the weather.

Days Four through Six had been progressively more gloomy—and not just from the weather. She wasn't an unwelcoming person, but if one more adventurous hiker had asked her directions to the keep or wondered aloud what it had looked like originally, she would have offered a few salty remarks.

During those three days, she had also had a few pointed conversations with People in the Know and others who had merely kept her company when she hadn't been haunting Raventhorpe. She had found a wonderful beach companion in Mary de Piaget Smith who had walked along the shore with her as often as she'd asked and been willing to be silent or give her as many stories about Jackson as she'd wanted.

Zachary had proven to be a font of information, though a discreet one. He had agreed that there were other gates through time, though it might take Jackson a bit to find one.

If he could actually go looking for one, of course, which was something Zachary very wisely hadn't added.

She imagined Jackson would have nodded in approval at knowing that on all six of those days, either Zachary or Kendrick or Derrick had come along with her to Raventhorpe to make themselves scarce while acting as guardsmen. She knew Oliver had been there every day as well, though she'd only caught random sightings of him. He was a ghost, that guy.

Day Seven had been difficult. It had been pouring with rain, which she thought might finally push her fully into that massive cold she hadn't quite caught yet, and popping in and out of the car to get warm had started to get a little tedious. It had taken until the afternoon for the onshore winds to finally drive away the rain clouds and leave just gloom, but that had at least allowed her to get out of the car.

The priest had come to visit her as she'd loitered near their usual wooden barrier. He had looked off at the ocean for a moment or two, then turned to her and offered a single observation.

"It'll be a lovely day tomorrow, lass," he'd said gently. "I'm certain of it."

She had clung to that, because seven entire days had gone by without a sighting of a man she had come to realize she absolutely could not live without.

She had also decided that on the current day, the eighth since she'd last seen Jackson Alexander Kilchurn V, that she was done pretending there wasn't a way to know the truth.

She'd gotten up early, showered, then dressed warmly including sturdy woolen socks. She'd put on the flannel-lined raincoat she'd been loaned by Stephen's wife Peaches, dug around in her suitcase for a hat Aunt Philly had knitted her for Christmas one year, then marched down the stairs with a confidence that was entirely manufactured from her imagination.

All of which left her where she was at the moment: walking out the front door, hopefully late enough in the morning that her guardsmen had exhausted themselves in the lists and staggered off to take mid-day naps.

She pulled up short at the sight of Zachary Smith leaning against his car that she'd been driving every day. She pulled the door shut behind her and decided the best thing she could do was simply bluster her way past him. She walked down the stairs with a spring in her step she most definitely didn't feel and looked at him pointedly when he didn't step aside so she could get his key into his door.

"Nice day for a drive," she announced.

He nodded.

She could see in his expression that he knew what she was up to, so maybe there was no reason not to be honest.

"I have to look today," she said quietly.

"I know."

"I'm not sure he's alive."

"I understand."

She was familiar with the story of how Zachary had brought Mary to the future to keep her alive, though even that hadn't been a sure thing.

"How did you get through it?" she asked.

"I trusted my brother-in-law's skill with herbs," he said carefully, "and I'll admit I did more than my share of praying. If Jackson's grandfather got him with that needle, at least Jake will have a starting place. Never discount the power of a medieval healer who knows what he or she is doing." He paused. "Want me to come with you today?"

"I'll be all right," she said, hoping that would indeed be the case. "Besides, Oliver follows me no matter who comes with me. Who knew I would have my own security detail?"

Zachary smiled faintly. "Life is full of surprises."

"I'm not sure I like them anymore," she said honestly. She took a deep breath. "He's either alive or … well, he's either found another gate or he hasn't. It might just take time."

Or she might just look in the graveyard and have all her questions answered.

The front door opened suddenly and Kendrick bounced down the stairs with the familiarity of someone who had grown up endlessly doing the same thing.

"Jack's uncles have arrived at the gates," he said cheerfully, "and I'm off to dish out a little payback. Why don't you dive into the back of that lesser automobile, Olivia, and allow Zachary to get you past them? Toss him out after he's outlived his usefulness. I don't think you'll be written up for littering, but I could be wrong."

Zachary rolled his eyes, then smiled at her. "Family."

Kendrick shuddered. "Two years in and I'm still trying to accept it."

"I'll meet you later in the lists."

"Try not to leave me snoozing through the experience, lad,"

Kendrick said, clapping him firmly on the shoulder. "Off you go, you two. Stephen and I will see to the rabble at the gates."

Olivia wasn't opposed to a little subterfuge to start the day off properly, so she got into the back seat and scrunched up as best she could before she hid under the same blanket Jackson had once pulled over her in modern-day Raventhorpe. She felt a little smothered, but fortunately Zachary stopped after only a few minutes. She crawled out of the car to catch her breath, then accepted the keys from him.

"You're sure?" he asked.

"I'll be fine."

"Off you go, then, and remember to drive on the left."

She glared at him so he would feel properly rewarded for that unnecessary comment, then got in the car and let him close her door for her. She buckled up, made certain she knew what side of the road she was supposed to be on, then set off on a trip she knew she couldn't avoid any longer. She glanced in her rear view mirror at one point to find the comforting sight of Oliver's car in the distance, but that didn't take care of the terrible ache that had lodged somewhere under her ribs.

An hour later, she parked a decent distance away from the church and got out before she thought too much about what she intended to do.

She walked up the path toward the church, then stopped outside the low stone wall and looked at the beautiful little kirk there. It was remarkably well-preserved, but maybe it had been too far north for any Tudor mischief and a bit too austere for anyone else to have bothered with it.

She stood there with her hand on the gate for so long, she wondered if she might ever manage to move again. She was no coward, though, so she took a deep breath, then opened the gate and walked through it.

She continued all the way to the church itself, but no one came out to greet her. Maybe her friend the priest could sense her rapidly disappearing ability to keep it together. She was all for the thrill of the chase and wondering what lay at the end of a well-crafted hunt, but there were answers in that graveyard there that she wasn't sure she wanted.

She stood there with the sea breezes washing over her and revisited again all the reasons why it was possible for Jackson to have missed meeting her.

He could have forgotten her cell number. Maybe he'd been distracted by her awesome self and memories of holding her in his arms had driven it right out of his head. He could have allowed his father perhaps one too many looks at his phone and run out of battery. It wasn't as if he could have recharged it.

He also could have lost his phone entirely. After all, he had rifled through the belongings of a troupe of innocent actors without so much as a flicker of remorse, so maybe Karma was having a little payback.

He could also have changed his mind. That one seemed a little farfetched, but she was trying to be thorough. He might have reconsidered one of his previous medieval dating partners and decided that the wonders of the future and a twenty-first century woman to go with them were just not to his taste.

Or it could have been something else entirely.

She turned away from the sea to look at the little graveyard there. She never read the last five pages of any book, because it was part of the deliciousness of any mystery, that not knowing.

The current bit of unknowing was entirely different. If she knew, she could deal with what she knew. It was the wondering that was about to do her in.

The graveyard was full of numerous headstones, most of them not quite as straight as they likely had once been, almost all of them bearing writing that had been worn away from years of weather. She started at one end of the cemetery and looked at every single marker there—because she was apparently a coward.

Or she was until she had no more headstones to examine and she was left with only what she'd come to look at.

She stood in front of a row of headstones nearest the footings of the church, on the protected side of the building which she was certain had been deliberate on Jake's part. She didn't stop to identify any of the children or their mates. There was a particular grave she was searching for and she looked at the row in front of her without stopping to brace for what she might possibly see.

Jackson Alexander Kilchurn V.

She felt the ground rock under her feet. For a moment, she wondered if the north of England had just experienced an earthquake big enough to knock what was left of Raventhorpe off the edge of the cliff into the ocean, then she realized she was simply trying to faint.

"Olivia!"

Great. Fainting, then hallucinations? She would likely pass out in a gloomy, almost-deserted graveyard in the north of England and she would drown in tears and rain before anyone bothered to come look for her. She was half afraid she might mold as well.

She felt arms go around her to break her fall. That would have been lovely if she hadn't felt as if she weren't quite attached to her body any longer. No paranormal activity? That was the last time she would ever say that out loud.

"*Olivia.*"

She supposed she would have to thank Oliver for catching her before she simply collapsed to the ground, so she opened her eyes and tried to focus on him.

Only it wasn't Oliver.

It was Jackson

The world slowed, then seemingly stopped for an endlessly moment before it suddenly began to spin again and she found that she could breathe again.

She threw her arms around him. She thought she might have

made a few sobbing noises, but she was honestly just too worn out to care. He was wheezing as well, so maybe he wouldn't notice.

"You're late," she managed, finally.

"Never again," he promised. "Never again, my love."

She held him for almost as long as she wanted to and wept almost as much as she needed to. Jackson was holding her with equal enthusiasm, though, so maybe he was going through the same things.

"Olivia?" he said finally.

"Yes, Jackson?"

"It's raining."

"Is it?" she asked, feeling herself burst into a smile worthy of any 1950s musical star. "I hadn't noticed."

He laughed a little. "To be honest, neither had I, but you'll chill out in the open here. Let us seek shelter by the church."

She couldn't bring herself to release him, so she kept her arms around him and stumbled with him over to the little porch at the front of the church. He leaned back against the wall, pulled her close, and sighed deeply.

"I'm not sure I can let you go," he said frankly.

"Please don't." She stood happily in his embrace until she almost believed she wasn't dreaming, then lifted her head and looked at him. "I want details, but I'm not sure I'm ready for them."

"I understand," he said. "I think I might need to hold you for quite a bit longer before I'm ready to give them to you, but I must at least know how you've fared. Has my grandfather vexed you?"

She shook her head. "He fell on that needle and your uncles carted him off to the hospital. We haven't heard anything since, though Derrick has been doing some investigating on the sly."

He looked around with a frown, then back at her. "Where are your guardsmen?"

"Oliver's somewhere, though I don't usually see too much of him. Today's the first day I haven't had some cousin or other shadowing me."

"Then they all live another day," he said, pulling her close again. "I'm sorry that I wasn't there to protect you."

She shook her head. "You got me out of the way and took your grandfather on yourself, which was more than enough. What happened after that?"

"I'll tell you everything when we're happily in front of a decent fire, but let's say that it took me until this morning to find a working gate." He shivered. "We might have to find that fire sooner rather than later."

She nodded, but couldn't bring herself to let go of him. "I worried."

"I did as well," he said quietly. "I'm sorry it took longer than I wanted it to." He looked at her. "I left my gear just outside the stone wall."

"I'll come with you to get it."

"I think that might be wise. Don't let go of my hand."

She nodded, then walked with him out through the little gate, watched him pull it shut behind them, then went with him to retrieve his medieval backpack. She happily kept hold of him as they walked back to the car and he put his gear into the trunk. He opened her door for her, looked glanced at his sword lying there between the seats. He took a deep breath, then looked at her.

"You didn't lose hope."

She shook her head. She imagined she didn't need to say how close she'd come to it, because she could see the same thing in his expression.

He took her face in his hands, kissed her softly. "Let's go home."

"All right."

"Where are we staying?"

She smiled. "Artane."

He hugged her briefly, then tucked her into the car. She waited for him, took a moment to breathe, then hoped she could stop looking at him long enough to get them back. He folded himself into Zachary's passenger seat, let out his breath slowly, then looked at her with a smile.

"Fish and chips on the way?"

And all was right with the world. She nodded happily, then turned the car around to head back toward the spot that had started their whole adventure.

TWENTY-EIGHT

JACKSON WAS TEMPTED TO CLOSE his eyes briefly to recover from a pair of days of sleepless travel, but found he couldn't. He might have missed something otherwise.

He was also torn between watching the landscape as it they passed it or watching his lady wife as she concentrated on getting them to Artane safely. Actually, the choice was easily made, so he shifted in his seat and looked his fill.

"Don't make me nervous."

He smiled. "I'm simply admiring the view."

She shot him a quick look. "I can't believe you're here."

He could scarce believe it either, and he supposed he had come very close to remaining in the past permanently. He suspected it might take him a few days and likely the extended haunting of some cousin's kitchen to find his feet fully under him again.

"So, now that you've had lunch and we're a captive audience for a few minutes, what happened?"

"The tale isn't terribly interesting," he said, knowing he was hedging but unable to help himself. "It would seem that whatever poison my grandfather intended for my father was fairly unpleasant."

"Fairly?" she asked skeptically.

He smiled and attempted a careless shrug, though he suspected she wouldn't believe that, either. The truth was, the concoction that had obviously been meant to kill his father had almost slain him and he'd had but a small sampling of it. He'd been senseless for several days, which he couldn't say he remembered, and been tormented by horrific dreams, which he remembered all too well. If he never saw another surly demon feeding the fires of Hell and waiting for him to wake so he could be tormented a bit more, it would be too soon.

"'Twas powerful enough to leave me unconscious for a bit," he conceded, "and I was simply scratched by that needle he was wielding. I woke, thankfully, embraced my family again, gathered up a few treasures for you, then spent a pair of days trying to convince the doorway up on the hill that it wanted to appear. I think my reputation for tenacity does not extend to these magical realms, for it was unresponsive to my polite invitations."

She smiled. "I'll just bet. So, what gate did you use?"

"Definitely not the one near Artane," he said uneasily. "I feared it might send me to an entirely different year."

She looked at him in alarm. "I could have been every day of ninety when you got here finally."

"And heart-stoppingly beautiful still," he agreed, "though I was actually more worried I might wind up in Elizabeth I's day. Fortunately for my modesty, my uncle Nicholas arrived with a map and a few suggestions. I finally settled on a very temperamental and dodgy little cluster of flowers rather closer to Wyckham than I wanted to travel, but it worked surprisingly well."

She smiled. "Did Sam and Theo come help you?"

"They were quite noticeably absent, which leaves me wondering if I should track them down to find out what they thought was more important than offering me aid." He paused. "I could begin, if I can use your phone."

She slid him a look. "Run out of battery on yours?"

"Blame my sire," he said lightly.

She smiled easily enough, though he could sense that she grieved for him.

"They will come and find us, love," he said quietly. "I'm sure of it."

She took a deep breath, then nodded. "I'm sure you're right."

He slipped his hand under her hair to attempt his accustomed goodly work of easing any tension she might suffer from too much driving only to have a quick warning look, then a laugh as his reward. He supposed there would be time enough to determine if she had changed her mind about him, though he would be the first to admit that patience was not one of his virtues.

"Do you still need a year and a day?" he asked, because he couldn't help himself.

She smiled briefly at him, then shook her head. "No. Do you?"

"I traveled over eight centuries to come find you," he said easily. "That was enough."

He would have said more, but he was distracted by the sight of Artane's gates open and Lady Gladstone standing to one side, waving at them. Olivia lowered her window as she stopped the car.

"What's wrong?" she asked.

"There are visitors up the way," Lady Gladstone said grimly.

Jackson realized with a start that he was wearing his medieval clothing and his sword was wedged rather visibly between the car's chairs, but there was nothing to be done about that. He leaned over and looked at the woman.

"Any ideas who, Lady Gladstone?"

"I believe, Lord Jackson, that they are your father's brothers."

Olivia bowed her head and laughed a little. Jackson couldn't decide if it were from the thought of his having to face off with his uncles or the knowledge that Stephen's ferociously efficient gate guard knew more than she likely should.

"Thank you, Lady Gladstone," he said politely. "I will go attend to them as quickly as may be. Might I come move a box or two for you later, or deposit several Elizabeth Reginas into your coffers?"

"Both," she said, then she winked at Olivia before she drew back and marched into her guard chamber.

"She's got your number," Olivia said, putting up her window.

"Does she?" he asked in alarm.

She laughed a little. "It just means she knows how to get you to do what she wants you to do, not that she has your phone number. I keep thinking she's going to want to use you in some guidebook about the castle, so don't be surprised." She glanced at him. "You're very handsome."

"But very married," he said with a light sigh. "I suppose she can take my photograph if she must, but any Future lassies who might also want to have my number will go away disappointed."

She smiled, then leaned her head back against the seat. "What do you want to do about the uncles?"

He looked down at his clothing, then considered. "Are there stables here still, do you think?"

"I'm pretty sure there are."

"And the lads are inside?"

"Most everyone you know, yes."

"Then might I borrow your phone? We're trapped in the automobile so you know I won't lose it."

She laughed a little and fetched it from her pocket. "I trust you with it."

He caught her hand as he took her phone, then carefully kissed the back of it. "Do you trust me with yourself?"

She looked at him in surprise, then color began to creep up her cheeks. "Ah—"

"You're blushing."

She glared at him, but 'twas half-hearted at best. "Yes, I do and yes, I am. I think I might have to go blush some more when you're not looking at me." She waved him on to his business. "You can take your pick of relatives for the delivery of different clothes."

He paused for a moment, then looked at her carefully. "All of them are here?"

She nodded. "They worried, I think."

"No doubt about what I would do to them if they didn't guard you properly."

"I'm sure that was part of it."

He cleared his throat and focused on her phone because that was easier than wondering if he might weep for the second time that day. He would obviously need time in the lists to help him get hold of himself before he was reduced to a swordsman of Zachary Smith's mettle. He found Derrick in the wee window of Olivia's phone and sent out a call to him. It was, he supposed, fairly reassuring how quickly Derrick answered.

"So, is this you, Olivia," Derrick drawled in French, "or did your boyfriend lose his phone and have to borrow yours?"

Jackson snorted. "Her *husband* needs to feed the battery in his, so he is using hers. Also, she will learn this tongue in time and you will cease to be safe around her and her awesome self-defense skills."

Derrick laughed briefly. "Welcome back. What do you need?"

"Clothing?"

"Where?"

"The stables, if you can manage it."

"Be there in five."

Jackson hung up, then looked at his lady. "He'll meet us in the stables, or so he says. He knew I was here."

"Blame Oliver, I'm guessing," she said happily. "And yes, I would like to learn your version of French. Genevieve promised to teach me all the most useful swear words."

He smiled to himself, then turned away from the keep as Olivia drove the car past the front door. He didn't see any relations cluttering up the stairs, but he wouldn't have been surprised to have found his aunt Peggy flying down them in a temper.

Jackson accepted clothing from Derrick at the stable entrance, then made use of an empty stall to quickly change into appropriate garments of the day. He put his medieval things in the boot, locked the car, then handed Olivia back the keys for safekeeping. He took his lady's hand and looked at her cousin.

"Thoughts?"

"What did your Dad suggest?" Derrick asked.

"Dying in front of my grandfather, though I'm not certain I can put things in my eyes to change their color."

"Well," Derrick said slowly, "that's the thing, actually. Your grandfather passed this morning, so it's just the uncles inside now."

Jackson nodded slowly. "If he fell upon his weapon, I can see why he wouldn't have survived it. Perhaps 'tis for the best. But why are my sire's brothers here? Did they come to announce that, or are they here simply to make trouble?"

Derrick shrugged. "I get the feeling they're just here out of curiosity, but you'll have to decide how much of that you want to satisfy. Stephen and Kendrick finally let them in the gates about an hour ago after leaving them outside for most of the morning." He smiled. "It's been an interesting day so far, but I'm guessing you could say the same thing."

Jackson smiled in spite of himself. "Aye, I could. As for those lads inside, should I introduce myself as a natural son of my grandsire's and let them make of that what they will? I could also be a cousin, if the irony won't slay me first."

"You certainly have enough of those, true. Why don't we just go inside and see how things play out?" He dug in his jacket pocket, then held out two disks attached by some metal business. "Sunglasses. They'll at least hide your eyes. I can pretend to be your lawyer, if you like, which would keep you from having to speak."

Jackson supposed if anyone could act the part of someone else, it would be the man in front of him. He nodded, then looked at his wife. "Shall we?"

She nodded. "Here goes nothing."

He made himself a brief mental note to ask Kendrick for a list of useful Future phrases, then walked with Olivia behind Derrick across the courtyard and up into his uncle's hall. Once inside, Olivia took his sunglasses from him and carefully rested them on his nose.

"I'll keep you from running into anything."

He saw immediately why that might be a concern, though his eyes had adjusted to the gloom by the time they reached the lord's table. He studied the field to take note of where the main players were. Stephen was obviously keeping the rabble under control and with him were Kendrick, Zachary, and … his mother's younger brother, John? Admittedly he hadn't seen the man in a score of years, but he had very vivid memories of being at his uncle's wedding when he himself had been a child. His uncle only nodded at him with a brief smile before he turned back to watching the visitors.

Those visitors were, as expected, his father's brothers. They were dressed in very fine apparel that he suspected might be pertinent to their business of making money, but that could likely be investigated later.

He walked with Olivia to stand just slightly behind Derrick who seemed to be quite comfortable taking a place next to Stephen. All that time as King Henry V had obviously not gone to waste.

"We understand that your father very unfortunately passed," Stephen said gravely. "My sincere condolences."

"He cut Jake out of the will three years ago," one of the uncles said with a snort, "so Jake might be the one needing condolences."

"Well," Stephen said politely, "feel free to offer them."

Derrick inclined his head to Stephen. "With your permission, my lord, I'll speak for my client."

Jackson glanced at Olivia, but she only shrugged slightly. He turned back to the battle at hand and concentrated on listening to Derrick inform his uncles crisply that he—or, his sire, actually—had enough money to survive quite nicely, but also enough to pay a great amount to a lawyer to maintain a switch that they didn't want him touching. He listened with half an ear to Derrick's words, but he was more interested in watching his father's brothers to see what words wouldn't reveal.

The elder two he immediately identified as belligerent but not necessarily dangerous. The youngest of the lot wasn't arguing, but instead merely listening. Jackson also found that brother occasionally glancing his way, as if he studied the field of battle as well.

Interesting, that.

"I never had anything against Jake," one of the elder brothers said suddenly. "Not really."

"Are you crazy?" the other said incredulously. "You wanted his business."

"I hate jewelry. Besides, it's all the in past. I'm executor of Dad's estate, and I have final say on things. Jake still gets nothing."

The second brother snorted. "You have the final say until Peggy stabs you in the dark, so maybe you should keep your mouth shut and watch your back. Let's just leave Jake alone and concentrate on dividing up Dad's stuff."

"Mother might have something to say about that," the third uncle put in mildly. "Unless you two have forgotten she's still alive."

"I'm wondering," Derrick put in politely, "if this is a conversation that perhaps you'll want to have in private? I think that might be your sister outside the hall door, wondering where you three are."

Jackson had heard his aunt screeching before, so he suspected Derrick was right about that. He hung back as his family members helped his father's uncles across the hall and out the front door, then he took the sunglasses off and looked at his wife.

"I might have too many relations."

She smiled. "You might."

"I think we might want to make sure the rabble gets out the gates."

"I'll come with you."

He put his arm around her and walked with her across the hall and out the door. He wasn't unhappy to merely sit on the top step and watch as not only Mistress Peggy, but his uncles were escorted out of the gates.

"Well, that's finished," he said with a shrug.

She looked at him seriously. "I'm sorry about your grandfather, but maybe it's for the best. It sounds like you might have a grandmother in the States, though."

He looked at her and felt a little faint. "I *definitely* have too many relations."

She laughed a little and leaned her head on his shoulder. "I'll come along and protect you when you go visit. I'm very fierce in battle as you might or might not know."

He rested his cheek against her hair and smiled, because he did know. He watched his family members walk back up the way to them, exchanged various pleasantries with his cousins and his mother's brother on their way up the steps, then patted his wife's hand.

"Let me go fetch my gear," he said. "I'll return immediately."

She lifted her head and looked at him. "Don't get lost."

"Do you want to come with me?"

"I do."

He smiled, then took her hand and pulled her to her feet as he rose. He fetched his sword and gear from the car and his medieval clothing from the barn, then turned to find his wife standing there with her hands outstretched. He sighed and handed his sword over, which at least earned him a sweet smile from his lady. He kissed her briefly, then nodded toward the hall.

"Hot shower, hot drink, hot meal, then we'll negotiate from there."

"Whatever you say, my lord."

He smiled at her as he offered her his arm, then found that he was halfway across the courtyard before he realized they weren't about to encounter a stray cousin, they were looking at an uncle—and not one of a medieval vintage.

"How did he get back inside?" Olivia whispered.

Jackson took a deep breath. "I've no idea, but once more into the breach, I suppose."

She lifted her eyebrows briefly, then walked with him across the courtyard to where the youngest of his father's brothers was standing. Jackson supposed there was little to be done about disguising himself at that point. His cousins had apparently gone back inside the hall, which left him to sort his own business.

He appreciated that, actually, though he realized immediately that Kendrick and Zachary were peeking around the corner of the keep. He glared at them briefly on principle alone, then looked at his uncle.

The man studied him for a moment or two, then held out his hand. Jackson looked at it to make certain it was weapon-free, then noted that the man's other hand was also in plain sight.

He shook hands, then merely watched his father's next-eldest brother without feeling the need to speak.

The man broke first, laughing a little. "Well, whoever you are, you have his stare."

"Do I?" Jackson asked mildly.

"I'm William."

"And so you are."

William smiled. "You look quite a bit like my brother."

Jackson only smiled politely in return.

"I am a big fan of the National Gallery," William said easily. "It's a funny thing, though. I was looking at a painting recently of Henry III and I could have sworn I saw my brother's signature on it." He paused and offered a long, unflappable stare of his own. "But that wouldn't be possible."

"Most likely not," Jackson agreed.

"I mean, Jake would have had to have scrawled his initials on a priceless piece of art."

"All too true."

William lifted his eyebrows briefly. "Life is strange."

"That is true, as well."

William studied him for another moment or two. "I'll keep my family in check."

"I'm sure I'll appreciate your efforts."

William smiled faintly and pulled out his folding purse, then removed a small piece of parchment from it. He looked at it for a moment in silence, then held it out.

Jackson took it, noted his uncle's name written there along with his phone number and other things he would study later, then looked at the man again.

"Prove me," William said quietly, "for as long as you care to, then give me a call if you're in London and want to meet for a drink. Pubs are discreet."

"I'll keep that in mind."

William hesitated, then looked at him. "I should have been a better brother to Jake. I regret that. I would like to try to make up for it now."

Jackson said nothing only because he wasn't entirely certain what, if anything, he should say. He watched his uncle walk all the way down to the gates, then waited a bit more until the noise of a car had disappeared into the distance. He took a deep breath and looked at his lady.

"Well," he managed.

"You're one cool cucumber," she said honestly. "I don't think even my grandfather could have outlasted you there."

"And your Aunt Philly?"

"Well," she said with a smile, "you'll have to try her and see."

He picked up his gear, then nodded toward the door. "What would you say to a visit so I might meet her? But no budget airlines."

"You've never flown *any* airlines, and how do you know about them?"

"My father warned me whilst I was puking my guts up into a bucket a few days ago."

"I might need more details," she said with a smile.

"I'll give you anything you want after I'm no longer faint from hunger," he promised. "After you, wife."

She snorted, then smiled before she walked up the stairs and opened the front door.

Three hours later, he sat at the work table in Artane's kitchens, much as he had innumerable times over the course of his life, and wondered if his heart might break.

There were things that were different, to be sure. Beyond finding himself occasionally startled by some Future marvel, he caught himself more than once looking up and expecting to find either his parents or a sibling walking into the chamber to join him at the fire. That would possibly ease with the passage of time, but perhaps not.

Being so near death in the past had likely been a blessing in disguise. He'd had hours of conversations with both his mother and father, perhaps almost enough to fill up the years until he saw them again.

He had a sip of his wine to pull himself away from those memories, then looked at the things that might not be so different from what they had been in the past.

First on that list was the comfort of family. He was profoundly grateful for the presence of his admittedly favorite cousin, even if her husband came along as part of the bargain. Kendrick was also a very welcome member of his current roster of cousins, Genevieve was a saint for enduring him, and their children were actually quite charming. The additions of Stephen and Peaches, Derrick and Samantha, and his own uncle John and his wife Tess were agreeable, as well.

He was also very grateful that he hadn't landed permanently in Renaissance times where he would have been alone.

Alone and missing the most important person in the chamber.

He sat back in his chair and looked at the woman sitting next to him. The light from the fire and the pleasing lights from the kitchen Future lamps fell softly on her and reminded him why he'd honestly been so startled by her when he'd finally had the chance to look at her properly. Not only was she lovely and courageous, she found him tolerable.

He could scarce believe that such a woman was his.

"So, Jack," Kendrick said pleasantly. "What's your plan?"

He pulled his attentions back to his cousin only to realize that Kendrick was smirking at him. Obviously he'd been caught mooning over his wife, but what else could they expect?

"Sell a few coins," he said easily, "find a labor to do, spend enormous amounts of time staring at my lady wife and feeling grateful that she was kind enough to wed me." He looked at his cousin. "I won't ask you for any other suggestions, thank you just the same."

"You can come work for me," Kendrick offered. "Open and close my gates, polish my boots, keep me from snoozing in the lists, that sort of thing."

"I'll remember that," Jackson said, vowing to repay his cousin for the suggestions at his earliest opportunity which hopefully would not be during the next fortnight or so.

"You're welcome to stay here as long as you like," Stephen said. "I'm nowhere near Lord Robin's level, but I'll meet you outside with a pair of dull swords occasionally."

Jackson watched several of his other male relatives raise hands as well, which he appreciated. Perhaps there would be other ways save running himself into the ground to keep from going to fat.

He set that aside to think about later, then looked at his wife. "You look weary."

He supposed in another time and place he would have repaid not only Kendrick but John for their chuckles, but he was a man firmly committed to action instead of words. He glared at them both, rose, then looked at his host.

"Might I raze your icy larder, my lord?"

Stephen waved him on, looking as though he might be struggling to stifle his own laughter. Jackson fetched what he thought might suit, liberated two spoons from his and Olivia's plates, then helped her out of her chair. Knight of the realm to the very last, assuredly.

"Can I offer any advice?" Kendrick asked politely.

"Your father already tried," Jackson said, shooting him a glare. "You don't want to meet his fate."

"You don't," Olivia agreed. "Lady Amanda promised to kill him and she wasn't kidding."

Jackson nodded his good e'ens to those surrounding the table, listened to Olivia offer hasty good-byes as well, then paused with her in the passageway.

"Forgive me," he said. "Did I pull you away from the festivities too quickly?"

She smiled and nudged him toward the great hall. "I think we have plenty of time to make nice with your family and mine tomorrow. I'm exhausted."

He looked at her in surprise, had a laugh for his trouble, then found himself pulled along with her into the hall and over to the stairs.

He reminded himself several times on his way up those stairs and down the passageway that he was indeed not a callow youth, but by the time he'd reached their chamber and shut the door behind them, he had begun to wonder.

He leaned back against the door and looked at her. "Cards?"

"Cards?" she echoed.

"I have gold this time," he offered.

"Are you out of your mind?"

He almost smiled, but managed to maintain a thoughtful expression. He considered the double-fudge bliss, then looked at his wife. "This will most likely melt."

"One could hope."

He laughed a little in spite of himself, then went to put dessert in a corner of one of the high windows there.

"Is that going to help?"

"This was my bedchamber in the past," he said, wedging the

pint into the draftiest spot he could find, "so this might at least slow the inevitable."

"We could always drink it tomorrow for breakfast."

He supposed they could, and if not, there would be time in the future to find more. He walked back over to his wife, pulled her into his arms, and decided there would also be time in the future to tell her how grateful he was to find himself in the same century with her.

Perhaps on the morrow, since they would see it together.

Twenty-Nine

Olivia walked into her bedroom, rubbing her arms against the chill and wondering where it the world she'd left her granddad's jacket. She didn't usually roam around Artane without it primarily because castles were chilly and secondarily because castles were full of things that might need to be investigated and her jacket pockets always contained useful things like a flashlight and a notebook.

She looked around the room that had apparently been Jackson's in the past to find it decorated comfortingly in things that were medieval *from* medieval times and not brand new because they currently resided *in* medieval times. It made her a little nervous to know she'd left something from that same era downstairs, some-*one*, actually, who she sincerely hoped wouldn't suddenly decide to rush off to jump up and down on a great big sort of X that might or might not lie on some unusual spot in the middle of a ring of mushrooms, flowers, or weeds. He wouldn't have gone without her, though, which was simultaneously endearing and terrifying.

Her life continued to be, she had to admit, a bit strange.

There were things, though, that were comfortingly familiar. Her aunt's stitchery was in a prominent place on the mantel, reframed in a more permanent sort of affair which she supposed might guide another three generations of Drummond-Kilchurns toward all sorts of adventures. Sitting next to that was a stack of note pads boasting Artane on the top of every page from the B&B down the hill, bought by her husband who was extremely persuasive and not unwilling to plunk down a few Elizabeth Reginas for the things he wanted.

She perched on the edge of a chair and gathered her thoughts. It had been almost a month of sheer bliss. She'd had such a happy mixture of medieval surroundings, medieval husband, and modern-day conveniences like ice cream and endless documentaries, she half wondered how she'd ever managed with anything else.

That business with his uncles had gone as well as it could, she supposed, though who knew what Peggy Kilchurn would do. Maybe the brothers would keep her so busy fighting over useless things in court that she wouldn't have time to stir up any mischief. The final nail in the coffin would probably have to be Penelope selling the physical shop in London, but maybe that would happen in time as well.

She looked at the coffee table in front of her that was covered with things Jackson had obviously borrowed from Stephen and reached over to pick up the book that had started her down a path she absolutely didn't regret. She opened it and smiled at the photo plate of Miss Eugenie Kilchurn. That was definitely a rapier she was holding, but it didn't look particularly Victorian. Perhaps she'd taken it as payment for room and board offered to some time-traveling Elizabethan guest.

And if the illustrious Miss Kilchurn had been born just a bit before Victoria had taken the throne, what had she traded to leave her time to take up residence in a different one? Was there some sort of cosmic inventory ledger that had to balance out perfectly once every so often? She could only imagine the sort of antique shop a woman who looked hauntingly like Jackson's younger sister might be running out of her barn—

Her phone beeped at her, making her jump a little. She pulled her phone out of her pocket to find she'd received a text missive from someone she was absolutely crazy about.

The fire in the great hall is hot, wife. Come sit with me? JAKV.

She smiled. She'd left Jackson there approximately ten minutes earlier, but maybe he'd gotten lonely. She set her book aside, found her jacket draped over the chair where she realized she'd left it earlier, then made her way down to Artane's great hall.

Jackson was indeed sitting in front of the fire, his nose buried in a book. She sat down across from him and watched him read.

"I would repay you for yet more of those lustful looks," he said, glancing at her briefly, "but I'm engrossed in this text."

"Well, you do have a few centuries to catch up on," she agreed.

"Indeed, I do."

"And here I thought you texted me for a particular reason," she said lightly. "Obviously you have no time for shenanigans."

He looked to be fighting a smile. "Is that what we're calling it now?"

"That was your word for it."

"A fine word, if I do say so myself, but aye, perhaps later. I'm quite engaged reading right now. Busy, busy, busy."

He said it in three languages, so he was obviously very busy, indeed. She leaned her head back against her chair and happily watched him read for another minute or two. There was something afoot, but she was content to let it play out how it would. He had invited her downstairs, after all.

She was tempted to pinch herself to make sure she wasn't living a dream. Jackson was just as intense as he had been from the moment she'd met him, sprinkled, of course, with a relentless curiosity and an endless desire to arrange things so everyone around him was safe.

But there was something else there that she realized had been steadily changing about him over the past couple of weeks, so slowly that she honestly hadn't noticed it at first.

He looked as if he were at peace.

"Just so terribly busy," he murmured, turning another page.

She smiled. "Your book's upside down, sport."

He closed his eyes briefly, then laughed and set his book aside before he reached out and pulled her over to sit on his lap. "I endeavored to give you a bit of peace from my awesome self, but if you insist … "

"We're in a public place, you know."

"I think everyone's either gone on holiday or away to their bedchambers to sleep," he whispered loudly. He looked at her purposefully. "I can pick the lock to Stephen's solar, you know. Lovely floor tapestry there."

"Jackson," she said, faintly appalled—and perhaps more appalled at herself that she was actually considering it. "I've been having a thought today, so don't distract me."

"Does it concern yours truly?"

"Actually, it does—and no, it isn't that sort of thought." She paused. "I might change my mind about that in a minute."

"I suggest you change your mind swiftly and follow that new thought where it leads," he said pleasantly.

"All right," she said, blushing a little. "But until I do, stop looking at me that way."

"I'm just looking."

"You never just look."

He shrugged unrepentantly. "I'm direct."

"That you are," she agreed. "So, about this thought."

"Which apparently doesn't involve me, but go ahead." He looped his arms around her waist and clasped his hands over her hip, then paused. "You're having *that* sort of thought."

She nodded. "Remember how we found that coin?"

"My coin?"

"The ownership of the coin is still in question because, if you remember, I left it on my side of the bed last night."

"Is it still there?"

"If it isn't, then you poached it which doesn't have anything to do—well, all right, finders keepers, losers weepers, and you're distracting me. This is important."

He leaned his forehead against hers. "I surrender. Not the coin, of course—"

"Jackson!"

He laughed a little and made himself comfortable. "Very well, Olivia, what are you thinking?"

She pushed out of his arms, but that was almost worse because she could see his face and the rest of him so she resituated herself on his lap and looked at him seriously.

"You know how Zachary says that you can't take items from one century to another?"

"Unless they've seasoned appropriately—"

"Or there's an exchange—"

"Which apparently James MacLeod finds alarming."

She shivered. "I'm almost afraid to visit him and hear all of that from the horse's mouth. But what if the coin was an exchange—alarming or not—for your key? What if you dropped it there, then that left one of those coins you got paid for marrying that couple in 1600 coming with you here?"

He considered, then shook his head. "I had all of them still in my hand when Sam and Theo pushed me into that gate. I put them in my purse where I arrived in this day."

"All except one," she said. "Which was upstairs on *my* side of the bed recently."

He smiled briefly. "'Tis still there, my love. I was just messing with you. As for the other, 'tis a fine thought, but I'm certain I didn't leave my key behind in Renaissance England—" He stopped speaking, then looked at her uneasily. "I did wake from cracking my head against a rock on my journey there only to find some vile youth trying to filch my boots, but surely he didn't shake anything loose."

"Do you think so?"

"I wonder if Stephen has a collection of keys somewhere, perhaps in some Renaissance cabinet."

She hopped off his lap, then pulled a flashlight out of her jacket pocket. "Want to go look?"

"Absolutely," he said pushing himself to his feet.

"Wait," she amended. "What if the case is locked?"

"I can pick any lock before me," he said confidently. "Well, with the exception of the lock in my father's shop."

"I think that one's booby-trapped," she offered, "so you probably wouldn't want to try."

He shivered and took her hand. "Let's see if we can find the key so that isn't necessary."

"Do we need a map?"

He shot her a look that made her smile, then he smiled as well. "I hope not. We'll come back and fetch your guidebook if we need it."

She walked with him down into the cellar, then along a path and back up more stairs that she certainly hoped weren't going to land them in a dungeon. At least whatever Jackson's experience with modern additions to the castle might have lacked, he made up for an uncanny ability to find unlocked doors. He finally opened the door to a more modern wing of Artane, peered inside, then made her a low bow.

"Use your wee torch to light our way and let's see what might be hiding in these collections of history."

She walked with him through the gallery and back through the centuries until she found herself standing in front of what looked like a likely year. She had hardly begun to really examine the goods before she heard the unmistakable sound of paranormal activity consisting of rather enthusiastic ghostly moans.

"That's not funny," she squeaked.

"I'm not making that noise," he managed, sounding as if he might be on the verge of squeaking as well. He turned around. "Stop moaning, you fiends, and show yourselves!"

Olivia pointed her flashlight at the shapes she could see standing ten feet away from them. Jackson put his arm around her shoulders, no doubt to give her courage, though he didn't feel all that steady himself.

There were three Scots and an Elizabethan gentleman standing there in front of them, watching them expectantly. She leaned closer to her husband.

"I know two of them," she whispered. "I saw them at the airport in Seattle."

"I know the other two," Jackson murmured. "I married one of them." He looked at her. "Or, not, in my case."

She imagined that might be a topic for a less perilous location, but before Jackson could begin what she was sure would have been an apology, the Drummond chieftain sighed gustily and waved them on.

"Pick the lock, young Kilchurn," he said wearily, "and let us be finished here. The suspense is killing me."

"Ye're already dead, ye fool," the Elizabethan ghost said shortly.

"And ye could be a bit supportive instead of critical, ye blasted Brit!" the McKinnon clansman exclaimed.

Olivia couldn't help but smile weakly at him. He had, after all, reminded her of the importance of genealogical research.

The Scotsman wearing a MacLeod plaid secured to his shoulder with a mighty silver brooch stepped forward and nodded to them both.

"Lady Olivia," he said politely. "Lord Jackson."

"Laird Ambrose," Jackson said. "A pleasure. Again."

"My sister would have things to say to you if your wee cousins hadn't put things to rights, but that's in the past." Laird Ambrose gestured for them to continue. "I won't spoil the pleasure of hunting for treasures that might or might not find themselves in locked cabinets."

Olivia looked at Jackson and thought she might have smiled if she hadn't been so unnerved by the additions to their number. Jackson took a deep breath, turned to the cabinet in front of them, then pulled a small collection of lock-picking tools from his pocket.

She leaned over and looked at them. "Where'd you get those?"

"A gift from Kendrick," he said with a faint smile. "For my twelfth birthday."

"That was a banner year for you, wasn't it?"

He smiled. "I daresay." He took a deep breath. "Fingers crossed, my love."

She smiled and held the flashlight for him while he, with an unnerving ease, got them into a cabinet containing what she guessed were priceless family heirlooms. He looked over his shoulder at their visitors.

"No advice?" he asked.

"Dig deeply?" Fulbert suggested.

She looked over the goods for likely piles to be dug into, then pointed her flashlight at a very weathered bucket full of keys. Jackson took a deep breath, then dug around in it for several long moments. He went still so quickly that she wasn't entirely certain he hadn't encountered some sort of deadly spider, but he only looked at her. He pulled his hand out of the bucket and held up a key.

The key.

As if in celebration, every light in the gallery came on. She jumped right along with her husband and found herself suddenly pulled behind him as he faced the new menace. He took a deep breath, then made someone a small bow.

"Humphreys," he said politely. "A good e'en to you."

Olivia peeked around his shoulder to find Humphreys standing ten feet away from them. He looked at them, glanced at the ghosts, then sighed deeply.

"Did you find what you sought?" he asked calmly.

Jackson nodded. "We did. Again, my apologies. Our haste was great."

"I will refrain from commenting about potential substitutions for the thrill of exercise in the lists of times past," Humphreys said with another sigh, "and how you might seek the same in another venue."

"The key is mine," Jackson offered.

"Which is why, my lord Jackson, I will not be calling the authorities."

"Humphreys, my gratitude knows no bounds."

Olivia caught the wink Humphreys sent her and smiled as he helpfully locked the cabinet back up, inclined his head to the ghosts still loitering there, then gestured for them all to proceed him out the door.

She waited until she and Jackson had reached the great hall and Jackson had retrieved the book he'd left there before she dared say anything.

"Miraculous," she whispered.

"Me?"

She laughed and put her arms around him. "You are, too. When do you want to go to London? We could take the train down and probably stay in Derrick's company flat. I still have that key."

"Let us send Penelope a text missive on the morrow," he said, taking her hand and pulling her with him. "I think we should go celebrate treasures found tonight."

She wasn't entirely sure he hadn't added *along with a few shenanigans* under his breath as well, which she would definitely ask him to clarify after they'd shut their own door. And bolted it. And likely stuffed a towel along the bottom of it to keep out any drafts and things.

Castle life was, as she was discovering, an adventure.

Two days later, she perched on the arm of a couch and watched her husband do some pretty fast talking to a woman who was coming face-to-face with a substantial bit of paranormal activity.

"Let me see if I understand this," Penelope said faintly. "You're Jake's oldest son?"

Jackson nodded solemnly.

"And your mother, Amanda, is the daughter of the man who built Artane."

"And was its first lord," Jackson agreed. "Rhys de Piaget."

Olivia found Penelope looking at her, quite possibly for help and most definitely for reassurance. She pulled two photographs out of the envelope she'd brought and handed them to her employer.

Well, her erstwhile employer. She wasn't quite sure what Penelope would end up being, but that might be something to discuss after they'd seen what Jackson's key would do to the safe.

Penelope studied first the photograph of the painting that Jackson had done of his family, then the one Jake had done of Amanda. She considered, then looked at them both. "Origins?"

"They are both paintings that find themselves currently in a private wing of the castle of Artane," Jackson said carefully. "The family is mine."

"And this is your mother?"

He nodded.

"Your father didn't paint this family portrait," Penelope said thoughtfully, "though if that's you, he did paint you in I'm guessing after the fact. He did paint your mother, though." She looked at him. "Did you do the one of your family?"

"Aye."

"May I keep them?"

"Of course, Mistress Penelope."

Olivia found herself the recipient of a look from Penelope that she understood all too well. "It seems fantastical," she offered, "but it's all true. I met Jackson IV in the past, and he is married to Amanda de Piaget."

Penelope let out a careful breath. "Then he's happy?"

"Very," Jackson said firmly. "You might be interested to know that my youngest sister is called Penelope, I daresay in your honor."

"Oh," Penelope said, putting her hand over her heart, "how lovely of him." She blinked rapidly as she looked at the photographs once more, then at them. "You said you found the key, though I don't think I want to know where. Shall we give it a go?"

Jackson nodded and rose, then helped Penelope to her feet. Olivia received the same courtesy, but she hadn't expected anything less. She looked around the office that had lured her all the way from her home on almost the other side of the world and had to shake her head. Of all the things she'd expected when she came to England, winding up with a man—and a *vintage* one at that—had definitely been last on her list.

She felt Jackson take her hand as they walked toward the inner sanctum.

"What if there's nothing there?" he murmured. "I might turn out to be poor as a church mouse."

"Do you think I'm standing here just for money?"

"I think you're barely standing there because what you want to do is pull me into your arms and thoroughly ravish me right here on this very lovely floor tapestry."

"Rug."

He smiled. "I know."

"Do you ever think about anything else?"

"Ice cream," he said promptly, "and swords." He shrugged. "You're always first on the list, though."

She found herself working very hard to muster up a glare. "You do that on purpose, don't you?"

"I'm endeavoring to distract you before you burst into tears."

"I'm not going to weep over you."

"Again."

She wondered if she looked as ill as she felt. "Jackson, stop it."

He closed his eyes, then reached out and pulled her into his arms

"If we find nothing inside the safe, will you still call me *my lord* occasionally?" he asked solemnly. "Just for old time's sake?"

She would have shoved him, but he was holding her too tightly. He was also trying not to laugh, which she supposed said a great deal about his ability to face unnerving things and not be intimidated.

She wondered absently how he would handle spiders the size of his head.

"I love you," he whispered before he pulled away, smiled at her briefly, then looked at Penelope. "Let's see if the key does what it should."

Olivia stood next to Penelope and watched Jackson open the outer door that hid the safe behind itself. He took a deep breath, then fitted the key into the lock.

The door opened, which was a bit of a relief, but Jackson didn't move, which left her wondering if something had escaped and slain him on the spot. Given the month they'd had so far, she wouldn't have been surprised.

"Jackson?"

He stepped aside and shifted to look at them. "I'm not sure what to make of it all. Would you two come look?"

Olivia hesitated. "Dead spiders?"

Jackson smiled uneasily. "Not inside, though I don't dare speculate on where he went to procure whatever might be in these wee bags."

"Would you like privacy?" Penelope asked.

Jackson smiled at her, looking slightly pained. "Mistress Penelope, this should likely be divided with you—"

"Oh, of course not," she said promptly. "Jake left me the business along with ownership of half this building. I could stop working tomorrow and never worry again. This belongs to you, Jackson. Your father obviously wanted you to have it and I agree with him."

Olivia watched him gather up a handful of velvet bags and a pair of thick manila envelopes. Penelope handed him a dark blue shopping bag with *Kilchurn, Ltd.* printed on the side to carry away the treasures, which Olivia thought might have been the most ironic thing she'd seen so far that year. Jackson glanced at her and she smiled reflexively because she suspected he was thinking the same thing.

She followed them as they walked to the outer office, then hung back for a brief moment. She had the same feeling she'd had on that final day in medieval England, that feeling that one door was closing so another could open. Obviously, her job with Penelope was going to evaporate, but maybe that didn't matter. She had just inherited a cool hundred grand thanks to her grandfather's having chosen a great broker to manage what had been held in trust for her until her birthday. And even if she hadn't, she could have pulled a few waitressing shifts at Artane's tea shop and Jackson could have chopped some wood.

It sounded like bliss, actually.

Her phone chirped at her, which she thought was a little surprising. Not many had her number, though for all she knew, one of Kendrick's kids had decided he needed some contraband junk food and thought she might be the gal to get it for him.

She pulled her phone out and opened it to find a text from Derrick.

I have an opening for an art assessor at Cameron Antiquities. Interested?

She bowed her head and laughed. Timing, as her grandfather would have sagely noted, was everything.

"Olivia?"

She looked up to find her husband standing there, looking slightly concerned. "I'm fine," she said managed. She motioned for him to come close, then leaned up and whispered in his ear. "Derrick just offered me a job."

He took her hands in his in that way he had that left her feeling cherished and protected and very, very loved. "So," he said thoughtfully, "does this mean I will become a kept man?"

"Do you even know what that means?"

"I do," he said with a smile, "but could never allow a woman, particularly *my* woman, to see to my keep. I will find a labor to do.

Until that time, perhaps my sire has left us a few of those ridiculous paper pounds to keep us from starving." He considered, then leaned close. "Have you an opinion on Mistress Penelope's future?"

She smiled. "Thinking to arrange things?"

"Well, it is what I do," he whispered. "Will she allow it any more willingly than the rest of you gels do?"

"It's worth a try."

He smiled, kept one of her hands in his, then pulled her back with him into the small lobby of the shop. Olivia found herself situated comfortably on the sofa while Jackson squatted down in front of Penelope.

"I wonder, Mistress Penelope, if a fresh start might suit you? I will offer what aid you'll allow no matter what you choose to do, but if you've no stomach to remain in London, I daresay there's no reason to."

She sighed deeply. "I don't suppose Jake and your mother will be popping down to London for a visit any time soon, so maybe there's no reason to stay."

"Let us exchange mobile numbers," Jackson suggested. "If I hear tell of some paranormal activity that will bring them to our day, I will ring you and let you know."

She nodded, then looked at him hesitantly. "Will your father's brothers still keep watch on the shop, do you think?"

"I don't believe so," he said seriously. "My attorney has sent along a few documents that have encouraged them to move on with their lives. Mistress Peggy might be less inclined to do so, but let that be my concern."

"You are so much like him," Penelope said quietly. "He must be very proud of you."

"I could only hope to be a shadow of him," Jackson said with a grave smile. "What I'm certain of at the moment is that he would ask you what, if you could do anything in the world, you would prefer to do? A new beginning, perhaps."

Olivia looked at him. "I love you," she mouthed.

He lifted his eyebrows briefly, smiled as well, then looked at Penelope. "My lady?"

Penelope looked as if she might have taken the first decent breath she'd had in three years. "I think I might like to open up an antique shop." She paused. "In Provençe."

Olivia was unsurprised. "My aunt would come help you scout through markets if you wanted company," she offered. "Her French is very good."

Penelope looked at her with a dreadful sort of hope in her eyes. "She did email me a couple of days ago, as it happens. Apparently, Belize didn't work out."

"Really?" Olivia asked in surprise. "The weather?"

"The boyfriend." Penelope smiled. "I think it was his inflexible commitment to bell-bottoms, but I could be wrong. Do you think two middle-aged women could make a go of a business in the French countryside?"

Olivia suspected there might be a few paranormal helpers more involved than either of them might want, but maybe those plaid-wearing, sword-toting Scottish ghosts only traveled to the States on their matchmaking missions.

"I think it would be wonderful," she said firmly. "It's such a lovely part of the world."

"And perhaps it will be full of equally lovely days," Penelope said. She took a deep breath and looked at Jackson. "If you're certain? I could sign the shop over to you—"

"Nay," he said quietly, "you should sell it and use those monies to begin anew in France." He looked around briefly, then turned back to her and smiled. "This was the work of his life until he took a different path. I have made the same choice to accomplish my own life's work. It is right that we respectfully close the door here."

Olivia watched him look at her briefly and didn't have to hear the words to know what he was thinking.

With his blessing.

She had heard both his father and mother tell him exactly that in the past and been the recipient of those very gracious words herself.

He rose and held down his hand to help Penelope up, then pulled her to her feet as well. She helped Penelope lock up, then held the goods for Jackson as he walked them through a thug-free hallway and down the stairs to the lobby. She stood just outside the building with her former employer and smiled.

"Thank you for the chance," she said, feeling a little uncomfortable. "I would say I'm sorry things didn't work out, but maybe they worked out for the best."

"It's been a bit of an adventure, hasn't it?" Penelope said. "I almost feel as if I'm in your shoes, thinking about a new life in a different country. I think I'll swear off—"

"Don't," Olivia interrupted, then she smiled uncomfortably. "Sorry. I'm nervous about making vows."

Penelope nodded at Jackson who was waving them over to a taxi. "Except with that lovely man there, I'm sure."

"He's definitely the exception to the rule," Olivia agreed.

Penelope stopped in front of the cab and hugged them both briefly. "You'll come visit me?"

"Of course," Jackson said. "I'll text you on the morrow after I've talked to cousins who will be able to aid you with the sale of the shop. If you want company whilst seeking out a spot in France, I daresay we would happily make a journey there as well."

Olivia nodded when he looked at her, then watched him help Penelope get into the cab. She waited until the taxi had driven away before she looked at the man left standing there next to her who could have been just any other absurdly gorgeous Englishman in a black leather jacket and jeans.

Only she knew better and loved him for it.

He shoved his hands in his pockets and turned to look at her.

"Hey, beautiful," he said with a smile, "feel like fish and chips?"

She pursed her lips at his flawless American accent. "The things you know," she said, shaking her head.

"I'm a dual citizen," he said with a shrug. "Or apparently I will be when Alexander's guy gets through with me. I'll want to blend in when we hit the Big Apple eventually." He held out his hand. "Sustenance?"

"Are you asking me out on a date, ridiculously handsome stranger?"

"Interested?"

"Very."

"Then let's go, cupcake. We'll drop off our treasures at the company flat, then see where our feet take us."

She smiled and watched him flag down another cab as if he'd been doing it his whole life. She crawled into the back with him, smiled again at the way he took her hand, then leaned her head against his shoulder,

She had come to England with warily high expectations only to find that they'd been exceeded in every respect. The possibility of a terrific job, a wonderful extended family, and endless numbers of vintage treasures to explore with someone who might just have an opinion on their authenticity? She was very glad she'd taken her grandfather's advice to keep going.

She could hardly wait to see what tomorrow would bring.

The one thing she knew was that if it included the man sitting next to her, rubbing his thumb over hers and humming a little medieval melody, it would be exceptionally lovely.

THIRTY

JACKSON ALEXANDER KILCHURN V RAN along the edge of the sea and realized that for the first time in his life, he was simply running for the joy of it, not to outrun things that tormented him. That collection of Hell's finest who had pursued him for so long had apparently wearied of the chase and gone off to look for riper pickings.

And why not? His life was full of so many wonderful things, he could scarce keep from smiling. All that good cheer was likely anathema to those better suited to grousing over their slag-lined accommodations below.

He was, thanks to Alex Smith's slightly nefarious connections, firmly planted in the current century. It had taken just a bit longer than usual to make certain he had a foot on either side of the Pond, but he imagined that would be worth it. He wasn't entirely certain that he wouldn't be paying a visit to his paternal grandmother at some point, so 'twas likely best to go as a proper Yankee grandson.

He was also, thanks to his father's meticulous planning, an exceptionally rich man. One of the envelopes he'd found in his sire's well-guarded safe had been full of things called stock certificates and other things called bank books. Derrick had proven his worth yet again by not only aiding him in understanding what he had inherited, but introducing him to Robert Cameron's accountant who was apparently accustomed to dealing with numbers that should have left him feeling faint.

He supposed he didn't care all that much for the funds, though the gems he'd been given were lovely and the ability to feed himself and his wife without worry was useful.

Then again, she had inherited that passel of funds from her grandfather, so perhaps they wouldn't have starved. Not that he would have allowed her to pay for his keep, but that had never been in question.

He had laid out a bit of current-day sterling to purchase a sedate car of modest size and pay for driving lessons. If Maryanne had tormented him with the occasional journey in her car that he coveted to an unwholesome extent, he had repaid her by herding her husband out to the lists and making him suffer.

He was also going to buy himself a ridiculously expensive automobile when he wasn't required to wear an L on the back of it. There were lines a medieval man of sense and maturity simply didn't cross and that was one of them.

But perhaps the most marvelous thing in his life was the woman a hundred paces away, sitting on a blanket, wrapped in more blankets, obviously having extracted from the shore all the shells she cared to search for that day. She was a hunter of treasures, keeper of his heart, and the very best thing the Future had offered him.

She ran with him when it suited her, or walked along the shore either with or without him when it didn't. She also occasionally simply waited for him as she was doing at present, which was something he never took lightly.

He slowed to a walk to catch his breath and looked up the coast. He could see what was left of Raventhorpe if he squinted, though he had made a journey or two there with Olivia just to roam over his prior haunts. The castle to his left, that monstrous pile of stones on that bluff, looked a bit more intimidating and substantial than it had in the past, but it was still a place of safety and security.

He was grateful to Stephen for the hospitality over the past pair of months whilst he got his affairs together, a hospitality he had repaid his cousin for by not destroying him in the lists. He had also dutifully moved any number of boxes for the intractable Lady Gladstone every time he walked through the gates, which she seemed to find pleasing enough.

All in all, it was a very good life. He had more than enough funds to build his lady wife a sturdy house on the sea, big enough to keep them, their future children, and the odd traveler who might be needing shelter safe. He had several frequent flier accounts set up, which he supposed might earn him a nod of approval from his father.

He also supposed he would eventually need to find a proper labor to do, but he was still trying to decide what that might be. He had considered painting, or procuring medieval antiques for Derrick's business, or even opening up a pub and spending his days chopping and cooking. What he did know was that his father had somehow known exactly what he needed and gifted him the perfect way to acclimate himself to the present day.

And that gift, the one in the other envelope that had been lurking at the back of his father's safe, was what he'd been thinking about since the moment he'd opened it.

He'd been looking for the proper way to bring it up to his wife, but in his defense she was very distracting and he'd been enormously distractible. Every couple was surely allowed some sort of nuptial tour, which he'd taken with her without hesitation.

But he'd caught her spinning the globe in Artane's library more than once, which he thought he just might understand.

He mopped his face with the edge of his shirt, then dropped down next to her on her blanket.

"Thank you for waiting for me."

She leaned over, kissed him briefly, then smiled as she straightened. "Least I could do. I understand you've already expended some energy with Stephen earlier."

"Aye," he agreed, "and unfortunately we left his security lads looking as though they might need a visit to the kegs in the cellar.

You would think they would be accustomed to this sort of thing by now."

She smiled. "It's because you're terrifying."

He couldn't deny it. "Fortunately for me, he has something in a different basement called a gym. 'Tis very new and intriguing with many things to lift and move about when there are no breathing men to endure the focus of my energies."

"I'm sure Stephen's security guys will appreciate that."

He nodded, then examined the lay of the battlefield, as it were. The picnic hamper was where he'd left it and the envelope containing what he'd brought along still rested beneath it. He considered his own situation, then took off his shoes and socks and happily let himself enjoy the winter breeze.

There were benefits, he supposed, to having grown up in the Middle Ages and the ability to smile whilst freezing was definitely one of them.

He looked at his lady to find her watching him as if she weren't quite sure what he intended to do. He smiled, then casually reached over and pushed her shoe off with his toes. That was yet another of the pleasures of the future he hadn't anticipated, that of scampering along the beach in his bare feet without having to bare more of himself than was polite.

"What?"

He looked at his wife, then shrugged. "Just looking."

"At my feet?"

He considered her. "They look itchy."

She laughed at him. "You aren't at all funny."

He pulled her over him, then rolled until she was comfortably arranged on the blanket and he was in a position to gaze down at her adoringly. "I am enormously funny," he said, "and I think you might love me almost as much as I love you."

She leaned up and kissed him briefly. "I think you might be right." She lay back and smiled up at him. "You ran a very long time this morning."

"I had thoughts."

"Spill 'em."

He considered, then looked at her. "I have something to show you."

"Should I be afraid?"

"Are you ever afraid?"

"Not as long as you're here."

"Well," he said modestly, "there is that. And if I am momentarily off in the loo, you do have your walking stick."

"Eugenie Kilchurn would be jealous."

He smiled. "I daresay she would be. We'll see what she says if she ever arrives at our door." He sat up, pulled Olivia up with him, then removed the envelope from its place. He pulled out what it contained, then handed that piece of parchment to his wife.

She studied it for a long moment, then looked at him.

"A map?"

He nodded.

"What are those Xs?"

"I don't know," he said slowly. "What do you think they are?"

She lifted an eyebrow. "I think they might be treasures."

"Shall we go look?"

"I think we should," she agreed.

He pulled his phone out of the picnic hamper. "I could ring Derrick to seek aid in booking our tickets."

She peered at his phone. "Aren't your contacts arranged alphabetically?"

"By level of sword skill, rather." He paused. "I'm a little surprised to find that Zachary isn't very last on the list, but I have to be fair."

She laughed a little. "All right, so you're very funny. Where am I on your list?"

"You are always first," he said solemnly. "And the other?"

She put her arms around his neck and smiled. "All right."

"Just all right?"

"Are you kidding? Let's go pack."

He tucked his father's map back into its envelope and handed it to his lady for safekeeping, then gathered up the rest of their gear and put his shoes back on. He looked out over the strand again, grateful that it wouldn't be for a final time, then looked at his love. Who could have predicted that an adventure that had started on the strand beneath his feet would have landed him in such a time, with such a woman?

He kissed her briefly, then walked with her back up to the castle that had, in the best of ways, started it all. He had the feeling he wouldn't be the last of the family to say as much, which was as it should be.

What a lovely life it was, indeed.

Epilogue

THE PIN BOARD WAS, AS it always was, full. A blond man leaned back in his chair, laced his fingers behind his head, and sighed deeply. The course of love didn't run smoothly or perhaps even not-so-smoothly, it simply ran forever.

He heard the front door open and shut, followed by the usual sounds of a pack being dropped on the entry hall table along with car keys. A jacket missed being shed atop the back of the sofa and landed on the floor. Curses uttered in a language that had fallen out of favor several centuries earlier accompanied all three, but it had been that sort of week so far.

Theophilus de Piaget folded his arms over his chest and watched his brother walk into the kitchen and continue on directly across the room to rummage about in the refrigerator.

"I thought you had rehearsal," he said.

"Canceled because of rain," Samuel de Piaget said, his voice muffled by both the door of the beast and whatever it was he was ruthlessly stuffing into his mouth.

"By the saints, what a gaggle of women you work with."

Sam straightened and imbibed a hefty swig of something in a color not generally found in nature, then replaced the bottle in the fridge and shut the door. "Slick floors and choreographed skirmishes fought by those not used to keeping themselves alive whilst up to their ankles in mud are not a good combination." He shrugged. "The perils of outdoor Shakespeare in the twenty-first century."

"Perhaps your director should hire people with better tolerance for weather."

"He should," Sam agreed, pulling out a chair and collapsing into it. "Or perhaps 'tis time I anonymously gifted the troupe a proper building."

"And then what besides inclement weather would you use for an excuse when you've other things to do?" Theo nodded toward the pin board. "Look at all that there. You'll be fortunate to make your entire run, never mind anything else."

"Well, it isn't as if I can simply drop out," Sam said reasonably.

"If only you were a terrible actor," Theo said with a smile. "Taking on lesser roles instead of leads would be less conspicuous."

"And you aren't out there as well?" Sam asked pointedly.

"Whilst mystery readers are an inquisitive lot, my lad, no one seems all that interested in discovering who TD Piaget really is. And I don't need to be *in situ* to meet my deadlines, if you know what I mean."

Sam shook his head. "One of these days someone's going to do a bit of investigating and decide that perhaps you're doing more note-taking and less inventing your tales out of whole cloth."

"I have no idea what you're talking about," Theo said mildly. "I'm just a regular bloke with a good imagination."

"You really should stop setting stories near stone circles and fairy rings."

"Write what you know," Theo said wisely. "Or so says my agent and she has yet to lead me—"

A knock sounded on the front door, interrupting him.

Theo looked at his brother in surprise. "Did you invite someone?"

"Of course not. You?"

Theo shook his head. They had three rules they never broke and not giving anyone the location of their flat was first on the list. He heaved himself to his feet and shot his brother a look.

"Where's your sword?"

"Under the sofa. Where's yours?"

"In the umbrella stand."

"Then what are you worried about?" Sam asked, shooing him away. "Off you pop and see who's there. Perhaps someone misdirected a delivery and we'll have something hot for supper."

Theo didn't dare speculate. He left his brother to his investigations of cupboards and walked to the front door, wondering not for the first time if they should have purchased a house out in the country. Losing themselves in London had seemed the wisest choice at the time, but now he suspected it hadn't been.

At the very least he should have installed a spyhole after any of the scores of times he'd told himself he should. He took a deep breath, then opened the door.

Four men stood there: three Scots in medieval dress and an Englishman garbed in Elizabethan finery.

Swords were obviously going to be of absolutely no use. Supper was also, unfortunately, not in the offing.

"Sam," he called. "We have guests."

His brother came up the passageway, working his way through a bag of crisps by the sound of it. The bag fell to the floor along with what Theo suspected had been his brother's jaw. He supposed it wouldn't have been polite to point out to his sibling that he had squeaked as well.

He took a deep breath, then stepped back, waving their visitors inside. He couldn't say he knew very many things when compared to the volume of knowledge contained in the current day, but he did recognize relatives and he recognized trouble. He was particularly adept at recognizing trouble-causing relatives arriving with luggage. Those four there fit that bill perfectly.

Minus the luggage, of course. They were who they were, after all.

"My lords," he said, making them all a sweeping bow. "Welcome to our humble abode."

John Drummond muttered a curse as he pushed past them and

made for the kitchen, Hugh McKinnon hard on his heels. Fulbert de Piaget looked them both over, shook his head, then followed his companions. That left only Ambrose MacLeod, laird of that same mighty clan during an era of food that tended to give Theo a sour stomach, standing there wearing a pleasant look.

"Lord Ambrose," Sam said weakly. "What a surprise—and a pleasure, of course. A surprising pleasure—or perhaps a pleasant surprise—ah ... "

Theo looked at his brother. "Stop."

"Right," Sam said weakly and backed away. "I'll make certain our other guests are comfortable."

Theo watched his brother hasten away, then looked at the man who had become rather infamous for attempting to direct the course of love over the past several years.

"'Tis an honor to have you here, my laird," he said politely.

"I have a few thoughts, young Theophilus."

"I am certain, my laird, that you do."

"Have you contacted Jackson and his bride?"

"Nay, my laird," Theo hedged. "I thought they might prefer the challenge of tracking us down themselves. Being who they are, of course."

Ambrose lifted his eyebrows briefly. "I suspect you might want to install that spyhole, lad, before Jackson finds you."

Theo smiled in spite of himself. "I'll take that under advisement, my laird."

"Now, before I turn my steely eye toward you and your brother to assure you of that same sort of happiness, let's go have a look at your map. You two did an excellent job with our last match, but time marches on and so must we."

"Of course, my laird."

Ambrose removed the mighty Claymore strapped to his back and looked around the small vestibule. He considered, then deposited the blade in the umbrella stand and stepped back to admire his work.

"Clever," he noted.

Theo made the hale and hearty shade another bow. "Thank you, my laird."

Ambrose smiled and walked away. Theo shut the door and did up the two extra bolts, then turned in time to see the last of their guests disappearing into the kitchen. He followed, paused at the doorway to survey the chaos, and came to a trio of conclusions.

First was that the course of love did indeed run forever and it occasionally benefitted from a wee helping hand now and then. That led to the second bit, which was reminding himself that he wasn't quite ready to break their rule about never dating the same person twice. That one had definitely pained him a time or two recently.

He noted the way the new arrivals had attempted to settle in with the elbow-room befitting their stations. Swords were, he was quite certain, going to be drawn sooner rather than later, which led him to the final, inescapable conclusion:

They were going to need a larger flat.

He also suspected—the thought of which left him suffering a slightly uneasy turn of his tum—that he wouldn't be able to dodge the slew of conversations in which he and his brother might figure prominently, but perhaps that could be put off for another day.

For the moment, he would pull up a chair, take hold of his own mug of drinkable ale, and enjoy yet another lovely evening spent in the company of family.

CPSIA information can be obtained
at www.ICGtesting.com
Printed in the USA
BVHW030204090222
628488BV00005B/112